# NIGHT MUSIC

## A Portland Melodrama

### A Novel

### Gehla S. Knight

Published by BookLocker.com, Inc., St. Petersburg, Florida.

BookLocker.com, Inc.
2021

Library of Congress Cataloguing in Publication Data
Knight, Gehla S.
Night Music by Gehla S. Knight
Library of Congress Control Number: 2021906978

This is for the lady with the cloud of auburn hair spun like cotton candy who read my very first story one rainy day and made the sun shine.

G. Knight

For Jack

# Books by Gehla S. Knight

Heath Street Stories
Buzzard Love
Plum's Pleasure
Zig Zag
Thrillers
Two Scoops of Seafood
Slab Town
Slap Happy
Old Wives' Tales

**Booksbygehlaknight.com**

## Ray Bates Mysteries

Blue Butterfly
Babylon Blues
The Camelot Club
Pontiac Pirates
Sweet Sorrow
City Serenade
A Cold Kill
Kiss of the Cobra

**Raybatesmysteries.com**

## Miles Brodie Mysteries

Slab Town
Hard Times

# Portland, Oregon
# 1944

# One

===========

**She** had the saddest eyes I've ever seen. They shone like twin Earths rising over a lunar landscape, evoking a pulse of longing and remorse in a stranded traveler's soul. I had never seen eyes like those, as brilliantly blue as drugstore glass, deep enough to wade in. And every once in a while when you caught her staring at the photograph on the Philco console, they sparkled like a Hollywood close-up. Not lit by tears, just memories breaching the light of day. That's how I remember her. First the eyes. And lastly a melancholy burning in my brain that is smoldering still.

Delilah was thirty-three-years old when I met her. Not met her actually in the formal sense as people did in those days. We weren't even introduced. I saw the sign in the front window, set my bag down on the sidewalk and rang her bell. It was a Tuesday, and I had slept on the oak benches at the Bus Depot on Fifth Avenue rather than cross the river and catch a streetcar to my father's bungalow on

Fremont Street. Ever since my sister Carla had snagged a good paying job with The Boeing in Seattle and left home in March, Pop was alone in the house. I realized when the spring term at Willamette University ended that if I showed up on his doorstep with baggage in my hand and an empty belly growling, I would never be able to break free. And freedom was what I was seeking that incipient summer of 1944. Even if it meant only modest accommodations in a rooming house on Portland's West Side with a chance to steer my own independent course while I completed my doctoral thesis.

Rooms were hard to find with the War on. Every serviceman and his sweetheart were camping out in the city's nooks and crannies along Broadway and Front Street. There was no room for a graduate student, a 4-Fer legally blind in one eye where my cousin Willis Soto had caught me with a fishing hook when I was seven. So I was alone, feeling small and ashamed of my strapping, healthy body which Uncle Sam had deemed unfit for service when all my friends signed up.

Delilah came to the door with a white turban wrapped around her hair and those bold, blue eyes staring at me. I didn't even notice her mouth, how sofa-cushion soft it was as it widened into an aloof gesture not unlike a regret. She wasn't wearing any lipstick or rouge, just those incredible eyes shining like Streamliner headlights.

There was no compassion in her gaze. I felt as if she were seeing right through me. I even turned to look back down the steps to discover who was pressing on my trail, hot after the furnished room I wanted. No one there. No one I could see anyway.

"Are you here about the room?"

"Yes," I said. "I saw the sign."

"Well, I'm sorry, but I just showed it to a lady who wants it."

I was driven to persistence by a pain in my backbone, stinky socks and a crick in my neck from using my duffle bag as a pillow. "Could I just take a look?"

"Sorry, but she's already made a deposit." The door closed in my face.

I stooped to pick up my bag and glanced at the bay window fronting the street. She was there, one hand at her waist, her blouse unbuttoned at the bottom and tied in a giant slipknot over sloppy dungarees. All I could remember was being disappointed that some brazen lady had beat me to the room and how those empty-ocean eyes made me want to drown my depression in a pint of beer. I trudged to a tavern at the corner of Main Street and Tenth Avenue, sat at the bar with my bag under my knees and ordered a draft. The bartender didn't even look my way as he set my beer down. Halfway through the suds, I realized I didn't want liquor at all. My head was ringing, and my belly ached. I was hungry. Down and out. That's what it was, and some stupid woman had beaten me out of a room within easy walking distance of the library. It wasn't fair.

I left the last of my change on the bar, pushed open the doors and hit the pavement again with no particular place to go. For no apparent reason, I found myself back at the 1909 Broadway house with the green shutters and wrap-around porch.

She came out to the porch with a stack of newspapers in her arms and nodded toward the bay window. "Say, if you still want the room, you can have it. That lady got another place over in Sellwood with her sister-in-law and asked for her deposit back."

"Oh. Swell." I didn't know if I should put my bag down to help her with the papers. Before I could decide, she had brushed by me, deposited her load at the corner, and indicated I should follow her up the steps and into the foyer.

She pointed up the stairs. "It's up there, at the back. The bathroom's at the end of the hallway, but there's a sink in your room. No cooking though, okay? No hotplates or anything."

I was nodding as I climbed the stairs behind her. Her hips seemed bound in one direction as her arms swung to the other. She smelled like ammonia. Her body was the shape of the dressmaker's forms in department store windows. Perfect symmetry. She had long legs and delicate hands I admired as she gripped the banister during our narrow ascent. Her tawny skin glowed like ecru silk without a flaw or permanent crease. It seemed as if she had never laughed, never frowned. Not a single inspiration or troubling thought was written on her face. It was impossible to read anything beyond those piercing, sad eyes.

"I change the linens every Monday, but you have to strip the bed yourself. Just put your sheets and towels in the hamper by the bathroom. Do you smoke?"

"Yes, I do."

"Well, make sure you don't smoke in bed. The last tenant I had nearly burned the house down. The spread has some holes in it, I'm afraid."

"I'll be careful."

"And use the ashtray. Lord knows I have plenty. That's how fires get started. People get lazy and careless."

"Don't worry. I haven't burned up anybody's house yet."

She turned around and drilled me with a military glare. "I'm serious. There's a fire extinguisher on the landing there just in case you need it."

"Let's hope not," I mumbled, trying to mend fences.

She pushed the door open and stepped aside to let me pass. "Will this be alright?"

The room smelled of musty newspaper, moldy carpeting and cigar smoke. "It's just fine," I lied eagerly.

It was better than the bus depot. Dry and quiet. And cheap. I could afford cheap. I set my bag down beside the bed. It sagged in the middle like a slaughterhouse nag. The iron rails were painted rusty brown. A chenille bedspread in pale blue with blushing rosettes long ago scrubbed into senile decline hung like a shroud over the metal carcass. I could hear the springs trembling even before I sat on the edge and thumped the lumpy pillow which flattened like a flapjack beneath my fist. The bed squawked and clanged but surrendered without a fight as I lay back and tested it with a few good bounces.

"And I expect the rent on the first of the week. You can leave it on the kitchen table downstairs if I'm out. If you want any extra laundry done, you have to pay on a piece basis."

"That's fine. I can manage."

She looked behind her at the smoky reflection in the dresser mirror. "Well, that's it. I'll have to have the first and last week's rent in advance."

"Okay. Sure." I stood up, dug in my trousers and pulled out my wallet, as thin as a slice of deli ham. "That's five dollars a week?"

"And laundry is extra."

"Sure. Here's five." I handed her my carefully folded bills. "Could I give you the balance on Friday when I get paid?"

In an instant, she glanced down at my shoes with a Hershey shine, the rain-splotched pants and corduroy jacket with a front button missing. "I suppose that'll be alright. I'll go down and get you a receipt."

She closed the door behind her, and I heard the sound of her steps on the stairway. A bus farted outside. Otherwise it was quiet. A good place to study with no annoying brats yelling and bickering outside my door. I was pleased with my good fortune as I sprawled back on the bed and shut my eyes.

When she returned, she laid a receipt for my five dollars on the bureau and handed me two fresh towels. On top were a bar of Palmolive soap and a safety razor. "The last tenant left these, so I guess they're yours if you want."

"Thanks." I took them.

"Mr. Peeler was a beer salesman. Do you drink much?"

"Not really." Couldn't afford to. I was barely able to manage food let alone booze.

"What's your name?" She was looking over my shoulder.

I glanced quickly in the direction of her stare. Nothing but a Coca-Cola calendar with the month of December hanging beside an old nail hole. "Nathan," I answered, uncertain she was paying attention. The calendar had a picture of a slim, young woman wearing yellow earmuffs. "Nathan McCarthy."

Her eyes never met mine. "I used to know a Gladys McCarthy. She was from Springfield. Would you be any relation, do you think?"

"No. I don't think so."

"I'm Delilah."

"Nice to meet you." It suited her perfectly—exotic, intriguing, sexy, beautiful. She was all of those things in her own way. As intriguing as foil-wrapped Christmas chocolates.

"Well, if you want to use the kitchen for anything, I leave it open until supper. You're welcome to the coffee if it's made, and there's usually leftovers in the icebox if you're hungry at night. But I don't furnish regular meals, you know."

"I understand."

"It's just that I have a lot left over, and it's no use going to waste if you can eat it. The lady down the hall in Number 2 doesn't eat much. Her name is Veronica Nigh, and she works at Kaiser. She's the welding superintendent's secretary, makes very good money but is so stingy she won't even spring for a streetcar when she goes to Albina to visit her mother on Sundays. I don't think it's fair for her to take advantage if she can afford the automat."

"Right." I stood like a mannequin, afraid to move my long arms, feeling completely stupid, hoping she would complete her verbal tour and leave me alone. I had an urge to expel some of the pent-up, gaseous contents of my lazy bowels, shed my rumpled clothes and sleep away my miseries.

"Well, you'll meet her. She's home every evening at six. And she doesn't like the radio played after ten."

"I like it quiet myself. I study in the evenings."

Her head tilted sideways to better examine my face, as if she'd only just noticed me. "You're a student?"

"I'm doing research for my doctoral thesis."

"That must be awfully important."

"I don't know that it's so important really."

"To keep you out of the service, I mean."

"Oh." I blushed with shame. My gaze couldn't stay fixed on hers. "I'm practically blind in one eye." Self-consciously, I adjusted my spectacles. I supposed they gave me a professorial appearance and masked my blatant youth.

She turned around and grabbed the doorknob. "Well, you're lucky, Nathan. Whatever it is, if it keeps you out of the Army, it's worth it."

"Roman history." I held her halfway in my space and halfway into hers.

"What?"

"That's what I'm studying. Roman History. My doctoral thesis is a modern history of the First Monarchy Period."

"Oh." The blank eyes turned away from me as the door closed partly between us. "Kings and queens, you mean?"

"Only kings, I'm afraid."

"I thought the Romans had emperors. Like Nero. He was an emperor, wasn't he?"

"Yes."

"And Caesar."

"Caesar wasn't really a single individual."

"I read about him in school. He crossed the Rubicon. I remember that part." She looked down and touched the tip of her nose, deep in thought for a moment. "I don't believe I recall just why he did that, but it was significant, wasn't it?"

"Yes. You could say that."

"Well, that was Caesar who did that so I'm sure he must have been a real person."

"That was Gaius Julius Caesar. But all the later emperors after Augustus were referred to as Caesar so the term applies to quite a few people."

Her eyes brightened with sudden enlightenment. "You mean it's like Your Highness? Something like that?"

"In a way."

"And why is that important?"

"Well, you see, Rome had a monarchy in the beginning. Then there was a republic, and then the first triumvirate filled the vacuum after the chaos and anarchy stemming from Caesar's rise to absolute power after the death of Crassus and the defeat of Pompey. Then came Julius Caesar's assassination, the second triumvirate with Octavian and Lepidus ending with the defeat of Mark Antony and the imperial period although many scholars argue the representative republic had actually disintegrated long before."

"Where was Caesar?"

"Oh. Well Octavian became Caesar Augustus."

"Not Julius then."

"Uh, no. That was Octavian's great uncle by adoption."

"Oh."

"It's interesting and instructive to learn how the monarchy evolved into a republican system of semi-representative democracy with an emphasis on civil law and legislative assemblies and then see how that failed in the end through military misadventure and political power struggles with Rome reverting to a tyrannical empire more repressive than the monarchy. That has important lessons for the present." I took a breath and felt my cheeks burn with embarrassment. She must think I was the most bombastic, pedantic, over-stuffed windbag she'd ever met. "That's the point, I guess. If there is one," I mumbled.

"So Rome had kings in the beginning?"

"Yes." In the midst of a great World Conflagration, how could anyone deem ancient history to be relevant? Doctoral academics were now at the bottom of the priority food chain, and my thesis along with hundreds of other liberal arts tomes would be buried on the scrap heap of postwar trivia. "I think there are important parallels to be drawn between the Roman Period and modern-day European monarchies. My thesis is directed at analyzing those similarities."

"That's nice to know then, isn't it? Maybe someone will think that's important someday."

"Yeah... maybe."

"Well, anyway I didn't know Julius Caesar was adopted."

I couldn't risk any more bad manners to clarify my verbal rambling. And by the time I thought of a retort, she had already turned her back. The echo of my nervous laughter rebounded off the wallpaper when she shut the door. She had cut right to the bone and made me bleed. Who cared what I was laboring on in the stuffy library stacks? What difference did Roman kings make when so many young men my age were being mowed down like summer wheat on the killing fields of Europe and bloody beaches of the Pacific? It sounded like such an inane, trivial pastime. Education, historical review, expansion of the intellect at a time when kids barely old enough to shave were being blown to bits by an Austrian paperhanger who flunked out of art school?

I sank on the bed and surrendered to its frumpy embrace.

Before I closed my eyes, I heard the sound of the front door opening downstairs, heavy footsteps plodding upward toward my door, thumps in the hall then the creak of a door opening. The walls shuddered as it slammed. My neighbor Veronica Nigh. I looked at my wristwatch: three past six. Right on time. As punctual as an Italian train.

I lay there for awhile, cataloging the noises in my new surroundings until I drifted off to sleep. When I awoke, it was cooler. Traffic swished from the street below signaling a break in the June heat wave. As I listened to the sound of the rain splattering on the gutter outside my window, I tried to quiet the hunger pangs in my belly and began to worry about where I was going to get the five dollars I needed by Friday. The truth was, I didn't have a job. I had lied. I had a slim prospect of a job, but I was hoping I wouldn't have to take it. I needed my nights free to study, and night clerk at the Roosevelt Hotel seemed like the best choice.

I stood up, unzipped my pants and kicked off my wrinkled trousers. My pockets were empty. The bureau mirror reflected a slovenly character with a bleary-eyed glare who bore little resemblance to the suave, aspiring intellectual I imagined myself to be. I needed to use that razor on my face before I went in search of a handout.

"Roosevelt Hotel it is," I resigned myself. Five bucks was five bucks, and there was something in those eyes of Delilah's that haunted me, made me want to avoid seeing them flare like spotlights, melting my defenses as I bared my baggy pockets and begged for an extension on the overdue rent.

It was deserted downstairs when I let myself out. On the sidewalk, pulling my collar up to shield my face from the rain, I heard the front window rising.

She hollered down at me. "Hey, Nathan! You need a key!"

She threw it down. It was tied to a maroon, Bakelite shoehorn. The number 3 was painted in black India ink on one side. I picked it up, and she had gone.

I put my head down and walked quickly to the corner. If I was Number 3, and Veronica was Number 2, who was Number 1? I had seen the closed door at the head of the stairs. Maybe I'd be lucky. Maybe my other neighbor would be a teacher, a retired musician from the symphony orchestra. A soul mate. Or maybe a salesman. Hopefully somebody quiet.

I spurted across the street in the watery wake of a Chevrolet coupe and headed for the Roosevelt Hotel to meet my rendezvous with mediocrity.

# Two

===========

**This** was the fifth year of war in Europe. The spring and summer of 1944 had been the hottest on record in Portland. The clusters of houses along Broadway's southern strip were sweating in the muggy evenings without even a hint of a breeze wafting upland from the sluggish Willamette River wending through the city. As I walked north into downtown, puddles splashed my socks from the stagnant pools filling the dips in the pavement. The morning rain had been a welcome balm for the sweltering residents. A few lights flickered on as I crossed Yamhill and ducked under the awning of a smoke shop and checked out the daily papers stacked inside the doorway. Headlines in the *Oregonian* and the *Journal* proclaimed Allied victory in Europe by the end of the year, but it was becoming evident that the enemy wasn't ceding any ground despite the Normandy landing in France. A long, grinding Allied advance across the Pacific promised sacrificial stars proliferating like snowflakes on the windows and storefronts of towns like Portland, Oregon. The Axis powers weren't beaten yet, and there were still plenty of pessimists like my father who believed peace wouldn't come until the last enemy combatant was killed or surrendered.

As the only son in a family of four children, my father had wept with joy when I was turned down by the draft board doctors. My sisters were all striking, fair-skinned brunettes who took after my mother Annette. I was the baby. All my doting big sisters smothered me with affection while I was growing up so I had no natural inclination to deprive myself for long of feminine company. My eldest sister Gladys was married to a doctor stationed at Fort Sill, Oklahoma. She had two little girls of her own. My second sister Carla was a bookkeeper for the Boeing plant in Seattle. She was dating a lawyer who escaped the draft because he was involved in "necessary war work." Frances, just three years older than I, was dating an Army Air Corps flier from Washington State. Although my father didn't know it, I knew that Francie was living secretly with her sweetheart in Tacoma.

Francie and I shared most of our secrets—even when it came to romance. Except that I didn't have any worthy secrets in that department. My affairs were brief, lackluster bouts of physical and emotional sparring that resulted in a platonic draw eventually. Accommodating but empty repasts that never sated my appetite for the flavor of a whole feast. Maybe I had received too much pampering by my sisters, too much affection from these lovely ladies to be tempted risking the pangs of febrile love. Perhaps I had been spoiled for the real world, for women with burdens of their own to carry and gaping spaces to fill in their lives apart from my needs.

My mother indulged me, too. Annette would always do anything to please my father, and what he wanted most in the world was a son. So she obliged him by bringing me into the world when she was forty-years old. I didn't make it easy for her. She spent the last three months of her confinement in bed reading through the entire works of Gibbon and Marcus Aurelius. I firmly held my mother accountable for my insatiable fascination with everything Roman. I was saturated in the womb with the likes of Pliny, Seneca, Julius Caesar, Suetonius and Claudius.

My father Thomas McCarthy owned a small emporium in northwest Portland. The neighborhood was enlivened by the influx of Greek and southern European immigrants at the turn of the century who worked in the drayage houses and trolley barns crammed together on the narrow, cobbled streets running north and south across Burnside Street. Our house was up the hill at the end of the trolley line where it crossed a steep ravine overlooking what was left of Guild's Lake, the site of the Lewis and Clark Exposition of 1905. We had a horse chestnut tree in our front yard that shaded the entire corner. That's where I fell when I was five and fractured my collarbone on a black-iron fence which protected our crab apple and cherry trees from the neighborhood gang of juvenile pilferers who plucked my mother's ripe fruit.

My sisters shared a large, open space on the second floor with their own bathroom. I had a room all to myself, big enough to ride a bicycle around on the third floor where I practiced sliding into home plate just like a big leaguer until my sisters complained about the plaster flaking off their ceiling below. But no one ever said a thing when I rigged up a giant slingshot with appropriated orange crates, my mother's silk stockings and the floor lamp from my father's study. I tied a bed sheet around my waist and armed with a carpet beater for a shield and a spatula sword stormed the walls of the barbarians' fortress with the daring of Hannibal.

I enjoyed this idyllic, sheltered childhood until I was nine. Then I received my first cruel blow in life. My mother died. I had been so preoccupied with my own self importance, shirking any but the most modest responsibilities in the household, I didn't even take notice of how she was wasting away before my eyes, taking more and more naps on the brocaded chaise downstairs. When she went to the hospital for the last time in December of 1930, it was very cold. I barely poked my nose from the down quilt when my father came into my room and told me to be a good boy and mind my sisters until he returned. I was too excited about the presents beneath the tree in the immense front parlor to worry about my missing mother.

I went to the hospital to see her one time before she died. My sisters were weeping, and I thought them to be unbearable sissies. Everybody knew that mother would be well again. I needed her, and she would certainly not dare to interrupt my ideal childhood by abandoning me. I had no inkling when she kissed me good-bye on Christmas Eve with a weak embrace and parched lips that I would never see her again.

When Annette died, it was a hard loss for me to bear, made all the more agonizing because I was finally forced to face my shameful selfishness. I was the one who cried the most at the funeral. Frances finally had to lead me out of the church, sit me down in the back seat of our LaSalle sedan and admonish me to stop my blubbering. I was only upsetting Papa, she scolded. I felt like such a failure, such a coward.

In 1931, when we were going through a series of housekeepers and cooks who never seemed able to please my sisters or my father for long, the stock market crash caught up with the family business. The credit customers couldn't pay their bills; the wholesalers wouldn't take credit from the retailers, and Papa was forced to close the store. Before long, we had to move out of the house, too. I cried the whole time the truck was filling up with our furniture: the India rug where I had spilled my watercolors, Mama's rattan chair with the polka-dotted cushion, our Victrola, the massive, black mahogany breakfront and dining table inherited from my maternal grandmother Adelpha Monroe. It was all gone.

When we arrived at our new house, a small bungalow on Fremont Street, none of our furniture arrived with us. Papa had sold it all. Now we were marooned on a pancake lot with a bare front yard, a concrete-slab porch and no place for me to play my war games except up in the attic with the spiders and moth balls. It was a dismaying downfall for a spoiled ten-year old. I didn't even have a decent tree to climb to escape the giggling gaggle of teens my sisters attracted. I was miserable for a whole year until Sally Bride moved in across the street.

Sally was blonde. When the sun shone on her head, she looked like a Botticelli angel sporting a gilded halo. She had big, green eyes and best of all, she could shoot marbles like a champ. Before the year was out, she had won all my best aggies and my prize steely. I hardly minded. Losing to Sally was a sinfully sensuous experience. Succumbing to someone so talented and sweet made my heart leap like a bullfrog. Sally was my first love, and I suppose my best. She never demanded more than I was able to give, sought my confidence, trusted my judgments on baseball, radio programs and spelling and gave me unbending loyalty. I loved her. She broke my heart when she grew up and went away to Corvallis to study music. While I was a student at Willamette University in Salem, we wrote each other every week, went to the homecoming dance together our sophomore year and made out in the back seat of her father's gray DeSoto.

My second life trauma came after Sally's first junior term. She was stricken by a cerebral embolism while riding a city bus when she was only twenty. I haven't gotten over it yet. God taking Sally so young was like plucking an orchid bud before it could bloom.

My best friend in high school besides Sally Bride was Mark Tanaka. His father owned the corner drugstore on Northwest Twenty-first Street where we could always mooch a chocolate soda on Friday nights if we helped him sweep up after closing. After Pearl Harbor, I spent a term at Dartmouth College on a fellowship grant from the Greco-Roman History department. When I returned to Portland in the fall of 1942, I was surprised to find the Tanaka's store closed. When I went around the block to their house, nobody was there. My sister Carla explained to me that the whole Tanaka family was being shipped off to Idaho.

"Why?" I had asked, stunned my friend had run out on me. There was some panic among Portlanders after the attack by the Japanese, but it wasn't enough of a reason for Mark to hightail it to the Idaho desert. He had talked about enlisting in the marines.

Carla had closed her eyes and turned her back on me. She resumed brushing her hair with a new ferocity as I hung in the doorway, begging for an explanation. "You're so wrapped up in yourself, Nat. You don't know, do you?"

"Know what?"

She sighed and whipped her dark locks into a fluff. "Haven't you heard anything about the resettlement plan?"

"The what?"

Her tone was as demeaning as the time she found me at the Sunday table licking the icing from her birthday cake. "Oh, Nattie. I can't believe you're so isolated at school."

"What's resettlement have to do with Mark? They were talking about moving enemy aliens away from the coast, and Mark's not an alien. He was born right here in Portland at Emanuel Hospital. And

Portland's a hundred miles from the coast. So why's he gone off to Idaho?"

"All the Japanese are being relocated to camps."

"Mark's not a Jap," I protested dumbly. "He's an American just like you and me, Carla. Hell, he even hates rice. He's as much a citizen as I am."

"Technically, I suppose. But Mark's ancestry is Japanese, Nat. All the Japanese are being moved out. It's happening everywhere—here, in California and Seattle, Vancouver, Canada. Everywhere on the West Coast."

I felt my mouth go dry. I looked down at the carpet. My heart sank to my belly button. "Why? What'd they do? Who says they have to go? What about the store?"

"I can't believe you didn't know, Nat. Janet Sato wrote you, I thought. She and her mother had to sell their dress shop and give away what wouldn't sell. It was awful. Janet Sato is third generation, and they treated her like a common criminal. Didn't you hear about it?"

"No. I didn't."

"Why don't you pay attention to the world? You can't live in your own, secluded, little academic ivory tower all your life, Nathan," she chided.

"I didn't know they were going to pack everybody off. Nothing like that. Not American citizens with no trial, nothing but the fact their relatives came from Japan. This isn't right, Carla."

"Everybody had to go down and register. Then they were allowed just enough time to pack some suitcases and get on buses which took them over to the stockyards."

"Stockyards?" My voice cracked in painful astonishment.

"They kept them there penned up like livestock until they shipped out to Idaho. It's just awful. Mrs. Ogura's father-in-law had a stroke, and it was two days before they could get a doctor to come in and see he got to a hospital. It's enough to break your heart. I can't believe it's happening right here in America. I heard the Watanabes left two weeks after Pearl Harbor and moved in with his sister's family in Kansas City, so they're safe for now."

"Jesus Christ. Mark's one of us for crissakes, and they put him in the stockyards like some slaughterhouse steer?"

"All the Japanese are being moved out. They're leaving everything behind. Mr. Tanaka just locked the door on their store and walked away. They're going to lose everything. They sold their Dodge to the German family who owns the butcher shop on Twelfth Street. He only got forty dollars for it."

"Oh, God. I didn't realize."

"Well, why don't you try reading a newspaper or your mail once in a while instead of all those musty, old Latin books? I swear, Nat, easterners don't have any idea what goes on out here in the Pacific Northwest. Aunt Tilda wrote and said she was astonished to learn that we had blackouts here in Portland. Apparently they still have all the lights blazing away on Broadway, and Brooklyn is lit up like a Christmas tree even with all the stories about enemy subs off the coast sinking ships right under our noses. You know, the Germans were shooting our freighters like ducks at the carnival. And they still kept the lights on. She says they were afraid to let the people know how serious a threat it was for fear they'd panic. Well, they sure let us panic out here. It's as if we were on another continent. Nobody thinks there's going to be an invasion at this late date. The war's really almost over, isn't it? I heard on the radio that our navy wiped out all the Japanese ships somewhere or another. So it just *has* to end soon. But they aren't closing the camps down until then so none of them will be coming home until it's finally all over."

"Carla, I didn't know. Honestly. When are they coming back?"

Her silence had the same force as the emotional sledgehammer that thumped me into a panic when my father couldn't tell me when my mother was coming home from the hospital. I knew what Carla's silence implied. Mark Tanaka wasn't coming back home. No more Friday night sodas at the drugstore, reading *Life* magazine and feeding the jukebox with rationed nickels. This stank. It was rotten. I stomped back down the stairs and slammed the door on my way out.

Since then, I had heard from Mark. He sent me a letter postmarked from Oakland, California. He had joined up after all: the 442nd Division bound for Italy. He'd gotten out of the camp even though he had to leave his mother and sister behind. His father passed away from a heart attack six days after Mark left the States. Mark was decorated twice, lost his left foot and took some Nazi shrapnel through his belly in Sicily. The Tanaka drugstore was taken over by an Italian immigrant family named Caprielli. Their house was sold for taxes to Herr Helmut Steinmetz who had fought in the First World War for the Kaiser and received the Iron Cross for killing fourteen doughboys at St. Denis. Life didn't seem fair at all.

Mark Tanaka was still up at the veteran's hospital in 1946. He'd had gangrene from the belly wound and had tubes draining out a thick, foul-smelling pus all the time. Stank like a privy. Every so often, these belly sores would burst, and bits of putrid cloth, wood and junk would ooze out of his wounds. He suffered a lot although he tried to smile when I visited him. Eventually he did heal. They gave him a prosthetic boot so he could get around pretty well. Except for the belly scarring and lingering intestinal problems, the rest of his life went on normally. He married, had a couple kids and spent his working days selling cigars and cigarettes at a St. Johns tobacco shop. The everlasting tragedy of his life was the government's short-stopping his potential. Mark had been headed for medical school and a bright future. What he lost, nobody or no official appology could give back.

I hadn't gone back to see him again after the war. I was 4-F, still pampered and sheltered from the harsher realities he had been forced to endure, and here he was, permanently crippled and wounded but not nearly as morally bankrupt as I was. I was ashamed to sit by Mark's bedside and tell him how proud I was of his sacrifice at the same time I was so terribly ashamed of my own shortcomings and of the disgrace I felt for Uncle Sam who had rejected its own. It was better for both of us if I stayed away.

So there I was in 1944 on my own for the first time, out of graduate school with no prospects. What I wanted to do was to teach at the University after I earned my doctoral degree in Roman History. With all my sisters occupied and living away, and my father in no financial position to support me, I had decided to go it alone. All I needed was a sparse room near the library to work on my thesis and a quiet summer to produce the century's greatest commentary on the Roman Monarchy. Delilah's empty room had seemed ideal. The only nagging detail left to attend to was the matter of employment to meet the rent, furnish me with change for the automat, laundry and smokes. Life seemed incredibly simple.

When I got to the Roosevelt Hotel, I slicked my hair back, brushed the toe of my right shoe on my trouser cuff and sauntered across the threadbare lobby to the desk.

A man with pince-nez glasses looked down his nose at me and sniffed. "Yes?"

"I'm here to see Mr. C. W. Ditnip."

He flicked lint from his lapel. "I'm Custer Worthington Ditnip."

"I'm Nathan McCarthy."

He looked me over as if he were choosing a grapefruit. No obvious bruises, but still. His steely stare focused on my rumpled jacket. "Have you come to inquire about the night desk-clerk position?"

"Yessir. That's right." I pressed both hands on the desk, hoping to demonstrate an eagerness for employment my heart did not endorse.

"Doctor Houghton sent you, I presume."

That was my brother-in-law. Gladys' husband. Before the war, he had a successful psychiatric practice in Portland. The doctor still had a few valuable connections for an unemployed, unskilled, artless relation looking for work.

Ditnip slapped the registration book shut and removed his glasses with a thumb and forefinger. "Young Man, you look robust and, if I may say so, in perfect health."

I knew what was coming. I had been here before. It would have been easier to lie, but the truth came out in a rush. "I tried to enlist, but I'm blind in one eye. Got a fishhook stuck in my eyeball when I was a kid. The army wouldn't take me and neither would the Coast Guard or the Merchant Marine."

He lifted his shoulders arrogantly. "I see. I believe Dr. Houghton said you need a night job to continue your studies?"

"Yessir."

"What kind of studies? Are you pursuing a medical career?"

"I'm working on my doctoral thesis in Roman history."

"Modern Italian history? Not fascism, I presume?" He peered skeptically at me.

"Ancient Roman history. The monarchy period."

He looked back down at his papers and dismissed me with a snort. "I thought Professor Gibbon had already covered that subject quite satisfactorily."

I pretended to look out the window and enjoy the distraction. In truth, my bowels were churning. I didn't want to work for this imperious, bigoted asshole. It might be better to take a job at the shipyards. I'd be sure to get on with some type of laboring job and sweat it out for a few months until I had enough saved to work in peace through the winter. But I was acquiescing to my father's insistence that his only son never engage in menial, brutish labor like a common immigrant. This sort of social positioning was very important to my father. He felt as though he had earned his son's blue-collar reprieve through toil in his grocery store. No heir of his was going to be swinging a shovel or standing on an assembly line. I was to be carefully groomed for the respectable sloth of academia just so my father could rest in peace once he passed on his inheritance to the next generation of McCarthys.

"Well, fill this form out. You'll need a uniform. We provide a jacket, but you'll have to pay for the cleaning and pressing."

"Yessir," I mumbled, starting to pull myself away. Last chance at freedom.

"I assume you have a pair of decent, dark trousers?"

"Uh, yessir."

"With a crease. No gum chewing, smoking or sleeping, Mr. McCarthy. Is that clear?"

"Yessir."

"We get a decent crowd in here. All respectable patrons. We don't cater to any of the riff raff who may come in looking to rent a room for the hour, if you understand my meaning,"

"Yessir."

"No loafers in the lobby allowed. Absolutely no salesmen. And don't waste your time chatting up every layabout who comes your way."

"Yessir, I mean no sir."

"We respect our country's servicemen here, but we will not tolerate loud, rude behavior, drunkenness or unbridled promiscuity on the premises. I trust that is clearly understood." He glared at me with his beady, rodent eyes, and I could smell the ginseng.

I had no idea what criteria distinguished unbridled from bridled promiscuity. It had to be a matter of professional judgment. Custer Worthington Ditnip looked like a man who would have a checklist for every possible vagary of the human species.

"You'll be on duty for the six to ten shift. Mr. Hardingware will take the desk from ten to eight in the morning. The pay is fifteen dollars a week, Mr. McCarthy, less cleaning and pressing for the uniform."

"Yessir."

"I expect you here behind the desk at six o'clock *promptly* every evening."

"Yessir."

"And your break is for ten minutes only. If you want to smoke, you can go in the washroom. Under no circumstances can you be seen loitering about in the lobby on your break."

"No sir."

"Every guest is to sign the register. No exceptions."

"Yessir."

He stepped back to take another look at his hapless charge and rocked forward on his toes. "Very well then, follow me."

"Yessir." I took a last, lingering look at the open doorway before putting my head down and following him back behind the row of mail slots. I was prepared to surrender my soul to the Roosevelt Hotel desk from six to ten four nights a week. It was a small sacrifice to make for the freedom Mr. Ditnip's absence would give me to pursue my opus undisturbed.

# Three

========

**By** the time Mr. Ditnip let me go, it was nearly six. I opened the front door at Delilah's and could smell onions frying. When I saw her stick her head through the doorway and smile, I took off my hat and walked into the kitchen.

"Hi there," I said, leaning against the counter. I flashed a jaunty smile and received a blank stare in return.

Her rich, chestnut hair coiled around her face, the cascading locks confined in a red bandanna. With one hand she stirred a sizzling pan of onions and tomatoes, and with the other she wiped a bead of sweat from her neck. "It's too hot to cook lately, but I thought I'd make some goulash for supper since it's cooled off some today."

"Smells great," I chimed, brazenly breathing in great gulps and hoping she would invite me to share her table.

She grabbed a pepper shaker from the stove top and seasoned the mixture as it steamed. "I have a relative in Astoria who gets meat for me." She looked up for a second in my direction, and those searchlight eyes lit on mine. "We all get by with a little help these days, don't we?"

"Sure."

"He manages a Safeway. He gets me some of the older hamburger. He's not supposed to, but he wraps up a bundle every

Sunday for me. He sends it in with his wholesale man." She stirred rapidly as the onion bits glazed. "Last week, he sent me a whole rump roast."

"Sounds good." I licked my lips as she dumped in a bowl of mottled meat the color of a prizefighter's pulpy mug.

A cloud of steamy grease rose over the stove. "God, it's so humid, isn't it?" She wiped her face with the dishtowel. "I can't keep any makeup on."

"You look great." She did—sweaty, blushed and ripe. I knew she was older than I. Men have an instinctive time clock for fixing females' place on their sexual calendars: virginal, ripe, upholstered, well preserved. No other categories ever seemed to apply. Delilah was deliciously ripe. Normal social intercourse couldn't commence until her position was firmly fixed. Thus my precipitate stupidity in blurting "How old are you?" Her eyes widened and caused me to swallow my bluster. "That is, I mean..." I was back-pedaling to keep my balance like the unicycle rider in the Barnum and Bailey Circus. "I have a sister about your age, I think."

"I'm thirty-three. How old are you?"

"Twenty-three in October. My sister Gladys is married to an army doctor. They're posted in Oklahoma."

She turned down the heat, splashed some catsup in the pan and took a can of creamed corn from the cupboard.

"Let me help you with that," I volunteered, commandeering the can opener. I twisted, flipped the top back and presented it as if it were a rose.

She dumped it in the pan. "Hand me the paprika."

I picked the Schilling tin off the shelf. "My youngest sister is in Tacoma. She's engaged to a B-17 navigator."

Delilah handed the spice can back. "Do you have a girl?"

"No." It wasn't until I saw the lips relax and the corners of her eyes tilt upward, that I realized it had not been an academic inquiry. I should have given her some indication that members of the opposite sex found me even a bit interesting. "I've been too busy lately to concentrate on my love life." My cheeks were stinging like nettles. "A thesis is rather a monumental task."

She shoveled the goulash onto a platter and set it on the table. "That's like a book, isn't it?"

"More or less."

"A story about Roman kings, right? Are their sword fights and damsels in distress?"

"Not exactly."

"Well, then I don't think anyone will want to read it, will they?"

There was fresh coffee in the percolator. She got down two plates and cups and began setting out silverware. I was salivating before she put down the bread and margarine.

"When is your little sister getting married?" she asked as she folded a napkin.

"Oh, Francie's my older sister. That is, they're all older. I meant Frances is my youngest *older* sister."

"Oh." She sat down. "For a writer, you're not very good at making yourself clear."

I watched as her fork raised and stuck in a mound of juicy meat. She scooped a share of goulash into her plate and buttered a piece of bread while I stood there. I made a tentative move to pull out the chair across from her. She never said a word.

"Uh, she's not actually engaged. Not technically, that is."

"You mean they're in love and sleeping together but nobody's supposed to know?"

"But they're planning to get married before he ships out."

"Maybe she should wait."

"Wait for what?"

"What if he doesn't come back?"

"I beg your pardon?"

"It's a shame to see so many young girls widowed by the War, don't you think?"

"I suppose it is, but if they're in love—"

"Maybe she should wait until he comes home. Besides, going over there changes them. Completely." She lifted her cup.

"Well, he's a terrific guy. He won't change. They're crazy about each other."

"I mean the war. Combat. It changes the boys over there. When they come back, they're not the same. It kills something inside them. Some of the lights go out, you know what I'm trying to say? Killing, being afraid of being killed any minute dims the light in your soul. You're forced to look into the mirror and see the person you really are underneath all the flash and polite facades we create in civilian life."

"Sure, but I think he's the kind of a guy who'd be true-blue to Francie, if that's what you're getting at. When couples are as much in love as they are, then war couldn't possibly do anything but make the bond stronger."

"No, no. Not that. I'm not talking about love. That's permanent, I agree. It's the killing that changes the way they look at life when they come back home. The things they see over there, normal people going through that, having to see women and babies blown apart, killing another human being just as scared and revolted by it all as they are." The eyes misted over and looked beyond me. "It's the deep-thinkers, the gentle ones who change the most. War makes them all rotten inside like bad fruit. Even though they look good from the outside, they go bad, shrivel from the inside out. I'd tell her to wait if I were you."

"How's it taste?" I made a last stab at waggling an opportunity to sink my molars into her goulash. "Smells de-lish."

"Needs salt, I think. Hand me the shaker, will you, Ethan?"

"Nathan," I corrected, forwarding the saltshaker. It was all too obvious that I had taken a wrong turn somewhere, but I had no idea how to get back on the right path.

There was a slam. The front door shook. A boarder started up the stairs.

Delilah looked up at the kitchen clock on the wall. "Hello, Veronica."

From the stairwell, a thin voice echoed back. "Good evening, Mrs. Goodknight."

"Good day?"

"Good enough."

"Good."

"Have a nice night, Mrs. Goodknight."

"Goodnight, Miss Nigh."

"Night, Mrs. Goodknight."

My jaw slackened as I studied the open doorway and tried to decipher the odd exchange between these two.

Delilah stirred milk into her coffee. "That's Veronica. She's always home at six. Hardly ever comes down from her room. You'll see. She likes it very quiet. I did tell you about the radio, didn't I, Ethan?"

"It's Nathan. Yes."

"She hardly ever goes out. Pins up her hair, has a bath and is sound asleep by ten."

I looked at the empty foyer once more then back at the place setting in front of me. Who was the spot being saved for? Who was going to arrive in time to enjoy my goulash?

"Oh, before you go up," she said politely, "could you put the milk back in the icebox?"

I picked up the bottle and turned around to open her Frigidaire. There was a fresh lemon pie inside. The waves of meringue, golden brown like the tips of ripe, summer wheat whetted my appetite even more.

I retrieved my hat. "I'll go on up then, I guess."

She barely glanced up at my departure. Our first social encounter hadn't exactly gone well. In my room, I jerked off my shoes, pulled off my socks and flopped back on the bed. Lacing my fingers behind my head, I gazed up at the ceiling. Every time I took a breath, I could taste the tangy goulash at the tip of my tongue. I should have figured Delilah would have a date for supper. Probably some slick, braided officer from the Merchant Marine showing up at the front door with a bottle of Greek wine and a loaf of feta cheese. Or maybe one of those mustachioed, vested bureaucrats working at the Federal Courthouse on Salmon Street.

I heard the sound of a toilet flushing down the hall. Then steps padded by my door—Miss Nigh on her nightly rounds. I would soon come to know the routine: fifteen minutes behind the bathroom door while she rolled up her frizzy brown hair, greased her face with the lardy poultice from the Pond's jar on the glass shelf over the sink and then ran the tub water. She never spoke to me if we passed in the hallway after she had adorned herself with her restorative appliances and potions. She would only lower her pointy chin and nod quickly as we passed, shoulder to shoulder, like toy soldiers on parade.

In time, I became intimately aware of all Miss Nigh's bodily odors and rituals of ablution. The bathroom we shared was filled with the damp residue of her perfumed baths, the detritus of her wear and tear: kinked hairs on the lip of the sink and on the rim of the tub, used tissues in the toilet bowl, strange-smelling odors from Eastern weeds and Oriental oils she rubbed, dabbed, splashed and sprayed on every part of her virginal body. With all that elephantine effort at refurbishing, she came and went, upstairs and down, each morning and evening with no discernible difference in her appearance. Miss Nigh was, after all that, still a plain spinster with hair like old mattress ticking, legs fit to hold up a highboy dresser and eyes like a badger.

But Delilah was, despite the turbans and dungarees, someone special. She moved in sensual rhythms. It was like watching Ginger dancing with Fred when she walked across the room. And those eyes. They were her most outstanding feature. There was a silver mist like an ocean fog that could cloud her gaze sometimes. She was so sad underneath all that submerged energy. I could not imagine Delilah entertaining some Dixie swabby from a Liberty ship, a shoe salesman from Meier and Frank or a pool-shooting shark from a Front Street dive. Delilah emanated a sense of class, a certain refinement that complimented her easy self-assurance.

That empty place setting at the kitchen table, I surmised glumly in my room, had to be reserved for a full Commander or a surgeon from the veterans hospital.

Upstairs, brooding in the twilight, I listened. It was as quiet as always outside. Just some errant sirens, a dog yapping far away, cars rumbling past and around the corner, the rattle of the streetcar starting up the hill. Veronica had said *Mrs.* Goodnight. So Delilah was married. Her husband must be overseas. That's why she had discouraged me from urging my sister to marry an airman. Maybe Delilah's husband was dead. My God, maybe missing in action, maybe a POW rotting away in some dreadful camp. And Delilah was keeping a patient vigil at home, renting the upstairs rooms to earn enough money to keep the house until his return. She must be reserving her table for her husband's best friend, maybe his squadron commander or the captain who had shipped her husband's things back home. What a dynamic drama.

I swung my legs off the bed, jammed my feet back into my shoes and hurried down the stairs, snapping my suspenders over my shoulders as I skipped through the foyer and craned my neck to see into the kitchen. It was empty. The plates were still on the table—one dirty, one as spotless and bare as when I left it. The percolator was still plugged in.

"Hello?" I called out softly. "Delilah?"

I opened the icebox. The pie was still untouched. Sitting down, I scooped the remainder of the goulash into the clean plate, stuffed my mouth and ate hurriedly. Before I even swallowed, I was flushed with sweaty shame. Here I was, a new boarder already in arrears with the rent deposit, stealing food from a poor, war wife, a grieving woman keeping the home fires burning for her brave warrior. What a miserable mouse, what a thieving rat. Revolted, I tipped my chair back, pushed the plate away, ran back upstairs to my room, closed and locked the door and listened to the blood thudding in my temples. I was half expecting some brutish fellow to crash through the door, push me up against the wall and choke the goulash out of me.

"Shit," I groaned, sinking back on the bed and closing my eyes. I felt lower than a common skunk for my cowardly kitchen raid.

As the room grew dark behind the saffron window shades blocking the summer sun, I played the same sad scene a dozen times in my mind. Delilah seated at the table, her faceted eyes burning holes in the dark-blue uniform seated opposite her, picking at the goulash on his plate.

*"You're a strong, brave woman,"* he would say in a rich, baritone just like Gary Cooper's. *"You've waited so long, Delilah."*

Her eyes glistened with dammed tears. *"I'll wait forever if I have to."*

His hand pressed hers. *"Delilah, you may hate me for saying this, but—"*

Her chin quivered. *"No. Don't. Please, Darling. I can't bear it."*

He leaned so far forward his tie dipped in the meat juice. *"It isn't fair."* Then he stood up and tipped over the bottle of milk. *"I love you, dammit!"*

I turned over, punched my yielding pillow and faced the wall. No. That wasn't right. She would never allow him to say it. He knew. She knew. It was the poignant silence that passed between them all these years. Since her husband had been gone. The tension was so thick she could cut it with a knife. But they never spoke of their tortured longing.

I played it again.

He gulped a mouthful of creamed corn. *"Delilah, it's been so long."*

*"Yes. I know. Three years."*

No. I turned over again as the bed springs screamed. Two years.

*"Two years,"* she murmured mournfully.

*"So long,"* he mourned with her. *"And you've been so faithful, Delilah. All these lonely years without him in your life."*

Suddenly my eyes flew open. I saw a black fly crawling over a plaster crack above me. What if she had grown tired of waiting? Two years was a long time. What if she had given up in despair of ever seeing him again? What if she had succumbed to temptation? I got up, reached for my cigarettes and lit one.

*"If he comes back... Christ,"* he said, hanging his head. *"What'll I do, Delilah? I can't give you up."*

She reached for his arm and laid her elbow in the margarine dish. *"He'll always come first, Gary, you know that."*

I blew smoke at the ceiling and dislodged the fly. Not Gary. Bradley, Stanley. No. Bruce. Definitely not Bruce. Nigel. Too British. Clark, Tyrone. Not quite. I drummed my fingers across my belly. Then the fantasy came back to life in a flash of poignant brilliance.

*"Oh, God, Nathan, I never knew it could be like this,"* she whispered.

The man across from her at the table was suddenly slimmer, younger, with wire-rimmed glasses and suspenders. He had a stain on his corduroy jacket and a corn kernel stuck on his lower lip. *"Don't worry about it, Baby. I can handle it."*

I grinned and sucked in a lung full of tobacco smoke. Now I could plainly see the two of us sitting downstairs at the kitchen table over the platter of goulash. Her eyes fastened intently on mine, our bare feet meshed beneath the table as her fingers tangled in my hair.

*"Oh, Nattie,"* she panted. *"I want you so much it's breaking my heart."*

I put down my fork and took a quick slug of cold milk from my glass. *"Keep your shirt on, Baby. There's plenty of time."* My smile transformed my face to a likeness of Jimmy Stewart, without glasses, of course. I could feel my toes start to tingle as I painted the picture. She was climbing across the table with her dungarees squashing the oleo. Her bandanna came loose, and her hair fell across her cheek. I licked off my milk mustache before we kissed. She arched her spine, moaning as I reached for a handful of flesh beneath the shirt. She was warm and fragrant with onions as I groped for her.

*"Oh, Ethan. I dreamed it could be like this."*

*"It's Nathan."*

*"Kiss me."*

*"Oh, Baby. Delilah..."* I came up with a handful of goulash, tomato paste and hamburger juice. Then the tablecloth slipped away from under her hips, and we both crashed to the floor. I held on to her with both hands. Her hair caught in my shirt button as we rolled together in a single embrace of eager bodies. Warm milk dripped off the table and splatted on her cheek. I slipped my tongue between her cherry lips and felt a niblet wedged between her front teeth.

My eyes opened abruptly. The dream dissolved. I reached over and put my cigarette in the ashtray. Sleep was beginning to pervert my fantasy. Before I could reconstruct the passionate coupling on the slippery linoleum, I was snoring softly with my legs curled up and my Lucky Strike smoldering in the souvenir ashtray from Hawaii.

# Four

===========

**He** sat there in the armchair, his knees rising as his ass sank in the spineless cushion. His fingers drubbed the threadbare upholstery while he peered first at the dresser and then at the lumpy bed with me sitting on it.

"Pop, it's only three blocks from the library," I blurted before he had a chance to speak, pointing out the window. My view was the bare brick of the Pythian Building. I had a slice of sky no bigger than a wedge of boardinghouse pie. "And the Roosevelt Hotel is an easy walk. I can save money on the streetcar." It was a puny rationale for deserting him but the best rebuttal I could muster.

He folded his hands in what I knew from long experience signaled grudging disapproval. "Nat," he admonished in his soft, phlegmy voice, "it's got no bathroom."

"It's down the hall, Pop." I rubbed the stain on my trouser. "It's cheap, Pop. Only five dollars a week."

"Don't tell me what cheap is. I can see cheap for myself. Shabby, small, a hole a rat wouldn't be proud to call home. That I can see for myself."

"Five bucks a week is all I can afford."

"That's thirty percent of your gross wages."

I looked down at my hands. It was impossible to argue with him. He always had the figures, statistics, rules and references at the tip of his tongue to rebut any defense I mounted. No matter what brilliant point of logic I tried to burn across home plate, my father always sealed the argument with a mathematical ratio of the total percentage of my ignorance. It wasn't that he tried to belittle his only son. It was just that to Pop life was all about numbers and cold, hard facts, and I somehow had failed to learn the proper lessons of accounting.

"It's not much," I answered meekly. "I can live cheaper." His pincer glare knocked me off the rails for a moment. "That is, I won't have much in the way of expenses."

"You need meals, laundry, cab fare, haircuts."

"I don't need cabs, Pop."

His bushy eyebrows rose. "You can't live like a bum, Nathan."

"Pop, I need peace and quiet, time to work without interruptions. I'm going to finish the thesis this summer."

He sighed heavily. Then he looked at the Smith Corona portable sitting on the table by the window and shook his head dolefully. "*That's* where you write?" Just like he used to squint at me with his right eye and ask if I intended to wear *that* shirt to class, the *filthy* one not fit for the ragbag. I'd spend the whole day at school peering down my shirtfront trying to find the offensive splotch.

"It's fine, Pop. I have lots of light from the window, and it's real quiet here."

"It's noisy at home? I could sell the old Zenith your mother saved for two years to buy me. Maybe I could cancel the newspaper so I wouldn't make so much racket in the mornings reading. I could kill the canary so his singing wouldn't bother you either."

"Please, Pop."

"You want quiet, why don't you move into the mortuary? Nobody to bother you there either."

"Please, Pop..."

"You gotta be independent, huh? Get away from your father so you can feel like a man, all grown up, does whatever the hell he wants to do for a change and everybody else be damned. Is that it?"

"Not exactly." It was. But I couldn't say so and break his heart.

"There's no toilet."

"It's right down the hall."

"You have a nice room at home. You can even play the radio all night long. I don't hear so good as I used to. And you can take a hot bath whenever you want."

"Pop..." I sank both hands in my pockets. My mouth was as numb as my brain. "It's fine. Just fine here."

"You got hangers in the closet?" he asked, twisting around to stare at my cubbyhole wardrobe. "You got no place to keep your good suit, the charcoal flannel I had tailored for your graduation. The moths'll eat it up in a week in this place. At home, I got cedar in the closets."

"It's fine, Pop."

"Who's gonna do your laundry, huh? You look like a bum, Nathan. No crease in your trousers. You should be at home with your family not living in some flop house with no toilet and no hangers."

"I got hangers. And there's a toilet right down the hall."

"Where you gonna eat? You got no hotplate for your coffee even?"

"Cooking in the rooms isn't allowed."

"So where are you gonna get a proper meal? How can you study all night, work all day and not eat right?"

"I'm working at the Roosevelt Hotel, Pop, from six to ten. I can catch up on my reading when nobody's around. I'll get by fine. The landlady says I can go downstairs and raid the icebox if I get hungry."

His eyes bulged. "Charity? You're that bad off you have to beg meals from strangers? Is that how you want to live? Like a bum? Like somebody who's got no home, no family? You want to shame me, Nathan? Shame the memory of your mother and me who tried to provide for you all these years so you could live like a gentleman?"

"Pop, please. There's an automat right on Broadway."

He snorted into his prodigious handkerchief. "Automat is not eating. It's for people who got no home, Nathan."

I had no more fingers to stick in the dike. I just had to sit and let him get it all out, his frustration with the unraveling ends of his life with my mother Annette gone for so long, his girls drifting into

41

busy lives of their own that did not include him anymore. And his pride and joy, his son Nathan Alexander slipping into a seedy semblance of anonymity without a struggle.

He looked up slowly, eyeing me like a shoplifter in his store. "Tell me the truth, Nathan. Is this about women?"

"What?"

"You gotta get away from home so you can bring women up here at night? Is that what all this is about?"

"Jesus, Pop."

"I'm not so stupid I don't understand what goes on these days. The war's turned everybody under forty into sex maniacs who can't wait to get their pants off. You can have as many women as you want, Nathan, until you get married. I'm not so old fashioned as you think. You don't have to move into a rat hole just to get laid."

My face was redder than my Uncle Herman's BVD's. This was impossible.

He tapped his fingers on a knee and jerked his head at the door. "You got a sink here for shaving. That's nice, huh?" He had finally found something on which he could bestow approval. "It's good you don't have to go out in the hall looking like a bum. You can shave and wash up right here in your room. But you got no bath, no toilet here." His face wrinkled in a frown. "You coulda got a nicer place, Nathan. Something with a bathroom, maybe draperies."

"Draperies? What do I need with draperies? I just want a quiet place near the library so I can do my research and write."

"All that time writing about all those old kings. Who wants to read about all those dead, Roman has-beens? This is modern times, Nat. You should be writing about Mr. Roosevelt, General Eisenhower or Winston Churchill. Real heroes. That's the kind of history people are interested in these days."

He'd hit a nerve, and I flinched. "We've discussed this a thousand times. I'm not interested in military history."

"Military? Who's talking about military? These are just people. Great people who happen to be famous. They're everyday news, Son. Everybody wants to read about General Eisenhower and his dog. What's his name? A bulldog, isn't it?"

"That's General Patton."

"Who cares what Julius Caesar did when Hitler is trying to take over the world? I ask you, Nathan—*who?*" He thumped his thigh with a hairy fist.

"I don't know, Pop. I just know ancient history is what I care about, what I want to teach. The Roman monarchy is what I've chosen for my thesis, and I can't change it."

"Well, you could write about some modern Italians, at least. Some popular people are Italian even with the war and that damned Mussolini. There's Fiorello Laguardia." He plumped his lips and drew the name for me with his forefinger punctuating the air. "There's Marconi for instance. He's very popular, very intelligent. And Giuseppe Verdi. They did something good for everybody. Who wouldn't want to read about those fellas, huh, Nattie?"

This was all an encore performance from the original diatribe at the time I announced my doctoral selection. "My thesis is on *The History of the Ancient Roman Monarchy With Parallels To the Decline of European Royal Dynasties*, Pop. That's it."

He appeared to be perplexed as if his reaction were entirely spontaneous. "Not even a mention of Marconi?"

"No."

"Not even a footnote to keep your readers interested?"

"No."

He rubbed his hands together the way I used to see him limbering up his fingers before he began stacking and arranging the produce in the store. His eyes roamed the room looking for another target. "You got no toilet here," he mumbled once more and put his hat on. "You got money for cab fare?"

"I'm fine, Pop."

"You can come over to the house on Sunday for a decent meal."

"I will, Pop."

"If you come over before four, I can walk up to the corner and meet your car, Nathan." Like I was still five-years old again, he never stopped looking after me. He tugged at the brim of his hat as he stood up. "You know, Francie is gonna marry that guy," he said without catching my eyes.

"He's a nice fellow, Pop."

"Nice? What's nice?"

"She's crazy about him. He treats her like a queen, Pop."

"I know she's living with him like they were man and wife already. She should get married, Nat. You tell her to get to church. Frances should be married before she ruins her chances to be with Mama in heaven. Living in sin like common, low-class trash would have your mother spinning in her poor grave if she knew what I know. I don't tell her anything about what Francie is doing with that Mr. Nice." He pointed toward the ceiling. "All my prayers upstairs just go on like Francie's as pure as the driven snow. You're her brother. You should do something."

What could I say? My father believed in the whole nine yards—heaven, hell, angels with harps and purgatory. All of it. As far as he was concerned, my mother was sitting upstairs somewhere behind a cumulus cloud, looking down on all of us, just waiting for a chance to get everybody scrubbed up for Sunday supper one more time. He looked on her death as just a trial separation in their marriage.

"Gee, Pop, Francie is really in love with the guy, and there's a war on, you know."

"Tell her to get to a church, Nathan. She shouldn't be ashamed to have me meet this Mr. Nice Guy she has to hide from her mother and me. I wanna see my little girl with a ring on her finger."

I tugged at my earlobe, a nervous habit that always gave away my chagrin. "She didn't want you to know, Pop. She knew you'd disapprove."

"I know what I know. I'm her father."

"She's gonna get married, but she's afraid that if he doesn't come back, and she gets pregnant—"

"Pregnant? Why is that such a sin for a married woman? Gladys already has two beautiful babies and a successful husband who's a professional man and takes very good care of her. She was married in the church wearing her mother's wedding dress and without any of this hanky panky."

I squelched a facetious grin. "You made it sound as if the church were wearing mom's dress."

He opened his mouth in mute astonishment at my digression. "What did you say?"

"Your progressive tense modifier. You misplaced it."

"What are you trying to say to me, Nattie?"

"You phrased the sentence so it sounds like the church was wearing mom's dress." I looked out the window, desperately seeking an easy exit. "Never mind."

"That's what I paid for?" He snapped his suspenders. "A fancy education so you can make fun of me, ridicule your own father with your fancy schemansky, big college brain, twist my words into some kind of a joke when I'm talking about your sister's future and happiness in the hereafter?"

"I'm sorry." I was. He was right, and I deserved more than the scowl he laid on me.

"You can show me some respect, Nathan Alexander."

"I didn't mean any disrespect."

"I'm your father even if you have left my house and turned your back on the family."

"That's not what I—"

"That's okay," he shushed my indignation with a quieting hand the way he would intimidate a frisky setter about to lick his face. "Never mind. You made your choice. So now I'm alone with all that house and nobody to live in it." He took a sidetrack before I could rebut his claim to martyrdom. "This would kill your mother. You know that, Nattie? If your mother knew what her children were up to, it would kill her."

"Pop, listen—"

"You tell your sister she should get this nice guy to a church, Nathan. And Carla should be thinking about starting a family herself," he took another sidetrack suddenly. "She's no spring chicken, you know. When is that fella gonna give her a ring? Or are they in such a hurry these days, they don't bother being engaged anymore?"

"Carla has a good job. They're saving their money to buy a house."

"Well, tell Francie she should marry her Mr. Nice anyway. If he goes overseas and doesn't come back, well, think how she'll feel if she has nothing left."

"Pop—"

"If she has a baby, at least she has something. I have your sisters and you, Nattie." His eyes were moist as he stretched to wrap both arms around me. "I have the jewels Annette left me. Her most precious jewels. That's a man's treasure in life, Nathan. His children."

I hugged him back. How frail and small he seemed these days. It was the store and losing the drive and purpose the business gave to his life. With my mother gone, the old house full of someone else's energies now, all of us gone, he was a fragile shell. "I'll talk to Francie," I promised. "Don't worry."

It didn't matter. He had said enough to let me know he knew we were concealing important parts of our lives from him. And our betrayal wounded his pride most of all. It made his heart ache to realize his children no longer needed him or his confidences.

We parted at the front step. He turned and walked around the corner to catch the Broadway streetcar. The last glimpse I had of him was the slouched shoulders hunched in the old fashioned, double-breasted overcoat as he trudged along like an old man bound for someplace where nobody was waiting for him.

As I closed the front door and started up the stairs, I saw Delilah coming down with an armload of towels.

"I was going to give you your fresh linen," she said. "Would you like an extra towel?"

"Thank you." I took the load from her.

She wiped her upper lip. Her neck and shoulders, bared by the low cut blouse, glistened with sweat. "It's so hot, I can't sleep. Would you like a fan upstairs?"

"That'd be great."

"Come on down to the basement after you put that away. I have some things down there you could use."

"Thanks. I will." I raced up the stairs and stowed my towels. Then I went back down, walked through the kitchen and peered down the stairwell into the cavernous basement.

A light came on, and Delilah called to me. "Come on down, Ethan. Watch your step."

I grabbed the railing and descended. It was cool down there in the musty dungeon.

She stood in a halo of electric light cutting through the murk like diamond shards. Her hair was pulled up over her ears, curled on top, damp at the temples. Her flame-tipped fingernails lifted the curls from the nape of her neck. She was wearing a pair of blue shorts with cuffs and a coral scarf knotted at her waist.

"It's over there on top of those boxes." She pointed, and I followed. "Be careful," she warned as I scaled the packing crates like a mountain goat. "There's rats down here."

"This one?" I tapped a box on top.

"I think so. Can you look inside before you bring it down?"

"Sure thing." I pried open a flap and looked in. "It looks like kitchen pots."

"Oh, well, try the other one next to the rug beater, Ethan." She handed up a flashlight.

"It's Nathan."

"Can you see anything?"

I directed the beam between the cardboard flaps. I saw the Westinghouse seal. "I see it."

"Oh, good. Bring it upstairs, will you, Ethan?"

I clambered up, laden like a pack mule and brushed the dirt off my one good white shirt.

She rubbed at a smudge on my chin. "Sorry about the soot and dust on your shirt. I can wash it for you. No charge."

"Oh, it's no bother. Don't worry about it." I lugged the box across the kitchen and set it down on the table. Delilah took out each item wrapped in newspaper and set it on the counter. I got the table fan, a reading lamp with a cowboy shade, a wool robe with maroon cord at the cuffs and a stack of *National Geographic* magazines.

"I thought you might like these. Maybe you could use them in your research."

"Thanks." I fanned one issue quickly.

"And you do need extra light if you're going to be using that typewriter at night. If you need a new bulb, you can take one from the floor lamp."

"Thanks. I will."

"It's so hot, isn't it?"

"Miserable." I wrapped the cord around the base of the fan and started for the doorway.

"I was thinking of taking my mattress out onto the porch tonight."

"Sounds like a terrific idea."

"Could you help me? It's awfully heavy."

"Sure." I put the fan back on the table and trailed behind her as we went through the arched entrance I knew lead to her bedroom.

She opened the door and stood back. There was a satin coverlet in salmon and tasseled pillows thrown up against the waterfall headboard. I could smell lilies and cigarette smoke. Luckies. Like mine. The glass ashtray beside the bed was filled with dead soldiers, crimson lip prints on each one.

She sat down on the chaise, kicked off her shoes and reached for a pack of cigarettes. She shook one free and looked up at me.

"Oh, sorry. Here," I said, fumbling for a match. Before I could strike a flame, she had picked up her silver Ronson and lit her own.

"Was that old man your father?" she asked as she put her head back and blew smoke toward the ceiling.

"He's just checking on me, I guess. I mean, the place, you know. Seeing if I'm settled." Sounded like a schoolboy, didn't I? I never made sensible conversation with Delilah. She probably thought I was another naive, pimple-faced college grad as dull as dishwater. Which I suppose I was.

"Does he live in town?" She crossed her bare legs and swung her foot. Her toenails were painted the same blood-red shade as her fingertips.

"Across the river on Fremont."

"So he's worried about you, Ethan?"

"He's lonely, I think. I was the last kid at home."

"Oh." She exhaled a cloud of smoke. "You're the baby of the family?"

I didn't answer that one. I pulled the spread off the bed.

"The poor old man must feel abandoned with you out of the nest."

"I suppose," I mumbled, wrestling with the covers.

"Why don't you live at home?"

I tugged and jerked the mattress off the box springs, curled it into a carpet-sized roll and heaved it over my shoulder. "You want this out the back door, through the kitchen?"

"Whatever's easiest."

I staggered through the doorway and didn't fit. The bulky mattress wedged itself between the door moldings and butted me like an overstuffed, Sumo wrestler.

"Are you sure you wouldn't like to tie it up with something?"

"You got any twine?'

"I have rope. Hang on." She squeezed by me, so close I could feel her nipples pressing against my damp shirtfront. "I'll be right back."

I wiped a dirty streak from my face, leaned against the wall and waited. When she returned, she looped some manila rope around the mattress, tied two neat square knots and stepped back out of my way. Slick as snot. But then I was brought up to expect womanly adeptness as routine.

"Thanks," I acknowledged weakly and dragged the bundle out through the kitchen to the sleeping porch in back.

When I unrolled her mattress and turned around to catch my breath, she was standing with her arms akimbo, blowing a lock of hair from her forehead. "It's so damn hot, Ethan. Maybe I can get some sleep out here."

"It's Nathan. Nathan Alexander."

"Oh." Her eyes fastened onto mine, and I felt as if my feet had caught fire.

"You keep calling me Ethan."

"I like the name, that's all. What's the difference?"

"Well, for starters, it's not my name."

"Don't you like it?"

"It's okay, I guess."

She brushed by me. "Well then, I think I'll call you Ethan, if you don't mind."

"I suppose I don't."

"Okay." She smiled slowly until I smiled back. "If you want to, you can call me Charmaine."

"Is that your real name?"

"It is if you want it to be." Goddam, I wanted to touch her, to make a carnal connection, but I knew better. She was already moving away, pressing her palms on the porch screen, staring out at the red-leaf maple shading the yard like a tattered umbrella. Her face paled as those sorrowful eyes abandoned me altogether. The silence that passed between us was as charged as an August thunderstorm

"I guess I'll go up then," I murmured finally. "Goodnight."

She didn't even look back at me as I left her alone.

That night, I pulled my window shade up and looked down at the tiny yard below. I could see the edge of the porch and a patch of dark screen shielded by the trunk of the tree. I knew she was down there, lying naked on the satin pillows with her arms thrown up over her head, staring at the stars. My entire body ached for a consummation of everything she had stirred in me, embers smoldering as I lay with nothing to quench the flames about to erupt.

I pulled my clothes off, set the fan on the bedside table and stretched the electric cord out to its full length. Then I got down on my hands and knees to peer under the bed for the power outlet. There wasn't one. I pulled the old chair away from the wall, peeked behind the dresser. Nothing. There were two outlets in my room. One under the bare bulb hanging over the sink and the other a single plug-in behind the wardrobe.

I put the fan on the floor and crouching on hands and knees tried to reach the outlet with my arm twisted behind the wardrobe. It was no use. The cord was too short.

I put on my trousers, looped my suspenders over my shoulders and started down the stairs. There was no light under Miss Nigh's door. Downstairs, the lights were off in the kitchen as well. I walked softly across the linoleum to the back door and rapped on the screen.

"Delilah? Are you asleep? It's Nathan."

There was the sound of soft purring, a fan stirring the summer night. She answered me in a thin, dreamy voice. "Ethan? Are you still up?"

"I can't plug in the fan. Do you have an extension cord?" Sweat droplets were dripping from my chin and nose.

"No. I'm afraid not."

"Isn't there one somewhere in the house?" I mopped sweat with my soiled handkerchief. "Can I have a look in the basement?"

I heard the rustle of cloth as she came to the other side of the screen and stood there looking at me. She was wearing a green crepe dress draped at one hip, black pumps and crimson lipstick. Her breath smelled of whiskey.

"I don't think so, Ethan. I'd rather you went back upstairs. It's late."

"Well, maybe tomorrow I can get one at the hardware store."

"That's a good idea. Goodnight."

"Night."

As I turned away, I could hear a second sound—glasses clinking and ice skittering into liquid with a soft plunk. Cigarette smoke coiled through the screen and up my nose. I stopped at the kitchen table and looked back at her slinky silhouette with the moonlight painting her hair the color of champagne. I saw only her shadow, smelled only her scent. Her hand floated upward to her face and then reached outward in a sensual caress to a lover beyond my view.

I heard her breathless sigh as I went out. "It's so hot tonight. Too hot. Too hot to make love. Let's just sit on the porch a while, shall we?"

I went upstairs, closed my door, stripped nude and lay down on my bed. I held my breath to hear her sounds from below. All I could make out was the slap of the screen door, and the music playing on the radio. It was a serenade.

# Five

========

**On** Sunday, I got up late, had a bite at the diner on Morrison and Third Avenue and then walked across the Morrison Street Bridge. On the East side of the river, I stopped in at a drugstore, bought a cheap cigar and a bottle of shaving lotion and grabbed the streetcar for Fremont Street. When I got off a block from the house, I could see my father sitting on the concrete-slab porch, reading the newspaper. He was still in his scruffy slippers, unshaven with his undershirt clinging like onionskin to his bulbous belly.

I hopped up the step, took off my hat and handed him the sack. "Hey, Pop, you forget it's Sunday?"

He looked up at me over the rim of his glasses. His mouth began to quiver. The milky eyes blinked back tears. "Oh, Nattie. I forgot. I didn't think you would come. I slept late. My ulcer is killing me these days, Nattie. Killing me. I can only sleep for an hour, and I wake up all the time, and I'm wondering why nobody is in the house except a tired, old man who forgets his son coming home for Sunday supper." He rose slowly and shuffled toward my arms.

I felt the stubble scrape my cheeks as we embraced. The strong, cheerful, competent man I had always known was turning into a confused, old codger with stains on his undershirt. "Hey, Pop. Forget it. We can walk down to Hollywood for some hamburgers."

He sniffled into his rumpled handkerchief. I opened the screen, and we went inside. The house was dark with all the shades drawn.

His shoes, trousers and coat were lying on the divan. Yesterday's newspaper was still unfolded on the dining room table.

"You came so early, Nattie. Nothing's ready." He waved his arms, raging at the increasing chaos in his life which reminded him each day how far he had come from the golden years when he owned his own emporium, employed twelve people and lived in the biggest house on the block.

"It's past noon, Pop."

"I slept a little late. My damned ulcer keeps me up these days."

I began picking things up. "You taking your medicine?"

He nodded and flopped down in his old rocker. "It's no good, Nattie. It doesn't work for me anymore. What I need is some of your mother's egg whites and nutmeg." He patted his paunch lovingly. "She always knew what I needed to make me feel good, Nattie. I miss her cooking. I'm not so good at it, you know."

I looked through the tiny dining area to the kitchen. The counters were stacked with dirty dishes, milk bottles and opened tins of soup. I had no idea my father was sliding so far off the scale. This wasn't like him at all. Maybe I should call Gladys and have her talk to her husband about taking care of Pop. Maybe he had more than a simple belly ulcer. Maybe our father was really sick with something serious.

"You shoulda called me, Nattie, and told me you were coming," he scolded.

"You don't even have a phone, Pop." I carried a load of dirty clothes into the kitchen and onto the back porch where the washing tub sat, unused for quite some time it looked like. The box of soap flakes was empty when I shook it. "You need some things done around here. How can you do your laundry when you're out of soap flakes?"

"I can't hear you, Nattie. And I don't need soap flakes. I got a full box right there by the washbasin."

I came back to the living room with an exasperated grin. I was used to my father taking care of things, looking after my sisters and me, and now I had to face the unpleasant fact that since I had left home, he was letting it all fall apart. "You know you can go over to the market and call me when you need something, Pop." The Fremont Market was only a half block away. Pop hated to go in there. The guy behind the counter had started in the business after Pop did, and he still had his store. He catered to more affluent customers, ones who worked in the offices downtown, whose wives had fur coats, hoarded butter and gas ration books and paid their grocery bills on time.

"What use is a phone if I can't call you up? You got no toilet. You got no phone."

"I told you there's a phone downstairs, and the landlady will come up to my room and get me whenever you call. You have the number written down?"

He shook his head as he blew his nose. "I don't remember. Maybe I put it right there in the kitchen somewhere, Nattie. Maybe it's on my smoking table. You find it for me, okay? I forget exactly where I put it."

"Jeez, Pop. You shoulda put it right by the bed or someplace handy in case you need me for something."

"What would I need besides a little company? I'm not a baby, Nat."

"Where are your glasses?" I asked, picking up another armload of clothes from the club chair. A withered orange was buried between the cushions.

"I'm not going over to that Fremont Grocery to make a call. I'm not giving that smarty bastard my money."

"It's only a phone call, Pop."

"No matter. That bastard isn't getting a single penny."

I went back to the kitchen and looked around. There was a loaf of stale rye open on top of the breadbox and a slab of cheddar cheese molding on the drain board. I returned to the living room and gathered up the old newspapers. "Pop, you need to take care of things."

"I'm fine."

"It's no good you living like this. Maybe you should think about moving in with Francie up in Tacoma."

"No!" He swatted at me with a hairy hand I easily avoided.

"She's got a nice little apartment, Pop. They have plenty of room. Their davenport makes into a double bed, and you could go to the pictures with Francie and get a decent meal." I picked up his slippers and fit them on his feet. I noticed his ankles were swollen as I pushed the deerskin shoes on. His skin felt like fresh dough, marbled with knotty veins and bruises. My father had aged so fast these last few years since the girls left, and I was away at school. Maybe I had been wrong to leave him on his own.

"Nattie, you're talking crazy. Just because you come early, and I didn't sleep too good last night, you start talking bullshit. What d'you think? I'm over the hill? Think I'm ready for the bone yard, the junk heap? You ready to toss me out of my home, Nattie? Just because I sleep late on a Sunday?"

I bent over and put my arm around him. He smelled like stale smoke and urine. I had been so busy with my own life, studying, writing and research while my father was wasting away to a pitiful, dumpy little grocer with a runny nose and fat ankles. What had happened to the strong, barrel-chested man with the bushy mustache who hoisted me onto his shoulders to see the Rose Parade floats go by not so long ago, the dapper guy with shoulders stronger than a pack mule's, a gold watch chain hung from his natty vest and the tang of shaving soap fresh on his cheeks?

I kissed him. "Hey, Pop. Don't worry about it. What say we clean the place up a little and then go out for some hamburgers?"

"No, Nattie," he demurred, clutching my hands in his. "It gives me a bellyache all that spicy, fried food. I wish I could have chicken and dumplings like your mama used to make."

"There's a swell new picture at the Hollywood. Greer Garson, I think. You like her, don't you, Pop?"

"No, no. I don't like the picture shows. Nowadays you have to sit through all those films about the boys being killed over there. Terrible things to think about. War pictures with terrible things going on, and then what all those young people are doing in the balconies these days. There ought to be a law, Nattie, that you have to go to a hotel for that sort of thing."

I sat down on the divan and sighed. "Okay, Pop, you tell me. What would you like to do? I got paid Friday. We can go out and have some spaghetti and meatballs if you want."

He was still shaking his head. "No, no. All that spaghetti sauce gives me a bellyache. Always that Italian food, Romans, emperors, kings and whatnot on your mind, Nattie. I miss your mama's cooking. She always knew how to fix a meal no matter what was in her cupboard. Your sisters should cook half as good as their mother."

"Pop, for crissakes."

"Don't swear at me. I'm your father, remember? This is my house. At your place, you can talk however you want. Here you show some respect."

"Yessir." I bowed my head, ceding the point to my elder, to the protector and mentor who had made such sacrifices on my behalf. Most of which, I was coming to realize, I never fully appreciated. Even now.

"Nattie, it's a shame you came so early. I was gonna fix something nice for you, something better than that automat crap you eat all week in town."

"You want me to fix something?"

He flashed a look of mock astonishment. "You cook? You can boil water and maybe fry an egg if I light the stove. And you call that cooking?"

"I can cook some, Pop. Hey, how about if I go see what you got in the kitchen?"

He flagged me to a stop. "Nattie, sit. Just sit down a minute and talk to me."

I settled on the sofa but avoided meeting his stare.

There was an unmistakable sadness in his voice as he reached over and took hold of my arm. "Nattie, I'm getting old."

"Aw, Pop, you have a lot of good years left."

"Be quiet. Listen. I'm talking to you, Nattie. You know how old I am?"

"Sure," I lied. I had to start figuring. Annette was forty-four when I was born. That was in 1921, so she'd be sixty-five if she were alive, and my father was nine years older. The years piled up like firewood in my mind as I counted the ravages of the decades on my father's bent body sagging like a bag of boiled potatoes. "You're not that old, Pop," I hedged.

"Seventy-four last May. I'm an old man, Nattie. Getting older every day."

"Heck, that's not so old."

He shushed me with a thick finger pressed against his lips. "Listen. I'm telling you, Nattie. You should pay attention. When you see your father has become an old man, and he's telling you something important, you should pay attention—"

"Pop—"

"—and you should not forget that this bellyache has been killing me for years, since before Gladys left home. Remember?" He groaned and rubbed his belly button. "I got sick at her wedding."

I hung my head. I remembered. Pop always had a funny stomach. "It was the excitement and all the champagne you drank, Pop."

"No. It was my damned belly. And it wasn't just an ulcer, Nathan."

When he closed his eyes, I stared uncensored at the yellow skin hanging like chicken flesh from his jowls. "Are you really sick, Pop? Do you need to see a doctor for your stomach?"

"No, Nattie. No doctor. I know what I got."

"You been taking medicine for that ulcer for years."

"It's no ulcer, Nattie." He turned his head and focused his bleary eyes on my face. "Nathan, you're my only son. You're the baby, but you've gotta be the one to do this."

"Do what?"

A redheaded kid with a brown dog ran across the front yard. A red-checkered taxicab stopped at the corner and honked. I remember that. I remember the sound of the cabby hollering out his open window at the brown dog darting across the street as my father heaved himself from his chair and kissed my forehead.

"You have to be the one to tell your sisters that I'm dying from the stomach cancer. I got a few months, maybe until Christmas the doctors said. That's it, Nattie. I'm sorry I have to burden you with this, but it's a son's duty to be the head of the family when his turn comes."

I sucked in a breath and froze. I could count every tick from the humped-back mantel clock keeping track of my father's time.

He slouched his shoulders and headed for the bathroom. "I wanna see Francie married in a church before I go, Nattie. You owe it to your mother and me to see your sister gets a proper church wedding. It's your duty, Nathan." He stopped and put a hand on the doorjamb. He waited until I could muster the courage to let my eyes meet his. "Promise me, Nattie."

"Oh, Jesus, Pop. Are you sure? What about running some more tests or something?"

"No more tests. I'm telling you, Nathan. Just promise me, Son. It's all I'm asking. You see to Francie. See she gets married in the church with a white dress and veil like her sister."

"I will, Pop. Don't worry. She's gonna be fine."

"And that man Carla is engaged to. Mr. Philip Somebody. He should be thinking about setting a date. Carla's not getting any younger, is she? He shouldn't keep her waiting."

"Pop, I..."

"You look after your sisters, Nathan. I'm counting on you to be a man." He sighed, and his undershirt wrinkled across his shallow chest. "You're a good boy, Nathan. Your mother's pearl. Everything's gonna be fine. We're all in God's hands. I could always count on you, Nattie. A professor someday. Imagine that. With a doctoral degree. Your mother would burst open with pride she'd be so proud, Nattie. Remember that. Your mother is counting on you not to let us down. You know we were so proud, a college graduate, someday a man of importance teaching at the university. Imagine, Nathan. A poor man like me having such a son."

I choked back my tears. There was so much I should have told him, that I wanted to say, words filled with emotions and a tidal wave of affection that seemed to drown my inhibition as I sat there fighting for control. But in the end, I couldn't say any of it. And then the moment slipped away, and I had never felt so desperate, so inadequate.

"You remember what I promised your mother, Nattie. I told her she'd never have to look down and see her boy with sweat on his back and dirt under his fingernails. You remember that promise and keep it sacred for me. I promised your mother on her dying day her son would have an education and be a real gentleman."

I hung my head and tore off my glasses, unable to speak, barely able to catch my breath.

"Now let me shave and wash up, Nattie, and we can listen to the ballgame."

I reached over and grabbed the paper sack I'd carried from the Rexall. "I got you some shaving lotion, Pop." I held it open so he could peek inside. "It's Aqua Velva, your favorite." I wanted it to be a treasure all of a sudden and felt ashamed at the paltry prize I had brought him. I had always taken so much for granted, and now I knew it was all going to be taken away.

He smiled and kissed me once lightly on the cheek. "That's nice, Nattie. Nice."

Then when he turned around to shuffle to the bathroom, I saw him at last as he was—old, misshapen, gray and sallow in worn underwear, urine stains on his old trousers and white stubble on his sunken cheeks. And as soon as he closed the door behind him and turned on the faucet, I sank to my knees and bawled like an abandoned baby.

# Six

======================

**It** was after ten o'clock when I clambered off the smelly bus and started up the street toward Delilah's. I still had the bitter taste of tears in my throat. My father and I had eaten supper together, canned green beans and macaroni with powdered cheese. But the food tasted like sawdust as it went down. I couldn't keep my eyes off the man seated across from me at the table. Nothing about him cheered me. All I could see now when I looked at my father's face was death's mask settling on him like a summer tan. None of us had suspected how ill he was. At our last reunion, he had never said a thing as we walked out the door one by one, forgetting to return his blown kiss as we scrambled to catch the streetcar and rejoin our busy lives.

This was going to be hard on my sisters, especially Gladys who thought of herself as the maternal head of the family since Mom had died. And Carla. She knitted socks for Pop and worried about his taking his medicine. She fussed over all of us. Francie would feel overcome with guilt for leaving home and living in sin behind his back. As for me, I was numb with shock and pain as I stumbled up the front steps with glassy eyes and a burning sensation in my chest. To lose my father, see the roots of my life smothered under the ground meant a face-to-face confrontation with my own mortality. It meant my youth was ended. My raging optimism and exuberance for life was crashing to the ground as I entered my stuffy room and sank down on the bed.

I wanted to cry some more but knew I could not. I probably wouldn't be able to lift the burden Pop had placed on me to be the man of the family, to carry on the family name, to amount to something, anything beyond what I felt so keenly as undeserving, miserably inadequate. I wasn't ready to face responsibility beyond my own selfish borders.

Sunday night, I lay sprawled on the center of my bed and smoked a half pack of Luckies. I blew smoke at the ceiling and listened to the sounds of traffic on the streets. I was miserable. My guts were churning like a Maytag. What was I going to tell my sisters? They were going to blame me for not taking care of Pop, for abandoning him. Maybe I had failed them all. What a goddam, miserable, selfish bastard I was.

I undressed, splashed tepid water on my face and switched on the light. Sitting down at my typewriter, I was struck with a passionate energy that seemed spawned from my misery and guilt. My sweaty fingers flew over the keys as the machine clacked and thumped its way through a sentence, a paragraph and then a full page. I tore the paper free and tossed it on the bed as I lit a cigarette and rolled in another sheet. *Clack, clack, clack...* the words flowed like hot breath after a race. There was no time to stop and read. I just worked at the keys until I noticed a dim, pink glow soften the walls of my room. My neck ached. My legs were numb. I stretched and heard Virginia's door open and her slippered feet pad to the bathroom.

I stood up and rubbed my eyes. The Hawaiian ashtray was full of Lucky stubs. The bedspread was littered with dozens of pages in no particular order. I stooped and began to assemble them into a manuscript. Then I fell back in the chair and tried to focus my eyes on the words as Miss Nigh ran her bath water and made the plumbing sing like Scottish bagpipes.

*"She had such sad eyes"* the first chapter read. *"The saddest eyes I had ever seen."*

My fascination with Delilah had begun to take shape and breath. Like it or not, good or bad, noble or base we were tethered as spiders caught in the web.

# Seven

========

**When** it came, Death introduced itself politely, sat in a near corner of the hospital room and waited patiently for us all to make apologies for our sins before slipping over to embrace my father as gently as an old lover. His dying was gracious in its intrusion and expedient in its exit. Pop keeled over getting off the streetcar in front of the Fremont Grocery. The owner rushed out and then called an ambulance so Pop got the guy's nickel after all. At the hospital, our father lasted only four days. In a peaceful sleep even if the doctors did call it a coma, it was blessedly easy to accept. When it was time for him to go, he heaved a last sigh fluttering his dry lips and quivered like a dreaming dog when Frances gripped his hand and kissed him good-bye.

We said our last farewells in sibling order: Gladys first, Carla, Frances and finally me. Then we huddled together in the hallway, orphans now as the doctors went in to confirm what we already knew. Pop was gone to a better place. Someplace where he hoped to meet up with my mother. Believing that much, he slipped away from our world willingly. It was the survivors, my sisters and I who cowered, shivered and whimpered at being left alone to face our own frailties.

Pop had made all the funeral arrangements beforehand. That was like him to spare us the details. He was organized in everything he did. Even his sock drawer had no singletons Carla discovered after she cleaned out the house and packed up his old clothes for the Red

Cross. After the simple chapel service at St. Michael's Catholic Church, we stood in a circle around the brilliant gladioli and pungent wreaths and sniffled into our handkerchiefs.

"This was what Daddy wanted," Carla said in a voice struggling for control. "He wanted to be with Mama."

"They're both at peace now," Gladys reassured us all with the authority of a firstborn.

"I'm so thankful he didn't suffer at the end," Frances sobbed. She had never quit crying since the moment we all left the house together and rode to the church from the funeral parlor.

"He was too good to suffer the pain of this world."

Gladys hugged her. "He's where he wants to be, Francie. With the angels."

I snapped the brim of my hat down and dug my hands deep into my trouser pockets. Just to please Pop, I had my suit pressed and cleaned for the funeral. Gladys stuck a carnation in my lapel and slicked my hair down as we got in the limousine for the drive to the Rose City gravesite.

"Nattie, you should get a proper cut. You look like Alfalfa." Gladys took a quick swipe at my cowlick.

"Lay off, Sis," I grunted, moving out of her reach. "That's what hats are for."

"Oh, Nattie," Carla joined in, fussing with my part. "You should really use a little pomade."

I ducked before Francie could get her licks in. As we rode the rest of the way, I sat back and looked from one stricken face to the other. My sisters held hands, fingers interlocking nervously, eyes flashing from the hearse in front of us to the figure perched on the jump seat with the unruly hair—their baby brother, the sole object of their feminine fixation now that Pop was gone. They were all brimming with motherly impulses.

Gladys folded her gloved hands over her pocketbook and looked directly at Frances. "So when are you getting married, Francie?"

"Don't you have a ring yet?" Carla jumped in.

Frances blushed beet-red, and her eyes darted to my face for a sign of rescue, but I ignored her plea for intercession. "We're on a limited budget. I don't really think a ring is that important what with everything else going on in the world right now."

"It's so romantic," Carla simpered. "You're not really formally engaged without a ring, are you?" She flashed her own modest diamond.

Gladys shot straight for the heart as usual. "You'd think he could manage to buy something on time for heaven's sake. Don't let him stall you with such lame excuses."

"I don't think this is the time to discuss my private affairs, Gladys. Can't we all get along for Daddy's sake?"

"What time *is* the proper time? When we're invited to the baby shower?"

Carla gasped and covered her mouth.

"Hey, Sis." I tried stepping in front of the speeding freight train. "Lay off."

"Be still, Nat. You know how Daddy felt about this, Fran. Now that he's in his grave, I would think you would want to get this put right as soon as possible. To ease your burden of guilt if nothing else."

"I'm not guilty about anything." Her lips firmed, but I could see the flush creeping up her throat and felt sorry for her. Frances was never a fair match for Gladys. Nobody was. Not even her husband the doctor.

"Well, I'd think you would be, Frances Gail. I expect to receive a wedding invitation before I go back to Oklahoma."

"Gladys, please!" Frances looked over at me for support, and I could only shrug helplessly. "Nathan? Will you talk to her, please? This isn't the time to discuss this. Besides, it's my life and not her business anyway."

"Gladys, let's lay off Francie, okay? Come on. Let's show a little respect for Pop."

"Me? You're asking *me* to show respect? I'm not the one living in sin, flaunting my behavior in front of the whole world, breaking my father's heart, disgracing the family."

Carla covered her face with both hands. Frances turned and stared out the window. Her chin was quivering with indignant resolve.

I patted Fran's knee. "Hey, nobody's casting any stones here. Let's not fight today."

"I'm not fighting, Nathan. Keep out of this," Gladys shushed me.

"Lay off her, Gladys. Pop hated for you to get after the girls."

"Nathan—"

"Draw in your claws, Sis. Come on, make nice." I tapped her gloves.

"Anyway, I'm going to stay on and help Carla with the house," Gladys said firmly, her fingers gripping the edge of her purse like a barn owl with a mouse. "I can help with your wedding gown. I've had mine in storage just waiting for you to make up your mind to do the decent thing. We can pad the shoulders and change the veil. I'm assuming you'll choose St. Michael's, Francie. You know the Doctor and I were just looking at our wedding portrait the other day and commenting on how splendid the whole affair was really. Yours won't be anything on that grand a scale, of course, but still..." She flashed a condescending smile. "Even a simple ceremony can be elegant if it's planned properly."

Frances hung her head. She chewed on her lower lip until it blushed scarlet. "We haven't decided yet on any wedding plans. We thought it would be best just to get married up there when the time comes. Walter may get sent overseas any day now."

Gladys let out an exaggerated sigh. "Then for God's sake, just do it. We'll come up there, won't we? Nattie will give you away. Carla and I can help. You might as well wear a suit then if you're not doing anything fancy. You can borrow my ecru French silk."

"We can let out the hem," Carla whispered timidly. Of the three sisters, Frances was the tallest, lithe and athletic with the grace of a gazelle.

"There's no need for all that," Frances sputtered, looking away. "We can take care of this without a lot of fuss. There's no rush now."

She squeezed out a flood of fresh tears. "With Daddy gone, it doesn't really matter that much anyway."

"Frances, for God's sake!" Gladys snapped. "This is what Daddy wanted. You know that. He was tortured by your 'arrangement'. Don't try to tell me it doesn't matter. We'll be up in Tacoma next week. You can get married on Saturday so Carla won't have to miss more work."

"Gladys, please," Frances pleaded.

"It's all settled then." She jerked her head in my direction. "Nattie, you can see to the details. I suppose the Doctor and I could finance a honeymoon of sorts. Maybe the Columbia Gorge Hotel for a night or two, but I suppose that's too far. Well, we can find a nice hotel in Tacoma. It's not exactly as if you needed the bridal suite, is it?" Her eyes darted back to Frances. "Does Walter have a proper suit?"

"He can borrow one of Philip's," Carla offered helpfully. She grasped Frances' arm and patted it tenderly. "What size is your Walter?"

Frances smiled through her tears, frustrated but proud as always. "He's tall. Taller than Nattie. And he has a good suit. It's navy-blue worsted with a gray stripe."

"Fine," Gladys seconded, straightening her back and lifting her chin. "September is a lovely time for weddings. Mums, I think. Mums would be wonderful in russet and yellow." Her forefinger rapped on Carla's knee. "You can wear that gold sheath, Carla. I think I'll have Henry send me my brown velvet two-piece with the gold braid."

As the car went beneath the wrought-iron arch at the cemetery gates, Frances reached over and squeezed my hand hard. "Nattie," she whispered as the sleek Packard glided to a stop. "You'll love Walter."

"Sure, I will," I replied, smiling back. "He sounds like a swell guy."

"Everybody likes Walter. He's just a prince of a fellow."

Gladys opened the door and swung a leg out to the running board. "Well, he can make you a princess then, Francie, in a church before God and everybody else."

My two older sisters got out and joined the line of mourners snaking through the tombstones to a gnarly elm under which my mother lay buried. Frances and I followed behind.

"Nat," she confided as we walked, "I'm not certain I should be telling you this, but I have to say something to somebody."

I turned my head and stared at her trembling lips and pale cheeks much too wan in spite of the rouge. She didn't need to say the words. Frances and I could always communicate in silent ways, interlocking brainwaves that needed no words for expression. I just reached over, wound my arms around her and hugged with all my might.

"It's wonderful news, Francie," I breathed into her ear. "I'm so happy for you."

She clung to me. "Don't tell the others yet. Promise?"

I laid a finger across my lips as I drew back. "Not a word, Sis. Promise."

She kissed me. "Gladys will have a stroke if she finds out."

"Don't worry about it."

"Thanks, Nattie. I love you, you know."

As we approached the tent, Gladys aligned us in birth order.

Just before the priest opened his prayer book and acknowledged the assemblage, I leaned over and whispered into my sister's ear. "When?"

Frances held up seven fingers. I smiled. Lots of first babies were short-timers. Gladys would be sore as hell when she found out. Carla would be embarrassed, but Frances would be thrilled. There was nothing devious or mean about Frances. Of all of us, she was the most deserving of good fortune and happiness and the one who suffered most for her bravery.

It began to rain softly as the service went on. I tipped my hat brim against the weather, put an arm around Frances huddled against me in her thin, cloth coat and looked around at the bleak stonescape.

They were mostly elderly people gathered to pay their last respects to my father, friends from the old neighborhood, customers from the store, all recipients who benefited from the many, small kindnesses my parents bestowed on those in need. Gnarled, pinched faces spoke in quavering falsettos of how my parents had sacrificed their savings to help those who were faced with ruin after the Crash.

"That's why he lost it all, the store, the house, and why his wife's health failed. They never could turn anyone away from their door. I remember times when he delivered groceries at Christmas and never sent a bill." They'd shake their heads with a doleful sigh and totter off to lay a flower on the grave, leaving me speechless, proud and ashamed that I had to hear this from strangers, too embarrassed to admit I never knew the depth of the man who lay beneath my feet.

Bracing against the wind like starched leaves on an autumn oak, they huddled in small groups, clutching hankies, ratty umbrellas and prayer books. Soon they'd all be gone, joining my parents in a graveyard like this one, alone at last in a cold, damp hole in the ground, feeding an elm or hawthorn. I shivered. Mortality was so specific, so closed to the expansive creativity of the human spirit. No matter what life played out, death was constant and final with no curtain call, no encore performance begged from the dress circle.

Gladys hung her head and wiped her eyes as the priest went on. Several old ladies behind me sobbed quietly. Pop would have hated this. He never liked to dwell on the negatives. Time was precious. "There's plenty time for moping in the grave," he would say a thousand times over to each of his children. "Life is for living. Be happy. Work at it. It's important."

Not anymore, Pop, I thought with a bitter wince as the prayers ended, and the dirt was sprinkled over his casket. Not anymore. Nothing mattered to Pop now. If I failed or succeeded, I could never hope to win his approval or disappointment again. I was on my own. For better or for worse.

"Ethan," the voice caught me as I looked up from the wreath of white roses resting on the polished coffin. "I'm so sorry for your loss. He must have been a good person for so many people to come out in the rain to say good-bye." She smiled warmly and embraced me.

I stood there like a store mannequin as my sisters turned to stare. I returned Delilah's embrace and inhaled her perfume and the fragrance in her hair. She was wearing a black hat with fuzzy polka-dots on the veil that hid her liquid eyes. I was touched by her genuine sadness and pleased beyond words that she had come.

"I'm so glad you came. How did you know?"

She took my arm and walked me back toward the road. Frances was on my left arm, and Delilah hung on to the right. Gladys and Carla were at my heels.

"I read the obituary in the paper, of course." She pulled her veil up, and I could feed on those eyes, Parrish blue in the steel-wool sky that framed her face as she gazed up at me. "I was disappointed you didn't tell me, Ethan."

"Well, I'm just a roomer, and I didn't think you'd want to be bothered."

"Nathan?" Gladys bolted forward and clutched at my sleeve.

"Uh," I fumbled to carry out the proper introductions. "This is my landlady Mrs. Delilah Goodknight."

She offered her hand to my sister. "Pleased to meet you."

"And this is my sister Frances and my other sister Carla."

"How do you do," Carla said demurely as she stepped forward to clasp Delilah's black-gloved hand.

Frances reached across my suit coat and touched Delilah's shoulder. "I'm Frances."

"Frances McCarthy," Gladys clarified loudly. "She's getting married next week."

Delilah broke into a wonderful smile that made the air warm around me. "Oh, Ethan's told me all about you, Frances. I wish you all the best happiness. Will your fiancé be going overseas right away?"

"We don't know the date for sure yet."

"Best of luck."

We walked to the car, and Gladys got in first. As I helped Carla step up into the Packard, Delilah bussed my cheek. My skin burned instantly where her lips had touched me.

"I have to run, Ethan," she pressed her hand into mine for a moment. "Maybe you'd like to talk when you get home. Come on downstairs if you like."

Gladys poked her head through the open window. "Why don't you come to the house for some coffee and cake, Mrs. Goodknight?"

"Please, do," Carla chimed in. "We'd love to have you come."

"Oh, no, thanks. I really do have to run. I just wanted to say hello to Ethan and offer my condolences." Then she turned and was gone before we could protest.

I got in the car and closed the door.

Gladys unpinned her hat and pulled at her glove fingers. "Did she call you Ethan, Nattie?"

"What?" I said, distracted as I watched Delilah disappear into a DeSoto cab.

"What did she call you?" Carla asked.

Frances was smiling. "She's very attractive, isn't she?"

"Who?" I could feel my face redden. My ears started to tingle.

All three sisters rolled their eyes in unison.

"Why does she call you Ethan?"

"Oh, did she? I didn't notice," I lied brazenly.

"Seems awfully strange to me. Doesn't she even know your name?"

"She's just my landlady, Sis."

"Well, I think it was nice of her to come," Frances helped me out. "Too bad she couldn't come by the house for coffee and cake."

"Too bad," Gladys slurred, pressing her head against the cold window glass. "Nattie could use some cheering up."

"We all could," Carla sniffled, twisting her handkerchief.

As the limousine cruised down Fremont, I looked out at the slate-gray pavement and pressed my fingertips together. Delilah had come to pay her respects for no particular reason. Just to be nice. She had kissed me, asked me to come downstairs and talk. No matter that I felt like an utter shit for closing myself off from the conversations of my grieving sisters for the rest of the afternoon, all I could think of was the smell of Delilah in my nostrils, and the sulky, soft lips branding my flesh as she kissed me. I couldn't even eat any of Gladys' cake. I was in a rush to get home. Nothing made any sense.

I kissed my sisters good-bye on the front porch of Pop's house, walked to the corner and caught the streetcar. All the way across town, I was glancing at my wristwatch, wondering if she would still be there waiting for me, those sad, sensual eyes shining like gemstones in the muted light as I stood there seeking solace. Maybe it was my own loss that united us now, a shared sadness. Surely, she had felt the pain of separation herself and sensed a kindred spirit now.

I walked quickly down the block to the house, fit my key in the lock and closed the door behind me. It was quiet. I took off my hat, went down the hall and looked into the kitchen. It smelled of lemons. On the kitchen table was an unopened bottle of milk and a battered pie keeper. I lifted the top. There was a fresh pie, its golden meringue waves making my mouth water.

"Delilah?" I called softly, looking toward the door. "Mrs. Goodknight?" My only answer was the hum of the Frigidaire. "Delilah? It's Ethan." Then I saw the note on the table. I sat down and picked it up.

"Ethan, have some milk and pie. I'm so sorry for your grief. Pain always passes in time. Charmaine."

I picked up a fork and sank the tines in the wispy meringue. After one bite, I realized I couldn't eat. My stomach was twisted in knots.

I opened the door to the sleeping porch and stepped across the threshold. An apricot-colored, silk slip was tossed casually over a wicker rocker. A half-dead bottle of Johnny Walker sat on the glass-topped table with two empty glasses. In the ashtray, a ruby-tipped cigarette still smoldered.

"Delilah?" I whispered hoarsely, straining to see more clearly in the dark. Shadows danced on the walls. I could smell her scent in this place where she spent her long evenings.

There was a wilted gardenia on the settee. A pair of nylon stockings hung over the back of a chair. The radio console glowed from the corner and hummed softly. I went over and rotated the volume knob. Cole Porter's music blared out at me.

The front door opened and closed. Heavy footsteps thumped up the stairs. The hallway above me reverberated as the tread beat moved from right to left. The trespasser moved to the end of the hallway and stopped. I heard the jingle of a lock being turned to room Number 1. The door clicked open and shut forcefully. Just before it sealed the privacy within, I thought I heard the voice of a woman, not laughing but sighing as a lover does just before the surrender. After the door snapped shut, I was left alone with the music and the aroma of fresh-baked lemons.

# Eight

=====================

I stubbed out the cigarette and flicked ash off my jacket sleeve. It was a slow night. So far, there had been only two guests register at the hotel. A traveling huckster with a beat up old calfskin bag who reeked of cheap cigars when he banged his way through the doors, and an older couple with a scrubbed, Midwestern sternness in their plain features.

I was bored with the newspaper, read through *Life* magazine and was about to head back to the lavatory to splash cold water in my face, when a click on the lobby tiles made me snap to attention. This time it wasn't my nemesis Custer Worthington Ditnip trying to catch me in some dalliance which could cost him an extra penny's worth of trouble. It was a woman with auburn hair in an upsweep tucked under a forest-green beret trimmed with ruby braid. Her lips were the color of fresh blood. And the eyes were looking right through me to the wall behind the registration desk. I knew those eyes so well and the illusory stare I tried so hard to penetrate.

"Hi," I said, feeling a little foolish in my starched jacket. "Can I help you?"

Her head turned slowly; the eyes focused, and the blood-red lips tilted upward. "Oh, Ethan. I didn't know you'd be here."

I blushed. All I needed to accomplish my complete humiliation was a silly cap and doorman's stripes on my trousers. "Yeah, I work here nights. It gives me time to study."

She nodded, completely detached. "You need quiet to write your book, don't you?"

"This is just to pass the time, earn a little extra mad money." How perfectly stupid, utterly childish and self-effacing could I be if I worked only a little harder at it? She must think I was a complete imbecile. I jerked my jacket down and tried to think of something to occupy my hands, some way to make myself seem more official. "Uh, I'm on duty for the night shift. It's the busiest. Pretty demanding at times as a matter of fact." She scarcely followed my glance around the deserted lobby. "Quiet night so far it looks like." My brittle laugh echoed off the grill work like ball bearings rattling in a tin can. "Lucky break, huh?"

"I suppose so."

"Uh, can I do something for you, Mrs. Goodknight?" I couldn't get her first name out. Which first name to use, I wasn't sure. Goodknight seemed safer.

"What?" The eyes finally fastened on mine. "I didn't catch what you said, Ethan." Her lips trembled as if she were going to ask me to vault over the counter, take her in my arms and kill the overwhelming sadness in her blank stare.

"I was wondering... Can... can I help you with something?"

She opened her purse and searched, ignoring me completely. *Ethan, I had to come tonight,"* I fantasized hearing as I waited for her to reconnect. I could almost see the words rolling off her luscious lips, the sultry stare zapping every nerve in my body. *"I couldn't help myself, don't you see?"*

*"Delilah,"* I tried to hold her off, to keep her from igniting a flame I knew would consume us both. *"Try to get hold of yourself. We shouldn't even be meeting like this."*

I imagined the dewy eyes pleading with mine. Her hand rose, the fingers gloved in black kid beckoned me closer. *"Oh, Ethan. I can't bear being alone anymore. I need you so."*

I saw myself bounding over the desk, seizing her in a Clark Gable embrace. Her hat fell off, and her hair flowed like a waterfall through my fingertips. *"Delilah, my darling, I can't say the words bursting in my heart."* No. Charmaine. She would want me to call her Charmaine. Ethan and Charmaine. That was our secret link—spirit to spirit. *"Charmaine, darling,"* I revised my fantasy. She would be closing her eyes then, surrendering completely to my suave, commanding charm.*"Kiss me like you mean it."* I could almost chew the real words in my mouth. In the final scene, Charmaine's lids fluttered to a close, and she swooned in my arms as my spectacles fogged up.

Too common. Banal. Ours was a celestial bond, two lost souls meshing in the infinite space of time and endless passion. Gable and Bogie were fine for other dames, but Delilah deserved Cary Grant.*"My beautiful, magnificent specimen..."* I could hear myself sighing in my hastily drawn dream. Jesus. Sounded like a chemistry experiment. God, if I could only remember the right words when I got back to my typewriter.

"Charmaine," I moaned with half-closed eyes.

"What?" She pulled a key from her bag and snapped it shut. "Did you say something, Ethan?" Her tone was all business as if she were asking me to change a light bulb, fix the leaky faucet or open a jar of pickles. I straightened up as the blood rose above my collar in a sudden flush of utter ignominy. My wakeful fantasies were a measure of my increasing insanity around this gorgeous, plaintive phantom.

"Uh... I was just wondering if I could do anything for you."

She walked past me and pushed the button for the elevator. The cage rattled and clanged and then started down from the fourth floor where the corn huskers had left it earlier in the evening. "No, thank you. I'll just go on up."

"Can I help you with that?" I rushed over and pulled the door back for her.

"I had no idea this is where you worked, Ethan."

"Well, it's just temporary until I finish the thesis. Keeps my nights occupied and gives me plenty of time to think..." I sensed I was wading into deep water. "About my research... and everything."

"Well, goodnight then."

"Wait!" I held the elevator door. "I came downstairs to see you after the funeral." I couldn't say anymore. I had crossed my emotional Rubicon. There was no way to turn back. "I wanted to talk. You said you'd be home, and I..."

"I'm so sorry about your father. It's hard to lose someone you love, isn't it?"

"It was thoughtful of you to come to the cemetery. My sisters were touched by your concern."

"I came for *you*, Ethan. You know that, don't you?"

"Uh... I was thinking..." My tongue was tying itself in slipknots. Thank God she couldn't see what I was construing in my ravished mind as I drowned in those languid eyes. "Can we talk some time, do you think? That is, if you're free some evening."

She stepped inside the car. With a slow, sweet smile that barely creased her face, she punched the button. Her answer drifted down from the second floor as the elevator rose to the mezzanine. "Oh, I forgot to ask how your novel is coming, Ethan?"

"Fine," I shouted up. Then I hung my head and leaned against the wall. She knew. She had read it. I must have been crazy to leave the manuscript out in the open in plain sight. She must have come up to my room to change the linens, innocently wandered over to the window, taken a quick look at the typewriter, seen the stack of paper and wondered how my project was going. And of course, as soon as she saw the first line, she had known it all. Known my deepest, most painful secret. My affliction.

"Oh, hell," I groaned returning to my post. It would have been only natural for her to be curious, to peek at a couple pages, a few more. I might as well go home, pack my things and sneak out before she came back. How could I have the nerve to face her? How could she find it in her to be so gracious and forgiving of such boorish behavior?

I slunk back behind the desk and lit another Lucky. The room service buzzer barked at me. I answered it with the cigarette still between my lips. "Roosevelt Hotel. Desk."

"This is Room 302. Bring up a bucket of ice and a pack of Camels, will ya, Bud?"

"302. Got it." It was the sloppy salesman who'd checked in on my shift. Too lazy to go out and get his own smokes. Too damned lazy to come downstairs and get ice from the machine.

I got the cigarettes, filled an ice bucket then skipped the slow elevator and took the stairs up to the third floor. Room 302 was just two doors to the right. I rapped three times. "Room service."

No answer. I had to go through the whole, lousy routine, hang around, hand over the goods and wait for the charity of the customer to deliver some silver to my palm. It was a bit like begging. Professional begging. But the tips fed the automat on Broadway and kept me in burgers and corned beef sandwiches.

I knocked one more time. "Room service."

The niggardly voice barked back through the door. "Just leave it, Bud."

A woman's giggly laugh leaked out into the hall. I waited for a minute to see if he would come out and leave some change on the carpet. He didn't.

Back at the desk, I smoked and pretended to leaf through a magazine. I was waiting for Delilah to come back down. I had no idea where she had gone. The elevator arrow pointed to the third floor. Who could she be seeing up there anyway? Her lover? A friend visiting in town? A relative? She had been searching through her bag for a key maybe. I checked the cubbyholes for a missing room key and found none. Did this mean she was a regular? A floozy rendezvousing with some bum whenever he hit town? I felt like tearing upstairs, beating down every door and dragging her back home.

Suddenly the elevator buzzed, groaned and clanked its way down the shaft toward the lobby. My heart thumped so hard my ears hurt. I crushed my butt and watched the car alight. It was the salesman in 302. His squinty eyes were shaded by bushy brows. Both cheeks and his bulbous nose were sunburned. His shoes were unshined. His tie was loose, and the top two buttons of his shirt were undone.

"Hey, Bud," he hailed me as he leaned both elbows on the desk. "Do me a favor."

"Sure."

"Tell me where I can find a drugstore."

I jerked a thumb toward the street door. "Go up a couple blocks to Broadway and head north. There's a Rexall on the corner of Morrison. Can't miss it."

"Thanks, Kid." He turned and strode across the lobby and pushed the doors open. No tip. Just the lingering tang of his cheap hair oil to keep me company.

I took a deep breath and sucked up the smell of the carpet, the mildew in the potted palms and the stale stench of the upholstery. Just like the rest of the wartime city, it was drab, dowdy and dreary. The only thing that had swept across my life so far and made me see all the colors of the rainbow, the dazzling, prismatic splendor of optimism was Delilah. She was magic to my starving soul. I was either going mad or hopelessly, insanely in love. Possessed may have been a better word. I hadn't even gotten close enough to describe what I was experiencing as love. Maybe it was better defined as fascination, fixation. Whatever it was, I couldn't stand to be there in that stifling, over-stuffed lobby with my ill-fitting jacket while upstairs Delilah Goodknight was scrunched in some slob's sweaty, lusty loins. It was too much pain to bear.

I ripped off my jacket, popping a button off the front and raced up the stairs. The phone jangled on the desk as I ran —second floor, third floor. I stopped in front of 302 and laid my ear against the door. It was quiet on the other side.

What in hell would I do if Delilah heard my labored breathing and came out? I pressed my eyes shut and saw the scene unfold in my fevered brain. She would peel the door back from her startled face. When she saw me standing there, a hand would flutter to her throat. I imagined her trembling. Only her shadow covered her body, as perfect as a Grecian nude.

*"Don't say a word,"* I warned as she fell into my arms.

*"Oh, Ethan, I was praying you'd find me."* Her rosebud lips greeted mine. Our kiss stole my breath away.

I staggered and woke up to the crushing reality of my agony, nose pressed against the door like a house dick, knowing she was only inches away, waiting for me, counting on me to be bold enough to slay her dragons. I knew what I had to do before it was too late. I took off my spectacles and tucked them into my pocket.

With a hefty charge, I pushed against the door which gave way with a loud bang as I lunged halfway across the room. Delilah wasn't there. I could have smelled her. I would have known if she had been here. She wasn't, and I had just broken into the dumpy salesman's room with absolutely no excuse to save me.

I panicked as I looked around searching for an explanation as I heard heavy footsteps pounding down the hall. Before I could move from the spot where my shoes seemed glued to the carpet, I heard a familiar voice grating from the hallway.

"*Mister* McCarthy."

I brushed my hands on my trousers and tried to look indifferent to my predicament. "I'm just finishing a room service delivery, Mr. Catnip."

Custer's beady eyes darkened, not amused by my obvious consternation. "*Dit*nip."

"302 wanted some cigarettes and..." I desperately scoured the room with my myopic eye for the ice bucket. It wasn't there. I barged into the bathroom.

"What the hell are you doing, you goddam idiot?" A frowzy woman with black hair was sitting on the toilet with her pudgy legs splayed around the bowl. She shoved the door closed and knocked me back into the room. "Get out! Get out before I call the cops!"

"Get out of this room immediately!" Ditnip shouted.

I beat him to the hallway. He was too upset to speak. I figured it was just as well. I had absolutely no answers.

When I got to the lobby, Ditnip cornered me at the desk. "What is happening here this evening, Mister McCarthy? I have a mind to call the police."

"The police? Nothing's happened at all. I was just up to 302 to answer a room service call for some smokes."

"You said you took up a bucket of ice."

"Well, yeah... smokes and ice."

"Without your jacket?" He shook it in front of my face like a bloody glove. "What kind of business are you carrying on in this establishment, Mr. McCarthy?"

"No business at all, Mr. Dimwit."

"It's Ditnip, if you please."

"Yessir."

"If you have been having a sordid relationship with that woman in this hotel, I'll—"

"Are you out of your mind?" I don't know which stung more. Caught being plain-assed stupid or Ditnip thinking I could have been banging that frump camped out on the crapper in 302.

"I've half a mind to discharge you right now." He wagged a finger in my face.

"Don't bother. I quit." I gave up my keys and vaulted over the desk as I'd already seen myself do in my dreamy duet with Delilah. I cleared the registration book by barely an inch.

"Young man! Come back here!"

I was already out the door and on the sidewalk, disgusted and too ashamed to admit I was more disappointed in not finding Delilah upstairs than in losing my job.

"Don't be impertinent with me, Mr. McCarthy!" he screeched. "I intend to talk to Doctor Houghton about this disgraceful incident. I'm warning you, if there has been any sort of illicit activity occurring on my premises, I'll make formal charges."

I crossed the street and never looked back.

*"Do you hear me, Mister McCarthy?"*

I didn't. I was still thinking about Delilah, wondering where she was. Was she looking down from the third floor of the Roosevelt Hotel to see me chased into the street, stripped of my clerking credentials?

As I hurried through the park, I met the huffing salesman returning to the hotel. He didn't even acknowledge me as we passed wordlessly in the night.

# Nine

=========

**Frances** was a beautiful bride. She stood before the Episcopal priest in the same dress my mother wore when she married Pop. My youngest sister looked like a Maxfield Parrish angel with pale blue ribbons in her hair and rosettes around the lacy bodice of her gown. That was Gladys' touch. To disguise Francie's generous bosom. Carla cried through the entire ceremony. The only dry eyes in the house were Walter's, the groom. He was a quiet, serious fellow with Cocker Spaniel eyes, a thick mustache that drooped over his generous mouth and arms like a trapeze catcher encircling Frances. I liked him. He ignored almost everything Gladys cautioned him about and stole every opportunity her critiques gave him to bolster his new wife's confidence. Frances had made a good choice. They made a great combination. Their kids would be terrific.

We sat knee to knee in the tiny front room of Francie's apartment. The newlyweds crowded together on the sofa.

Gladys laced her fingers together and tossed her head back. "I don't suppose you've time for a proper honeymoon."

"I'm shipping out next Wednesday," Walter confided with a loving smile for Francie cuddled beside him.

"Well, I only meant that—I mean..." Gladys hemmed, "it's not as if you haven't actually... that is..." She stumbled to a stop and began to blush.

"Gladys, why don't you get the coffee?" Carla whispered.

She grabbed the chance to extricate herself from the scowls of her sisters and left the four of us alone.

"Walter," I said, trying to sound more mature than I felt, "I want you to know I'll look after Francie while you're away. I don't want you to worry about her."

"Thank you, Nathan. It means a lot knowing Fran will have someone to take care of things while I'm away."

"Will you be flying in combat as soon as you get overseas?" Carla interrupted. "I mean, over Germany? Maybe you'll be assigned to a training unit for a while. They say the war is winding down since the invasion. Isn't Hitler just about ready to surrender? Doesn't he know he's better off stopping it now before the Russians get to Berlin?"

Walter smiled at her naive optimism. "The Germans are far from beaten, I'm afraid. Now that we're on their turf, they seem to be fighting harder than ever."

"Well, maybe they'll give up before you get shot down." Her tongue skidded to a stop. "I mean, well, you know. Anything could happen, couldn't it?"

Frances reached over and touched her. "Don't worry, Carla. Walter's coming back to me safe and sound." She looked at him with adoring eyes that made my belly warm. They kissed sweetly, and I felt like a voyeur watching them. Time was so short, and they needed to be alone.

I stood up. "Sis, never mind the cake and coffee. It's late already, and we have a long ride back to Portland."

"Oh, no, Nattie. Don't rush off." Frances grabbed hold of my arm to stay my departure.

Walter was a perfect gentleman. "Stay a while yet."

I pulled Carla to her feet and stopped Gladys in her tracks as she came into the room with a coffeepot in her hands. "Thanks, but we really have to get back. Besides, I have an appointment tomorrow morning I need to get up early for."

"What appointment?" Gladys blurted. "On Sunday?"

I took her arm and steered her back to the kitchen. "Yes. With the Priest. Confession."

"Nathan," she protested as I swung the door closed, "you're too much."

"Let's beat it," I scolded my sisters. "He's leaving in a few days. They need to be alone. Get your coats. I'm going to find a taxi."

Gladys put the coffeepot down and blocked the back door. "Nathan, the train doesn't even leave until ten. What are we going to do? Wander around the station for four hours?"

"Yes. Get your coats and powder your noses. I'll buy you a sandwich and a Coke at Union Station."

"I think Nathan's right," Carla backed me up. "They should be alone. I mean, after all, Gladys, he might never come back, and this is all Francie would have to remember him by."

My older sister's eyebrows arched critically. "She's got a lot more to remember him by, believe me."

"Girls," I cautioned, reaching around Gladys to open the back door. "Don't be catty. I'll be back in ten minutes."

I went out and walked three blocks to a telephone. When I returned, both sisters were on the sidewalk with their valises, hats in place, bags on their shoulders and frowns on their faces.

"Well, they didn't insist we stay," Gladys pouted as we waited for the cab.

"Walter's awfully nice, I thought," Carla said to no one in particular. "He's very tall, isn't he?"

"Do you know what he's going to do after the War?" Gladys snarled.

I was noticing the shadow of the lovers embracing behind the window shades. Then the lights went out. I had to smile. Frances looked so happy.

"Shoes." Gladys jabbed her elbow into my side. "Shoes, Nathan. Shoes."

"Uh huh."

"He's going to be a common shoe salesman for God's sake."

"That's nice."

Her voice rose. "*Shoes*, Nathan. Plain shoes. Work shoes, boots, logger's corks, that sort of thing. Not even stylish shoes, men's dress wear. Work boots, Nathan."

"Uh huh."

"You know what that means. He's never going to be able to make a decent living. Frances will be scrimping and saving, wearing old clothes, sacrificing for the sake of the children. It's all so utterly common. So sad when you think about it."

"Gladys, let up on her, for crissakes."

"Don't swear, Nattie. You know what I mean."

I knew but didn't care. Gladys was never satisfied with anything or anybody. Life in general was the biggest disappointment for my eldest sister. None of us ever managed to measure up.

"Look, if Frances is happy, who cares what he does for a living? Pop was just a greengrocer when he married Mom. So what?"

"Daddy had potential," Gladys corrected me sternly. "He was a businessman. Our father was respected. He owned his own establishment with a certain stature in the community."

"I think he's very well mannered, Gladys. Don't you, Nathan?"

Our eldest sister brushed her off. "Oh, Carla, be quiet. Don't either of you realize what I'm trying to say?"

"What?" I asked her with a tired shrug. The cab was overdue.

"Francie is going to cheat herself out of everything Mama and Daddy worked so hard for. You know she was their favorite. They wanted the best for Frances, and now she's going to have nothing in life but hardship and struggle."

Carla whined "I think Walter is awfully nice."

"Gladys, just shut up," I barked as the taxi swung around the corner and bore down on us. The old DeSoto stopped, and I jerked open the back door. "Get in and just be damned glad she's got a few days to be happy. Don't spoil this for her."

"Nattie, just listen—"

"Get in." I pushed, and Carla meekly followed.

It was a long, silent ride to the station. I was thinking about other things by the time the train pulled out southbound for Portland.

Carla fell asleep while Gladys switched on the overhead light and read. I was left alone to consider my shortcomings, the fact that there was no one waiting for me, no prospects for the kind of joy Francie had found with her Walter. There was no passion in my life to match what they had experienced. I had only a silly fantasy constructed in my imagination of what it would be like to want to die for somebody rather than lose him. I ached with an emptiness inside me that demanded to be filled.

When I thought about making a stab at romance, filling my lonely nights locked up with my typewriter in my stuffy room, I thought of coming in with lipstick smeared on my shirt, my hair in my face, smelling of ripe perfume and musk. Delilah would greet me at the stairs, stare through me with those soulful eyes and make me hate myself for settling so cheaply.

I knew what I wanted, who I wanted. Only she was completely unapproachable.

Gladys put her book down as the lights flickered along the tracks nearing Vancouver. The Portland station was just across the river. Twenty minutes more, and we'd be home.

My sister studied me carefully before slipping the book in her bag and buttoning her jacket. "Nathan, what's the matter with you lately?"

"What do you mean?"

"You're not yourself, frankly. I've been thinking maybe it's something to do with the War."

My eyes stretched wider to take her in. In the murky light, with shadows crisscrossing her face, I couldn't see her eyes clearly. "How do you mean? My being rejected for the draft? Is that what you mean?"

"Yes, to be frank. We think it's affected your—"

"My what? Affected my what?"

"Well, to be completely frank with you, Nathan..."

"What? Say it, Gladys."

"Well, your manhood. We think it's affected your self confidence in some way."

86

I sagged back in the seat and looked away. The train was pulling across the river. Below, the water was as black as soot. "Who's we? You and the Doctor?"

"Nathan, don't try to put me off by being rude. We've discussed this, of course."

"Of course."

"Henry is a doctor of medicine, Nathan. He's seen lots of cases like yours."

"Cases like mine? Now I'm suddenly a case? Jesus, Gladys."

She took out her compact, flipped up the mirror and began rolling lipstick on her mouth. "If you need to talk to someone about it, Nathan, you know you can always come to the Doctor and me."

"Christ, Gladys."

"If it's keeping you from meeting someone, falling in love—"

"Gladys, will you be quiet? Just lay off, okay?"

"I only want what's best for you, Nattie." She closed the compact and pressed her lips together. How she could apply her war paint in the dark without smearing red on her nose and chin was beyond me. My sisters' many talents always amazed me.

"Just lay off me and Francie and Walter. Okay? I'm grown up now, Gladys. I don't need you to mother me to death anymore. Fact is, none of us do."

"Nattie, for heaven's sake, don't be so sensitive about this."

Carla woke up and rubbed her eyes. "Are we coming into the station?"

"Not yet," Gladys said perfunctorily. "Nathan, I want you to take this seriously. I can have the Doctor call you."

I laughed. "Gladys, do you tell the girls to call their father Doctor Daddy?"

"You can always call him Henry, Nathan. You know that. Don't be so damned sensitive about everything." She crossed her arms defiantly. "You see what I mean? You didn't act this way before the war. You need to see the Doctor before it's too late, and you mess up the rest of your life."

"Are you sick, Nathan?" Carla asked me sleepily.

"No."

"He just won't admit it," Gladys added with a hurt look. "He won't even talk to Henry about it. Nattie, you're much too sensitive about this. The Doctor sees dozens of patients with symptoms like yours every month."

"What's wrong, Nattie?" Carla straightened her hat and retrieved her purse from the seat. "I have some aspirins in my bag."

"Oh, Jesus," I breathed, banging my head on the overhead rack as I stood up.

When the train pulled in, I off-loaded my sisters' suitcases and put them in a cab. I told the driver the address on Fremont Avenue, kissed them good-bye and walked toward home.

Headlights flashed by. Neon winked overhead as I turned down Broadway. Sailors crowded around a bar door on the corner of Washington Street and bummed cigarettes off me as I passed.

When I got to the house, I slipped my key in the lock and stepped inside. I could see the glow of an electric lamp from beneath the bedroom door and wished I had the nerve to knock, the guts to do something instead of bite my nails like a lovesick schoolboy. I hated my miserable cowardice. Maybe Gladys was right about being too sensitive to think logically about my problems.

When I got to my room, I saw a beam of light cascading out onto the hall carpet from beneath my door. Tentatively, I put a hand on the knob and turned.

"Good evening."

Delilah was sitting on the bed with my manuscript spread out around her. A cigarette coiled smoke from her fingers as a scarlet nail picked a tobacco shred from her lips. She was wearing a violet nightgown under a white angora sweater. The auburn hair was long and free and made me hold my breath until I adjusted to the awful truth that she was reading my most intimate fantasy.

"Hi," was all I could answer as I came inside. I just stood there beside the bed, watching her in a catatonic daze.

After a minute, she looked up as she flipped a page. "You wrote all this?"

"Yes. But it's not finished yet. This is just a rough outline really." I couldn't bear to think she had read the chapter about the hotel tryst. I wanted to go up in a puff of flames and disappear.

She tapped ash into the palm of her hand. "It's really very good, Ethan. I think you're quite talented."

I couldn't even begin to think of a sensible answer to that one. I wasn't sure if she was mocking me or too ignorant to understand my dilemma. It didn't matter.

"Can I have the ashtray?"

"Uh... sure." I turned around and knocked it onto the floor. "Damn!"

She bared a delicious, flawless thigh and retrieved the Hawaiian ashtray with the hula girl. "I guess you've been up in Tacoma for your sister's wedding."

"Yes."

"She must be very happy, Ethan." She settled back on the pillows, rested her head against the wall and crossed her ankles. "Is her husband going overseas?"

"Yes."

"How much time do they have?"

I couldn't focus my eyes any longer. I wanted to fall on her and taste every inch of her delicious body. Instead, I licked my lips and mumbled "Three days."

"Ohhhh..." she sighed wistfully, blowing smoke toward the ceiling. Her eyes closed. "So short a time to be happy."

"He's coming back home. Frances is sure he'll make it since things seem to be going so well in Europe. Winchell says the German air force is kaput."

"I don't think it's that simple, Ethan." Her eyes opened. "They must be very much in love."

"Walter's a great guy."

"I can tell, Ethan. There's something in the eyes that tells me. Something so sad, it almost speaks to me." She sighed. "I can always tell."

"Tell what?"

A faint shadow of a smile slipped across her mouth. "Tell me, Ethan, when will you finish the book?"

"I don't have an ending yet."

Her hand brushed against my cheek. "Sit down and talk to me, Ethan. Tell me about Charmaine."

Goddam. My head was about to burst open. This was like letting her see my dirty underwear. Worse than letting her squeeze the zits off my chin.

I didn't dare sit down with her on my bed, the scene of a hundred frenzied fantasies where she had lain in my arms and surrendered to my concocted desires. "She's just a fictional character," I lied.

Another intriguing smile played across her lips. "You know what I think, Ethan?"

I didn't think I could bear to find out. I just stood there rooted to the rug like a fir tree.

"Charmaine is me. And Ethan is you. And this is the way you'd like it to be between us. The two of us together in a passionate romance."

My eyes were bulging. I couldn't even think about checking my fly. Not even a fleeting thought in that direction. "It's just a story. I don't write fiction really. It's just something to pass the time, a change of pace."

She stretched forward and took both my hands in hers and drew me down so close I could smell the Luckies on her breath. "You came upstairs looking for me at the hotel, didn't you, Ethan?"

She undid the first button on my shirt, and I bit down so hard on my lip, I could taste the salty flesh puncture. "There was a call for room service in 302." She pulled gently on my necktie and drew me closer. Now both knees were on the bed, and it groaned with a plaintive wail I longed to hear in my fantasies. "What are you afraid of?"

Our lips were so close I could feel the heat from every pulse beat. She gently removed my glasses and smoothed the hair from my brow. The clocks must have stopped. There were no sounds in the house except the air filling her lungs and the tobacco burning in her cigarette. I was suspended in space somewhere between heaven and hell. Completely, totally lost in a paradise I had only glimpsed in daydreams.

Then she switched off the hula-girl lamp, and I could see nothing but the glow of her cigarette smoldering in the dark. "I know you want to kiss me."

"Delilah," I begged, reaching blindly for her. The bed springs screamed as I groped on the mattress, delirious with wanting to consummate my dreams in warm flesh and silky, scented hair, but she had escaped.

"Goodnight, Ethan. Sweet dreams." The door closed, and she was gone.

I couldn't breathe until I heard her steps going down the hall and treading lightly on the stairs. It was a long time before I could fall asleep. I don't remember dreaming only waking up and smelling her scent on the sheets and reaching for her shadow floating like a gilded apparition above the bed.

# Ten

========

I suppose I should have been grateful that Ditnip didn't call the Doctor and sic Gladys on me, but I didn't think much about my employment fiasco. What I did consider, especially on the first Saturday I awoke without enough change in my trouser pockets to buy breakfast at the Woolworth counter, was that I was broke again with no prospects of improving my financial fortunes. I had blown all my resources on Tacoma, trains and Francie's wedding. And now, I was bitterly reminded as I stared at the empty club chair where my father had sat not long before railing at my lack of *in camera* sanitary facilities, there was no one to whom I could turn for assistance. I was on my own.

I lit my last Lucky Strike, crumpled the pack and tossed it on the bed. Then I sat down in the overstuffed chair and considered my meager options. I could go down to the lunch counter and scrounge the want ads from the newspaper always left lying on an empty stool. Or I could try calling on a few friends and pleading academic hardship. Professor Ruth would be sympathetic. He was my mentor in the history department of Willamette University where I had been his star undergraduate student and lectured for his freshman classes while in graduate school. But he was probably as poor as a pauper himself if his raggedy cardigans and scuffed shoes were an indication of his prosperity. Besides, I reminded myself, he would no doubt ask to see the manuscript. And so far, despite the beneficial circumstances of my residence, I had written scarcely more than a few pages of my Roman history since moving into Delilah's house.

Perhaps, I should rely on my natural instincts bent toward more percipient backers of my struggle to succeed in a blue-collar world at war. I picked a shred of tobacco from my lip and suddenly knew exactly what I would do. There was a way I could avoid having to succumb to simple arithmetic and take on another tedious, menial job. I was a scholar. And I had a right to assume that my primary occupation in life would be the pursuit of intellectual sloth. Because to be a writer, a chronicler of ancient history, it was necessary to meditate, research, cogitate and incubate ideas in a mind at peace with the world. So far, to my knowledge, the planet had not produced a wellspring of Pulitzer prize winners from accountants, supervisors and night clerks.

Getting up with a burst of newfound energy, I squinted through the cigarette smoke, retrieved my socks and shoes and finished dressing. In five minutes, I was pulling on my jacket and skipping down the stairs. At the front door, I was stopped.

"Going out so early?" Delilah asked. She was wearing the turban again, the one I had seen around her hair the first day we met. Only a spongy layer of burnt-cinnamon curls poked out from the wrap. Her eyes were sparkling.

"I have to see someone about a job."

She leaned against the doorjamb, rested one hand at her hip and poised her chin on the end of the broom handle. She could have been a chorus extra in a Buzby Berkeley musical, about to do the swabby-sailor number with Gene Kelly. This morning, Delilah Goodknight was as cute as a blue-eyed bug.

"You lost your job at the hotel, huh?"

"In a manner of speaking."

"You stormed into that room and scared a woman half to death, Ethan." She was trying hard not to laugh at me. I almost wished she would. "She made an awful racket. I thought she was going to call the police."

"You heard all that?"

She cocked her head to one side and twisted her lips in an insouciant grin. "You broke the door down, Ethan. The whole hotel must have heard it."

"You were up on the third floor the whole time, weren't you?" Of course, she was. We both knew it. Only I didn't know which room she was in, except I knew for a certainty she was not in room 302 with the pudgy salesman.

"I heard you break the door down, if that's what you mean." She turned around and started back for the kitchen.

I followed her. "Delilah." I paused until she could dispose of the broom and look at me. But she didn't do either one. Instead, she began sweeping the linoleum floor with an unrestrained energy. "I realize I don't have any right to pry into your personal affairs."

"No. You don't," she said as simply as ordering ham and eggs.

"I just thought, what I mean to say is you went upstairs that night, and I thought—" My tongue was swelling until it blocked my throat, and I gagged on my own words. "That is, I was wondering if you were... maybe you were visiting a friend... or something."

She tidied up the floor with a few, deft strokes. Then she put the broom aside and finally looked at me. "Ethan, for heaven's sake, say it. Go on." She emptied the dustpan into the bin, wiped her hands on her skirt and struck an expectant pose. When she put her head back and fixed me with an inquisitive stare, I melted into a mushy sap who would have confessed anything to have her put on a dreamy face like the one she had worn when I found her lying in my bed, reading my manuscript.

"I was just wondering, that's all," I stammered in a husky whisper I hoped sounded sexy rather than influenzal. Sweat beads broke out like blisters on my brow.

"Ethan, may I tell you a secret? I get so lonely sometimes. Can you understand? I manage through the days mostly, but sometimes the nights just seem to go on forever." She raised herself on tiptoe and planted a cool kiss on my cheek. I felt her eyelashes caress my skin, and I could smell ammonia and Ponds cold cream. Wonderful flavors. "I need someone sometimes." She leaned against me only for an instant. "Do you think I'm so bad, Ethan?"

I reached out to hold on to her, but she moved away and sat down at the kitchen table. Unable to answer with anything appropriately meaningful, I pulled out a chair and sat down across from her. "You're not bad at all, Delilah. I think you're wonderful as a matter of fact." Spoken like a true rube, I winced internally.

"Why don't you call me Charmaine? Does it make you think I'm crazy to want to have a special name between us?"

"No." I had absolutely no idea if she was crazy or not, or whether she was making me crazy. Such basic trivialities didn't even factor into my equation.

"Tell me about your novel, Ethan. Have you written more since Charmaine and Ethan made love on the kitchen table?"

I felt my jaw slacken. My eyes bulged, and I may have started drooling for all I knew. "It's just a silly story," I mumbled. "I wouldn't take anything from it."

She folded her hands over mine. "Oh, no. I love it. It's a beautiful story. Charmaine and Ethan are so desperately in love, and yet, there is something between them, isn't there?"

"Well, I don't have the plot worked out yet."

"Ethan loves her so much. He'd die for her. He gives up his teaching job at the University to enlist in the Army Air Corps, and then when he's wounded in the skies over Dunkirk, he decides he can never come back to her because he's less than a man." She was warming, blush colored her porcelain cheeks and swelled her lips like cantaloupe flesh. "Don't you see, Ethan?"

I gulped, stalling. I wished I could have come up with some profundity worthy of Hemingway or Sinclair Lewis, some great verbose recipe for the meaning of life as it applied to Portland, Oregon and the two of us in particular. But my brain was a dry well. Nothing sprang to mind but the idea that we could be entwined like blackberry vines on the drop-leaf table, moaning and sighing, lost in passionate madness.

"Ethan?"

I reached for her and knocked over the sugar bowl. "Oh, Jeez." I scooped up the mess while she watched me with a flicker of compassion. "Clumsy. Sorry."

"Don't bother. I suppose I shouldn't have said anything."

"Pardon?" I looked up.

"About the book. The plot."

"Oh." I dusted off my hands. "Well, it needs some work."

"I think it's lovely. What a wonderful, touching love story."

"Well..."

"Don't you see it, Ethan?"

"What?"

"The fact that he's been wounded doesn't matter to her."

"He's burned pretty badly," I reminded her for the sake of literary accuracy.

"It doesn't matter because it's his soul she loves." Her hand pressed over mine again. I could feel grains of sugar grating between my fingers. "What he looks like doesn't matter to her. She's in love with what's inside." Her hand fluttered over her heart. "That never dies."

Something in her seemed to fade as she recalled the sentimental trash I had scribbled upstairs. Delilah looked at me, widened her eyes and then saw something hanging behind me, something in the air, in the atmosphere unseen by any other mortal. I could never focus her attention completely when we spoke. It was if there was always someone between us, a flesh and blood presence, temporarily unseen, intruding on our conversations.

I stood up to break her spell. "I better get going."

"Have you any money for a decent breakfast?"

She startled me with her tactless assumption I was flat broke. I suppose I didn't need to pretend I wasn't looking for a feeble excuse to avoid her charity.

"Here. Let me fix you something." In a flash, she was up and banging pots and pans, running water in the sink and cracking eggs in a bowl. "You could use a decent meal. Get some dishes down from the cupboard and light the stove, will you?"

Delilah whipped me up a feast with ham slices as thick as cedar shingles, scrambled eggs and toast with raspberry jelly. I washed it all down with three cups of coffee and took my plate back to the sink.

My belly was full, but my ego was trampled flat. Here I was, destitute and pitiful, sponging a meal in her kitchen, making her feel sorry for me when I should have been a tower of strength for her soulful loneliness.

I rolled up my sleeves and helped her clear the dishes when I was through. Delilah hadn't eaten a thing.

"Where are you going to apply?" she asked me as I plunged both hands up to my wrists in hot, soapy water.

"What?"

"Your job. You said you had an interview this morning as you were going out."

"Oh. I'm going to call a friend of mine who works at The Multnomah."

"Can he help you get another position as bell clerk?"

I handed her a slippery plate and grabbed my coffee cup. "He said to call him if I was looking for something light."

"Light?"

"Something to give me time to work on my own." It was like loafing, wasn't it? How could I explain the need to let my creative, intellectual brain cells idle in neutral during my work shift so that I could return and pour out my energies on the typewriter?

"To think about your writing, you mean?" she came to my rescue right on cue.

"Something like that, I guess."

"What does your friend do?"

"He's a waiter. We roomed together in college."

She closed the cupboard door and folded the dishtowel on the counter as I rinsed the sink clean. "Why didn't he go in the service?"

"Same as me. 4F. He had TB real bad as a kid, got in his bones and crippled a leg."

"Oh."

"We're the cripples and misfits left here at home, aren't we?"

"Don't think that, Ethan. You're lucky. You don't know what combat can do to people."

I turned around and leaned back with my hands braced on the linoleum counter. "You talked about that before."

"I remember." She was drifting away from me again.

This time I had the nerve to grab hold of her arm and draw her attention back. "Did you lose someone over there?"

Her eyes misted. "We've all lost someone, haven't we?"

"What do you mean exactly?"

"You just lost your father."

"That's different. I'm talking about the war, Delilah."

She reached up and put both arms around my neck. "Call me Charmaine."

"Charmaine," I whispered, barely able to breathe in she was so close, pressing up against me like winter underwear, warm and plush. I knew for certain now I had been right. There was someone she cared deeply about, someone who left her here in this drafty, hollow house and broke her heart. It must have been the dark-haired Major with the eastern accent. Maybe the Army captain with the blue eyes and bronzed tan from the Pacific Theater, rotting away in a Jap jungle POW camp.

"I'm so sorry."

We kissed. One second her mouth was pressing on mine, writhing and moving like an Amazonian serpent, and the next, when I was able to reopen my eyes, she was hanging limply from my embrace, staring at me with those dispassionate, disengaged eyes as if I were another kitchen appliance. Just before I started to protest her detachment, she shushed me with another quick kiss and thrust her hip into my thigh. The fantasy was alive as I held on and bent her backward while my mouth lunged for her neck. She was mine at last in a fatal frenzy of lovemaking I had dared to write about cramped over my typewriter while she danced in the dark below me and listened to the plaintive tunes on the radio.

I lifted her onto the table. Then I pressed her back over the sugar bowl. This time when my lips bore down on hers, her mouth opened.

"Ethan..."

There was a bump, a thump and a slam as the front door swung wide, and Veronica Nigh, wearing green slacks and a silly scarf tied over her pin curls, clomped into the kitchen. "Oh, Mrs. Goodknight, are you alright?"

Delilah pushed both hands against my chest. My left hand was two thirds up her thigh. The right was cradling her head. My mouth was swabbed in crimson paint from Delilah's luscious lips, and my head throbbed like Midwest thunder.

"Fine. I just fell, slipped on something when I was cleaning up." She scrambled down and pulled at her blouse. "Lucky for me Mr. McCarthy came downstairs."

Virginia peered at us for a moment, and then set a bottle of cream on the table. "Well, I wanted to thank you for this the other evening. I didn't mean to use it all."

"Oh, think nothing of it, Virginia." Delilah took the cream and opened the refrigerator.

"Well, I'll go on up then and wash some things out if you don't mind."

It took me a moment to realize she was speaking to me. "Oh. Uh, sure."

"Well, if you don't need to be in the bathroom."

"No. Fine." I waved her back.

"Well, I'll go on up then. Nice to see you, Mr. McCarthy."

I feigned a cordial smile. "Same here, Miss Nigh."

"You've been keeping pretty late hours, haven't you?"

"Uh, sorry if my typing bothers you."

"Not at all. I just noticed your light on late, that's all. Working on your book Mrs. Goodknight tells me."

"It's nothing really."

"He's working on a wonderful book," Delilah gushed. "It's all about tragic love."

"Oh, my. I didn't realize. I thought you were a history teacher, Mr. McCarthy."

Delilah touched my shoulder. "He will be. He's taken a sabbatical to write a novel."

"Oh, my," Virginia said, her penciled eyebrows wriggling like night crawlers. "Isn't that something? Imagine. Another Hemingway right here in our midst."

Delilah adjusted her turban and left, leaving me breathless and disturbed. I was an acrobat stranded on a high wire with no way down. I needed help, and she had abandoned me aloft with Miss Nigh.

"Well," I said, moving toward the doorway. "I better be going."

"I'd love to read your book sometime, Mr. McCarthy."

"Well, it's a long way from being finished yet," I demurred, inching toward the stairs.

"Good luck."

"Thanks." And I was through the front door and outside.

At the end of the block, I looked down and saw my manly lance still poised for the joust. Virginia Nigh must be the horniest old biddy on the block, talking about my book all the while her beady eyes were glued to my fly. My clumsy courting had turned into boardinghouse burlesque.

It turned out my friend was no longer at The Multnomah Hotel. He'd come to work with a few too many gin fizzes in him and got the sack the day before. Timing was everything in life, wasn't it? I talked to the manager and got the job anyway. Turned out he knew my father and used to shop in the store. So thanks to Pop, I was gainfully employed once more.

# Eleven

===========

I worked second shift from six in the evening until ten when my replacement made an entrance clutching his Orphan Annie comic books. An odd lot these night clerks. My four-hour stints didn't require more than a night-light spurt of brain power. Perfect for my need to drift off in mental forays far from graduate school pursuits. My tips alone were enough to keep me in automat lunches. Although ever hopeful, I never saw my room lit up again as I topped the stairs. In fact, I went almost two weeks without seeing a trace of her. There was nothing to remind me of our nearly completed coupling on the kitchen table but the rampant replay running through my mind every time I came downstairs and peered into the deserted kitchen.

On a Friday evening when I let myself in and walked down the hallway for a quick peek, I smelled a delicious, tangy aroma. My nose tracked the scent to the kitchen counter. Atop the breadbox was a fresh pie topped with snowy swirls of meringue. I scraped my nose on the flaky crust and inhaled the lemony perfume. Delilah probably baked this for her lover. Maybe in memory of her sweetheart's favorite delicacy from happier times. Who relished these succulent desserts now? I never saw Delilah eat any sweets.

I poked a finger through the stiff egg whites and reached the creamy filling. Scooping out a trench full, I licked my prize and nibbled at a chunk of broken crust. It was delicious. I hadn't had anything like this since Gladys left home. Overcome with a ravenous appetite after working all night watching others more fortunate than I stuff themselves, I picked up the pie plate, placed it on the table and searched for a fork. Armed, I sat down and began to eat. As I relished my reward and licked my lips, an eerie spark of libidinous excitement began building along the base of my spine. I was symbolically having her, possessing the only part of this woman I could conquer—her culinary creation. For now, it was enough to fill my aching belly and lull me into a peaceful sleep when I returned to my room. I left the ravaged dessert half eaten, a gaping, oozing yellow wound proclaiming my guilt in plain view for Delilah to discover my raid. Maybe she would notice, would care enough to talk to me, try to see me. I wanted so much just to believe she missed me these past weeks. Missed me enough to wonder where I was, why I had eaten her pie, spoiled her perfect surprise for someone more fortunate than I.

She never did mention my midnight raid. In the morning, when I looked in before going out for breakfast, the pie was gone. So was she. I wondered where. She must have gone out of town to visit a relative. Maybe the brother-in-law at the coast she had mentioned. The one who gave her the extra meat rations. Or maybe she was at the Roosevelt Hotel with him, whoever he was, and she never thought of me at all.

On impulse, desperate for an answer, even a negative one, I scribbled a note and left it on the kitchen table before I went to work. During my whole shift, I kept watching the entrance to the restaurant, searching the faces for a familiar smile, hoping she would care enough to answer.

I finished work and walked up Broadway for home. At the corner of Broadway and Yamhill, a taxi swerved to the corner. The driver leaned across the front seat and opened the door. Delilah Goodknight wrapped in cashmere and black fur hurried out from a neon lit bar. She was wearing black kid gloves, platform pumps and a crimson veil. Just as she started to step inside the car, she looked up and saw me. Before I could speak, she had slammed the door. The driver shifted gears, and the cab jerked away from the curb. Delilah never even looked back at me standing there in the drizzle with a dumbstruck glaze on my face.

When I got home, I expected to see her there in the hallway, waiting for me to catch up, but it was dark and empty. Upstairs, I could hear the sound of Virginia Nigh snoring. Downstairs, my note was still undisturbed on the dinette. Disgusted, sick at heart, I ripped it loose and wadded it into a ball. I was going to get over this silly crush. The whole premise was preposterous anyway. Here I was still a kid, a naive, nearly virginal, idle dreamer imagining this fascinating, intriguing woman would find me the least bit interesting, and all the while she was carrying out the love affair I could only try to write about.

In bed, I scrunched my pillow under my head and turned to stare out at the blank wall beyond my window. Maybe even now, she was racing into her lover's arms. Maybe he was on a short furlough from the front. She had gone to the Roosevelt or somewhere to steal a few secret moments of happiness. I was only an intrusion, an occasional amusement.

Before my eyes closed, I heard the faint sounds from downstairs seep through the floorboards. I listened hard, afraid to breathe in. It was real. I wasn't dreaming again. Delilah was there. On the screened-in sleeping porch, sitting in the dark, listening to the radio, dreaming of him. Maybe she had been home all the while, watching me from the shadows as I crept into the kitchen and looked for her. Guarding her privacy from my infatuation. Goddam it.

I rolled out of bed and opened my door. The music was louder. I could hear Dick Haymes' mellow voice flowing like expensive liquor from under the door at the end of the hall. A stream of light painted the carpet in front of room Number 1. I padded soundlessly down the hall, listening and trying to discern the melody of voices from behind the door. Driven to the brink of sappy melancholia by her illusive charms, I pressed both palms against the wood, laid my ear on the brass numeral and held my breath. Then I heard her. Her short jabs of expiration punctuated the silence between the lull of the music and her childlike sobs.

Delilah was crying.

I should have turned the knob and stepped into her life right then. But looking back, I can still feel the pit of my stomach opening up, my ears ringing like Ma Bell and my sweaty hands gripping the door frame. Her sadness overwhelmed me and left me feeling woefully inadequate and helpless to act. I sensed she was caught in the eddy of some emotional whirlpool where even I could never hope to reach her. It was all so hopeless, so pointless and so godawful, unendurably painful.

I turned around and crept back to my room. With the door shut, I lay in the dark and listened for the muffled sounds of the radio. Only a few times since I had moved in had I seen a light from under the door of Number 1 and heard a sound. I had never suspected it was Delilah who was behind that door, crying softly while the radio played swing tunes meant for happy couples. When I thought about it, I had no idea who occupied Number 1. It could have been some mysterious, reclusive boarder who avoided both Miss Nigh and me. To be truthful, I had never wondered that much. It was a room like mine perhaps but closer to the alley, probably colder and quieter than my space. But it didn't matter who my silent neighbor was. I was eager to avoid unwanted socialization and concentrate on Delilah.

I lit a cigarette and sucked until the end glowed cherry red in the darkness. I began thinking in logical steps about this new wrinkle on my hopeful romantic notions. I could plainly hear the radio playing from the end of the hall. Why hadn't Miss Nigh been complaining about the noise? She seemed unable to sleep if I knocked ash on the carpet. I was certain the clacking of my typewriter keys into all hours of the morning irritated her. So who was in room Number 1 crying her eyes out if it wasn't Delilah? Who was with her anyway? Was there some secret resident upstairs with Virginia and me? Someone whom Delilah wanted to keep away from my prying eyes?

I blew smoke toward the foot of my bed and curled my arm under my head. Maybe it wasn't some dashing serviceman or impeccable society snob she was secretly romancing. Maybe this was some beer-swigging longshoreman, some bus driver or married sap with three kids and a wife working the night shift at Jantzen.

The blood pounded at my temples. I was being eaten alive by irrational jealousy, my rage at being bested by some unknown swordsman who never even had the guts to show me his face even if I wasn't prepared to meet him. Whatever it was, whoever he was, he was making her cry. If I could, I would have liked to crash through the door and deliver a Joe Louis punch to this heartless interloper. Yes. I closed my eyes and painted the scene in my mind: I was up from the bed, my Lucky stubbed to death in the ceramic hula girl's feet, down the hall and in front of the door. I paused in my daydream only a second to confirm Delilah's pitiful whimpering, then I put a shoulder to the wood and crashed through like Elliot Ness raiding a speakeasy.

*"Oh, Ethan!"* she would moan as I leaped into the room and came face to face with the slob who was standing over her, his red face contorted in a leer. *Don't! Be careful!"* Naturally, she would be afraid for my safety, a healthy concern for my personal welfare I would shun with gallant disdain.

*"What the hell do you want, Mac?"* he would snarl, his thin lips twisted in a scowl.

And without a word, I would recoil like a Navy destroyer's deck cannon and shoot him all the way into the hallway with one punch. As he skidded across the carpet and banged his head on the balustrade, Delilah would be up and clinging tearfully to my arm.

*"Oh, Ethan! Don't kill him! He didn't mean anything by it!"*

There would be blood all over the bastard by now, and I would be standing there wiping my knuckles, restrained by Delilah as the sonuvabitch got to his knees. *"You ever come back here again, and I'll finish what I started, Mister,"* I would bark just like a movie tough guy.

Then as he stumbled down the stairs, slinking off like a wounded hound, Delilah would fold herself into my waiting arms and wet my sleeve with tears and maybe even a little snot from her runny nose. I wouldn't mind at all.

*"I can't stand to see anyone make you cry, Baby,"* I would say in my Bogie baritone.

*"Oh, Ethan. Hold me, hold me tight and don't let the rest of the world inside."*

I had to take a deep drag on my cigarette to keep the fantasy from driving me over the edge. It was as if I were dreaming with my eyes open, my muscles ready to fire in the right direction, but my mind still weak. It was a joke at best. What would I know about saving maidens in distress? The most experience I had ever had was killing spiders in the sink for my sisters and carrying a college date a quarter mile through the mud once when her dad's old Ford broke down. That didn't amount to much in the scheme of Don Juan heroics.

Now the picture changed as my mind clouded over with a dose of lethal reality to distort my melodrama, and I spun another version of my fantasy. Delilah was standing in the middle of Room Number 1 with her arms akimbo, her hair cascading over one eye, her lips curled back in a spiteful snarl. *"You idiot! You maniac! Look what you've done! You've broken his jaw!"*

*"I didn't realize. I thought he and you, that is..."*

Her hand came out and swiped across my cheek, blazing a trail of angry, red welts. *"He's from the finance company, you moron! Now he's going to repossess the Frigidaire."*

*"I didn't realize. Honest. I'm sorry."*

*"Miserable, interfering creep,"* she hissed as she stomped off to offer aid and succor to the creditor with a swollen jaw.

There was a muffled thump. "Goddammit," I mumbled, too miserable to re-open my eyes as my mirage fizzled to a merciful ending.

A door opened with a muted click and closed. Footsteps moved down the hallway for the stairs. Then I heard the click of Delilah's shoes on the steps. For a moment, I wasn't sure if I was able to move in the right direction. My father's words filled the room suddenly. *"Nattie, forgiveness is always easier to obtain than permission. If you think something's right, do it."*

I had to do it or I would consign myself to a miserable, rodent-like existence in this house, always in the borders of her shadow, afraid to step into the light. She could be angry with me for interfering, prying into her affairs, but at least I would be owed an explanation, an answer. I had to do it.

I was out the door and following on her heels in a split second. When she reached the bottom step, I was right behind her.

She turned around so slowly I nearly knocked her into the entryway. "Ethan? What's wrong? You startled me."

I caught hold of myself balancing on the last tread and spoke before my brain had time to catch up to my feet. "I heard you crying. Are you okay?"

"Oh, Ethan, grow up."

She went into the kitchen, and I followed like a lost puppy. When she flicked the light on, I could see red in her eyes and tracks of smeared mascara on her cheeks. Dream or fantasy, boy or man, I was driven to jump down the well with her.

"I want to know what's wrong. Is there a man bothering you?"

"Never mind. Just leave me alone."

"That's not a good enough answer, dammit."

Her eyes glistened as she tried to peer through me. I took a step closer and caught hold of her shoulders. Tonight she seemed so small and vulnerable. Eggshell fragile.

"Ethan, you don't understand. Please, don't make things complicated." She shrugged off my awkward embrace. "Just leave me alone."

"What is it for crissakes?" I pleaded as much for my sake as hers. "Tell me."

"There's nothing to tell."

I had hold of her once more. My lips came to rest on her hair. It felt like cotton candy and smelled even better. "Jesus, Delilah, tell me. I want to help in some way. Any way."

I could feel her muscles tighten, her backbone as rigid as a curtain rod. She was not yielding a centimeter. I might as well have been begging for mercy from a statue.

"You don't understand at all. It's nothing. Besides, who gave you permission to question me about anything? You have no right to pry into my life."

"Yes, I do."

A hand suddenly lashed my forehead. I didn't have time to feel pain or shock, just surprise. At least, she had reacted.

"Get away and leave me alone! You're being a pest!" She switched off the kitchen light and marched off to the sleeping porch.

For a few moments, I stood there at the sink, my head stinging where her nails had raked a bloody trail across my brow. In a moment, I heard the radio playing.

Since I had gone this far, there was no logical reason to retreat. I followed her to the sleeping porch, feeling my way in the dark. She was sitting in the corner, her feet tucked under her, smoking a cigarette and watching the shadows dance on the screened windows.

"Go away, Nathan."

It was too dark to see her eyes, but I knew she was staring right through me. "I can't."

"Why? Dammit, why won't you just leave me alone?" She bolted out of the chair and turned her back on me again.

As the radio played the Andrews sisters, I longed to understand her aching. "Charmaine, you don't have to be alone tonight if you don't want to be."

"Go away, Nathan, and leave me alone."

"Call me Ethan if you want to. I like it."

"Please, go back upstairs."

"Charmaine, I won't go away. Not unless you tell me you don't trust me."

"Please, go back upstairs. I just want to be left alone."

"If you make me go, I'll never finish the book, you know."

She turned around immediately, and even in the murky shadows, I could see the diamond reflection of those eyes. "Oh, Ethan, don't stop writing. You have to finish the book."

I held her in my arms, triumphant. As we kissed, her tears wet my cheeks. I didn't know if I should speak or just let her lead me into her embrace. She seemed as hungry as I was, searching for my hands and lips as I shook so much I could barely place myself in time and space as we meshed. Our bodies danced in the dark. I was not even aware of the radio, the persistent jangling noise from the hallway, only Delilah's whispers and shivers flowing into my veins like opium.

"Ethan, wait. I have to answer that," she gasped, taking hold of my hand caressing her pliant, warm breast at last. "I have to go. I have the block phone. It might be an emergency for someone. Please, Ethan."

She pushed me away, and I staggered into a wicker chair, panting, sweating and drunk with a throbbing lust while she left to answer the telephone. She spoke in a hushed voice I couldn't quite overhear. Then she came back and stood a safe distance from my waiting hands. "Nathan..." I knew from her tone the spell was broken. I looked up obediently. "It's your sister Carla."

I still couldn't react. Blood roared in my ears, and my eyes could focus only on her blurry silhouette. "What?"

"Your sister Carla says there's something wrong with your sister Frances."

"Is she sick?"

"Nathan, she needs to speak to you right away. Your sister is in the hospital."

"Oh, God," I moaned, staggering out to the hallway and the telephone stand. I picked up the receiver. "Carla?"

"Nattie, darling, I hate to alarm you, but the doctors feel you better come up right away. It's Frances. She's had some female trouble, and it's very serious."

I felt my bowels sinking. "What is it?" I knew, didn't I? I knew.

"She's in surgery, Nattie. The doctor says it's urgent that you come right away."

"How is she?"

"It's bad, Nattie. They had to operate."

"I'll take the first train in the morning."

"Do you have train fare?"

"Of course, I do. I'll be there as soon as I can. Is she going to be alright?"

Carla sighed heavily, and my spirits sank. "She's very sick, Nattie. The doctor says she lost a lot of blood. She's very weak. She didn't know me when I saw her just before they put her under. She looked so pale, Nathan." Now my sister was sniffling. "The way Mama was at the last. I couldn't bear to look at her lying there like that.""

"What's wrong with her?" Why couldn't we say it?

"The doctor will explain everything when you get here."

"Were you with her when she got sick?"

"I spent the weekend with Francie. Since Walter left, she hadn't been feeling too well. And we were at the pictures, and she just got so sick, threw up all over everything, and we had to go out and get some air. She had these awful pains." Carla paused to blow her nose. "I have to call Gladys now, Nattie."

"Okay. I'll be up as soon as I can, Carla. What hospital is she in?"

"Tacoma General. Don't forget she's Frances Clippendale now, Nattie."

I pulled at the back of my neck. Delilah hovered behind me.

"I'll be there on the first train, Carla. Don't worry. Francie'll pull through." I thought of Walter and the silhouettes on the window shade. "Have you called the Red Cross? Walter needs to get home."

"I know."

"I'll call Gladys. You go back and stay with Frances."

"She's still in the recovery room, Nattie."

"Well, for God's sake, go wait for her."

"I will, Nattie. Do you think I should pray for her?"

"It can't hurt. Just be there when she wakes up, okay?" I hung up the phone.

Delilah put her arms around my waist and snuggled against my back. "I'm sorry, Nathan. This is the price we pay for being happy."

"Why Francie? Goddammit!" I wanted to take Delilah back in my arms and bury my pain in hers, but before I could turn around, she pulled away and blew me a kiss from the door.

"I'll call you a cab. Why don't you get out at the Interstate Bridge and hitch a ride?"

"Yeah." I resigned myself, defeated and disgusted. "Sure. I'll get my jacket."

I went upstairs, shut my door and bit my lip. Frances had to be alright. She couldn't be punished for being happy, being in love. It wasn't fair.

I grabbed my jacket, scraped change and my wallet off the bureau, threw some things in a bag and closed the door behind me. When I got downstairs, Delilah was gone. I picked up the telephone and dialed the long distance operator. If I was lucky, the Doctor wouldn't be home to answer the call.

# Twelve

===========

**We** stood around the bed in a semi-circle like mourners at a wake. Our sister lay with a white sheet pulled up to her neck, an oxygen tent draped over her torso, her skin drawn tight across her cheekbones. A glass bottle hung beside the bedpost, and a gray rubber tube snaked from the coverlet to a bag half-filled with cloudy, amber liquid. The surgeon had told us he made a seven-inch incision through her belly, removed her uterus, ovaries, Fallopian tubes and snipped out her appendix for good measure. Frances was only twenty-six, and she had lost the essential elements of her womanliness. She was doomed to be barren, empty forever for so long as she lived without a living soul to inherit her genes and the promise of immortality. I felt so sorry for her, so guilty for not being with her, doing something to spare her this ordeal.

"You look so tired, Nattie," Carla whispered, squeezing my hand. "Did you get any sleep on the way up?"

"I was too worried about Francie to sleep."

I could barely remember the trip. I was wedged in the back seat with an infant on my lap and a chubby teenage boy crowding me against the window. A dairy farmer from Tillamook had picked me up in Vancouver and given me a lift all the way to the hospital. He and his family were on their way to Bellingham to attend a funeral. Their church and neighboring farmers had all chipped in their gas ration cards so they could make the trip. Nice folks. But I hadn't slept at all.

"You should lie down. The nurse said we could use a cot in the hallway."

"I'm fine." All I could think about was poor Francie lying there like a broken doll. I couldn't bring myself to go off and leave her for fear she might slip away from us. She was so pale and fragile, an autumn leaf fallen on the snow.

"The doctor said she would sleep all night, Nattie."

"I know. You go. I'll stay here for a while."

"No. I'll stay." She patted my shoulder and wiped her eyes. She must be even more spent than I was. "Oh, Nattie." She heaved another sigh. "It's so awful. Poor Francie. When is Gladys going to come?"

"She'll take a train out as soon as she can get away. She has to find someone to stay with the girls."

"It's just so awful for her. Poor Francie. Poor Walter, too. I think Gladys should be the one to tell her, don't you?"

"Tell her what?" I knew what Carla was getting at, but I just didn't want to talk about it. If we didn't discuss her mutilation, we could go on thinking of our youngest sister as the golden child a while longer. I wanted to think of her as the happy bride, mellowing into motherhood.

"You know, Nattie. Somebody has to tell her the bad news. I think Gladys should be the one to do it. I suppose the doctor will tell Walter though, won't he?"

"I suppose."

Carla wound a coil of hair around her finger. "He should be the first to know. He's her husband now. I suppose they'll tell him, and he can break the news to Francie."

"Doesn't matter."

"I suppose not. But I wish Gladys could tell her. Frances always listens to Gladys, don't you think?"

"It doesn't matter, Carla."

"Well, I can't tell her. I couldn't do it, Nattie. I just couldn't tell poor Francie something so awful."

"It's not awful."

She rubbed the bed rail. "It is, Nattie. You know it is."

"Look, Carla, the important thing is for Francie to get well. The rest doesn't really matter. Frances getting better is what's important."

"I know. But I was just thinking—"

"Well, don't. Forget it."

"If she had a baby already, before this had to happen, then it'd be different, don't you think, Nattie?"

"Oh, Carla, for crissakes." I hung my head, tired and spiritually depleted. "Don't even think about it. If what they did saved Francie's life, then it's worth it."

"I know. Only if she and Walter had just married sooner." She defended herself against my warning glare. "What I'm trying to say is that Daddy and Gladys wanted her to get married last Christmas, and if she'd listened to them, then maybe this wouldn't have happened."

"Stop it! Just stop it, Carla. There isn't any reason."

"Okay," she whimpered, offended by my outburst. "But it's so unfair."

"Francie has never done anything wrong in her whole life, and nothing she did or didn't do had anything to do with her getting sick."

"I suppose. What do you think Walter will do when he finds out, Nattie?"

"What do you mean?"

"Well, if Francie can't ever have children. They just got married, Nathan. What do you think he'll do? He wants to have a family, doesn't he? And if Francie can't—"

"For crissakes, he loves her." I pushed her toward the door. "Jesus, can't you think straight? Walter won't care about anything so long as Francie is okay."

"I guess not." She meandered down the hallway and left me alone with my sister.

Frances had nearly died on the operating table. The doctors said it was an ectopic pregnancy. The fertilized egg had started to grow in the Fallopian tube instead of in her uterus. If she had been alone when she started to hemorrhage, there was a good chance she would have died. As it was, they weren't certain they had saved her. When she woke up, she would hate what they had done to her, ripped away her chances for a future full of kids. Lost the only child she and Walter would ever have.

Walter wasn't able to make it back to Tacoma before Frances got out of the hospital. He arrived two days after she came home, with Carla acting as her nursemaid. One look at his face when he saw her lying on the sofa, pillows at her back and blankets piled around her shoulders, convinced me he didn't give a damn what the surgeons had done to save his wife's life. Frances started to weep for the first time when she saw him. So did Carla. I just tried to get the hell out of the way and give them as much privacy as I could.

Walter was home for two weeks, and then he was headed overseas to his bomber squadron in England. He would be flying out on a brand new Flying Fortress B17 ferried from Boeing Field to its base in Surrey. Gladys arrived with her two little girls prepared to stay for a month and never once said an unkind word to Frances. She turned out to be an angel of mercy. As soon as Gladys had unpacked, scrubbed the kitchen floor and starched and ironed the curtains, Carla returned to her job at the Boeing plant, and I prepared to take the train back to Portland.

Gladys came out and kissed me good-bye as I loaded my bag in the taxi. "Nathan, take care of yourself, Dear. We worry about you down there on your own in Portland."

"I'm fine."

"I felt better knowing Daddy was there to look in on you."

"Don't worry."

"Are you finishing your research?"

"It's coming along."

"You know how proud Daddy would be to have you published, Nathan." She bent over and kissed me. "We'd all be so proud."

"Sure. Well, take care of yourself and the girls."

"If the Doctor can come out to get me and the girls, we'll stop off in Portland on the way home, Nattie."

"I'll look forward to it."

"Good-bye, Dear." A dry kiss brushed my lips.

When I arrived at Union Station in Portland, dishwater clouds scudded across the sky. Mt. Hood was veiled in a buttermilk haze, and the streets were still wet with yesterday's shower. I grabbed my bag and walked south to the Hoyt Hotel. I spent my last buck for a cold beer and sipped slowly as I watched the lobby traffic.

I needed to regroup, get to work on my book—the real book, not the farcical fantasy of Ethan and Charmaine. I had consumed enough poison to kill a grown man chasing that frustrating phantom. Francie's misfortune had sucked the life out of me, killed my spirit to risk another failure. All I wanted was to escape into my comfortable, secure academic stupor and bury myself in the stacks at the library, finish my Roman history and get on with my life.

I had been struck by a wild bout of infatuation. But now I had to take a long, critical look at myself and decide what the hell I was going to accomplish by diverting my energy and time writing drivel about a sappy romance between two characters who could contribute nothing to mankind's understanding of the world. The publication of my doctoral thesis *The History of the Roman Monarchy* would mark me as a man of substance, harvest the bounty from years of study and hours of solitary reading in dreary libraries. Delilah Goodknight had been a distraction, a detour. That's all. The sooner I understood the situation from a realistic perspective, the better for everybody.

I wiped away a foam mustache and smiled. Christ, I mused. I'd go home and chuckle over our romantic interlude on the sleeping porch. Some joke, huh? She must have enjoyed a good laugh after I left, probably regaled her lovers with stories of my clumsy bumbling on the kitchen table. Now that I could see everything clearly, I would approach Delilah as a pal, someone who might like some company once in a while, and if she didn't, hell, there were plenty of lonely women around these days. What the hell was I worried about?

I finished my draft, zipped up my jacket and started for Broadway and home. By the time I got to the Park blocks and the

Roosevelt Hotel, it was drizzling. I stuck my head down and hurried on. She practically ran me down she bolted out the doorway so fast.

"Damn!" I blurted, regaining my balance after dropping my bag in a puddle.

"Oh! Ethan! It's you. You're back." She straightened her hat and pulled her collar up to ward off the blustery wind hurling rain at her.

"I'm on my way home." I picked up my bag and started across the street. "Let's get out of this weather." Despite all my insightful ruminations at the Hoyt, my heart leapt at just hearing her voice.

Delilah followed me across the wet grass, holding on to her hat and double-stepping to keep up with me. "How's your sister?"

"Better, thanks. She's home now."

"Did her husband get leave?"

"Two weeks. Ten days actually. His unit was still stateside training, but he has to fly to England to rejoin his squadron."

We got to the house, and she took out her key. Inside, we stood dripping and shaking water from our clothes.

"Poor Ethan." She helped me shed my jacket. "I hope Frances will be okay."

"She's fine now. My oldest sister is staying with her for a couple months."

"I thought about sending a wire."

I stopped and watched her unpin her hat. "You didn't need to bother."

"I didn't know if I should call to check with the hospital."

"It's sweet of you to be so concerned."

She shrugged. "I didn't expect to run into you so soon."

I knocked water off my hat. "You almost ran me down."

"Well, I couldn't get a cab, so I thought I'd just run for it."

We stood facing each other. For once, her eyes stayed on mine, engaged and connected. "I had supper at the Roosevelt this evening. Didn't feel much like staying home and eating alone." She hung up her coat. "Well, I don't suppose you'd like a cup of coffee?"

"I'll go up and drop my things off."

"Don't be long," she chimed as I started up the stairs, two at a time.

I went up to my room and unloaded my baggage. I needed a nice hot bath, a shave and some fresh underwear. But that would have to wait. My toes and fingertips were tingling. I could feel an acrobat doing somersaults in the pit of my belly. I hadn't taken control of the situation yet and felt more than a little chagrined at my giddy delight in seeing her. That seemed to be all that had changed.

Delilah had the coffee perking when I came into the kitchen. She motioned me to a spot at the table and set a plate in front of me. "I have some pie if you're hungry," she offered.

"Lemon?"

"It's fresh." She cut a slice and scooped it onto my plate. The meringue glistened like an Atlantic ice floe. "It's from the bakery. I just don't seem to have the time anymore. There's always so much laundry to keep up with."

"I can always send my things out."

She brushed me off and licked lemon filling off her finger. "Oh, no. I don't mind. It keeps me occupied after all."

I took a bite of pie. The crust tasted like week-old newspaper. "Is lemon meringue your favorite?"

She poured my coffee and sat down with her own cup half full. "I thought everybody liked lemon."

I swallowed another mouthful and retired my fork. "You always seem to have a lemon pie around, Delilah. I thought it must be your favorite."

Her eyes locked on to mine, hard as diamond drill bits. "It's nice to have something special, don't you think? It helps break the boredom, doesn't it?"

"Boredom?" I asked skeptically, watching her click her fingernails against the cup. "Are you that bored, Delilah? Is that it?"

"What? Is that what?"

"What's eating you."

"Finish your pie, Ethan. I'll bet nobody cooked for you in Tacoma."

"My sister Carla took good care of me."

"Did she bake any pies?"

"No."

"Well, I'd think you'd be pretty hungry for a good desert then."

"Once I came downstairs when you were out and saw a lemon pie on the counter and helped myself."

"Oh."

"I didn't know if you minded or not," I confessed. Her eyes never gave her away. She was completely indifferent. "I thought you'd baked it for someone special."

She brushed crumbs away and sipped at her coffee. "Oh."

"Was it?" I prodded.

"What?"

"For someone special."

"Oh, not particularly."

I'd run into that stone wall she threw up whenever I honed in. I pushed my chair back and dabbed at my mouth with the napkin. "Thanks for the pie."

"You haven't finished, Ethan. More coffee?"

"No, thanks." I stood up. "I'm beat. Think I'll go up and hit the sack."

"Ethan, are you going to start work on the book again now that you're back?"

"I'm way behind on my research. I'm going to have to hit it hard if I want to finish before the end of the year."

"The Roman book? About the kings?"

"I'm way behind schedule."

She stirred sugar into her coffee. "Are you planning on going back to school next term?"

"Yes."

"Well, you still have time then, don't you?"

I sank both hands deep into my front pockets, pulled off my glasses and pinched my brows together. "Some, I suppose. But I have to get back to work in earnest. The research takes a lot of time and effort, and to get ready for submission, I need to start work on the final composition by the middle of next month."

"Oh. Well, is there any time to work on the other one, do you think?"

"The other one?" I hated to bait her, but I needed to hear her loneliness named, stamped and certified so I could count a small victory.

"The love story. Ethan and Charmaine. You're planning on finishing it, aren't you?"

"I can't say."

"It's important, too."

"It's just a stupid story. A waste of time really. I was never serious about it."

She got up and pushed her hair back from her face. Her hat had shielded only her crown from the downpour, and the limp curls hung loosely around her face as she gripped the back of the chair. "It's important to me that you keep working on it."

"I better go on up. It's been a long day."

"Please, try. For me anyway."

I got as far as the telephone stand in the hallway before I knew what to say. It was a daring thrust to best her parry. "Delilah, who are you seeing at the Roosevelt Hotel?"

"No one."

"Who was up on the third floor of the hotel the night I got fired?"

"How should I know?"

"I guess I don't have any right to an answer, do I?"

"It's not that."

"Thanks for the pie and coffee."

"Ethan, wait." She tugged at my sleeve. "Would it make a difference if there *was* somebody?"

Maybe it wouldn't. Maybe I was better off with concocted suitors pursuing Delilah across the landscape of my fertile imagination. There was a good chance I didn't have the balls to face the real thing anyway. "Just tell me. Is there someone special or is it just anybody?"

Instantly, her lips hardened in an ugly gash splitting her face, eyes narrowing to serpentine slits. "I didn't think you could be so mean." She turned her back and walked away.

# Thirteen

==========

**It** wasn't easy. I had neglected my historical research for three months. All my mental reserves that had stored up such optimistic energy for the book had wilted. I scarcely had the stamina to revive my flagging interest. For the first time in my life, the Roman Kingdom seemed incredibly archaic, trivial and mundane. Every time I sat in front of the typewriter, my fingers found the keys which flew to another tryst between the ardent, wounded soldier and the beautiful, tortured woman who possessed him. After two weeks, Ethan and Charmaine were charging through chapter ten, and I was emotionally exhausted. Their love finally consummated, albeit on paper, my vicarious hunger was sated.

When the gray skies pressed at my window and shadows danced on my wrinkled wallpaper, I would peer through the cigarette fog and see the fictional figures dancing a close two-step on my rug. Charmaine's eyes were lit like foundry coals. Ethan was smiling in a half leer, half dreamy smile with his scarred lips. They were drinking from the fountain of life, and I was still standing in line at the automat. Their love was more tangible than my still unmet bursting need to bloom.

I saw little of Delilah after my return from Tacoma. I left for work at five just as Virginia Nigh was coming up the stairs.

"Good evening, Mr. McCarthy."

"Good evening." I held the door open for her.

"Off to work?"

"Yes."

"How is the book coming, Mr. McCarthy?"

"Slowly, I'm afraid."

"Oh, my yes. There's so much research to do with a thing like that."

"Yes."

"Kings. Who would have thought someone had the inclination to write about that?"

I barely managed to force a civil smile. "Yes. Who?"

"Will you be mentioning *Il Duce*, Mr. McCarthy? I suppose he's a king of sorts, isn't he?"

"This is an ancient reference work, Miss Nigh. The twentieth century is gratefully excepted."

"Oh, my. Well, I thought a biography of Mussolini would certainly add a little dash of excitement. History can be so dull, can't it, Mr. McCarthy? It's all such old news."

"But that's the point, isn't it?"

Her skinny eyebrows wrinkled. "I beg your pardon?"

It wasn't worth pursuing. Miss Nigh was only one poor soul in a sea of such critics. "Well, I'm late for work. Goodnight."

I worked at the hotel restaurant until ten, stacking dishes, scraping plates, cleaning tables, folding linen. When I got home, the house was usually dark. Once in a while, I would hear the radio playing downstairs, but I never heard her voice, never had a sign she was watching me. I quit stopping downstairs in the kitchen, looking to see if the glow from the Philco console could be seen from the sleeping porch. I just bounded up the stairs and went straight to bed. Most nights, I slept without dreaming.

One Sunday a month after I started working at the hotel, I woke up early. A car horn was honking below. Virginia was running her bath water down the hall. Bacon was frying downstairs. I sat up and reached for my watch. Eight-thirty. Too early. I could sleep another hour or so and then saunter downtown for some fresh coffee and doughnuts before coming back to write. So I put the pillow over my head, closed my eyes and drifted off as the water pipes hammered and gurgled in the walls.

Suddenly without realizing I had been asleep, I awoke with a start and raised my head. Delilah was sitting in the cushy chair where Pop had sat bemoaning my accommodations. My manuscript was in her lap, and she was holding up a single page, cigarette smoke from her Lucky Strike curling over her head like a genie's vapor trail.

I sat up and pulled at my cheeks with both hands. My tongue felt like a fir tree, and my eyelashes were sticky with sleep.

She spoke without taking her eyes off the page. "Good morning. It's late, you know."

"What time is it?" I fumbled to reach my wristwatch on the nightstand.

"Almost ten. I had breakfast and did the ironing already."

I flopped back on the pillow. "I thought I smelled bacon."

"Too late. Virginia joined me this morning. She usually visits her mother in Albina on Sundays, but she's not feeling too well."

I had no reason to care about any of this, but I appreciated the tender attention she was lavishing on my creative fruit. She never once looked away as she read.

"I didn't even hear you come in." I was still too fuzzy to figure out why she'd slipped in like a house detective.

"You were sleeping so I didn't wake you. You don't mind, do you?"

"I guess not."

"I like it that Charmaine forgives him. I think this is even better than the first part. He realizes that love isn't something you can barter for." She turned her head to look at me. "Do you know what I mean, Ethan?"

"No. Doesn't matter though." I swung my legs out of bed and waited to see if she would watch me emerge from the rumpled covers, hairy and bare as a newborn in my skivvies. She didn't even sneak a glance.

"I think he's going to win her in the end, Ethan. He has a good soul, don't you think?"

I scratched. "Soul? What's that?"

"You know. His heart is pure."

"Nobody's heart is pure, Delilah." I grabbed my undershirt and stood up.

"Why do you say that?"

"Ethan isn't altruistic at all."

"What do you mean?"

"He's a lost soul. Maybe Charmaine can help him find out where he's headed." My literary clarity amazed me. I doubt if I had formed the thought before it passed across my lips. I thought I was writing a recipe for carnal adventures to feed my own ravenous appetite. But maybe something else had emerged after all.

She scoffed. "Don't be maudlin. I don't like it." She slapped the page on her lap and took a long, hard drag on the cigarette. "How would you describe it?"

"It's a stupid, sappy, maudlin story about a lovesick moron and—"

"What?"

"I don't know. A sorceress maybe." I hopped into my pants and buttoned my shirt.

"That's rubbish, and you know it. Ethan is honest and loyal. He's so much in love he can't bear to see her suffer for him. She has no hold on him except true love."

I stifled a yawn. I couldn't stand to have her excise my labors with her scalpel-sharp wit. "It's just a story. They aren't real people anyway so what does it matter?"

"They *are* real people. And you know that, too."

I zipped up my trousers and stood so close to her I could count the hairs rise up on her forearm. "Who are they then?"

"You know who they are. Don't play such stupid games with me, Ethan." She stood up. We breathed in each other's air.

"Me and you? Is that it?"

Her cheeks flushed. "Well, damn you then."

She brushed against my chest on her way to the door. When she went out, she slammed it behind her so hard that the hula girl danced in the ashtray. I put my glasses on, bent down and picked up the scattered pages of my manuscript. I couldn't help myself. I read a paragraph where she had left off. The edges were still curled from her finger hold.

*When she looked at him, he saw through the icy aloofness and recognized the child hurting inside, crying to be let free.*

*"God," he whispered as the darkness folded over them. "I've tried so hard to keep from loving you." She touched him, and he wept.*

# Fourteen

========

**Everybody** in the hotel kitchen was crowded around the radio for the evening news. Edward R. Murrow was broadcasting from London, and he was talking about the Allied drive through the Lowlands. Our troops would be on German soil before long. Maybe the War was going to be over by Christmas, and the boys could come home.

"Oh, Lordy," the sous chef Maxine groaned, clutching her apron with both hands. "I don't see why they don't give up and save what's left."

Melvin the cook swabbed a puddle of grease from his grille and wagged a finger at her. "We ought to pulverize those Nazis, plow 'em under for crissakes, the rotten bastards. Nathan," he commanded, aiming his bony forefinger at my navel, "you're the historian. Tell 'em what the Romans did to Carthage. Sowed the soil with salt, by God. Right, Nathan? Salt."

"Hush, Melvin," Maxine scolded. "Who cares about that?"

"Nathan, tell 'em. Salt. Sowed the ground with salt and plowed 'em under. Never hear about the Carthage army causin' nobody any grief now, do you, huh? Salt, by God. Ought to plow the whole goddam Nazi fatherland under six feet of salt and forget about the bastards."

My dish-washing partner tapped the cook on the shoulder. "Hey, Mel. I'm Dutch-German."

"Yeah? So what of it?"

He drew back slightly. Mel was almost twice his size. "Well, we ain't all Nazis."

Mel waved him away. "Aw, get buggered, Kid. Ought to take all them goddam krautheads out and line 'em up against the wall. World'd be better off."

Maxine whispered "My Joey's in the South Pacific, Mel, an' he never even saw a single German the whole time he's been in the service."

"Krautheads, Japs. Ought to just plow the whole lot under, I say. Be done with the sons a bitches." He scratched his bald knob and switched off the radio. "Get back to work. Ain't nothin' happenin' tonight. Goddam politicians don't know a goddam thing anyway."

Maxine shrank back to the dining room door and rang the bell for service pick up. "Well, I say Mr. Roosevelt will bring 'em all home for Christmas. That's what I say."

"Bullshit," Mel spat. "War ain't gonna be over until we kill all those bastards. Ever last one of those slant-eyed bastards. That's when your Joey is comin' home, when the Emperor himself gets the hot seat." Mel nudged me with a hard elbow. "Hey, Nathan, how come you couldn't make it into the army? Hell, they take queers and drunkards for crissakes. What the hell's the matter with you anyhow?"

I pointed self-consciously to my injured eye, useless except for the lightning spark when the doctor shone a light directly onto my retina. Everyone stared at me, waiting for me to expiate my abstention from duty. "I'm blinded in one eye," I explained. "Accident when I was a kid."

"Oh, shame. Damn shame." Mel turned his head and spat into the dishwater. "Too bad you can't be over there killin' Japs like Maxine's Joe."

"Yeah. Real shame," I relented.

"I'd be over there myself knockin' the balls off those damn krautheads if I was ten years younger and didn't have this damn hernia." He limped a little getting back to his grille and spatulas.

"Damn shame we gotta have widdas right here in town when there's some a these fuckin' draft dodgers sneakin' around."

"What do you mean by that crack?" Maxine challenged him.

"I seen 'em at the bar las' night. Draft dodgers. Cowards. Goddam cowards. No balls. One of 'em said he was in defense work. Shit." He spat again. "Defense work my ass."

"He work at Kaiser?" the pimply-faced dishwasher asked. He was only nineteen and had a gimpy leg. I doubted if he could do much more than read a racing form and tie his own shoelaces. He never seemed able to dip both oars in the water at once.

"Naw. He don't work at Kaiser. He's a goddam salesman. A cheap huckster in a J.C. Penney seersucker for crissakes."

"What's he sellin'?" Maxine asked.

Mel tossed the answer over his hunched shoulder. "Beer."

"Beer?" the three of us echoed.

"Booze. The bastard is beatin' the pavement sellin' beer for crissakes, and he's as strong as an ox. Oughtta strap his rosy ass to a Howitzer and ship him on over to General Bradley. That'd make a man out of the s.o.b."

The swinging door opened, and the maitre d'hôtel came in with a scowl on his pasty face. He almost never smiled. "Melvin," he snarled. "We have a complaint from Table Number Four."

"I ain't got time for no complaints from those fat asses," he shot back.

"You undercooked their steaks. Here. Rewarm them." He plopped two T-bones down on the grille. "Let's hustle back here. We got customers out front waiting on their entrees. Cut the gab and do your fucking jobs like you give a shit!"

Mel headed for the reefer and pulled out a baking pan with yesterday's meatloaf. "Hold your piss. We're on it."

My turn next. "*You.*" He stabbed me with a capped fountain pen. "Table Number Six has dirty linen."

"Yessir." I was out the door ahead of him. At least in the dining room, nobody asked me about my 4-F status, whined about the meat shortages or threatened to fix me up with his niece in Scappoose—

the one with the three little brats and the ex-husband in the state penitentiary for armed robbery. The Allies didn't know how lucky they were to have Melvin sidelined with a double hernia.

At ten past ten, I was out of the kitchen, on my way home, carrying my jacket and my hat as I rounded the corner at Yamhill. The sound of billiard balls clacking together, glasses tinkling and the soft laughter of a woman drew me to a halt at the door of Murphy's Saloon. I turned and pushed open the door. Inside it was smoky, dark and musty. I sat at the last empty bar stool and ordered a draft. Halfway into my third swallow, a beefy guy with a raincoat, red cheeks and a bushy mustache crowded in beside me, leaned across the bar and ordered a boilermaker.

"Hey, 'scuse me, eh, Bud?"

"Okay." I tried to move away and sip my beer in peace. When I saw the bottom of the glass, I was heading home to bed.

My anonymous stool mate got up suddenly and left, and the heavy intruder plopped his ass down beside mine and folded the raincoat across his pudgy thighs. "Hey, Mac," he said out of the corner of his mouth. "How's the world treatin' you, huh?"

"No beefs."

"Nothin' like a straight shot after beatin' the streets all day, huh?" He put his head back and flung the whiskey down his throat. Then his beady eyes fastened on my profile. "Say, you look familiar, Kid. You work around here?"

"Close."

"Yeah. I seen you somewheres before. Makin' my rounds. You tend bar at the Multnomah?"

"Nope."

"I swear I seen you before, Bud."

"I wash dishes—clean up."

He grinned. "Yeah. I knew I seen you. The Multnomah, right?"

"You got it."

"You're the guy who comes and takes my dirty dishes."

"That's me," I said with an obliging smile.

"Bus boy, huh?"

"Yep."

"You stop in here a time or two, huh?"

"Some."

"Yeah. This is one of my steady customers. I'm in beer, wholesale for Northwest Spirits Distributors."

"You must have a lot of business with the war on."

"You better believe it, Kid. Business is good. Whatchya drinkin' there?"

I raised my glass. "House draft."

He sniffed my brew and wrinkled his nose. "Hey, that ain't our stuff. That's horse piss. You should try some good beer."

"This is fine, thanks."

"You live uptown?"

"Yeah." I drank faster. Another few questions from this fleshy truant, and I'd be late for the door.

"I just moved into a nice place over on Burnside. Got me a great deal." He shook his head. "Jeez, decent places are scarce as hounds' teeth, you know what I'm sayin', Kid?"

"Sure."

"I moved in with a buddy from the company. He's just split from his missus, and him and me used to hang out together in the old days."

"Uh huh." Who cared about this lump of humanity?

He smacked his thick lips. "I used to stay up on Broadway—big, green house there rented out three rooms upstairs."

"Uh huh."

"Landlady had her husband off in the Navy somewheres, I think. Midway, if my memory serves me. What the hell. She was one cold-hearted bitch. Nice looker." He shuddered and took another slug of whiskey. "Brrrrrr..." He gave me a lascivious wink. "You get my drift, Kid?"

"Sure."

"Where you stayin'?"

"Broadway."

"No shit?"

"Yeah. Big green house. Rent an upstairs room."

"No shit? You stayin' with that redheaded broad and crazy old maid in the same place up on Nineteenth and Broadway?"

"Beg your pardon?" I said with deliberately slowness. I couldn't say why exactly, but I was offended by his offhand slurs.

"Ain't it a small world? I move out. You move in, huh?"

"Yeah. Seems that way."

"You know the crazy gal?"

"Miss Nigh?"

He brushed me off. "Naw. The landlady. The redheaded dame. Weird, crazy fuckin' broad. Never could figger her out."

"What the hell are you talking about?"

"Deborah I think it is, right?" He drained his beer. "Nice looker. She's got great eyes."

I pushed my glass away.

He clamped a hand over my arm and pinned me to the bar. "Hey! Have another drink."

"No, thanks. I gotta shove off."

"I'm buyin'. Take a load off, Mac." He snapped his fingers for the bartender. "Hey, Sammy, bring me another round and get the kid here some decent brew for crissakes."

I was still trying to pull free. "I gotta shove off."

"So you're the new boarder, huh? Bet the old maid creams her panties havin' you bed down within arm's reach."

I wanted to smash his face in and erase the leer spreading across the fat cheeks. What a creep. Maybe just this once, Melvin was right in his character assessments. "Look, I gotta go. Some other time, okay?"

The bartender sloshed another beer in front of me, and the hustler pushed my ass back down on the bar stool. "I gotta ask ya, Bud. You ever see the old maid's tits?"

The guy had a hundred pounds on me, not to mention a paunch big enough to squash me as flat as a Model T tire. "No."

"Hell, like a washboard with a couple rubber nipples." He laughed. My stomach was turning too much to enjoy even the beer. "But the redhead—shit, she's nice."

"Who?" I asked naively, hoping he would spare Delilah.

"You know. Deborah. The broad who owns the place. The crazy dame."

"Delilah?"

"Yeah, that's it. Nice looker. I told you I roomed upstairs for a while. Same as you, Buddy." He toasted me with a shot glass. "Me and you're sack mates, Bud."

I bobbed as he swung an arm in my direction, bent on embracing me in a pungent hug to enforce our fraternal links.

"Hell, I tried to get a rise outta that dame, but she's frigid as an Eskimo, Buddy. Ain't interested in a workin' stiff like me. Shit. What a frosty-eyed bitch, right?"

I don't know what spurred me to risk my life in trying to insult this behemoth, but I blurted it out before my common sense could muster caution. "You must have the wrong place in mind, Mac. Delilah Goodknight is a classy lady, real, genuine class. She's a lady, understand? A real lady." I took a drink of beer while his eyes rolled. "Gotta shove off. Thanks for the beer."

As soon as I got up, he put a leg out to bar my path. "You shittin' me, Kid?"

"Pardon me." I pushed, but he didn't move.

"The green place on Broadway? Nineteen hundred block? Redheaded knockout dish with a few bats upstairs and an old maid, knock-kneed, no-tits broad up in Number 2? Lives in the goddam bathroom, makin' a racket all night with the friggin' pipes?"

"That's Virginia." I grinned facetiously.

"Well, I'll be goddammed." He pulled at his double chin. "Sorry if you took offense. I guess you got past first base. Good on you, Bud." He thrust a fist into my abdomen and nearly knocked the wind out of me. "You're okay. Say, I'm Abbie."

"Nathan."

He glommed on to my fingers and shook until the circulation was cut off, and my fingernails turned blue. "Abbie Peeler. Pilsner and draft delivery Tacoma to Yachats."

"Nice to meet you."

He released me, and the blood started to flow again. "Nathan, huh? Nathaniel?"

"Pardon?"

"You a Nathaniel?"

"No. Just Nathan."

"I'm Abraham. Everybody calls me Abbie."

"Nice to know you." I drank some more beer. Might as well. At least it was free.

"It's a nice enough place, don't get me wrong."

"Sure."

"But she just never warmed up to me, you know?"

"Uh huh."

"I figger hey, she's a war widda, right? She's gotta be dreamin' about it, don't she? Nice lookin' woman like that, on her own. I think she had some brother-in-law or somethin' at the coast, used to get her extra rations."

"Uh huh." I rested my chin in my palm and stared at him from the reflection in the mirror behind the bar. I was thinking about lemons. Fresh from the tree.

"But on her own, you know. Seemed nice enough but hadda few loose screws if you ask me."

"How do you mean?"

He signaled for another boilermaker. "Like she never seemed interested."

"Uh huh." That was a point in Delilah's favor.

"But then I see her ass draggin' around town all hours, you know? I see her comin' outta the Roosevelt Hotel at three in the mornin' for crissakes. What the fuck am I gonna think?"

That one hit home. "Uh huh."

"She's gotta be gettin' it on the side somewheres. There's all kinda scum on the make these days, you know what I'm sayin'?"

"Absolutely."

"But she acts like she don't even know me. Damn frigid bitch. Waltzes right on by me without so much as a hello. Like I didn't see her or somethin'."

"Uh huh."

"Yeah, well, I seen her all right. And she's gettin' in taxi cabs all hours, goin' here and there. I figger she's got some uniform swordsman she's seein' on the sly."

"Sounds logical." I sipped at my beer. I thought about the similarities in our experiences with Delilah. I'd run into her at the Roosevelt Hotel, seen her jump into taxis, heard her dancing with someone on the sleeping porch, crying in room Number 1.

"So it's this way, see." He hunkered down over his drink and whispered conspiratorially. "One time I get up to take a pee, and I hear this noise at the end of the hall, down at the far end in room Number 1."

My ears pricked up. My left foot started to tingle. "Uh huh."

"And I go down to the other end of the hall and put my ear on the door, see. Just to see what the hell is revvin' up this broad's motor."

"Uh huh."

"And I hear her sighin' and moanin' and whatnot, groanin' and grindin' like a twenty-dollar hooker."

"Uh huh."

"And I figger what the hell? I ain't gettin' to first base with this bitch, and some damned Gyreen is layin' pipe like a crazy-assed plumber in there." He swigged down the last of his whiskey. "What the hell. Can you figger?"

"What the hell," I repeated.

"So the next mornin', on my way out, I close the door an' all, and then I forget I left my case upstairs. So I open the door, and I hear this click. The door is comin' open on Number 1 upstairs, see."

"Interesting." It wasn't. Not strictly speaking. But to me, it was more intense than anything Mr. Morrow had had to say about the Invasion Forces this evening.

"So I'm thinkin' what the hell? So I duck back in the doorway, see, and keep real quiet, and pretty soon she comes out and walks right on down to the bathroom. So up I go. I get right to the doorway, and she comes out. But I get a quick look into the room before I go get my case."

"Uh huh." My good eye began twitching. My ultimate fantasy—opening the door to room Number 1 and seeing for myself what this jerk had seen with his two good eyes: the real Ethan, the lover who made Charmaine come alive.

"Shit!" He slapped his hand down on the bar with a smack loud enough to draw a concerned stare from the barkeep. "I look in the damned room, see. And you'll never guess what the hell I see with my own two eyes."

"What?"

"Hell. There's this sonuvabitch in the bed, just lyin' there, on his side so's I couldn't make out his face exactly. Sleepin' it off. An' you know what else I see, Bud?"

"Some officer. Navy man maybe?"

"Hells bells, some poor, randy bastard wearin' silk pajamas for crissakes." He poked me again. "Silk. I saw it with my own two eyes. Lyin' there sleepin' one off like he was Clark Gable or somebody, stiff as a fuckin' board."

My eyes were as big as hubcaps. "Must be an officer."

He nodded. "Damn right. Saw three gold stripes on his fuckin' jacket sleeve hangin' in the wardrobe, Bud." He slashed his finger across his upper arm. "Three big ones. Ain't no secret why she gave me the cold shoulder. She goes for the big-brass boys who can pay her way, if you get my drift."

"Yeah."

"Whiskey bottles dead as door nails on the floor. Cigarette butts everywhere, panties and unmentionables hangin' over the furniture. Looked like a fuckin' Chinese cat house."

"Was he—"

"Asleep." He jerked his head toward the bar. "Or drunk on his ass. Didn't even move when I went by. I see his jacket there hangin' up, shoes under the bed all shined up like he was headin' for a fuckin' parade."

"A full commander," I sighed wistfully. My fictional hero named. He was no longer a figment of my over abundant imagination. This obnoxious peeping Tom had seen him *in intimis*. I felt horribly inadequate and foolish all over again.

"Full fuckin' commander my pink, rosy ass," he bellowed, sloshing beer foam on his sleeve.

"What?"

"So he's got this fancy uniform hangin' up, see. And I spot his skivvies lyin' on the chair there. A goddam jumper."

"What are you getting at? His jumper?"

"Hells bells, Bud. He's a goddam gunner's mate."

"I don't follow."

"Looky here. It's this way, Bud. This asshole is paradin' around with commander's stripes on his sleeve, gettin' in the lady's panties slick as snot."

"Uh huh."

"And he's some snot-nosed gunner's mate. I oughtta call the goddam Shore Patrol, the FBI, and the cops."

"What?" I interrupted his stream of wishful vengeance.

"Bastard's a goddam impostor for crissakes! Damn broad's too stupid to tumble to him. Somebody oughtta wise her up, Bud."

"Oh." I had it figured out at last. No dashing, thin-lipped Commander with shoulders decked out like the USS Yorktown. This couldn't be. A gunner's mate. He could be my age.

"Impersonating an officer is a federal offense, Buddy," Peeler snarled. "Somebody's gonna turn his ass in."

"You're certain about this?" I just didn't want to believe Delilah could be fooled so easily. She wasn't like that—gullible.

"Hells bells. I know what I seen. I see a full commander's jacket hangin' up bold as brass, an' I see the fucker's jumper with his rating, a lousy gunner's mate second class. I ain't no fool. My brother's in the Navy, Mac. I know what I seen, okay?"

"Sure. I guess so."

"Ain't nothin' to guess about. He's a goddam impostor. She oughtta wise up."

"Maybe the jacket belonged to somebody else?"

He shook his head and belched. "My thoughts exactly. A classy lady, huh? Who's she tryin' to kid? What's she pullin'? Fleet night?"

That stung. "She's not like that."

"Hell. They're all like that, Bud."

"She isn't."

"You ever break in on her when she's entertainin' the Allied Forces out back?"

"Pardon?"

"She's got this sleepin' porch, see, off the kitchen."

"I looked in a time or two, I guess. Just curious. Not much to see."

"She brings these schmoes home, see, an' screws 'em on the back porch. Probly so Miss Holy Drawers upstairs won't find out. Christ, one time I come home early from a road trip down to Medford and K Falls, and I hear this music, see."

"Uh huh." The Philco console.

"And I hear booze bein' poured and laughin', and I go on in to take a look-see." He shoved his shot glass away with a meaty hand. "And by God, there she is, standin' there balls ass naked, drinkin' good gin and swishin' her butt around for some john sittin' on the couch."

"The same guy?"

"Hells bells, Bud. Never turned the fuckin' light on to see a goddam thing. She sees me and starts shoutin' and carryin' on. Think I'd peed on the rug or somethin'. Hell, I packed my bags and moved out. Crazy fuckin' broad."

"What about the guy? The fellow downstairs on the couch."

He turned to look at me as if that question hadn't occurred to him before. "Him?"

"Yeah. The guy on the couch."

"What about him? Him and me didn't start up a conversation exactly."

"Was he the same guy you saw up in room Number 1?"

"How the hell do I know? Weird fucker. Never said a goddam word. Too busy puttin' his pants on, I guess. She did all the hollerin' and bitchin'. I can't think if I got a word off to him or not come to think of it. Probly both drunk on their asses."

"Drunk."

"Me, I'm in the business, see."

"Uh huh."

"I know how to hold my liquor. These broads who get stinkin' piss me off, you get my point, Nathan?"

"Sure." I couldn't begin to see Delilah reeling in an alcoholic stupor, loud-mouthed, vulgar, sloppy. She wasn't like that.

"Bitch must be screwin' the whole damned fleet. But her ass is too good for me, a workin' man. She gets it from a full commander for crissakes. Phony as a three-dollar bill. Well, fuck her pink, rosy ass, right? That's her business if she wants to lay down for every sonuvabitch in a uniform."

"She's different."

"Bullshit!"

"I mean maybe he was her husband or sweetheart."

"I told ya. You don't know shit, Kid. She's a war widda. Ain't no husband. Ain't no sweetheart neither, if you ask me. She's got her legs spread every time a fuckin' ship comes in."

I knew I should have aimed my best punch at this loud-mouthed asshole's mouth, but I couldn't justify fending off his heavyweight counterattack at a time when I was down to less than twenty bucks in my pocket. Dental bridges and stitches were expensive. Delilah would never know I had failed to defend her. In my heart I was loyal, but my flesh was weak.

"Nathan, if you're gettin' along with the lady, my hat's off to ya." He had a hat, a sweat-stained fedora with red satin lining. He swept it up in a grandiose gesture and broke open his face in a hearty laugh that made me smile as well. "Get it while you can, Bud. Hey," he leaned close again, "she givin' you a break on the rent?"

"No," I admitted sheepishly.

"Hells bells, Nathan," he chastised me with an evil wink. "You ain't goin' for the long end of the stick?"

"But she makes me lemon meringue pie," I blurted. God. Just how stupid could I manage to make myself look anyway?

Abbie Peeler grinned and thumped me on the back. "Lemon pie? Hell. That's better'n a poke with a sharp stick, huh? You're okay, Kid. Okay. Have another beer. On me."

I shrugged. My head was buzzing already. What the hell. Besides, Abbie was buying. He already had the money on the bar before I could hold up another finger.

# Fifteen

===========

**It** was almost two o'clock in the morning when I staggered up the stairs, tried to fit my key in the lock and almost fell backward off the porch. Both my legs had turned to jelly. Either that or the house was moving, dodging and weaving as I tried to hit the keyhole with my finger. Abbie Peeler had poured more beers in me than I could count before I managed to duck out the door. Fumbling with the damned lock that refused to remain stationary long enough to punch my key in the slot, I twisted into a human pretzel with both knees locked, butt dragging, one arm swiping at the porch light chain and the other still trying to unlock the doorbell.

The door flew open, and I stumbled over the threshold, fell on the stairs and sagged to the floor with my feet splayed. When I looked up, an unfriendly face with disapproving eyes and a thin, schoolmarm mouth glared down at me. Without my glasses, it looked just like Gladys.

"Hi, there," I burped. "You know, you look jush like my shister."

Gladys was not amused. "Nathan, do you have any idea what time it is?"

"Nope." I tried to get up. Even the balustrade seemed to be trying to avoid me as I toppled into the telephone table. "Oops. Sorry."

A strong arm grabbed hold of my jacket and pushed me up the stairs. The good Doctor to the rescue. "Come on, Nathan. Let me help you to your room."

"I'm fine," I protested with a squeak as Dr. Henry Houghton steered me down the hallway. It was not without difficulty. The damned walls kept moving in and out like bellows.

"Nathan, you know you can't drink. My lord," Gladys scolded from the foyer below. "I can't believe you're doing this in front of the Doctor."

He opened my door and sat me down on the bed. Before I had my shoes off, my sister was in the room, standing guard like a prison matron as her husband pulled off what was left of my clothes.

"Are you alright, Nathan?" he asked me in a professional tone I resented immediately. I recognized that condescending attitude. It always preceded a sneaky shot in the ass or a horse's snout full of castor oil.

"I'm perfectly fine," I answered, trying hard to appear sober.

"Nathan, you are *not* fine. You're drunk. This is so humiliating."

"Gladys, calm down." He shooed her away. "He's fine. Why don't you go down and get us some coffee?"

"How could you do this to me, Nathan?"

"What?" I mumbled meekly as the Doctor rolled off a sock.

"You're disgusting. I'm only glad that Daddy isn't here to see this for himself."

"Gladys, go downstairs and leave us alone for a few minutes." Doc had me down to my skivvies. I needed both hands to hang on to the mattress whirling around the room like Dorothy and Toto in an Oz-bound twister.

"I'll bring up some coffee, strong, black coffee." Gladys went out and stomped down the stairs.

"Now tell me, Nathan," the Doctor began, sitting on the edge of the bed and peering like a professor assessing a dissected frog, "what's troubling you, Son?"

"Nothing. I'm fine." I reached for a Lucky, and he lit it for me. "How the hell are you, Doc? Lots of shick folks in Okiehoma to keep you busy?"

"Nathan, we're quite concerned about you."

"Me?" I sucked in a lung full of satisfying smoke and hugged a lumpy pillow to my chest. "I'm fine, Doc." I saluted. "A okay." *Hic.*

"Gladys thinks perhaps you're suffering from delayed grief over your father's death. Would you like to talk about it?"

I blew smoke in his face. "Gladys doesn't know what she's talking about, Doc. I'm fine."

"You don't appear fine to me, Nathan."

I leaned back against the headboard. He looked ready to whip out a stethoscope and stick a thermometer in my mouth. To be safe, I pulled the sheet under my chin. "I think I'm a little tight. What's your professional opinion, Doctor?"

"You've stated the obvious. The question is why do you have to drink yourself into this kind of condition in front of your sister?"

"I didn't. I was at Murphy's with a very boring, *hic*... overbearing, extremely shweaty gentleman who sells beer. We were sampling his product, and I was indushed to make a comparison between the house offerings and... whatever he was selling. *Hic*... I never laid eyes on my shister otherwise for your... *hic*... information."

"Nathan, don't play that game with me. I'm family. I want to help you. For Gladys' sake."

Ever since I met this officious prick at the wedding rehearsal, I wondered how my parents could have professed such love for Gladys' husband. Doctor Henry Houghton was right about everything, condescending to the point of criminality and unbearably vain even for a medical man. Pompous, self-righteous, glib and, sadly for my sister, hung like a bumblebee. I stood alongside him at the urinal in Union Station once. When he was through, he tapped his puny spout as if he were testing a melon. Not a manly shake, not even a good choke. It was a *tap, tap, tap* like my mother would visit on Pop's three-minute egg.

"Look, Henry. Can I call you Henry?"

"You can call me doctor, Nathan. There's no need to be afraid of the fact I'm here to help you in a professional capacity as well as a familial one."

The impeccable prick, my brother-in-law was convinced Gladys' entire family was a psychological train wreck. Humor always seemed to defuse his ardent practice on me and my sisters. "Hey, Doc, you're right." I stuck up my foot and wagged my left toe in his face. "I gotta ingrown nail that's drivin' me nuts. *Burp*. You got any shuggestions?"

"Nathan, I want you to think about the effect your behavior is having on your sisters."

"You ever get soused, Doc?"

"We're not discussing my wayward habits, Nathan."

"Ever get shit faced when Gladys wasn't around?"

"Absolutely not."

"I accept your denial, Doc. How come you doctors always say 'the patient *denies*' et cetera, et cetera? You make it shound, *hic*, 'scuse me, please, like the patient is a damn liar. You guys don't trush any of us peons, do you, Henry?"

"Let's stick to the point, shall we?"

"It's 'Mr. McCarthy denies exsheshive beer drinking.'"

"Nathan, for God's sake."

"'Mr. McCarthy denies a history of prior insanity'."

"Now see here..."

"—pregnancy, VD, pimples or uncontrolled flatulence.'"

The door opened, and Gladys reappeared. This time armed with a percolator, a cup and a bib for crissakes. She poured the coffee, tucked the bib under my chin, put out my cigarette and pressed the crockery into my shaky hand. "Drink this, Nathan."

"I hate black coffee," I protested as the hot liquid scalded my lips. "Christ!" I spewed coffee out like a Yellowstone geyser, dousing Gladys and spraying the good Doctor in one terrific blow.

"Oh, Nathan!" She got up and wiped her dress off with my sheet. "For God's sake! Look what you've done!" Then she was bleating, out the door and racing for the bathroom at the end of the hall.

I was hoping the Doctor would follow. He didn't. He lit his own smoke, a thin-stemmed pipe and puffed in silence. "Nathan, I'm asking you to talk about this man to man. In strict confidence, of course. Your sisters need never know what's really troubling you. I'm a doctor. I understand these things completely."

"Fine." I was rubbing my lips with a tentative, probing fingertip, expecting blisters to form by morning.

"You can talk to me like a brother as well as your physician. You know you can always speak frankly."

"Thanks, Henry. What if my lipsh are scalded off, and I can never pucker again?"

"Your sister is terribly shocked by your behavior this evening." *Puff, puff.* "And I must say, Nathan, hurt and confused. She expected you to be down at the station this evening to greet us and see the girls."

"The girls are here?"

"Of course. Didn't Gladys tell you we were coming?"

I had to think for a moment. There was that conversation when I left Tacoma. Gladys said the Doctor was coming out to take them back to Oklahoma, and they might stop by. How in hell was I supposed to know it was this evening? Tonight? My one evening of debauchery at the local tavern, and Gladys and her prick-perfect husband had to show up and write me off as a Front Street stumble bum.

"I work till late, Henry." *Burp.* I was beginning to feel an urge to make a run for the bathroom. "What time did your train get in?"

"At ten. We had a bite to eat downstairs with your landlady. Gladys expected you home a little after twelve. We put the girls to bed downstairs on the sleeping porch. Mrs. Goodknight was kind enough to offer her hospitality for the night. We have to catch a one o'clock train tomorrow."

"Oh," I burped again, somewhat contrite. "I am sorry, Henry. I didn't know what time you were coming. Gladys should have phoned or shumthing."

"I'm sure she tried to reach you. You know Gladys is always conscientious to a fault."

"A fault."

He put a hand on the door and made my heart stir with hope of being abandoned. "I should let you get some sleep. We'll talk in the morning."

"Fine. The girls okay?"

"Splendid."

"See you topside, Doc." *Burp*. Whatever I had wolfed down for supper was working its way back up. If the Doctor stood between me and the john, he was definitely in harm's way.

"Goodnight, Nathan. Let's just tell Gladys you'll see her in the morning then, shall we?"

"Fine." I swung my legs free from the covers and felt the blood rush to my head. My ears were pounding, and I could taste copper pennies in my mouth.

"Goodnight then."

"Stand aside, Doc. I'm comin' through." I bolted upright and lurched out to the hall, pushed the Doctor against the wall and slammed the bathroom door behind me a second before everything I owned that wasn't permanently nailed down came up and exited in one violent gush. *"Ahhhhgggg..."* I exploded, drooling and red-faced.

I grabbed the sink, turned on the tap and splashed cold water in my face. Empty, I felt much better. When I looked up, I saw all Virginia's potions, lotions and notions splattered with my foul-smelling brew and felt a rush of shame singe my ears. Miss Nigh was not going to like this. As a matter of fact, she was going to be extremely pissed.

I cleaned myself up, took a few paltry swabs at the stained tile and felt my way back to my room. They were all gone, thank God. I fell into bed, pulled the sheet over my head and waited until the Tilt-A-Whirl slowed down enough for me to slide off to sleep.

# Sixteen

======

**Scrubbed,** shaved, shaken and as white as Delilah's meringue, I sat at the kitchen table.

"Ohhh, Jesus..." I moaned, downing a half-cup of black coffee strong enough to strip house paint. I felt as if I could drink a small lake dry, pack myself in dry ice and hibernate for a few weeks. In short, I wanted to turn myself inside out, dive in Delilah's washtub and hang myself out to dry on the backyard line. This was fucking awful, worse even than having the doctor stitch up my eye or enduring bee stings when I had chicken pox.

A cool hand swept the hair back from my brow and patted my cheek affectionately. "Poor thing. Would you like some cream?"

"No, thanks. This is fine." I sipped the coffee and tried to focus my eyes.

"Wouldn't you like something to eat?"

My stomach did a few double axels at the thought of greasy eggs and bacon sizzling in an iron skillet. I shook my head and gulped my java in lieu of a more civilized demurrer.

"Poor thing," Delilah clucked, sitting down beside me. "Are you sure you're not ill?"

"No, just stupid." I put the cup down. "I must have puked up my guts last night." Now I blushed and shook with shame. "I'm sorry... really."

"Don't think a minute about it. It's all cleaned up. No fuss at all."

"I feel so goddam rotten about this."

"Drink your coffee. I'll get you some juice." She got up and opened the fridge.

"Oh, no, please. I can't even think about anything solid yet."

"This is good for you. My brother-in-law taught me this recipe." She shook up a can of tomato juice, punched it open, poured a glass half full, added a raw egg, a generous dollop of Worchester sauce, salt, pepper and squeezed in a slice of lemon. Then she stirred the glop and approached her reluctant patient with a sweet smile. "This is just what the doctor ordered."

"No, really. I can't. This is fine." I toasted her weakly with the coffee cup.

"Drink this. It'll make you feel much better."

She put the glass to my lips, and I obediently opened for her. It went down as easy as Quaker State. My eyes fluttered closed as I swallowed. Not bad. My stomach was beginning to assume a stationary position for once.

"Is that better?"

It was. I wet my lips and handed the glass back empty. "Yes. Much better."

She sat down again. "Cody says it cures every kind of hangover there is."

"Thanks."

"What were you drinking to make yourself so sick?"

"Beer, I think."

"Just beer?"

"Maybe boilermakers. I can't remember so well," I admitted sheepishly. Somehow, this fiasco had made me more manly in her eyes, subject to all the failings and foibles of lesser suitors.

"You don't drink much, do you?" she mused, pouring more coffee.

"No."

"Your sister seemed awfully upset."

"She likes to mother me. Gladys is the oldest sister and feels like she has a duty to keep me in line."

"Her husband's very successful, isn't he?"

"The Doctor?"

"He seemed awfully smart. He spoils Gladys and his daughters wonderfully. Do you ever think maybe your sister has too much?"

"Is that possible?" I hadn't thought about it. Gladys wasn't quite filthy rich, but Henry was making progress, and she was certainly better off than any of the rest of us. Much better off than Mom and Pop had ever been. Financially, at least, Henry was a good catch.

She got up and squeezed the lemon into a juice glass, prompting me to ask a silly question. "Where do you get all these lemons with a war on?"

She dried her fingers on her apron. "Cody gets them for me. He tries to help me out. He gets extra rations, you know."

"You said he works at a Safeway?"

"He's the manager."

I lit a cigarette and felt the surge of nicotine vitalize me. I tossed the burnt match in my saucer and studied her through the haze of bluish smoke. "Tell me, Delilah, how is Cody related to you exactly?"

"He's my brother-in-law."

"Your husband's brother?"

She poured herself some coffee. "Yes." She knew where we were going with this conversation, but this morning, she didn't try to derail me. "He and Lionel were four years apart. Lionel was older."

"Lionel is your husband then?"

"We were married in '42. I met him at a dance in the Roseland Ballroom. My girlfriend and I went to have some fun and hear the band, and Lionel was there with his brother. We hit it right off." Her eyes were downcast. She put the coffee cup down and massaged her fingers. "He had the most serious eyes. He had so many plans of what he wanted to do with his life. Always so serious, so absorbed." She sighed wistfully. "You know, Ethan, I knew from the very first moment we danced together that I was going to marry him." She laughed. "Does that seem silly?"

"Yes." It was love. True love. Romance, like in the novels she read. It was Ethan and Charmaine meeting at the train depot in my corny novel.

"He lived with their mother who was crippled with arthritis. This is her house, you know."

"Whose? Your mother-in-law's, you mean?" I took a quick look around. Of course. The collection of Danish blue plates on the kitchen wall, the crocheted doilies on the buffet in the dining room, the photographs of the spectacled couple peering down from the mantelpiece. Grandparents had houses like this. Not newlyweds. Not Delilah. Not even Lionel. I should have known.

"The Goodknights lived here for over thirty years. I think the house was built in 1899."

"Is she gone now?"

"Last year. She had the room downstairs." She tilted her head sideways. "Lionel and I moved in to help her take care of the place after Cody and Susie moved over to the Coast."

"Susie is Cody's wife?"

She nodded. "Lionel went overseas in April of '43. We were married for ten months before he left. Just ten months."

"He's still overseas then." It didn't need to be a question.

"Now it's been seventeen months."

"Oh." I had no words. She was drifting away from me again. Those sad eyes were staring at the kitchen wall, looking right through the Vargas girl with the pink shorts and striped parasol. "He must be due for a leave soon."

"His ship was in Australia. They were hit by a Japanese submarine on their way home. They almost went down but managed to make it to a friendly port. Their ship's being repaired though." She continued to stare blankly at the wall and ignore me completely. "There's a lot to do. It's a big ship, you know, and they're so busy at all the shipyards these days trying to get our Navy boys back out to sea again."

"I see." So she wasn't a widow. Only a temporary one still tethered to someone beyond my reach. I wasn't even a poor substitute for what she had with Lionel. A comic stand-in at best was all I could hope for.

She pushed a lock of hair from her forehead and smiled dreamily, miles away from me and the cozy kitchen. She was dancing again, in someone else's loving arms, swaying to music only she could hear. I couldn't bring myself to speak for fear of jarring her back to some painful reality she was escaping.

"They'll be home for Christmas though. You'll see. I'm counting on a long holiday leave. Lionel ought to get a reassignment when he gets back, maybe some shore-side duty for the duration, don't you think?"

"I don't know."

"After all, he's been at sea now for fifteen months. Don't you think it's logical he'll be able to sit out the rest of the war from somewhere stateside?" Her question didn't begin to address me really. The eyes were locked on to a space filled with images animated only by her wishful thinking. Loneliness seeped from her skin like sweat from a steam presser. My poor Delilah lonely, lost, waiting for her Lionel. "You know, I've been thinking I should make certain Cody can bring me lemons this winter. Lionel loves lemon pie. It's his favorite. I made it for him once before he left, and he said he knew now what heaven tasted like." Her lips drew back in a fleeting smile. "Time goes by fast. He'll be home before we know it, won't he?" Suddenly, she turned to face me, and it was like staring at a Lucky Strike billboard. No connection whatsoever, as if I'd disappeared through a hole in the floor. All we shared was kitchen space. "I'm sure he'll be home soon, Delilah."

"Ethan, why were you out drinking? It's not really like you at all, is it?"

"I suppose not."

"Your sister was so worried about you. You know, I liked her. She's so concerned about all of you. She told me about your sister Frances. Is she going to be alright?"

"Yes."

"She said her husband Walter has gone back overseas."

"He could only get an emergency ten day leave."

She took a deep breath. "Frances must miss him terribly."

"She does, I'm certain."

She began to gather up our dishes and clear the table. "Are you still worried about her?"

"She'll be fine. She's the toughest one of the bunch in our family."

"That's not the reason you got drunk, is it?"

"Does there have to be a reason?"

"There always is with someone like you."

I picked up a dishcloth and joined her at the sink. I could hear that fat creep Peeler telling me about Delilah and the impostor in her bedroom, maybe the same sonuvabitch who had made her cry the day I went by room Number 1. The more Peeler had talked, the more my skin broke out in goosebumps, and my belly lurched. Poor, sad Delilah, abandoned by her sweetheart shortly after a honeymoon, spending days and endless nights wondering where he was, worrying about his safe return, torturing herself with not knowing. The aching loneliness it must have caused her. Maybe she thought of him cheating with a girl in Australia or maybe her concerns were directed at his health, his own longing to be with her. It made me sick to hear Peeler talk about Delilah as if she were a common slut, a mattress-back for every serviceman in town for a weekend leave of boozing and whoring. Delilah wasn't like that.

But I had seen and heard it all as well as Peeler had—the man upstairs, the men on the sleeping porch, smoking, drinking and dancing with her in the dark. Then there was the meeting at the Roosevelt Hotel and her third-floor rendezvous. I'd even seen Delilah jumping out of a taxi in front of a downtown bar. I had seen it all, but I refused to believe any of it. It was loneliness, Delilah's desperate attempt to dull the pain somehow. That's all I saw. All I let myself see or wanted to see.

She handed me another cup. "Well? What got you so messed up, Ethan? A woman?"

I was just too weak and cowardly to lie anymore. "Yes."

"Why do you let her hurt you this way? You mustn't. I can tell you it's not fair to punish yourself like this."

She scrubbed a plate and paid no attention to my hungry eyes locked on to the sensual curve of her neck, the stray auburn curls framing the line of her chin and exposing the faint blush coloring her cheeks as the steam rose from the dishpan. I wanted to crush her in my arms and extinguish all her pain. All I could muster was a hopeless ambiguity. "What *is* fair?"

Delilah stopped with her dishrag in a glass, leaned a hip against the sink and sighed. "Oh, Ethan. It's *all* so unfair, isn't it?"

"Seems that way lately." I dared to hope we were talking about the same topic. Our mutual despair, a shared emptiness that could be healed by our spiritual bonding. And, of course, a mingling of our flesh in the fires of passion. I could already feel the desire blooming in my corduroy crotch.

I shut my eyes and saw my delusion lit in vivid color, cerebral cinema—Delilah panting in the steamy kitchen, waiting for me to fasten my teeth on her silken neck. I swept her up in my arms, carried her out to the sleeping porch and laid her on the wicker sofa. I was pressed against her hot mouth, inhaling her expelled breath, tasting her musky richness as I felt the room rock and sway. All of a sudden, the Philco console turned on as if by magic, its strains of Tommy Dorsey reverberating along my entire backbone, my fingertips and toes trembling in rhythm to the bass backbeat. In the dim glow from the radio, we clung to each other and made love like two survivors lost to the rest of the world. I rose slowly to the peak, dizzy with mounting frenzy as she pulled me farther and farther into her delicious warmth. And then, just as I was about to explode like a Fourth of July rocket, she dug her nails into my shoulder.

"Ethan!"

I snapped to attention, opened my eyes and jumped back as shards of dinnerware skittered across the kitchen floor. "Christ, I'm sorry, Delilah."

She knelt down and began to pick up pieces of the plates I had dropped. I bent down to help her.

"Oh, they're broken!"

"I'm sorry. Really. I lost my concentration, I guess. Let me clean this up for you."

She was picking up the pieces and trying to fit them back together again. "This was a wedding gift from Cody and Susie." Tears began to brim behind the lashes.

"Jesus, Delilah. I'm sorry. I don't know how it happened."

She pushed me back and herded the bits of porcelain in a pile. "It's all broken. Look at this!" She was on her knees, sweeping up the debris with both hands.

"Delilah, let me fix it for you. I can glue the pieces back together."

"No, you can't! It's all ruined."

"I'm sorry."

She slapped me across the face. Hard. "You broke it!" Her eyes were as cold and mean as a jailer's. In a flash, it was as if she didn't recognize me. I was fortunate she didn't have a carving knife at hand. "How could you do such a mean thing?"

"Delilah, I'm sorry. Jesus. Really sorry. It was an accident. I don't know what I was thinking. Let me help."

"No! Just leave me alone!"

I stood there like a moron, not sure if I should insist and get a broom and dustpan, sign an IOU for my firstborn to repair the damage or just beat a quiet retreat. "Delilah?"

She didn't hear me. I stood and watched her salvage each shard, tenderly tucking it into her apron pocket. After every proposal to make things right was rebuffed with an icy glare, I gave up and retreated, feeling lower than a peeing pooch.

Upstairs in my room, I sat in front of my typewriter and stared at a blank sheet of paper. My fingers flexed over the keys. I listened to the sound of a man yelling on the street, heard a garbage can clatter on the pavement. There were no words left for the page. Nothing. I tried to force out a single sentence to prime the pump. All I could think of was my conjured coupling on the sleeping porch. Dreams were more comforting than reality.

Exhausted and too disappointed to think about Delilah anymore, I slumped in the easy chair, put my head back and let sleep take me to a better place.

# Seventeen

===========

**Gladys** hadn't been home long enough to warm the covers before she sent me a long, tutorial letter advising me on the perils of bachelorhood evidenced by drunkenness, womanizing and the habits of a wastrel. The good Doctor seemed to have a great deal of input to her diatribe. Apparently my bout with demon rum had inspired others besides Delilah to assume there was a woman at the root of my problem.

I folded Gladys' letter and tucked it under the socks in my bureau drawer. I couldn't bring myself to throw it out. I still required her maternal lashing, I suppose. She was someone able to assume responsibility for my lapses of leadership. I was the man of the family, the one who was supposed to present a fatherly role model for my sisters and nieces. And I had miserably failed them all. Carla and Frances had no doubt been filled in to the last, unseemly detail of my disgrace by Gladys and the Doctor. Carla would be concerned for my mental well-being naturally. She was a born alarmist. When we were kids, she had crawled into bed with me once to shiver in fear because it had dawned on her that the sun might decide not to come up in the morning.

"Why would you want to think something so dumb as that?" I had snarled, tugging at the covers to reclaim my share.

Carla had poked her nose from under the quilt and peeked through the window at the starry night sky. "Don't you ever wonder, Nattie, what would happen if it didn't come up?"

"No," I replied in as snotty a tone as I could master as the runt of the litter. "That's stupid. Why would it do that?"

"Well, what if it did?"

"That's stupid."

"No, it isn't, Nattie. Think about it. The whole world would be dark... forever." She huddled against my back and shivered.

Cripes. I felt butterflies swarm in my tummy. She was scaring the shit out of me. What if she was right? Maybe she had a point there after all. Who said there was an absolute guaranty about anything anyway? I didn't want to think about any of it. I feigned sleep.

Carla whispered in my ear. "Think what it would be like if the whole world was black. It'd be so scary, Nattie. All the bugs and snakes and bats would come out, and nobody could see anything."

"Snore... snore... snore..."

"Nattie, are you asleep?"

By then my toes were starting to curl up with rampant terror just thinking about the whole neighborhood swarming with hungry, blood-sucking bats and creepy crawly things running amok in the backyard. No more sunny days to play ball, nothing but inky black forever. Cripes.

"Nattie, if there isn't ever another sunrise, I'm going to stay in bed forever. I'm never going to get up again."

My eyes blinked open. It was blacker than licorice whips. "You'd have to go to school, Carla," I said, hoping my logic would snap her back to reality and undue the scary story.

"I'll just starve myself to death right here, Nattie. I'm not going out there to let the creepers get me."

"What's a creeper?"

"Big, slimy things with bigger teeth than a crocodile. They're just waiting for the time it gets all dark so they can come out of their hiding places and eat us."

"Where are they hiding, Carla?"

"Everywhere, Silly."

"Even in our house?"

She never answered me. I still didn't know what sort of unnamed monster was waiting to get me the day the sun failed to rise above the horizon. For years after that, I hated to get out of bed in the dark and tiptoe down the hall to the bathroom. What if the creepers were there just waiting for some hapless fellow to stumble into their lair? Maybe they were like the ogres hiding under the bridge in the storybook my mother used to read to me. Carla knew about them so they must be real. And after that night, I was never so confident about my security. Carla used to scare the shit out of me when I was a kid.

Frances, on the other hand, when she heard how I had hung one on, spat hot coffee in Gladys' face and insulted her husband, would only shrug it off and say her brother was probably just letting off steam. That was Frances. I could always count on her support no matter what. We were pals, true buddies. Besides, she knew if I was truly hurting, I would tell her all about it. And of course, she was right. I would. Only I couldn't tell her about this, discuss Delilah with another living soul. It would have been like trying to describe a nighttime dream half-forgotten in the light of day.

But a week later, after Miss Nigh had snubbed me coming up the stairs, I did venture to poke my head into the kitchen before leaving for work. Delilah was gone. The oven was warm, and the smell of pastry was fresh in the air. I saw a pie sitting on the counter. Lemon meringue so redolent I could flick out my tongue and taste the tartness. I walked out to the sleeping porch and stood in the center of the room for a moment, looking out at the handkerchief-sized back lawn. The maple tree was starting to turn, its leaves tinged with a sallow spatter of gold and the lawn painted with a scattering of fallen umber to mark the approach of fall.

My gaze was drawn to the Philco radio and the silver-framed photograph on top. I couldn't take my eyes off it. It had to be Lionel. He stared out at me with bright optimism. He had a straight nose, even brows and a pencil thin mustache over thin lips, splendidly handsome in his dress uniform with his hat set at a rakish angle. Scrawled across the bottom of the photo was a flowing, brash signature: *All my love forever, Darling... Lionel.*

I stared with the rapt fascination of a voyeur mesmerized by the thought of this young man possessing all the love and beauty in the whole world while I was only an impoverished bystander. In the photograph, he looked barely older than I. There was no hint in his expression of the wistful sadness Delilah's eyes echoed when she thought of him. He was confident, eager and strong the day he posed for the photographer. Now where was he? Pining for Delilah in some dingy outback bar? Or was he locked in a sweaty dance with some Aussie nurse?

I pulled my cap down and headed for the front door. Miss Nigh came downstairs and turned to avoid my glance.

"Evening, Miss Nigh," I offered lamely.

She grunted an unintelligible reply and went past me to the dining room. Well, I hadn't exactly endeared myself to her. I heard her throwing out bath salts and cold cream jars contaminated by my bathroom upchuck. I suppose she wasn't interested in explanations to mitigate my guilt. Didn't matter. I didn't have any really.

I walked to the Multnomah Hotel to start my shift. In the kitchen, I wrapped my apron around my waist, ran hot water in the sink and waited for the foam to rise to elbow level before plunging in.

Melvin handed me a crusty soup pot. He had a cigarette butt clamped between his lips, and his potbelly was stained with the residue of last night's special. "Say, Kid," he started at me. "You fixed up for Saturday night yet?"

"Thanks anyway," I lied. Melvin could not be trusted for feminine referrals. Seems he always had a stray niece or cousin looking for companionship on a Friday or Saturday night. They were always over thirty with stringy hair, runners in their hose, pierced ears and cheap gin in their purse. Most of them also had beefy boyfriends on parole or in the Shore Patrol Brig on Swan Island.

He rested his thumbs on his apron strings. "Well, I gotta hot little number in Vanport can't wait to get her panties wet."

Maxine walked by and glowered at him.

"Oh, shit," the cook cussed her. "The boy's gotta get laid, Max. He's a man for crissakes even if he is a one-eyed geek." He flashed me a quick wink.

"Don't you listen to him, Nathan," Maxine scolded. "He'll do nothin' but get you into trouble."

"Yes, Ma'am."

When she had gone out through the swinging doors, Melvin nudged me in the ribs. "You got a little honey hidden away someplace, Kid?"

"Sure, Mel. More than I can handle in one shift."

"See, it's this way, Kid. These women go stir crazy." He aimed another painful jab at my midsection. "Some of 'em been crossin' their legs for over a year, see, with the old man outta the pitchure. They're horny as toads, Son. Get my drift?" He punctuated his lesson with a lascivious wink.

"Sure."

"Easier to get laid these days than to take a piss, Kid. Hey, you see that black-haired tootsie over at the bar?"

I wasn't interested. Mel was like a gnat, an annoyance, but harmless and best tolerated if ignored completely.

"Great looker. Probly got the hots for me," he joked, stepping on his cigarette butt and grinding it into the floor. "I'm off early tonight. Think I'll saunter on over and give her first chance," he bragged, jiggling his crotch out of sight of the dining room door. "You want me to fix you up, Kid?"

"Thanks anyway."

"Suit yourself, Kid. Pecker's gonna shrink up like a peanut if you ain't careful." He untied his apron, tucked his shirttails in, hitched up his pants and swaggered through the kitchen door to the dining room.

Melvin was back before I finished the dirty pot. He lit another smoke and put his apron back on. "Damn dyke."

"No dice, huh?" I asked him with a concealed smile I was enjoying.

"Naw. She's gotta be one a them lesbos."

The pimple-faced dishwasher raised an inquisitive eyebrow. "What's that? She's a foreigner?"

"No, you dumb shit," Melvin cursed, grabbing hold of the meat locker door and jerking it open with one tug. "A damn bulldagger, man hater, ball breaker. Tell by lookin' at her."

My cohort looked at me for an explanation. "You mean she ain't gonna go out with you, Mel?"

"Aw, shut up, Stupid." He slapped a beef loin on the cutting board and reached for the cleaver. With two quick chops, two steaks plopped on the steam table. "You two know absolutely nothin' about women, you know that? A couple a real losers, both of ya."

"Nathan's got a girlfriend," Pimples spoke out.

I looked away and tried to get even busier with my dirty pans.

"Who? Nathan?" Mel shot me an incredulous stare that made his eyes bulge. "You got a ripe little tootsie you're hidin' away, Nathan boy?"

"Naw."

"She's a real classy lady, Mel. She's got red hair, too. Don't she, Nathan? Tell him. She's beautiful, ain't she, Nathan?"

Melvin was smirking with suppressed glee. "A real looker, eh, Kid? Redhead, huh?"

She's okay," I hemmed uncomfortably.

"And her name's French," Pimples boasted. "Charmaine. Ain't that pretty? She's beautiful, too, ain't she, Nathan?"

"Sure. Gorgeous."

Now Melvin was interested. "You shittin' me, Kid? Who is she? How come I ain't seen her?"

I splashed water on the floor as I labored with another heavy pot. "Hey, do I look that stupid?"

"Shit, Kid. Mighta known. It's always the silent types get all the best nookie."

"You gonna marry her?" Pimples asked with an admiring, wide-eyed stare.

"Sure. Someday. Sure. Why not?"

"Shit," Melvin spat, attacking another piece of meat with a giant whack. "He ain't gonna buy the cow when he's gettin' the milk for free you stupe."

Melvin chopped his meat while Pimples rinsed out the soup pot. I stood at the sink with dishwater dripping onto my shoe tops and hated the breach of my secret fantasy to this crude crew. It had slipped out just once at lunchtime. I had mentioned her to Pimples as we munched on baloney sandwiches and drank milk straight from the bottle. We were just making idle conversation about nothing in general, and then he had mentioned that he had a girlfriend once. As incredible as it seemed that a member of the fair sex would find Pimples' company attractive, I encouraged him to tell me about the illusive lady. Turned out she worked at Woolworth's behind the lunch counter grilling toasted cheese sandwiches and scrambled eggs. Her name was Sylvia, and she lived with her widowed mother in St. Johns. They had come out from Albany, Georgia, to work in the defense plants. Sylvia had taken the test to be in the steno pool but flunked. She was barely literate it turned out. Her mother got a job as a riveter while Sylvia wound up at Woolworth's bending over the stove. Same job she had back in Georgia tending to her five brothers and two sisters.

"How about you, Nathan?" he had asked me finally. "Do you have somebody special?"

I hadn't, had I? But then I had thought of Delilah and diverted to her fictional heroine Charmaine, and her named popped out of my mouth. "Charmaine."

"Oh, that's pretty, Nathan. Is she French or somethin'?"

I couldn't say much more. I sensed I had stepped out of bounds voicing the figment of my own creation in public. I was embarrassed at the lapse in judgment. Pimples would probably forget about it anyway. No harm done. My secret was still secure.

"Sylvia has brown hair. Her eyes are the same color."

"Uh huh. That's nice."

"I'll bet Charmaine is real pretty, huh?"

"Sure."

"Does she have blonde hair like Betty Grable?"

"What?" I put the milk bottle down and bit off a generous hunk of my baloney sandwich.

"You know. Like Betty Grable. I think she's the greatest. She has those legs and all."

"Uh huh."

"Is she?"

"What?"

"Blonde."

"Nope."

"Hedy Lamar is real pretty, ain't she?"

"Uh huh." I reached down for the milk bottle before Pimples could grab it.

"She a brunette?"

"Who?"

"Your girl."

"Nope."

"Sylvia has brown hair, kinda straight, I guess. She pins it up on Friday nights though, and it looks swell for a while."

"Uh huh."

"It gets kinda curly if she don't get it wet. I like it."

"Uh huh."

"Is hers curly like that?'

"Who?"

"Your girl Charmaine. She curly-headed?"

I had to think about her now, see the halo of auburn curls fit like a crown over the sky-blue eyes. "Wavy. Thick and wavy."

"Is it brown like Sylvia's?"

"Auburn."

"Like the car you mean?"

"No. Auburn's a kind of red. Dark red. Like polished mahogany."

"Gee. She sounds real pretty, Nathan. A real nice lady, I'll bet."

"A real nice lady."

Pimples grinned and put out a hand to request the milk bottle. I gave it up and finished my lunch.

Now I regretted that one quick lapse of the tongue which had exposed my secret torment to Melvin's prurient inquisition.

When I finished my shift at the hotel, I went straight back to my room, sat at the typewriter and tried to recapture the picture I had painted of the two of them, Ethan and Charmaine wrapped together like Christmas tinsel on the sleeping-porch couch. My fingers began to fly across the keys slippery with my own sweat until I heard the toilet flush down the hall, the pipes banging in the wall and the sound of Miss Nigh gargling her minty, forty-proof mouthwash. The sun was washing through my blinds before I finished the last chapter.

I got up and stretched the kinks out of my back. It was seven o'clock. Behind me, strewn on the floor like snow from a Cascade blizzard were more than fifty pages of manuscript. Reaching down to gather them up in a pile, my eyes fell to the bottom of a page.

*She fell limply across the couch, an empty receptacle for his needy passions, surrendering completely to his embrace. She was lost somewhere beyond his reach. Tremulous with a wanting he was helpless to restrain, he bent down and came to her unmasked, his soul naked for the very first time.*

# Eighteen

=========

**It** was a Wednesday. I remember that especially because it was a cold, drizzly, gray day in Portland. The streets were swept bare by an easterly wind that had sheared limbs off the elms in the park blocks. Leaves huddled together in clumps across from the courthouse. Rain dripped from the leaden skies and gushed from gutters. It was bleak. I remember that. As if the sky were crying, the trees weeping as their leaves were stripped by autumn reapers.

Carla was on the phone when I came downstairs to answer Delilah's call. It was almost five o'clock in the evening, and already the lights were on along Broadway as if the War were a million miles away. This was November of 1944, and nightfall crept in early. The fighting in Europe had turned into a bloody slug fest with German Panzer divisions regaining ground our boys had paid so dearly for last summer and fall. Everyone was depressed with the bleak news from the Western Front and the blustery, mean winter weather.

As I stood there by the telephone table and gripped the receiver, I could turn and see into the cheery kitchen where Delilah was kneading pie dough on the breadboard. There was a spot of white flour on her cheek, and on the counter were a half-dozen lemons.

"What is it?" I asked hesitantly. Delilah had already told me it was my sister Carla calling person to person. "What's wrong?" As soon as she heard my voice, Carla started to cry. "Come on, Carla. For crissakes, tell me. What is it?"

"It's Francie, Nattie," she whimpered.

I rubbed my temple, a cold wash of dread chilling my innards. Behind me, I could hear Delilah thumping the dough on the board. "What's wrong?"

"Poor Francie, Nat!"

"Jesus! What the hell's wrong? Tell me."

"It's not Francie exactly."

"Well, what is it for crissakes?"

"It's Walter. Oh, God, Nattie. It's terrible."

My heart sank into my belly. I should have known. Nothing Francie touched ever turned to gold. Her table was always set with pewter dishes. I could see poor Walter lying in some foreign ditch, muddy and ragged, his body torn to bits by German flak shredding his bomber like confetti.

"Is he dead?"

Carla blew her nose and sniffled. "It isn't that, Nattie. It's so awful."

What could be worse than being planted in some dank, forgotten grave in the stubble fields of France? What?

"Carla, for crissakes."

"He's been wounded. Francie got the telegram from the war department yesterday that said he was shot down over Holland. His plane went down in the ocean."

"Oh, lord," I sighed.

"But then she got a telegram from London. He's in the hospital there. He bailed out of the plane before it went down, and a boat picked him up and got him back to England."

"Thank God," I heaved and leaned back against the wall. I felt a warmth beside me, and when I turned my head, Delilah was standing there with a floured hand on my sleeve. "Then he's going to be okay. He's coming home."

Carla let loose with another torrent of tears. "Oh, Nattie, it's so awful. Poor Francie. It's not like that at all."

"What's wrong? What the hell's going on? Will you quit crying and talk to me?"

"He's all burned up, Nattie. His face and everything. His lips are all burned off and his ears—he doesn't have any ears anymore."

"Oh, no..." Delilah leaned her head on my shoulder. I barely noticed for once. "Who told you all this?"

"We got a letter from his squadron leader. He wrote it for Walter because Walter's fingers..." Her voice cracked, and she sobbed out the last. "Oh, Nattie, his fingers are all burned off."

"My God."

"Frances just fell down when she read it. She passed out cold."

"Where is she? Is she okay?"

"I called the doctor. He came out and gave her a shot of something so she would sleep. She just stared at me, Nattie, when she woke up. She wouldn't even talk or anything. Oh, Nattie, you've got to come up and help me..."

I felt as if I'd been hit by a log truck. My knees were buckling beneath me. All I could think of was my poor, dear, sweet sister Frances suffering as if her world were coming to an end. "Carla, I'm coming right up. I'll take the next train or hitch a ride."

"Oh, Nattie, what'll we do? Maybe she's gone completely crazy."

"Carla, for crissakes sake, stop it."

"She won't even talk, Nattie. It's just like she was sleep walking. What'll we do?"

"You stay there and watch out for her, Carla. I'm on my way."

"Don't you think you should call the Doctor? Maybe he can help."

"I'll call Gladys when I get there."

"Oh, Nattie, I'm afraid for Francie. Poor, poor Francie. Walter's whole face is just burned off. Can you imagine how hideous he must look?"

"Shut up. Just shut up, Carla, and get ahold of yourself."

"I'm sorry. I just can't help thinking how cruel it is for Francie, that's all," she sniffled.

I shut my eyes. It was soothing to reconstruct a reminiscent portrait of my favorite sister, a silhouette on the window shade, stepping into the arms of her bridegroom on her wedding day. "I'll be there as soon as I can." I hung up.

"What is it, Ethan?" Delilah leaned into me. "Is it awfully bad news?"

"Walter. He's been wounded."

"Frances' flier?"

I could barely nod. "His plane was shot down over Holland."

"Was he badly hurt?"

"Burned."

"Oh, my God," she whispered in a voice so soft I could barely hear. "It's just like Ethan and Charmaine, isn't it? In your novel. It's all true, isn't it?"

"It's just a story for God's sake, Delilah." I didn't want to think about my stupid machinations at the typewriter being a blueprint for life. Especially not for Francie's life. This was just a cruel coincidence playing on my guilty conscience for ceding control of the family circle. That's all it was. What I wrote upstairs to mollify my infatuated fantasies had nothing whatsoever to do with real life. I would not let myself even think about that. It was just a combination of coincidence and fate. Nothing more. It couldn't be.

She wrapped both arms around me. I wanted to cry, to let out my anger and rage at what the world was doing to young men like Walter, tearing apart the lives of so many people who deserved to be happy. Instead, I just moved away from Delilah's comforting warmth and started up the stairs.

"Ethan? Would you like me to pack you a supper for the train?"

"No, thanks. I'm not hungry."

"Will you be away long?"

I couldn't even answer as I trudged up to my room. I stacked my manuscript, set it beside my good shoes in the closet, took out my bag and loaded it with what clean underwear I had from the bureau. I folded in my cardigan, a wine-colored pullover Gladys had knit for me, set my hat on my head and turned out the light.

Downstairs, Delilah was standing by the door, tears glistening on her face. I bent down and kissed her cheek. "Goodbye."

"Will you let me know if you need anything?"

I punched my right arm into my jacket. "I'll drop you a line. Don't worry. Things'll be fine. At least Walter's alive. The war is finally over for him and Francie this way."

She touched my arm. "Ethan, tell her not to worry. No matter what has happened to him, he's coming home. That's all that matters in the end, isn't it?"

I looked back at her and saw the tears falling, streaming down her cheeks. I was overcome then with the sadness for Francie and Delilah, both of them losing part of what they loved so much. I wished there were some way for me to cure the pain, some way to make up for it all.

"Lionel is coming back to you soon, too. You'll see."

"I'm thinking Christmas we'll hear something."

We hugged once more on the porch before I stepped out into the soft rain. I think she watched me walk to the end of the corner. At least, I felt her eyes following me as I hurried up Broadway toward the train station. I'll never know if she stood there with that incredible sadness clouding her eyes as I walked out of her sight.

I stopped at the hotel, spoke to the maitre d' and explained that my sister was seriously ill in Tacoma. When I told him about Walter being shot down, his voice softened.

"Well, go on then and do what you can for her, Nathan."

"Thank you."

"You're the only son, aren't you?"

"Yessir."

"Well, let me know when you get up there. We're shorthanded as it is, Nathan."

"I understand. I'll get back as soon as I can."

He sighed and flipped a linen towel over his shoulder. "We'll make do for the rest of the week, but I can't really spare you longer than that. I'll have to see about a replacement if you can't make it back by then. I hope you understand how it is."

"Sure. I understand. Thanks."

He shook my hand perfunctorily, and I took off for the station with its cinnamon-red brick tower jutting into the oyster-shell clouds. The clock face shone through the evening mist and reminded me I had only twelve minutes to make my train. As I waited for the engine to pull into the station, I saw Delilah's plaintive eyes burning through the smoke, searching my mind for answers, secrets to security I couldn't find.

The train was packed. Bodies of damp sailors, marines and recruits jammed together on the car with babies crying, mothers scolding, men joking and old men snoring as the wheels clacked over the northbound rails. It rained all the way into Tacoma. I took a taxi to the apartment. Frances was asleep in the bedroom. Carla was curled up on the sofa in the living room. We made coffee and sat up the rest of the night talking in hushed whispers about a future made more uncertain by a lucky German shell tearing through Walter's unlucky B17 and changing all our lives forever.

# Nineteen

═══════════

**Frances** stood in the middle of the living room with her blue wrapper drawn tightly around her thin shoulders. Her sunken eyes were outlined with dark shadows, the lids puffy from crying, and I noticed a new sharpness to her cheekbones since we last saw one another. She looked old, weak, beaten. While she dabbed at her runny nose and fidgeted with a handkerchief balled in her robe pocket, I pretended to be cheerful.

"Was it a crowded train, Nattie?" she asked me with a vacant smile.

"Not too bad at all."

She sneezed and blew her nose. "I seemed to have caught a helluva cold, Nattie. Carla's been making me chicken soup every day. I eat much more, and I should start growing feathers."

"What's the doctor say, Francie?"

She stuffed the handkerchief back in her pocket and sat down. "About the cold?"

"Well, about you in general."

"I'm fine." She flashed me another reassuring smile meant to quell my concern. I noticed instead how gaunt she was. "I'm fine, Nattie. It's just a cold."

"About the other thing—the surgery. You're getting around okay now?"

"Honestly, Nattie." Her hand brushed against my knee. "Don't be such a worry wart. I'm just fine."

Carla came in from the kitchen carrying cups and saucers. I started to reach for a slab of shortbread, but Frances waved her away. "Carla, could you be a dear and leave Nattie and me alone for a few moments?"

"Now? Aren't you going to have your coffee?"

"Just for a few minutes, Carla. We need to talk over some things. Do you mind?"

"You two have secrets from me? I thought we'd outgrown all that silliness."

"Please, Carla. Just for a minute or two. I need to talk with Nattie alone."

She pouted. "Well, I guess so. But don't be too long. You don't need to keep anything from me, you know." She had a slightly hurt edge to her voice.

When she was gone, Frances grasped my wrist. "Nattie, I'd like you to read the letter I received from Walter. Do you mind?"

"Of course, not, Francie. But I thought, that is, can he write?"

She took a folded letter from her pocket and handed it to me. The paper was damp from sharing a pocket with her handkerchief or from the tears which must have fallen as she read it for the hundredth time.

"This is from Captain Pilstrom, his squadron leader. Walter asked him to write it. When I received the telegram from the War Department telling me Walter had been shot down, I felt the life go out of me, Nathan."

I didn't know what to say. What to do. "Fran, I'm so damned sorry about all of this."

Her hand stilled me. "But I was thinking that he was going to make it back to me. It was just a thing between us, Nattie. A promise he made me. I believed it. I knew in my heart that Walter was coming back to me." Her eyes lingered on the letter drooping from my fingers.

"He'll be home soon, Sweetheart. Then this will all seem like a bad dream. Nothing more. Just a dream, Sis."

Her head was shaking slowly. "Nattie, he's not coming home. Ever. That's what's breaking my heart in two." She opened her mouth and let out a whimper like a wounded fawn. She rubbed a fist against her mouth and muffled the sobs welling up in her throat.

"Francie, don't." I tried to hold on to her. "Please, don't, Frannie. It's going to be okay. They'll take good care of him over there, and as soon as he's well enough, he'll be coming home. You'll see. It'll be alright."

"Read it, Nattie. Read it aloud, will you?"

I didn't want to. It was like prying into their private lives. But I understood she needed me to obey, and I dutifully unfolded the top sheet and began to read. It was like reciting a death sentence to a condemned inmate before the switch was pulled.

"Read it to me, Nattie." She rocked slowly back and forth in the chair, her arms hugging her waist and her eyes tightly closed as I began to read in a hoarse whisper. "I've read it over a hundred times, it seems like, and I still can't believe it."

I started reluctantly. *"Uh... my darling wife Frances. I am sure you have received the official notice from the War Department of our plane going down. We were limping back towards England and home after a raid on Holland when a Junkers 87 cannon got us when we were separated from our fighter escort. We had to drop down to four thousand feet because the starboard engine froze up and the vibration from the damaged props nearly knocked us out of the air. Me and Harry Howenstein, the waist gunner, are the only ones that made it out when we got hit. I never even saw him, but he was close enough that I could hear the cannon fire. It seemed to be only seconds before the whole fuselage was in flames. I didn't bail out, Sweetheart. I was blasted out through the bomb bay when our belly got ripped open. I can remember seeing my boots on fire and smelling smoke and cinders on my gloves when I tried to put my hands up to my face. Sweetheart, I'm having my squadron leader Tommy Pilstrom write this for me cuz I have no fingers. No more hangnails. What luck, huh? And I seemed to have lost my wedding ring but I didn't break my promise to you, Sweetheart... I never took it off my finger. Somewhere at the bottom of the English Channel, my finger and your ring are both lost. I have bandages over my face and breathe through a little pinhole where my nose used to be. Just like Lon Chaney in the Mummy's Tomb movie. Now don't feel too badly, Darling Fran. They're taking good care of me over here, and they tell me that they can make spare parts for me when I get back to the States. Just like the Tin Man in the Wizard of Oz.*

*Darling, I think about you every single minute I am awake, which isn't much with all the morphine they're giving me. I don't dream anymore just nightmares of being on fire, seeing the smoke and trying to scream as I'm falling through the air like a human torch."*

I paused to catch my breath and swallow a lump growing in my throat. Frances was still rocking herself like a fretful baby.

*"You're so young and lovely, my darling Fran. Life has so much still to offer you—too much for you to waste yourself with a hopeless cripple. Before you cut me off here, listen. You're so kindhearted. That's one of the reasons I fell so madly in love with you, my darling girl. No one on this earth is such a sweet, loving, gentle angel as you Frances. I know you would tend to me like a mother, the most loving nurse a man could hope for. But I couldn't bear it, Darling, to have you waste yourself on that kind of life. It will be years the doctors tell me before I am able to be a man again – to do all the things you would expect from a husband. I will be confined to a hospital while all the operations are going on to try to make my appearance acceptable to people. I won't be able to go back to my job to earn a decent living for us. I'm going to come home a monster like Frankenstein sewn together with spare parts, helpless, Fran. Someone who can't do for himself any better than a baby."*

I let the letter page flutter to the floor. My eyes were filled with tears and suppressed anger. How could Walter reject her like this? How could the truth be so unbearable? How could this man who obviously loved my sister so much abandon her altogether, cheat her out of the last shred of happiness she had clung to? I couldn't read anymore.

"He's not coming back to me, Nat," she said in a monotone, too much in pain to inflect, mouthing the sentence Walter had passed onto her. "I'll never see him again."

"Oh, Fran, come on. This is just his hurt talking. He's still in shock. You know he loves you so damned much," I blubbered, losing my own self-control.

Frances got up and stood gazing out the window at the empty street. "His pride won't let him come back to me like he is now, less than a man, barely human."

"Stop it, Fran. That's not true, and you know it. He's bound to be depressed, think the worst about everything, imagine his life is over. He's been hurt, terribly hurt, but he can get better. They do all sorts of marvelous things with surgeries these days. I read about some RAF boys burned in the Battle of Britain. *Life Magazine* had a piece on it."

"Nattie, he's burned terribly. There's a good chance he won't even survive, I suppose. Infection takes so many of them long before they can heal. Henry told me that."

Goddam the Doctor. Just what poor Frannie needed to hear—abject pragmatism when her heart was bleeding. Gladys should put a muzzle on that guy.

"I'm sure he's getting excellent care, Fran. They take the best care in the world of our boys over there. Everybody says so."

She sighed with a long breath. "I've lost him, Nattie. There's nothing I can do about it. If only I could be with him, touch him, tell him just once more that I love him."

"Francie, you'll get another letter soon. You'll see. He'll be doing better, and he'll apologize for being so depressed. This is natural. He'll be making plans to come home. Just wait." I draped an arm around her shoulder and felt the cold bones beneath my skin chill me as well. "You'll see, Fran. You've just got to keep the faith a while longer."

"He's never coming home, Nattie. I know it. I just wanted you to understand, that's all. Carla and Gladys can't accept the truth."

"You have to have hope for Walter's sake."

"I have to remember him the way he was, how incredibly optimistic he was, how happy he was to know that I was going to be well." She pulled at a lock of drab hair, unwashed, lifeless. "I've been praying that the Lord will take him away from me, Nattie. Walter would want it that way, wouldn't he?"

"Francie, don't say that. Don't talk that way."

"I feel my prayers are going to be answered. Walter's too good to suffer like this."

I reached out to hold her, but there was no response, no recognition of the healing bond we had always shared.

Carla came back into the room and stared at the two of us standing like storefront Indians by the drafty window. "Fran? Wouldn't you like some coffee? I can fix some eggs and toast if you'd like something to eat, Nattie."

I shook my head. "Thanks, Carla. I'm not hungry."

"Frances? Won't you have something?"

My sister continued staring out at the rain-slick street. When I looked into her face, I saw the same distant emptiness reflected in Delilah's eyes. The same dead pain, an unhealed scar bleeding from a wounded heart. My poor Frances. There would always be an impenetrable curtain between us. I felt like the little, lost brother once again begging to crawl up into my sister's lap when frightened by a snarling dog.

I was in Tacoma for three days, and during that time Frances never mentioned Walter's name again. His picture was wrapped carefully in white tissue and placed in her cedar chest. The only vestige she left intact was her wedding band. The more Carla and I insisted she excuse Walter's letter as the result of shock and depression from his serious wounds, the more Frances would retreat from us.

Frances was right, of course. Walter was too badly burned to survive. He died twenty-four days after being retrieved from the ocean and was buried in Coventry in the same churchyard where his ancestors had farmed before the American Revolution. As far as I know, Frances burned the letter the squadron commander had written for her husband. I never saw it again or heard her speak of it. I think

Frances buried Walter that day when I read the letter to her. She erased the agonizing picture of him lying in a hospital room, swaddled in bandages, blinded, suffering incredible pain, striving to be noble for her one last time, and saw him forever after as the dashing, laughing, gentle man he was when they had last embraced and said good-bye beneath the dome of the Tacoma Union Pacific station. That man and that loving image she continued to mourn for the rest of her life.

I rode back to Portland on a coach filled with families, young children asleep on their mother's laps and babies tucked up in blankets. When we got back, I grabbed my bag from the rack and started walking up Sixth Avenue. At Burnside, I stopped and ducked into a bar for a drink to warm my insides from the November chill, I told myself as I sat down at the bar. But really to restore my spirits after leaving my sisters behind. Their teary farewells rang like a dirge through my mind. The family was beginning to unravel, and I was powerless to prevent it. I ordered a beer and took a long swallow before I looked up and noticed the fellow sitting next to me, bent over a whiskey, puffing on a short cigar. I knew him.

"Say, small world, isn't it?" He swiveled around to face me and extended his hairy hand. I took it. "You look like hell, McCarthy. You haven't been under the weather, have you?"

"I just got back from Tacoma. My sister's husband was shot down over Holland."

"Ohh, damn, what a dirty shame. I'm sorry to hear that. Carla?"

"Uh, no. Frances actually. But she's doing much better."

"Good. This war is ripping so many lives apart. It's going to take a whole new generation to heal the wounds."

"I suppose."

"So how's the work coming along?"

I needed another beer already. Meeting this phantom was my penance, after all. I deserved to be flung in front of a mirror and forced to look my failure in the eye. Professor Harlan Ruth was bound to be a confessor tonight. No sense in prolonging my agony with rationalizations. "Professor, I haven't been making much progress, I'm afraid."

His face sagged with disappointment. "I'm sorry to hear that, Nathan. Family troubles keeping you from your studies?"

"No, Sir. That's not a very honest excuse."

He toasted me with his glass. "Well, I was disappointed not to see you back at school this term. I hope you haven't scuttled your doctoral project all together."

"I don't know if I have or not." When I said it, no one was more stunned than me. Consciously, I had no inkling that I had made such a decision to terminate my education.

"Well, I hope to see you back on campus at start of spring term, Nathan. There's plenty of time. What with the war on, we all have to rearrange our plans somewhat, don't we?"

"I suppose so," I said, acknowledging his graciousness in letting me off so easily.

"Well, I do hope you find time to pursue your doctoral studies. I believe you'll make a contribution."

I laughed derisively. "Roman history? Who cares?"

"You have a wonderful grasp of the early period. I must say, I was looking forward to reading your paper this term."

I wiped a foamy mustache off my upper lip and pulled out a cigarette. While I lit it and took a long suck of nicotine, the Professor watched my reflection in the mirror. It struck me suddenly how much he reminded me of my father. He could be posed to ask if I had a private bathroom in my boarding house.

He was kinder than that. "Nathan, tell me something." He puffed on the stogie a bit. "Is this what you want to do with your life? History, teaching?"

I was stumped by that question for the first time. Multiple choice would have been easier. I rubbed at my temple, tentatively weighing my answer, testing my certainty. "What else would I do?"

"What else are you considering?"

"Nothing." I looked up and met his gaze through my beer glass. "Maybe writing something."

He nodded as if he'd heard more than I said. "I see."

"When I finish the Roman history, I suppose I'll keep on writing one thing or the other. Maybe I'll try the literary novel on for size. For fun, that is. You know, an avocation outside of academia, perhaps, to get the feel of it."

He finished his whiskey and fit the cigar stub between his teeth. "Fiction, is it?"

"Oh, not really. Just something to get me primed, I guess. I sort of hit a dry spot."

"I see. Literary fiction?"

I shrugged, blushing behind the cloud of cigarette smoke. "Just something stupid, Professor. Nothing actually with any purpose."

His finger doodled in the beer puddle I'd created on the bar. "I see. Well, you'll need a publisher, Nathan. Let me know when you've finished a first draft. I have a friend at Yale Press who might be able to offer some encouragement if you're interested."

"Thanks, but it's nothing serious yet really."

He stood up and laid some money on the bar. "Well, keep in touch. If there's anything I can do to help things along, let me know." He offered a final handshake.

"Thank you."

"Take care of yourself. And if there's any way I or the department can be of assistance, you only have to call."

"Thank you, Professor."

"Once the war is over, we'll be looking for professors, Nathan, to rebuild our faculty." He buttoned his overcoat. "Hope to see you back on campus for spring term."

"Yessir. I hope to be back. Just have some things to sort out first."

He nodded affably and set his tweed cap on his head. I watched him go out into the rainy evening and then turned around to finish my beer. I had crossed over the line, hadn't I? No longer was I bound to the destination my father and family had ordained since I was a child playing with toy soldiers in my room. Now history and Roman kings could be the avocation, and the literary novel could become my mainstay, my calling.

I leaned on the bar and peered at my image in the glass. Was that the face of an author looking back at me or the last vestige of my youth deserting the man? Where had I let my imagination lead me? To a new starting point or toward a dead-end road like the path Frances had followed? It was nearly the end of November. Christmas was less than a month away. Lionel would be coming home, and I would have to find a way to end Ethan and Charmaine's journey. I would have to give up my hopes of requited love, steel myself for the pain of rejection I knew was in store. My salvation was waiting for me upstairs in my room where the silent machine waited for my fingers to turn virginal paper into my imitation of reality.

# Twenty

===========

**Carla** and Gladys were so concerned over Frances' mental health after Walter's death that they insisted she move in with one of them. Since it was clearly out of the question for Frances to relocate to the Midwest and take up residence in Gladys' full house, she moved in with Carla. They shared a one bedroom apartment in a four-plex in the University District of Seattle. Frances seemed to take a very long time to recover her strength and even longer to evidence any zest for living. Nothing any of us thought of to cheer her up had any affect. I could see my sister turning into another version of Virginia Nigh, headed nowhere with nothing to accomplish but passing time.

I sat down to a crowded Thanksgiving Day table with my sisters and Philip, Carla's steady suitor and official fiancé. We passed the platter and talked about Philips' law practice, tediously avoided talk of Pop and Walter and toasted the hope that the Germans would be pushed across the Rhine before Christmas, and all our boys would be homeward bound by New Year's. Sadly, those dreams were dashed when the Wehrmacht mounted their Belgium offensive barely two weeks later, and the Battle of the Bulge began the last stand on the Western Front for Hitler's Third Reich.

Frances would turn to look at me, stare with those sad, gray eyes and remind me of Delilah. Only now I understood what it was she was seeing as she looked right through me. No doubt there was a smiling Walter there somewhere in the haze obscuring her view of the present. It was an uncomfortable holiday. Our family seemed splintered like pine kindling. Pop was gone. Mother was with us only in a distant spirit with her framed portrait smiling down at us from the dining room wall. Gladys and her husband's family were in Long Island for the holiday where the Doctor was speaking to a medical convention on the *Psychological Makeup of the Hypochondriacal Patient.* One would have thought that with the War on there were plenty of genuinely maimed and sick patients on which the good doctors could concentrate their labors.

While I was finishing off a slab of turkey breast, I tried to think of what Delilah was doing, where she was sitting and at whom she was gazing. She had gone to the Coast to be with her brother-in-law Cody and his family. I had been invited to dine at the Imperial Hotel with Miss Nigh and was fortunate to have an honest excuse to keep me from sharing her tight-lipped company.

The second week of December, Carla announced she and Philip had moved up the wedding date, and Gladys had a fit. Philip was divorced with three children, and he and Carla would not be married in the Episcopal Church but by a Justice of the Peace. There was nothing for Gladys to do in the end but give her consent. If it mattered. I was the titular head of the family, and I went along with whatever made Carla happy. Besides, Philip seemed like an alright sort of a fellow to me. He had class. Not a snobbish effeteness which plagued Doctor Henry Houghton. Philip was a New Dealer with a certain intellectual flair which I admired. He would be a welcome addition to the family, a spark of new genetic material to produce nieces and nephews who would be worthy opponents for Gladys' rapier criticism.

Gladys was infuriated with my complacency in the face of what she considered rampant heresy. "Nathan, aren't you going to talk to your sister?"

"About what?" I whined over the telephone, as I stood in the foyer in my bare feet on a Saturday morning.

"You know this would have killed Mother and Daddy."

"Gladys, for crissakes, lay off her. There's nobody to care about that anymore. Carla loves this guy, and they're getting married. That's it."

"No, that isn't *it*, Nathan." She heaved a heavy sigh burdened with the frustration of my ignorance about such matters. "You can't let her make a decision that will ruin the rest of her life. It just isn't right, and you know it."

"What are you talking about for crissakes?"

"Marriage. It's vital that this union be sanctified in a church."

"Sweet Jesus..." I groaned.

"I know it can't be *our* church, but certainly, Nattie, they could find *someone,* even the Methodist Church would be a suitable substitute. To think that our sister is going to be married by a Justice of the Peace like a common clerk stamping a trolley pass. I just can't allow it."

"It's not your decision, Gladys."

"He's a divorced man, Nathan. Do you know that?"

I yawned. "So what?"

"He has children."

"Carla loves kids."

"He has three children by this other woman, Nathan. Carla knows nothing about her."

"Jesus, Gladys. He has three kids. So what? Are you against kids now for crissakes?"

"Of course, not. Don't get fresh with me, Nathan. We don't know where these children even came from now, do we?"

"What the hell does that mean?" I barked "Are you trying to impugn the stork now for crissakes?"

"Do you know their mother? What kind of woman is she? She's a divorcée after all."

"Gladys, give her a break. She's gonna marry the guy, and I'm sure they'll be very happy. Carla is crazy about his kids."

"Are you telling me that you're not going to do anything to prevent this shabby spectacle called a wedding?"

"I'm gonna get my suit cleaned."

"Are you prepared to accept responsibility for our sister making a grave mistake which may cause her all the unhappiness and pain that Frances suffered because she made an unfortunate match?"

That was too much. My temper flared. "Shut up, Gladys."

"Nathan, don't you dare talk to me like that."

"Just shut the hell up. Leave her alone. She can marry whoever the hell she likes when she likes and where she likes. I don't give a damn if he has six kids, three ex-wives and a bone through his nose. Carla loves him. If she wants to get married by a Justice of the Peace or some Holy Roller pastor, it's fine by me. Besides, he's a nice guy. You'd like him. He's a graduate of Columbia for crissakes. His father is a Circuit Court judge."

"Well, I won't attend the ceremony."

"Fine. Stay home."

"She won't be married in the Church, and you know it won't be recognized, Nathan."

"Look, Gladys, goddammit. Mom and Pop weren't married in the Church. They eloped because Mom's pig-headed father was just as unreasonable as you are."

She yelled over the wire. "Don't you drag our parents into this, Nathan McCarthy!"

"Granddad was just as stupid and stubborn as you're being right now. And Mom and Pop turned out just swell, didn't they? Priest or no priest. So lay off, Gladys."

"This is different, and you know it."

"No, I don't."

"Well, she won't have my blessing, Nattie."

"Fine."

"And I won't be sending a check."

"Fine. Don't bother."

"And I won't be sending Christmas presents for those children—whoever's they are."

"Oh, Christ, Gladys. Knock it off, will you? Who appointed you to be so goddam righteous and holy?"

"Nathan McCarthy, you forget who you're speaking to."

"Like hell I do. Don't tell me you and the good Doctor are so fucking pious you can pass judgment on your sisters."

"How dare you speak to me with such foul language."

"Oh, grow up, Gladdy. It can't be that pure out in Oklahoma."

"We have a good marriage and a wonderful family. All I want is for my sisters to have the same happiness Henry and I have found."

"Well, just lay off Carla, okay? One peep from you about those kids, and I'm gonna tell Carla to forget she knows you."

"Listen to me, Nathan."

"I mean it. Lay off. All you should care about is whether or not Carla is happy."

"That's what I *am* concerned about. How can you be happy not knowing whose children you're raising?"

"Gladys, dammit."

"Ruining your chances of starting out married life on the right foot by having your marriage sanctified in the church. You think that's some sort of black mark? I only want what's best for Carla."

"Bullshit."

"Well, I'm sorry you feel that way, Nathan. I expected you to support me, to be the man of the family now that Daddy's gone and set a moral example for Carla and Frances."

That stung. An arrow shot right through my heart. I swallowed a growing lump in my throat. "Gladys, save a nickel. Don't call me again. If you love Carla and really want to see her happy, then be nice. Pull in your claws and send her a big, fat check for the wedding."

"I'll have to think about it."

"Fine. Do that." I put the receiver down and sank both hands deep in my trouser pockets. Goddam woman was turning into a female version of Henry Houghton—prejudiced, narrow-minded, bigoted, arrogant. I was also glad my parents weren't alive to see this, to hear their eldest daughter condemn her sister as if she were some tent-packing Christian crusader looking for sinners in the backwoods.

Before I could get back up to my room and dress for my Saturday automat breakfast, the postman came up to the porch with a handful of mail. I got a letter from the University Registrar's office. Miss Nigh got a plain brown package from Baltimore, and Delilah received a few bills. She came from the kitchen and took her mail from the ding room table where I left it.

"Good morning, Nathan. Was that your sister on the phone?"

"Didn't you recognize the whine?"

She smiled. "I thought I did. Are she and the children doing well?'

"Fine."

She read the return addresses on her mail, fit the envelopes in her apron pocket and opened the draperies. I watched her fussing with the chairs, straightening the tablecloth, dusting the buffet and wondered if her letter, the one she must be hoping for every day was still to come with some word of Lionel, news that his ship was on its way across the ocean. Home for Christmas.

"Any word from Lionel yet?"

She barely looked up at me. "Virginia! Mail!" she hollered toward the stairs. "Oh, he'll probably be sending a wire."

Virginia hurried downstairs and retrieved her package without a word to me.

"What do his letters say?" I inquired boldly, pretending to peruse my own missives.

She stopped dusting for a moment and peered at me through a lock of wild, glossy hair drooping over one eyebrow. "I beg your pardon?"

"I mean about the repairs. How his ship is doing."

"It takes time for these things."

"I'm sure it does. Was it heavily damaged?"

"They need to have special parts flown in, and with the war going on in the Pacific the way it is, that takes time."

"I see."

"But he'll be sending me a wire."

"Is there a chance he'll get a leave before Christmas while his ship is laid up?"

"They couldn't do that. It wouldn't be fair. They couldn't send all the crew home, could they? It wouldn't be fair for the officers to come home and leave their men behind, Ethan."

"I suppose not."

"He has to be there to supervise the repairs. There's just no way that he could come home before the others. It's just not possible as much as I wish it were."

"Well, I didn't know."

"As soon as the ship is repaired, they'll sail home. I'm making plans for New Year's." She bustled about the room cleaning, polishing and chasing cobwebs only she could see.

"You miss him very much, don't you?"

She swiped at the picture frame above the buffet. "Loneliness is like a disease, Ethan. It's a cancer that eats away at you until after a while there's nothing vital left inside." She looked at me. "Do you know how long he's been gone?"

"I believe you said it had been about fourteen months."

"It's been eighteen months, a week and two days." She pressed her fingertips against her cheeks for a moment. "I have accounted for every minute of that time, Ethan. Sometimes it seems like a dream, as if I only knew Lionel in a dream, and none of this is real. Our marriage, the time we had together before he went overseas. It all seems like a dream sometimes."

"It must be hard on him, too."

She shrugged off the suggestion and resumed her dusting. "Well, he's busy. Very busy. Night and day. There's so much work to do. He doesn't have time to be as lonely as I do. It's his duty to be there for the people who rely on him."

"I understand." Maybe her rationalization was a defense against the disturbing thought of Lionel pursuing romantic interludes as she had to ease her aching loneliness.

"But he'll be here after Christmas. They won't be away much longer. I expect a wire any day saying their ship is underway."

"Where is he exactly?"

She turned her back on me and bent to beat the chair cushions. "It's a long trip across the Pacific, of course, but at least I'll know he's on his way home."

"Which port is it in Australia?"

"So I'm making plans, Ethan. It's going to be the best holiday season ever knowing he's coming home soon."

"I can help you, if you'd like."

Her eyes grew wide with a silent question.

"Put up a tree, I mean. Decorate the house. Anything you like."

She paused, put a hand to her hip and bit her lower lip thoughtfully. "There's a ladder in the basement. I'd like to go up to Corbett and get a tree, a big one with lacy branches. If he makes it home in time to see the tree, he'd feel more normal. You know, be able to put all those war memories aside."

"Sounds terrific."

"Ethan, can you drive?"

"Yes."

"Well, if I could get us a car, would you drive me up to Corbett to cut a tree?"

"Sure, I would, Delilah. Where are you going to get the car?"

"Cody has a Plymouth coupe. The tires are getting so bad he won't take it over the mountains, but he's driving Mr. Solomon's truck to Portland to pick up a load of turkeys for the store. We could use the truck, Nathan. But you'd have to promise not to tell anyone."

"My lips are sealed."

She wiped her cheek with the dust rag. "Alright. Then I'll tell Cody he can leave the truck parked here at the house overnight after he picks up the turkeys. I always make him supper when he comes over."

"Okay."

"And then we can go get the tree."

"When is Cody coming over?"

"Tomorrow. Is that too soon? Do you have other plans?"

"I have Sunday off."

"Good. Then it's settled." She got down on her knees and began to polish the legs of the dining room table.

"Okay." I sensed I'd been dismissed. "I'll see you tomorrow afternoon then."

As I got to the foot of the stairs, she stopped me. "Oh, Ethan."

"Yes?"

"Not in the afternoon. We're having supper about four."

"Okay. You tell me what time you want to go."

"Well, Cody won't go to bed until after eight."

"Pardon?"

"We have to be sure we don't wake him up when we leave, Ethan. So I don't think we should go until nine or maybe nine-thirty."

"What?" I was as dense as old growth fir. "You mean Cody won't know we're taking the truck?"

"Well, he'll think we're just walking out to a show or something. Don't worry. He won't want to come. He goes to bed early, especially since he has to deliver those turkeys first thing in the morning."

"Why can't you tell him we're taking the truck to Corbett?"

"Because he'd never let me have it, especially if he knew we were going all the way up to Corbett. It's his boss's, and he gets extra gas rations because it's for picking up goods for the store. And if anybody stole the turkeys off the truck, Cody'd lose his job."

I shrugged. What the hell. Life was dangerous as it was. While my answer hung in the air, I imagined the two of us locked in a furry embrace, hip deep in powdery snow, a Wagner opus thudding somewhere over the horizon as the sun set on the mountain slopes. I would have stolen the truck and eaten all the damned turkeys if she'd asked me. This might be my last chance to be alone with Delilah before Lionel made an appearance and hastened my exit.

"Will you do it or not?"

"Sure, I will. Just let me know when you're ready."

Upstairs, I shaved, dressed and read through my mail. The university was officially reminding me that if I was going to go back to school, I needed to register for the spring term. The history department needed me to commit to my assistant teaching position. It was time for me to make a decision. My lowly job at the Multnomah Hotel was enough to keep me in smokes and automat lunches while I finished my book, but after that, I might be adrift again on the unemployment seas. Gladys would be screaming at me to be a man, take a real job and make something of myself, and this time, she would be right.

I decided to go out to the library, plant myself in the stacks and ruminate. At least, assume the position. Pretend I was pursuing my research, see if I felt pangs of guilt for my extended absence or itch to find my way out the door.

As I went down the hallway, I noticed the door of room Number 1 ajar. I wanted to push it open and steal a peek, but I was afraid of being caught in the act. I stopped at the stair rail and listened hard. Delilah was running the carpet sweeper in the foyer. What the hell. I tiptoed backward to the door, put a hand against the knob and pushed slightly. The door swung open. I went in and pulled it closed behind me.

The room was dark, shades drawn. The bed was neatly made with a silk throw boldly embroidered with Hawaiian hibiscus flowers. A cheery *Aloha* was swirled across the center. It suddenly dawned on me—the source of the Hawaiian spread, the hula girl ashtray in my room. Lionel must have sent these gifts as tokens to his bride. His ship probably sailed from Pearl Harbor.

On the bureau, I saw his picture. Lionel in a white shirt with the collar open, a pipe in his hand in a suave salute to the photographer. At the bottom was the printed inscription *Lionel M. Goodknight – January 4th, 1939*. In a porcelain box beside a sterling silver brush set lay a pair of earrings, tiny anchors fashioned in gold with rubies.

The whole room smelled of her perfume. A phonograph sat on the easy chair by the window. Records lay on the floor. An ashtray, filled with crimson-stained butts overflowed on the nightstand. A glass with a swallow of amber whiskey sat on the windowsill. It was a scene set for a one-night stand. Peeler had been right. There was a black, USN Class A jacket hanging in the closet with gold braid on the sleeve. A Commander's coat. This must be Lionel's. The gunner's mate jumper Peeler had seen must have belonged to a Saturday night remedy for the blues. This couldn't be right. Delilah had to have an explanation for this, something besides the obvious. I couldn't accept that she would resort to something so tawdry. Not in this room with Lionel's portrait dominating her dresser. Not with his jacket hanging within arm's easy reach. I didn't believe it. There had to be more than what it seemed to be.

I went out and closed the door softly behind me. Delilah was still raking the sweeper back and forth over the carpet downstairs. If she were this lonely, this bereaved at bearing the separation and uncertainty, I could forgive her anything. And if she took another man into her bed to comfort herself, then she could take me to her breast as well for succor. We had nearly come to it, hadn't we? If we hadn't been interrupted, then what? Would I have been invited to stay in room Number 1 like the gunner's mate? Maybe there was a parade of such men, visitors moving in and out through the long, cold nights, faces without names, shadows without shame. It made me shiver just to think about it. I was hurt by not being among their number.

She looked up as I came down the stairs. "Going out to eat, Ethan?"

"Thought I'd catch a quick bite and go to the library for a while."

"Aren't you going to write today?"

She meant the book. Ethan and Charmaine. "Maybe later. I need to catch up on my doctoral research."

I closed the door and walked off. One more word, and I would have stayed. Rushed upstairs and pounded the life out of the typewriter keys to please her and prove to myself I could do it. Find an ending to what had to be a tragedy. There was no way out for Ethan. No way to avoid what was happening to him. My plot was hopelessly stymied. The hero was losing the girl.

# Twenty-One

═══════════════

**On** Sunday, Cody Goodknight showed up at three o'clock in his truck. The bed was covered with a tarpaulin. Beneath it, he explained to Delilah with a wink, were two-hundred turkeys ready for the Christmas market at the Astoria Safeway. He came inside and swept off his wrinkled hat.

"This is my brother-in-law Cody." She took his coat. "Ethan's my upstairs boarder."

Cody shook my hand. "So the beer huckster took off, did he?"

"Ages ago," she said.

"Nice to meet you." I decided against correcting my name. By now, Delilah had me answering to Ethan without a second thought. "Ethan McCarthy."

"Same here, McCarthy. Dee tells me you're a writer."

I looked quickly at Delilah, but she moved off and avoided my glance. "Uh, in a way."

"He's writing a love story. It's going to be published, Cody. It's based on a true story, and it's wonderful. Ethan's going to be famous someday."

I gulped and felt my ears sting with embarrassment. "Well, not exactly."

Cody was impressed by such a generous buildup. "Oh, yeah? A writer, huh? That's somethin'. What kind of a love story? Something like *Farewell To Arms?* I read that one. Hemingway. I like him. You write like that?"

"Oh, God no. Nobody does."

Delilah brushed by me on the way to the kitchen. "He's much better, Cody. And he's going to be much more famous someday, too."

"I'll be damned," Cody mumbled, following her to the table.

"I'm not a real writer. Not yet, that is."

"Nonsense," she shushed me. "Don't be so modest, Ethan. Would you be a dear and go down to the basement and bring up that ladder for me? You can straighten up the work bench while we finish supper."

"Now?" I whispered, looking over her head to the table set with crispy fried chicken, biscuits, mashed potatoes and sliced cucumbers. Since I had been recruited as her midnight cohort on the truck caper, I had expected to share a place at the supper table. Wrong again.

"Here. Take the key." She pressed a skeleton key into the palm of my hand.

"Nice to meet you." Cody nodded as he took a seat in front of the chicken platter.

"Where'll I put the damn thing?" I asked her in a stage whisper.

She gave me a gentle push in the direction of the basement door. "Just take it around the front and lean it against the porch for now."

As I unlocked the door and started down the steep, rickety steps, I heard Delilah passing plates to her brother-in-law.

"Ethan and I might take in a show this evening, Cody, if you don't mind being left alone."

"Hell, no. You two take off. I'll read the paper, listen to the news and hit the sack. I gotta get up at the crack of dawn to start back over the mountains with those turkeys."

"Well, I'll get up and make you breakfast before you go."

"Don't bother, Dee. I'll take off around five. No sense you getting up that early."

"It's no bother at all, Cody. I owe you for the groceries you brought."

"My pleasure. Forget it. Catch a few extra winks. I'll stop at Elsie and grab a cup of java on the way to tide me over."

The basement door clanged shut and slapped me in the butt as I bumped my way down the stairs. I banged my head on the overhanging furnace duct, stooped and looked around to get my bearings. A light chain tickled my face as I stumbled forward, and I reached up and yanked. As the bulb swung back and forth like a metronome, shadows bounced off the boxes piled up against the pockmarked cement wall. Delilah's massive old furnace stood in the center of the space like a battleship with its steel funnels and boiler hissing and steaming. A clothesline was strung north and south, punctuated by clothes pins sitting like wooden birds on the wire. I searched the clutter for my prize. A ladder shouldn't be too hard to spot.

Upstairs, I could hear the sound of the Philco penetrate through the floorboards above me. Mood music, conversation and succulent supper. Maybe they'd leave me some leftovers. It seemed incredibly rude of Delilah not to invite me to share dinner with them. Maybe she assumed I would get the ladder, attend to our secret business and then come to the table. That must be it. I could take the ladder out front, wash up and then claim a place for my drumstick and spuds. Of course. She hadn't intended to exclude me at all. Business first. That was it. Nothing to get my nose pressed out of place.

I moved a rake, pushed aside a galvanized wash bucket, peered over the stack of firewood by the fruit-jar pantry and got my bearings. There was enough junk down here to stock a five and dime. I'd have to reconnoiter before I started tearing into piles. No wonder she'd sent me down here first.

My eyes stopped suddenly on a steamer trunk partially covered with a worn tapestry and a hatbox. I laid them carefully aside. The top of the trunk was pasted with travel stickers: Singapore, Manila, New Delhi, Honolulu, Macau. On the top right corner was an oval seal in tangerine with a blue border. In the center was a hula girl with flowing black hair, upturned breasts and a grass skirt parted to show dimples in both knees. She was the cousin to the girl upstairs fastened to my ashtray. I jiggled the lock free and raised the lid. The smell of musty paper and dead flowers filled my nostrils and initiated a false sneeze. Mums. I bent down and put my hand around a withered bouquet. A card fell out: *With all my love and kisses, L.*

I sucked up a breath and rubbed my nose. The pungent, moldy dampness was starting to make my eyes water and my nose run. I lit a cigarette and let it burn to clean the air. Then I reached down and picked up a pair of lieutenant j.g.'s bars pinned to a pair of silk, striped pajama tops. Size 42. A silk handkerchief with *USS Hammann* embroidered on it caught my eye.

I pulled up the wash bucket, turned it over and sat down. Beneath the dried bouquets, there was a wool watch coat lovingly laid to rest with tissue paper. An envelope bore the address of the Naval Training Station at San Diego, California. There was a scrapbook with the gold letters L.M.G. embossed on the cover. I opened it. Snaps of Delilah with bows in her hair, spectator pumps and a polka-dot dress standing on the running board of a '36 Ford Roadster; Delilah and a blonde woman in shorts standing below Multnomah Falls; Delilah holding a picnic basket, a bandanna tucked around her hair—*1938/Silver Creek Falls* written in white ink beside the photo. I focused on snaps of Lionel in a linen suit with his hat cocked at a jaunty angle, sun in his eyes as he tried a serious pose in front of a giant redwood. Lionel again, waving from behind the wheel of a light-colored Packard roadster stopped on the St. John's Bridge. Lionel in a tailored overcoat looking very chic with one arm around Delilah in a gray suit and silly cocked hat. They were standing proudly behind a wrought-iron gate enclosing a Tudor house with three stories and a Lincoln parked at the garage door. Happier days. I couldn't take my eyes away from the pictures. They were so innocent, so enthused. How had Delilah gotten here from there? What had happened to make those bright, laughing eyes so sad?

Underneath a straw hat with a floppy, red crepe hibiscus, was a packet of letters tied with pink ribbon. The return addresses were Oakland, California, and Honolulu, Hawaii. Love letters. I stared down at them in awe. These were the real thing, the ending to my story lay here. This was the beginning and end of Lionel and Delilah, Ethan and Charmaine. All the love and hope they had shared was in those letters mixed with all the misery and longing of their separation. I wanted to tuck them in my pocket and steal away to my room to read in blissful privacy.

The door opened, and Delilah was haloed at the top of the stairs. "Ethan, did you find it?"

"I got it. Be right up." I dropped the letters back into the trunk and hoped she hadn't caught me snooping.

"Take it out the side door then. It's locked from the inside. You'll have to be sure you put the lock back on when you're done."

She slammed the door and went back to her company, her chicken dinner and the radio.

I closed the trunk lid, put the hatbox back in place and folded the tapestry. When I turned around, I tripped over the rung of the ladder. So I had found it. I hauled it from under the corner of the woodpile and hoisted it over my head to make my way to the ground level exit. I struggled to force the rusty bolt back and push open the door. Old leaves and branches littered the side yard as I clambered out with my trophy. I carried the ladder around to the street side of the house, rested my load against the porch railing and went back to the basement to secure the back door.

When I finished and started up the stairs, I heard the dishes clattering in the sink. I switched off the light, went up and let myself back into the kitchen. Cody had two hands around a chicken thigh, and Delilah was dishing whipped potatoes onto his plate. When she saw me, she looked up expectantly until I nodded to confirm my accomplishment. Then she put a finger to her lips and motioned me to go out to the hallway.

When I turned around, she came up so close I could count the flecks of ebony in her irises. "Wait upstairs for me. I told him we're going out to see a show later."

I still wanted to lobby for supper. I felt entitled, emboldened by my conspirator to demand equal rights. "Why don't I just join you at the supper table?"

She shook her head adamantly. "Oh, Cody isn't very sociable, Ethan. He's so tired from making that long drive he'd rather not have to make polite conversation at the table. Just as soon as he finishes, he'll put his feet up and listen to the news. Then we can go."

"But—"

She stretched up on tiptoe and kissed my lips. "Thanks, Ethan."

And she was gone. All I could do was stand at the doorway and watch as Cody crunched his way through the last drumstick and splotched gravy on his napkin.

# Twenty–Two

===========

**I** lay on the lumpy mattress, listening to the faint strains from the Philco, sweet melodies that floated up the stairwell from the sleeping porch. I could hear Cody laugh every once in a while. Then the pipes in the wall banged and gurgled. Delilah scraping the dishes clean of giblet gravy and golden-fried chicken whose aromas made my mouth water. Cody retired to the porch, I could see the fingers of light stripe the backyard below my window when he turned on the lamp.

I smoked a Lucky and reached out to start the hula girl's hips wriggling on my ashtray. The Philco grew louder with Charlie McCarthy. I couldn't make out the words, but I could catch the ripple of laughter from the radio audience after every gag line.

I put out my cigarette and folded an arm behind my head. I wasn't comfortable with the idea of borrowing Cody's truck without his permission, but any transgression short of a capital crime was worth an opportunity to be in Delilah's debt. And to have her all to myself for a couple of hours was enough to prime my fantasy figures to perform on the window shade. First, there was my seductive heroine Charmaine with an auburn ringlet hiding the curve of her neck. And then there was Ethan, my alter ego. Dying, of course. A symbolic sacrifice for my expiring love, no doubt. But tonight, the lovers were together. One last time. One last, desperate moment to be consumed in the fires of their passion. That was good: *"fires of their passion"*. I started to get up and reach for my pencil. No need. I could hear this dialogue raging in my brain like bombshells exploding on the firing range.

Ethan would hold her close and slowly disrobe her like peeling leaves from an artichoke until her marblesque limbs were exposed to the shimmering moonlight. *Shimmering*. Yes, that was it. I could close my eyes and see the snow glistening like sugar crystals in the reflected light of a silver-dollar moon. I could smell the fragrant fir boughs and bracing Cascade air chilled until it made my cheeks flush. Just as the two lovers meshed in a heated embrace, a burning sensation stirred in my loins.

"Ethan?" Delilah was rapping on my door.

I bolted upright, a hot, tingling sensation still flaring in my groin. "*Jesus!*" It was a real burning. I had dropped off to sleep and shed hot ash on my trousers. My crotch was smoking, and my pants were scorched. Christ!

Delilah rushed into my room. She was wearing a camel hair coat and a knit hat with a sable-brown, pheasant feather at the crown. Despite my excitation, she stayed calm given the fact that her boarder was on fire.

"Ethan! You're smoking." She began to beat me with a pillow.

"Jesus!" I swatted hot ash from my pants and rolled off the bed. I was intact thankfully. Embarrassed and distressed but unhurt. "I burned the hell out of these pants. These are my good trousers. Dammit!"

She brushed ash off the bedspread, shook both the pillows like a terrier with a rat, grabbed up my matches and cigarette and set them in the sink. "Ethan, you should be more careful. If I hadn't come up when I did, you could have burned the whole house down." She circled the room, peeking behind the blinds, looking in the wardrobe and slapping the hula girl's shade. "My God, you might have started a fire. Do you realize what you nearly did?"

I surveyed the mess on the bedcovers. "Sorry. I'll try to be more careful."

"*Careful?*" she gasped, wrapping her arms around herself. "My lord! Careful?" She shuddered. "What good does that do if you fall asleep like that? You could kill everyone."

I held my arms out, palms uplifted. "I am sorry. Truly."

"You scared me, Ethan. Honestly, you'd think you could be more considerate."

"I'm sorry. What else can I say? It was just an accident. No harm done."

"Look at your trousers."

"Except for my trousers, that is."

"I'll put it all in the laundry tomorrow anyway." She looked around the room quickly as if expecting someone or something else to burst into flame. "Are you alright?"

"I'm fine. Embarrassed and chastened but fine." I tried to elicit a smile to signify my atonement, but she stiffened her shoulders and walked past me for the door.

"Don't ever do something like this again, Ethan. Never!"

"I promise. I'm running out of trousers anyhow."

"Well, are you ready? Cody's fallen asleep downstairs."

"Let me get a coat."

"We'll have to be quiet. He'd be awfully upset if he knew we were taking the truck."

I punched my right arm into my jacket and grabbed my hat. "Are you sure we ought to go through with this?"

"Of course, I'm sure. You said you'd help me, didn't you?"

"That's not it."

"Well, just try not to make too much noise when we're outside."

"I just want to make sure this is what you really want to do."

"I said it was. How else could we get up to Corbett for a tree?" She switched off my light and opened the door.

"We could just ask Cody to borrow the truck, couldn't we?"

She pressed her fingers against my mouth as we went out to the hallway. "*Shhhhh*. Come on. Be quiet."

We crept down the stairs like burglars, went outside and carried the ladder to the truck. With her help, I slid the ladder under the tarp and opened the driver's door. Delilah was hugging her coat around her to ward off the cold breeze making little white clouds from her breath.

"Do you have the keys?" I asked her.

"*Shhhhh.* Of course, I have the keys. I took them from his coat pocket after dinner."

I held my hand out. "Well? Get in, and I'll start it up."

I might as well have suggested we moon bathe on the sidewalk. Her face crinkled in a frown. She pointed to the end of the block where there was a mailbox and a huge rhody bush crowding the sidewalk. "Ethan, you'll have to push it up the block. You can't start it here."

"What?" I strained to keep my voice down. "Push this thing all the way up the block? For crissakes, why?"

"Cody will hear it start up. Just start pushing."

"Oh, Jesus." This was not to be a winter tryst beneath the starry skies. I was being employed as a stevedore, a driver and no doubt a lumberjack before the night was over. "Get in then."

She climbed in. I put the gear box in neutral, released the brake, got out, braced myself against the door post and pushed so hard I got dizzy and saw ink spots floating in front of my eyes. I was one step from a coma when the wheels started to turn.

"Steer," I choked as the truck inched forward.

She slid across the seat and gripped the wheel. Her skirt hiked up above her knee and exposed a beautiful shank of creamy, white thigh to my hungry eyes. I strained and pushed, grunted and leaned into the old International until the truck gained momentum and raced me for the corner. Just as we rolled into the intersection, I heaved myself aboard, slipped the clutch and started the engine.

"Turn on the lights, for God's sake," she nagged me as we swung onto Broadway.

"Where the hell *are* the lights?" I shot back without trying to be civil. I'd nearly given myself a double hernia pushing a truck full of goddam turkeys down the street. I fumbled around in the dark until one of the knobs I pulled switched the lights on.

Delilah snapped open her bag, took out a cigarette case and tamped down the tobacco in a Chesterfield. "Smoke?"

"Yeah. Thanks."

She lit one for me, stuck it between my lips and sucked on her own cigarette as I drove across the Burnside Bridge and headed east out of town toward the sleepy village of Troutdale. The heater didn't work in the truck, and before we had passed the orchards and holly farms which decorated the gorge foothills, my knees were locked in a stiffening, cold cramp, and my teeth were chattering. Delilah rolled her window down a crack and flicked ash into the slipstream. So far she had ignored me. Not that I had that much to contribute conversationally. I was debating whether or not I should assume I was a social companion along for the splendid company and charm of my personality or whether I should just play the part of hired hand and make up my mind to spend a cold, miserable night schlepping fir trees.

"Jesus, it's cold," I chattered as the truck bounced over the Sandy River Bridge.

"You're not complaining, are you?"

In the dark, her face was barely lit by the reflection of the dash light and the flicker of occasional headlights as we chugged along under the pall of overhanging firs. "I'm just cold, that's all. Both my feet are frozen."

She blew smoke at me. "First you nearly burn your balls off and then you complain about freezing." She laughed first and drew me in. I suppose from an objective viewpoint, the situation did merit some humor.

"Your husband's gonna like the tree, huh?"

"Of course, he'll like it. Wouldn't you if you'd been gone a year and a half from home?"

"Sure I would." I let my cigarette hang from my lower lip as the truck gyrated and shimmied around a pothole. "So are you going to cook up one of those turkeys?" I jerked my thumb toward the back where the two-hundred headless birds bounced like bowling balls every time I hit a bump.

"Maybe I'll fix a ham. Lionel loves ham."

"Cody can get you a ham?"

She grinned knowingly. "Cody can get me a ham if I want one. He gets me lots of things."

"Nice."

"What?" she replied suspiciously.

"I said nice. It's nice he can help you out like that."

"He does a lot for me."

I wrenched the steering wheel to the right as I took a tight turn that slid Delilah's warm thigh against mine. "He's Lionel's brother you said?"

"Cody's four years younger than Lionel."

"So how old is Lionel?"

"Are you trying to find out if I married an older man, Ethan?"

I could hear the amusement in her voice and knew it was safe to press on. "I'm only twenty-three, you know."

"You're a child, Ethan. Just a kid. Maybe even a virgin."

My ears started to burn. She was right mostly, but the words still bruised my pride.

"Lionel's older than I am," she admitted with a diffident sigh. "He's eight years older. It doesn't seem like so much really, does it? Eight years?"

"I suppose not."

"He was engaged before we met." She flicked ash on the floorboard. "Did I tell you that?"

"No."

"Her name was Dorothea, and she was a blonde. They were engaged to be married for three years while Lionel was finishing college. I think her family had a great deal of money. Even more than Lionel's."

The photos from the album flashed across my mind. Lionel looked like the end product of good breeding, class and privilege. The Tudor mansion and the Packard must have been his. "So why didn't he marry her?"

Her hand rested on my leg as I shifted gears to coax the truck up to Crown Point. "She was really quite attractive, tall and slim with green eyes. I've seen her picture."

"Uh huh." I could only concentrate on the warm fingers massaging my pulsing thigh.

"She must have been very much in love with him."

"So why didn't they get married?"

She turned and stared out the window at the black bluffs. Sterling chains of water fell like lacy veils from the rock crevices high above the highway. "She died," Delilah said dryly.

I braked to avoid a branch that had fallen across the road. "How'd she die?"

"She drowned in the river."

"What happened?"

"She was out on the river at night, just her and Lionel. The two of them took the boat out from Hayden Island. They took along some champagne and tomato sandwiches and were going to make love on the water in the moonlight." She sighed and took another drag on her cigarette. "It must have been very romantic, don't you think?"

"I guess so."

"It was a warm evening in the middle of August, and Lionel suggested they go for a swim. So they stripped down and dived in the water. There was practically no current in the river that evening. Lionel swam out to a sand bar and lay down on the beach, waiting for Dorothea to join him."

"And?"

"She never did. He waited and then went back in the water to look for her. He got back in the boat to see if she had swum back by herself. He called and walked along the beach looking for her. But he never found her."

"So they assumed she drowned?"

"Almost a week later, they found her body wrapped around a floater log."

"That must have been hard on him."

"He swore he'd never marry anybody else. And he almost didn't, I guess. I mean, he did wait a long time, didn't he?"

"How long?"

She stifled a little laugh. "Well, he was almost forty. Nobody thought he'd ever marry. I think his mother had given up hope of ever seeing him married after Dorothea died."

"So why did you wait so long?" She was so beautiful in an ethereal, translucent sort of way. I couldn't imagine how she had resisted marriage for so long herself, long enough to find Lionel. "What were you afraid of?

"Afraid of? What do you think I'm afraid of, Ethan?"

"I don't know. Love maybe. Losing somebody you love. Something like that."

"You can't love without taking risks. That's part of it, isn't it?"

"I suppose so." Her hand was moving up my trouser leg. Much higher, and I was going to drive the truck off the damn road. "Why did you wait so long before you married?"

"Because it took that long for Lionel to find me."

There didn't seem to be an appropriate sequitur. Delilah was fading on me, distancing herself behind that veil of solitude she could draw closed around her. I wanted to keep her close, keep her hand kneading my flesh and kindling my lust. "You love him a lot, don't you?" I said in a hushed voice, unable to control my trembling.

"You know how you wake up in the morning and see the sun shining in through the window, Ethan? And it makes you feel safe, believe everything is normal in the world, in its proper place?"

"I suppose."

"That's how I felt when I met Lionel. And now that he's gone, it's like waking up in the morning to find the sun hasn't come up, isn't going to come up ever again." She exhaled a cloud of smoke. "That's how I feel about Lionel."

The truck groaned and whined as it pulled us up the steep crest of the hill until we could see the outline of the Crown Point Lookout, a Hellenic silhouette in the night sky as it stood a lonely watch on the gorge bluff six-hundred feet above the river. I parked the truck alongside the rock wall and set the brake. Far below, we could see the mouth of the Columbia River Gorge yawning like a serpent's mouth, the strip of silver water glinting like a dragon tongue in the gloom. Wind whipped around us and rocked the truck as if it were a cradle swinging on a branch.

"What about the other men?" My voice broke the hush and interrupted the whine and bluster beating against the windows. A cold slap of wind whipped across my face from the crack in the window or from her icy stare. I wasn't sure which. "Why, Delilah? I know how lonely you must be without him, but still..."

"You don't understand, Ethan. You just don't understand."

"Tell me what I don't understand."

"What do you mean by that? Tell me. I want to try and understand all of this, why it's necessary for you to have these other men in your life. I need answers.""*You* need answers?"

"I don't want to think they're just..."

"Just what?"

"Necessary, I suppose." I lacked the courage to expose my true fears. Fears that she was no different than all the other fallen angels the War had cursed, and that I would never be able to assuage the pain of lovers like Francis and Delilah.

"Necessary? That's what you think? Oh God, Ethan. You have no idea. No idea at all."

"Explain it to me."

"I can't understand why people pretend to be so happy anyway, content with things the way they are," she said dreamily, staring out at the stark tableau.

"What do you mean?"

"Well, it's all just a dream, isn't it? We all pretend every day."

"Pretend what?"

"That this is going to turn out alright. I see people laughing, joking, pretending they're fooling somebody, winning something. And it's all a lie. A filthy, rotten, dirty little lie."

"What is?"

Her face turned toward mine, and I could see the wetness in those luminous eyes. "Life. We're all just waiting for it to happen, Ethan. Most of us don't know when and how it will happen. We're just waiting like sheep at the slaughterhouse." She looked out at the nacreous ribbon of the Columbia winding toward the horizon and shivered. "We all have to face it. Maybe it's something awful, painful, lingering or maybe it's mercifully quick. But each of us has to face the suffering at the end, the dying part." Her eyes found mine again. "Death is waiting for us, Ethan. No matter what we do or how much we try to be happy and pretend, it always finds us in the end."

"Well, sure," I stammered. "That's how it is in the general scheme of things, isn't it?" How profound, I thought regrettably. I must sound like some simpering freshman essay.

"There's just no point in being happy and pretending it solves anything. No use at all. So I don't try to pretend. I go through the motions every day, live my life. And I don't regret anything, Ethan. None of it. There's no point, is there?"

"But we still have to do what we think is right. Morality makes the living worthwhile."

She looked out the window again and ignored my profundity. "None of it matters. Nobody matters. Lionel is the only one who matters to me, and that's only temporary, you see. That can't last. Nothing does."

That didn't explain the other men, the sleeping porch redolent with cigarette smoke and whiskey, a midnight rendezvous in the glow of the Philco radio.

"I wish you didn't need anybody else," I murmured.

"You don't understand at all, do you?"

"I *want* to understand, Delilah."

"What I do is absolutely none of your business, Ethan. So there's nothing more for me to say, is there?" She withdrew her hand, cranked down the window and tossed out her cigarette. She shuddered with the cold and stuffed both hands deep in her coat pockets. "Let's go on up to Larch Mountain and get the tree. It's getting late."

Her eyes glazed over, a thousand miles now from me. There was no use in trying to say any more. There was going to be no confession, no contrition, no falling into my arms with a plea for sympathy and compassion. She didn't seek or need my understanding. I had lost her once more.

"Sure," I grumbled, my teeth chattering. "That's what we came for, isn't it?"

"I put a hatchet in the back. I'd like to pick out one with snow on the branches. They look like ballerinas in their ball gowns with the branches all decorated with snow, don't they, Ethan?" Her eyes stared dreamily out the windshield and saw visions of happier, warmer people who never graced my field of view. "Just like beautiful ballerinas. I want a tall one with snow on it."

"Yes, Ma'am," I replied as I made the turnoff onto Larch Mountain Road and saw patches of white in the fields beside the pavement. I'd be damned lucky if I got through this trip without getting the truck stuck in the damned snow, getting lost or freezing my ass off.

Then as I felt the rear wheels slide off on a slick spot on the pavement, her hand gripped my arm as the truck danced off the road and headed for the shallow ditch.

"Dammit! Hold on!" I jerked the wheel around and wrestled the truck back onto the slippery shoulder where it shuddered to a stop beneath a giant red cedar with a trunk as big as a foundry smokestack. A shower of snow fell on the windshield. We sat there in silence for a moment, shaken by the sudden jolt.

"Ethan, would you like to kiss me?"

My mouth was covering hers before she could hear my answer. My hands, frozen like icicles, sought the warmth beneath her coat as our breath clouds mingled in the chilly cab.

"Ethan," she whispered against my face. "Just hold me for a little while to keep warm."

"Dammit, Delilah," I moaned with my lips in her hat feather. "I want you so much."

"I know," she whispered back gently, capturing my cold hand on her bare breast. "That's what love does to you, Ethan. It makes you want things you can never have."

She let me kiss her, cradle her body in my eager arms and pet her silky thighs and perfumed hair, but she kept me from the heart of the fruit. I was only allowed a sip of the nectar. Just enough to make me crazy with wanting her, afraid I would burst apart with my pent-up want. But it passed. Like the cold and the aching numbness in my arms as I hacked and sawed at the mature fir she picked out.

By the time I parked the truck back in front of the house and set the brake, Delilah was snuggled up against my shoulder, fast asleep. I bent and kissed her until she woke up and focused her eyes on mine.

"Home?"

"Home." I stole another warm kiss.

Then she took the key, got out of the truck, walked up to the porch, opened the door and left me alone to drag out the tree and the ladder. I fell into my bed half-frozen and spent of all my manly ambition to win this woman's frigid heart.

# Twenty–Three

========

**I** knocked the water off my hat and rang the bell. I stood on the stoop for a moment and listened for sounds on the other side of the door.

"Nathan?" he said when he swung the door away from his face and saw me. "Nathan McCarthy, come in. How are you? What a pleasant surprise."

I swept off my hat and unbuttoned my jacket. The house was uncomfortably warm. I could see the flicker of a fire in the living room to my right. The smell of fresh-perked coffee was in the air. "Thank you, Professor. I was hoping I would find you home."

"Well, I'm flattered, Nathan. Really. Come on in and have some coffee."

"Thank you." I followed him dutifully to the front room and waited until he motioned for me to sit on the divan. While I ran my fingers around the damp brim of my hat, he went to the kitchen and brought back two cups of hot coffee.

"How nice to see you, Nathan. How's the book coming along?" Professor Ruth set my cup down and wiped his face with his free hand. His baggy eyes seemed to gleam, and I knew he was genuinely pleased by my visit. That in itself was worth the bother of coming here, changing buses and getting soaked to the skin in a brisk shower.

"I'm not sure I can finish it before the start of the spring term, Professor."

His face never betrayed any disappointment in the admission. "I see," he said simply without a hint of judgment in his voice. "Are you keeping yourself busy then?"

"Well, in a way."

He stirred cream into his coffee. Then he leaned back in his chair, crossed his legs and balanced the saucer on his knee. "You know, Nathan, there's more to life than getting your doctorate right away. Since the war, well, some might say that it seems trivial, perhaps, to be pursuing an advanced graduate degree when so many other things of worldly import are hanging in the balance. I can certainly understand your reluctance to commit yourself to another term."

"It's not just that, Professor. Quite honestly, well... I've been wondering if a teaching position is right for me."

"I see."

"I mean, maybe I'm not cut out for academia, Professor. Not suited to the profession the way you are, I mean."

His kindly smile warmed my frostbitten bones. "Nathan, let me make a confession. When I was your age, I was just back from France. I served in the infantry, a terrible, frightening experience, and I wasn't certain what I wanted to do, but I was positive that I had to make an important contribution." He chuckled to himself. "Whatever that was. You see, I was consumed by youthful altruism and patriotism. The war had permanently changed my perspective of the world. I was involved. Intimately involved, Nathan. Whatever I decided to do with my life, I had to feel it was an important contribution to something beyond my own personal agenda."

"So you chose a teaching career."

He shook his head and sipped at his coffee. "Oh, no. Drumming all the failed policies and beliefs of my parents' generation which had led us into war and slaughter for no meaningful betterment seemed terribly feeble. Instead I applied for entrance to the Willamette University Law School."

My eyes widened with respect. There were more facets to this man than I had imagined. "You were going to become a lawyer?"

"Oh, yes. I was going to defend the underdog, stand up for the downtrodden. It seemed to be a very noble aspiration at the time. I was swept up in the fervor of my generation to change the Old World order."

"I'm amazed, Sir. That is, in truth you've always seemed so stable, secure in your own decisions. You set an impossible standard to follow, I'm afraid."

"At one time, Nathan," he paused to wink at me, "I was a member of the Communist League. They seemed to have all the answers at the time. I was eager to do away with the old aristocratic stranglehold on world politics, relieve the suffering of the masses. In retrospect, they may have been somewhat less radical than the New Dealers."

I smiled. That thought had crossed my mind.

"So I was bound to be a barrister and champion the injustices of the underclass."

"But you didn't become a lawyer. What changed your mind?"

His eyes crinkled. "*Who.*"

"Pardon?"

"Not what but who. Madelaine Beutry. My wife. I caught first sight of her at a fraternity party and fell madly in love. So much in love I couldn't see straight for weeks. Fortunately, she took pity on a poor love-struck fool and agreed to go out with me. Probably just to keep me from pestering her. I couldn't concentrate on anything but Maddy. I was fatally smitten. Terminally infected. A mortal affliction of the heart."

"So you gave up your dream of practicing law?"

"In six months, Maddy and I were married. And ten months later our daughter Beatrice was born. I was working at Miller's Department store selling shirts by then."

"You mean you quit school?"

"My economic situation forced me to retire from academia for a while. But I didn't mind really. Maddy and I and the baby were so wonderfully happy in those early days. Whether or not I was becoming a lawyer had little importance."

"You didn't care?"

"Not a fig. It was my wife who finally urged me to go back to school and pursue my education. Not law. We just didn't have the money for it. But I was able to manage a few classes per term when Maddy took a job at the telephone company. It took me seven years to get my M.A. and then another four years to earn my doctorate. Our daughter Beatty graduated high school before I finished my dissertation."

"Eleven years?" I was flabbergasted by his confession, unable to comprehend waiting over a decade to fulfill a dream. I was a short-termer when it came to labor and reward.

"By the time I received tenure here, I was quite comfortable with my choices. The detour didn't account for much in the long run."

"Do you ever regret not following the law, Professor?"

"Heavens, no. Teaching has more lasting impact than haggling with the illusory vagaries of the law. Teaching is a long-term investment, Nathan, planting seeds for the generation's future in its most important resource—its youth."

"I'm not sure I'm cut out for it," I admitted.

"Well, there's certainly no rush required. You have plenty of time to figure this all out, Nathan. If you let it, life will lead you in the right direction."

"But I want to finish my thesis, Professor. Everyone expects me to do it."

"Don't worry a minute over what anybody else expects you to do, Son. There are lots of works on Roman history. If yours is a good one, it can wait."

"I want to do it."

"What about the other work? The novel you're working on."

I looked away. "It's getting in the way of my serious study, Professor. That's the problem."

"Well, perhaps it isn't a problem, Nathan. Maybe you just need to relax and write it."

"I don't know."

"Maybe you're not meant to be an historian at all. There could be a great literary novel within you."

"I'm not really a *writer* at all. It's just that, well... this story seemed to come together in my mind, and I felt obligated to write it down for some reason, and it's ended up consuming all my energy and taking me away from my studies."

"I see."

"Along with some other personal complications."

"Mhmmm."

"And what I really want to do is get the history finished, come back for the spring term and complete my studies."

"Naturally."

"But I don't feel I can just walk away from this other thing."

He put his saucer on the coffee table and leaned forward to study my face. "Nathan, I suspect this is a case which involves a certain attractive, young lady."

"In a way," I hedged.

"Rejoice!" He reached over and slapped my knee. "That's what life is all about, Nathan. Don't see love as an impediment in your life. It's a gift full of brand-spanking marvelous, new opportunities."

"Maybe you can put it that way but—"

"You know, I can recall another student of mine, some time back. Long before the war, in fact. He was the prodigal son of a noted, fine old family. There were two sons, in fact. One was tall, handsome, reserved and quite decent. A very serious student who excelled in track and field sports, courted a respectable young lady from an excellent family and made his parents proud. But this young man, my student, had a brother. Another kettle of fish altogether The other son was, as I say, the dark side of the coin. He was brash, headstrong, impetuous, stubborn and rebellious. His entire nature seemed to be in conflict with his environment. He was a trial to his parents, teachers and associates although we all recognized a streak of genius and tenacity in this young man."

"He was a graduate student of yours?"

He shook his head. "He could have been. But he dropped out of school his senior term. What a dreadful waste it was. At the time, he was rebelling against the reins of his parents who were trying to steer him into the proper social circles. Cody could never adjust, never fit into the mold."

"Cody?" The name made my lips tremble.

"He dropped out of school after a drinking incident with some coeds made the newspaper. His father gave him a position at the bank, and I think Cody was just miserable with that style of life. As much as his elder brother was obedient, reserved, excelling in all his endeavors, Cody rebelled at preordained rules and regulations. Rather than following the rules like his brother Lionel who always succeeded at everything, he eventually ran off with a girl who worked at the fish cannery. Rumors were that he had gotten her in a family way and was one or two steps ahead of the shotgun. But as it turned out, that wasn't the case."

"What happened?"

"He had a falling out with his father over his precipitous marriage, and it changed his life. He left his position with the bank, moved out and settled down with this cannery worker. He never had much to do with his father after that. It was as if he had never been born and raised in the same house with Lionel. That's how estranged the two were."

"His family cut him off?"

Professor Ruth nodded. "Financially, of course. But they also refused to accept Cody's decision to marry this woman with whom, by the way, he's enjoyed a blissful family life working at a blue collar but honest occupation, and probably better off for all his supposed failure."

"I don't understand your point, Professor." Why was Cody ahead of the game carrying Christmas turkeys over the Coast Range instead of working six floors up in the Jackson Tower? It didn't make any sense to me.

"It's just that happiness can't always be defined by material success, Nathan. You should keep that in mind. Your completing your education and teaching— maybe that won't bestow the measure of satisfaction you hope it will. Don't overlook the present for a promised future that has no guarantees other than old age and death. The doors we open in our youth decide all our fortunes in the end."

"This young man you were describing, your student who dropped out of school and was disowned by his father. Was he Cody Goodknight?"

"Why yes. Do you know him?"

"I'm rooming at a boarding house owned by Delilah Goodknight. Cody's her brother-in-law."

"You see what a small world it is."

"I suppose so." Now I knew why Lionel was posed in front of fast cars and Tudor estates, and Cody was schlepping crates at the Safeway. "Why would Cody's father turn away from his son just because he disapproved of his wife?"

"Well, you'd have to ask Mr. Goodknight about that. I suspect there were other factors involved. We'll never know. It doesn't matter, I suppose. Many young men with tremendous promise have a falling out with their fathers, and it changes the course of their lives."

"It seems so cruel."

"You recently lost your father, didn't you, Nathan?"

"Yes."

"Well, perhaps, you need to re-examine your priorities in light of your abandonment. In one way, although I'm sure you feel an obligation to your family, you're free to chart your own course now, Nathan. Think about it. Be sure you're chasing your dreams, not anyone else's."

"Yessir. I've been thinking about that. A lot."

"You're wrestling with yourself right now, and I can understand your dilemma. Don't force yourself into making a final decision just yet. There's plenty of time."

"Maybe I should just take a regular job and help out my sisters, establish myself."

"I know since your father passed away, you feel you should take up the mantel now. But is this a burden you have placed on yourself? Has anyone else made any demands on you?"

"No. In fact, my sisters want me to finish the history and return to teaching."

"I see."

"But I'm not sure that's what best for me at all." I put my head in my hands. This was all garbled. I had planned on making a clear, concise dissertation on my choice to delay graduate school and the book, but now I was sounding more like an adolescent than a responsible adult. This was a mistake.

His hand gripped my shoulder. He reminded me once again of Pop and the way he used to sit back and listen to my disjointed dialogues and then fit it all together neatly in one candid reply. "Nathan, listen to your own heart. That's the best advice I can give you. There is no master plan for life. You have to make it up as you go along."

"But I feel as if I'm letting everyone down."

"Don't. Learn to be responsible for yourself alone. This is your life, Nathan, and you have a long time ahead of you to make decisions. Take your time. Give yourself a chance to explore before you make a commitment."

"I hate to let you down, Professor."

"You're not letting me down, Son. Not at all. Someday, if you finish the history, I'm certain it will be well done and well received. And should you decide to come back and take on teaching, then the faculty will be well rewarded by your contribution to the department. But if there is something else you need to accomplish first, then by all means, go to it. Doctoral theses and teaching will wait for you."

"I don't know what to say." I didn't. I was stalled. At the moment, I lacked even the encouragement to work on the novel. Ethan and Charmaine had reached an impasse, and my fingers froze on the typewriter keys when I tried to write.

"I hate to have to find a replacement for you this late in the year. You're an outstanding teaching assistant, Nathan. But if you want my blessing to delay completing your doctorate to finish your novel, then you have it. Most definitely."

I looked up. "I don't even know if I *can* finish it, Professor Ruth."

"Well, then you'd better give it a damned good try, hadn't you, and find out? How do you know if those new shoes fit unless you walk a bit in them?" He stood up and started back to the kitchen.

"And now, how about some fresh ginger snaps Maddy made this morning?"

Walking back to the bus stop, I tried to make myself think that I had been absolved of all the sins of lassitude and disaffection toward my studies. If my mentor, Professor Harlan Ruth, head of the History Department, had so much faith in me, then I was remiss in not believing more in my own abilities as a writer. Maybe I could complete a great work of literary fiction. Perhaps Nathan McCarthy would become a household word or at least a byline at the library index file. He was right about one thing: I had to give it a decent try. Without the guilt and the feeling of self-deprecation I had soaked in since Pop died and left me in charge of the family. From now on, I decided as I splashed through a puddle, I was going to let my sisters take charge of their own affairs, and I was going to pursue my destiny. Whatever the hell it turned out to be.

# Twenty–Four

================

**As** December came, I pounded out chapters of my novel. I could see the two of them, Ethan and Charmaine, moving through the windows of my mind as I sat crouched over the typewriter, my back kinked and my butt numb as I worked through the night after my Multnomah Hotel shift was finished. I heard Miss Nigh's trips to and from the bathroom, smelled her pungent aura after her ablutions but never laid eyes on her as I left the house and crept back to my lair long after everyone else was asleep.

I was enthused with the heady conceit of the artist. This book was going to be a literary salve to save the souls of a million bleeding hearts ripped asunder by the war's forced separations. I might be hailed as the generation's greatest author. My fantasies were only bounded by my ego. In other words, I let my optimism run away with my reason and convinced myself that the world was waiting for my opus to be delivered into the hands of an eager publisher and bestowed on a grateful public.

Downstairs in the front room, Delilah had set up the Christmas tree I had chopped down. She had popcorn strings twined around the branches, paper rings, glass balls and snowflakes crocheted from white and silver thread hanging from every limb. And every day she would sit in a chair and gaze at the tree as if it were a lover, sighing and fussing with an ornament, adjusting the gold star at the very top of the tree. It was clearly all for Lionel, and I sensed his arrival must be imminent.

It was confirmed for me on the twentieth of the month when there was a ring at the doorbell just as I was preparing to go to work. Western Union was at the door with a telegram for Delilah. She rushed in from the kitchen, took it and gave the messenger a couple quarters.

When I came down the stairs, she beamed at me. "Hello, Ethan. Have a good day today."

I was amused at her exuberance. I was hung over from a sleepless night working on my unraveling plot. Three hundred pages into the abyss by now. "Good news?"

She pressed the telegram close to her breast. "It must be. It must be. Because it's so close to Christmas, isn't it? I knew he'd be home for Christmas, Ethan. I told you so, didn't I?"

"I hope he's on his way."

She ripped open the envelope and read. Then she thrust the paper under my nose and kissed my cheek. "See? I told you so. He's really coming. He's really coming home to me, Ethan." Tears moistened her eyes as she waited for me to read the telegram.

*Dec. 19, 1944/USS Hammann – US Naval Base, Brisbane, Australia*

*TO: Mrs. Delilah Goodknight – 1909 Broadway, Ptld., OR, USA*

*Darling: On my way home. Stop. Set to sail at midnight, Aussie time tomorrow. Expect to arrive US Navy Operation Base, Hawaii on 25th. Dec., sail 27th Dec, dock Oakland Naval Shipyard 3 Jan. Stop. Await your loving arms to welcome me home for holidays. Stop. Love and a thousand kisses, Lionel. Stop.*

Before I could speak, she snatched the telegram from my hands and folded it into her pocket. Then she wrapped both arms around my neck and kissed me, letting her lips linger on mine. "Oh, Ethan. Isn't it wonderful news?"

"Sure," I murmured, wanting to kiss her back. "Wonderful news."

"Are you happy for me?"

"Of course." My lips brushed against her hair. "I'm very happy for you, Delilah."

She raised her face and slowly closed her eyes. Her mouth was tilted toward mine. I felt as if I had to kiss her, as if she expected more than this. I pressed my lips down on hers until she leaned into my arms. Then her mouth opened, and I was inside this luscious woman. Standing there with the front door wide open, exposed to passersby, we kissed like long-lost lovers.

"Come up upstairs with me. Please," I choked.

My words broke the spell, and she pulled herself away. "We can't, Ethan. Not now." She turned around and straightened her dress. "Now that Lionel is coming home, I have to get everything ready for him. Maybe you could help me on Saturday."

Hot and cold. Fire and ice. How could she turn herself off and on like that? I was still shaking, limp and pale with an erection the size of Mount Rushmore.

"Maybe you could help me with the shopping, Ethan. Do you mind?" She waved cheerily and started back to the kitchen. "You can help me hang a garland on the plate shelf in the dining room."

"What the hell," I muttered to myself. "You want me to cart groceries, hell, why not?" I closed the door behind me and stomped down the porch steps. "Why the hell not? What a stupid, goddam chump."

I put my head down and set off for the Multnomah Hotel and another routine shift washing dishes, scrubbing pots and pans and setting tables. If Lionel was coming home, I was going to have to find another place to live. I wasn't sure how I was going to explain my reasons to Delilah, but, dammit, she shouldn't need any reasons. Should she? I was determined not to let her make an even bigger fool of me than I already was.

At the hotel kitchen, Melvin was leaning up against the sink smoking on a stained cigar butt. "Hey, Kid," he greeted me as I came in. "How's tricks?"

"Terrific," I fired back at him. "Just fucking terrific."

He flashed a smug grin at my pimpled accomplice and sent the butt flying down the drain. "So what's gotten up your ass, Bud?"

"Nothing. Absolutely nothing," I lied, tying on my apron.

"Nothin', he says," he kidded mercilessly. "Okey-dokey. So you get beat outta the sack by some uniform, huh? That what's eatin' you, Kid?"

"No." Then I threw my shoulders back and tightened my lips in a sadistic snarl. "Damned right. Goddamned right. So just lay off me, Mel, okay?"

Melvin stepped back and gave me a wide berth at the sink. "Hey, Kid. Suck it up. These Navy boys get all the good pussy these days. Right, My Man?" he asked Pimples with a sly wink.

Pimples was flattered to be included in the conversation for a change. "That's right, Melvin. It ain't fair, is it?"

"Hells bells," Melvin barked. "What's fair got to do with it?" He looped a sweaty arm over my shoulder. "So who's been gettin' in her panties, Son, beatin' your time?"

"It's her husband. He's coming home from Pearl."

"Ooh, shit O'Shea." Mel seemed impressed by my frankness. "So she's been playin' you for a chump while the old man's at sea sinkin' Japs. So that's it, huh?"

"Yeah," I admitted with a sour face. "That's it." I was angry with her for betraying *me* not Lionel. To hell with Lionel. It was her rejection of my advances that infuriated me and gave me a sudden instinct to strike out at her and sully the image I had created of an innocent heroine. "She's been fucking around on her husband, and now he's coming home, and she's got her legs crossed."

"Balls, Son. Damn women. So you got the shove, huh?"

I nodded as the suds blew up my nose. "Yeah. That's it."

"That's rough, Kid. Really rough. Bitch."

"Bitch," Pimples echoed sympathetically.

"So when's he comin' home?"

"His ship's leaving Australia on the twenty-fifth."

"That's Christmas day," Pimples added with a vapid smile.

"Where's he at?"

I scrubbed on a pot as if it were her shining face reading the good news. "Some Aussie base where they repair US ships damaged by the Japs. He's headed for Pearl Harbor then home, I guess. He's an officer on the *USS Hammann.*"

Melvin reached for his cleaver. "No shit?"

"She got his telegram this morning." I heard a tremendous whack as Melvin split a lamb shank in two.

"You say she got a telegram from her hubby this mornin'?"

"Yeah."

"And he's on the *Hammann* comin' home from Australia?"

"Yeah. Sailing at midnight."

"By way of Pearl?"

"That's what it said. He'll be in Frisco after the New Year."

Another deafening whack as Melvin buried his cleaver in the cutting board. "A Western Union telegram, you say, Kid?"

"Dated December 19th."

"He saw the telegram, didn't you, Nathan?" Pimples asked, trying to back me up. He caught the suspicious flare in Melvin's squinty eyes when he looked over my shoulder. "Tell him, Nathan. You saw it, right?"

I slowly turned halfway around to look at Melvin who was poised with his cleaver in the air. "So what if I saw it? What difference does that make for crissakes?"

*Whack... whack... whack.* "There ain't no telegrams, Son. Ain't no such animal."

"What do you mean?"

*Whack... whack.* "Dontcha know nothin', Kid? You that wet behind the fuckin' ears?"

I pulled both arms out of the dishwater. "What the hell do you mean?"

Melvin chortled as he chopped. "Hells bells, Son. Ain't no telegrams tellin' when the fuckin' ships're sailin' or comin' in. For crissakes, use your head."

Pimples nudged me. "Loose lips sink ships, Nathan. I know that."

"What do you mean exactly?" I asked, not afraid to display my considerable ignorance. My curiosity was greater than my shame. "Are you saying the telegram wasn't legal or something?"

"Hell, no. There ain't no telegram sent from the *USS Hammann*, or any other fuckin' US ship advertisin' when it's comin' into port. *Midnight?* It said he's sailin' outta Australia at midnight?"

"Yeah. I saw it. That's exactly what it said. So what?"

"And it was dated December 19th? You saw it?"

"I just said I did."

"Navy uses military time, Bub. Midnight's twenty-four hundred hours. And they put the month ahead of the day. Nineteen December. Ain't no way that telegram is legit, Lover Boy. Your lady is puttin' you on."

"What do you mean?"

Melvin wiped the cleaver on his apron and reached for a rump roast. "You're tellin' me that she showed you some Western Union wire said her old man was sailin' home from Australia on the *USS Hammann,* headed for Hawaii?"

"Yeah. I saw it."

"Balls. An' it said he was gettin' into Pearl? And arriving in Frisco on a certain time and date?" *Whack... whack.* He flipped gristle onto the floor. "Bullshit. In the first place, there ain't no way he coulda got a wire off announcin' his sailin' dates to Western Union. Or the ports he was puttin' into. Jesus H. Kee-rist, Kid. You got oatmeal between your fuckin' ears." *Whack... whack!* "And second—this is the juicy part." *Whack... whack!*

"What?" The hair was standing up on the back of my neck. The same feeling I got when I discovered a pickpocket had lifted my watch at the Oregon State Fair in Salem my junior year in high school. It was the engraved railroad watch my Grandfather Nelson had left to me.

"And besides, ain't no such animal in the United States Navy, Kid. She's been fuckin' with your head, Sonny Boy."

"What animal?" I was almost ready to grab his meaty neck and squeeze the answers out of him. "What the hell are you talking about?"

"The *Hammann* went down in '42 comin' back from Midway, tryin' to save the Yorky. Got cut in two by a Jap sub and broke her back."

"Who's the Yorky?"

"USS Yorktown. Carrier. You really that stupid you don't know that?"

My mouth went dry. I couldn't believe any of this. Obviously, Melvin was putting me on, enjoying making a complete ass of me. That's what it had to be. Even if I did smell the scent of truth in his laughing eyes. This was Melvin's distorted idea of a joke. It had to be. "You must be mistaken."

"Nope. Ain't. My ex-wife's baby brother Robert was chief engineer on the *Hammann*. Bobby was on the salvage crew that got aboard the carrier to try and save her. She's still got his official Navy Department posthumous citation he got if you wanna see it."

I blanched and steadied myself against the lip of the sink. "I don't believe it. It must be another ship then. Maybe I misread the telegram."

"Ha! Misread, my pink, rosy ass. She's shovin' it up your butt, Kid. Playin' you for a first-class sucker. Ain't no *USS Hammann* comin' home from nowhere. It's home for the fishes at the bottom of the fuckin' Pacific Ocean."

I turned back to my dishwater.

"Is she two-timin' you, Nathan?" Pimples whispered.

I ignored him. It was so much more than that, wasn't it? If it were true. And why wouldn't it be true? Melvin knew I could check out his story. If the *Hammann* went down in the Pacific, I could find out. But why would she lie? What else was she lying about? And why? What was the point.

"There must be a mistake."

Melvin threw down another hunk of meat and wiped his blade. "Ain't no mistake. She's playin' you for a grade A asshole, Kid. Grade A. Her old man is probly dead as a door nail. Even he made it off somehow, the censors would never let a piece of shit like that through. Use your head for somethin' besides holdin' your hat on. You need to go home and show her where the bear shit in the buckwheat, Kid."

"There must be a mistake somewhere," I repeated.

"If she's tellin' you she's got an old man comin' home on the *Hammann,* then she's a goddammed liar. Plain and simple as a pimple on my butt." *Whack... Whack.* "There's a sucker born every minute, ain't there, Pimples?"

"What're you gonna tell her now, Nathan?" Pimples whined.

"Maybe he was one of the survivors."

"Dream on, Kid. He'd a been in Pearl for the little thing back in Hawaii when Bobby got his award. You been had, Buddy."

All I wanted to think about now were the dirty dishes bobbing in the greasy water. I couldn't handle anything more complicated like why Delilah had lied about something so important to her. I couldn't even begin to ask myself other questions about Lionel, about the other men she had been seeing. Suddenly, nothing seemed to make any sense.

Melvin was back at the sink in a few minutes, lighting a smelly cigar and thumping my shoulder with a beefy hand that might as well have still held the cleaver. "Hey, Kid, cheer up. They do this ever so often when they get to thinkin' they can pussy-whip some poor sonuvabitch. Don't take it so hard. You just go on home and drill her a couple a times, knock some sense into her head. Chances are, she's got the hots for some swabby in town and wants to put you to pasture for a while. My advice?" He bent close enough to let his scruffy, two-day old beard scratch my cheek. "Knock her up. Keeps 'em home. Once they have a kid, they settle down, you know what I'm sayin'?"

"Sure."

"Forget this crap about splittin' up. Show her who's boss, okay? For crissakes, don't let her pussy-whip you, Son." He winked and stifled me with a cloud of noxious exhaust from the stogie. "Gives us all a bad name, you know what I'm sayin'?"

"Sure. Thanks."

He gave me a final slap of encouragement and returned to his cutting board.

I spent the rest of my shift with my elbows in dishwater and my head wrapped in cotton wool, unable to absorb any of the thousands of painful thoughts waiting to scream at me for answers. When I left and started home, I decided I would find out for myself why anyone would want to deceive me about something so important. There had to be a better explanation. Lionel was real. I could feel it. The *USS Hammann* was real, too. Melvin had confirmed it. Maybe there was a mistake, a misunderstanding. I could have misread the name of the ship on the telegram. Maybe the name I saw in the trunk down in the basement, the *USS Hammann,* was the ship he had served on before it went down. And maybe he was on another ship now with a similar name. Maybe the *Longhorn* or the *Louisiana* or the *Louisville*.

I couldn't think of anything sensible. But I was going to get some answers.

The minute I got home, I went straight down the hall and through the kitchen, took the basement key from the nail by the back door and let myself down the basement steps. Jerking on the single bulb, I uncovered the trunk and pawed through the keepsakes until I came to the album. I crouched down beneath the light, settled myself in on the bottom stair and laid the photo album across my knees. Then I opened it up and started looking for clues.

# Twenty–Five

====================

**I** picked up a ride at the gas station and shoved my jacket in the back seat as the Chevy pulled out onto the highway. I exchanged pleasant greetings and stilted introductions with the driver as the road wound along the river and left St. Helens behind in the swirling mist of a dreary, gray winter day. It was only two o'clock in the afternoon, but the Chevy's headlamps illuminated the black pavement lying like a licorice whip on the rain-soaked delta.

The Chevy pulled off the highway at Tongue Point, dodged a gaggle of sailors and merchant seamen congregating under the shelter of a hemlock and let me out before swishing away in the drippy gloom. I pulled my hat down, buttoned my jacket and started hiking along the gravel shoulder into town. By the time I got to Commercial Street and spotted the parking lot of the Safeway Store, I was soaked clear through to my shorts.

I went in the store, swept off my sodden hat and squished my way to a cashier. "Hello," I said, hoping my appearance was better than my attitude. "I'm looking for the manager."

His head jerked toward the center of the store. "Mr. Goodknight?"

"Yes, that's right. Can I see him?"

"You a sales rep?"

"No."

"We ain't hirin', you know."

"I'm here about a personal matter."

He sniffed and pointed around a stack of tomato soup cans. "Sure. He's in the office. Go straight back through those swinging doors past the produce. Upstairs."

"Thanks."

I made my way to the rear of the store and ran right into Cody.

"Mr. Goodknight? I'm Ethan McCarthy. Remember me?"

He turned around and took a moment to recognize me. "You're the guy who rooms with Dee in Portland. The writer."

"Yes, that's right."

"How are you?"

"A little wet but okay otherwise."

"What can I do for you? You lookin' for a job?"

"No. Nothing like that. I was wondering if I could buy you a cup of coffee."

"Oh, yeah?" His eyes narrowed. He leaned against the doors and wiped a hairy hand across his face. "Look, uh, Mister —"

"McCarthy."

"McCarthy. Look, I can't do you any favors. Dee is family, you know, and I help her out when I can, but, uh..."

I waved my hat. "Oh, no. I'm not looking for anything like that, Mr. Goodknight."

"Yeah?"

"I just thought you could spare me a little time to talk."

I could see the cords in his neck bulge. His mouth tightened. "What about?"

"Delilah." He stared at me without blinking. I had no idea if he was going to throw me out of his store, welcome me into his office or swing the door shut in my face.

"What's this about?"

I shuffled my feet, twirled my hat and felt my ears redden. "I'm worried about her, that's all, and I thought you could maybe talk to me."

"What's wrong with her?"

"Nothing really. That is, I hope not." My hollow laugh echoed in the confined space and elicited no change in his expressionless eyes.

He flicked his knuckles against my chest. "You and her got some kinda thing goin' on, is that it?

"Oh, no," I gulped, realizing this guy was big enough to knock me thorough the wall if he wanted to. "Nothing like that."

"Well, what is it then? I'm kinda busy."

"I'd like to speak to you in private if you don't mind."

"What for? I got work to do, McCarthy."

"Please," I persisted. "It's important. Just a few minutes."

He studied me for a few seconds more, taking in my soggy shoes and dripping jacket. "You hitch all the way from Portland to see me?"

"I picked up a ride in Burlington."

"So you wanna talk to me about Dee?"

"Yes. It's important."

"What's your connection to my sister-in-law?"

"I'm in love with her," I blurted. Couldn't help it. It just came out in a burst like an explosive sneeze.

His demeanor instantly changed. The face sagged, and his shoulders hunched. He pushed past me and started up the narrow stairs. I followed close behind. He opened his office door. "Have a seat."

I squeezed in between crates of South American oranges and sat down on a wooden chair. He flopped down behind a crude desk piled with invoices, bills and receipts. Boxes were stacked up to the rear window along with cartons of produce and canned goods. Time cards, pencils, ashtrays, rubber bands and stamped ration books littered the desktop.

He leaned back against the wall and laced his fingers behind his neck. "Okay, shoot, McCarthy. What's on your mind?"

I sensed I was being put on a timer like an egg boiling in the pot. I had three minutes or less to make my point and convince him it was worth his while to indulge me. "Mr. Goodknight, I need to know about Lionel and the *USS Hammann*."

He brought his hands down slowly. "What's Dee told you?"

"Not much."

"Why don't you ask her? Why come all the way over here to ask me for crissakes?"

"Look, this is difficult."

"How so?"

"Your brother Lionel—I know he's not coming home."

He raised an eyebrow. "No shit."

"What I mean is, I know why he isn't coming home."

"So? There's a war on. Lots a boys ain't comin' home."

I reached inside my jacket and pulled out my purloined paper. Without looking directly at him, I handed the telegram across the desk and waited for him to read it.

"What the fuck is this?" he grunted, scanning it quickly and tossing it back.

"I think she sent it to herself."

"Jesus." He pulled at his neck and wiped his lips with a callused thumb. "Look, McCarthy."

"Nathan."

"You care a lot about Dee?"

"Yes, I do."

"She's a sweet kid."

"I know, but frankly she scares the shit out of me with something like this."

"See... me and Susie, my wife, we thought she had pretty much got over this, you know. It was hard as hell on her."

"Lionel was on the *Hammann* when it went down, is that right?"

"His body was never recovered. Eighty-two men I think went down with her. Eighty-four maybe. They lost a lot anyhow. She was a destroyer coming back from the Midway Islands. Lionel was an officer, and he had just come off watch when they got hit. The communications officer went to Lincoln High School with my brother. They both lettered in track. He made it back and came all the way from San Diego just to tell Dee about Lionel and what happened." He sighed and pinched his eyes closed with a thumb and forefinger. "She saw a lot of action in the Battle of the Coral Sea, made a rescue of some stranded fliers. It was written up in the papers. Then after the Japs got their butts beat at Midway, the Hammann was part of the group trying to save the Yorktown from going down. She'd been badly damaged, and the Hammann was part of a screen picking up a salvage team and the Yorky's captain trying to get her ready to tow her back to Pearl when a Jap sub fired four fish right at 'em. Two went under the Hammann's belly and hit the carrier, and one got her amidships. Lionel was just gettin' in the sack after his watch when they got cut in two like a loaf of bread. Just bang, and that was it. The guys on the bridge, up on deck, some of them made it and then got blowed up by an explosion after she went down. Lionel and the rest of those poor bastards, they just went down before they knew what the hell had hit 'em."

Poor Delilah. What torture it must have been for her replaying that nightmare over and over again.

"He *was* comin' home for Christmas. They were supposed to put into Pearl and then head back to Oakland for a refit. Lionel was gonna get an XO spot on another tin can so he'd a had leave that December. He was pretty excited about that." He drummed his fingers on the desk. "Everything always went smooth as goose grease for my brother. School, sports, business. Whatever. Lionel made it all look easy. Me?" He held both hands up in front of his face. He had calluses the size of marshmallows on his giant paws. "I fuck up. Everything I touch turns to shit. Lionel was somethin' special."

"So it's all in her mind, isn't it?"

"Two and a half years ago now. Funny part is since Lionel was a kid when we were growin' up, I always figured he'd outlive me, you know? It was real hard to figure he couldn't beat this thing, that he didn't find a way to make it back home."

"I'm sorry. Really."

"But I guess he just used up all his lucky days and ran short this time."

"Are they sure? I mean, is there any doubt about whether or not he might still be alive somewhere?"

He swiped a finger as thick as a Polish sausage under his nose. "Naw. The escort ships, see, they picked up survivors and bodies. They swept the area pretty good. They figger Lionel's body was still in the ship with a lotta the other bastards who didn't make it out. Dee wanted to make out like he coulda got rescued, maybe be in some Jap camp or something, but that's bullshit, and she knows it." He hit the telegram with a fist. "This shit. This is fuckin' pitiful."

"She doesn't suspect that I know anything about this." I was trying hard not to offend this man who was obviously suffering with my forced recollection of his brother's death. "I haven't said anything."

"Well, it's just the grief, that's all. She doesn't mean a thing by it."

I sat and waited while Cody pulled out a handkerchief and blew his nose. He folded his hands over his gut.

"All these poor bastards over there. They ain't ever comin' back, and their families got nothing here to help 'em get through the grief. No funerals. No cemeteries to go put flowers on the graves. Nothing. So all they got, all the people they left behind, got virtually nothing except memories—some good and a lot pretty damn bad. I don't think about what my brother went through when his ship got blown in half. My hope is he went quick, but who knows? Damn certain I'll never know and neither will Dee. That's a shitload of heavy grief to bear."

"I've thought about that. She has his pictures and souvenirs from Hawaii and probably lots of letters, but—"

"What's this all about, McCarthy? Why the hell are you here anyhow?"

"I need to know about certain things, and I can't get any answers from Delilah."

"What things?"

"Lionel and Delilah. About their marriage."

"What about it?"

"Tell me about Dorothea."

"What?" His face wrinkled in puzzlement. "Who the hell is Dorothea?"

"Lionel's fiancée before he met Delilah."

"Never heard the name."

"You never heard of Dorothea who drowned in the river?"

"Nope. Lionel was married to a gal named McCoy. Charmaine. She was injured in an accident, and they got divorced."

I felt a rock hit bottom in my gut. "Lionel was married to Charmaine?"

"Yeah. Two years or so, I think. They had a kid. That's the only thing that didn't work out exactly right for Lionel, I guess. Not the way he planned it anyhow."

"She isn't dead?"

"Dead? Hell, no. Charmaine's back up in Washington. Tacoma, I think. Their girl's livin' up there with her grandmother."

"They had a daughter? Lionel and Charmaine?"

"Yeah. Dottie. She lives with Charmaine's folks. Lionel was nuts about her."

I stood up and tried to pace in the cramped office. None of this was making any sense. Either I was crazy or Delilah was completely, hopelessly demented. "So Lionel's first wife is living up in Washington?" "Yeah. Last I heard. Susie and me keep in touch with my niece. Like I said, Dottie's a sweet kid."

"Why did Lionel and Charmaine split up?"

Cody wiped his mouth and erased a sardonic smile. "Look, let me put it this way. They were both kids when they married. Charmaine was a beautiful woman, and Lionel was always working. One thing leads to another, you know? You wanna grow a good garden, you gotta stay and tend to the weeds, you know what I mean?"

"I guess so."

"But Lionel was crazy about her. They were really nuts about each other."

"Then why did they divorce?"

"You might say Dee broke it up. My brother had a temper, and when he and Charmaine had a row, he'd move out. Usually, he'd

234

come and stay with me for a few days until things smoothed over. One time when they were on the outs with each other, he met Dee, and one thing led to another. Pretty soon they were serious, and Lionel had to decide what he wanted to do with his life. Well, he chose family and his kid, and he left Dee and went back to his wife. But Dee, she wouldn't let Charmaine and Lionel get back together. Dee was always in the middle, stirring things up. If Lionel was at home with Charmaine and Dottie, Dee would call him up and threaten to kill herself if he didn't come back to her." He shrugged. "You know. That kind of thing. Dee means well, but she was really head over heels. Lionel just couldn't decide which way to turn."

"So he chose Delilah in the end over his wife and child?"

"Not exactly." He pulled a pack of Camels from his shirt pocket, lit one and tossed the spent match on an overloaded ashtray. "Smoke?" he offered, holding the pack up.

"Thanks."

"Anyways, after Dee threatened to do herself in all the time if Lionel didn't divorce his wife, Charmaine finally went through with it."

"With what?"

"Suicide. She tried to burn the house down and kill herself. Lionel got out, pulled Dottie outta bed and carried her up to the attic where they got helped down off the roof before the whole thing went up. But Charmaine was burned up pretty bad, all over her head and face and legs. She's crippled, permanently crippled. I don't know how many operations she's had, but she's pretty bad off. She was in the hospital up there for a couple years."

"This is unbelievable."

"Dee didn't tell you about any of this?"

I was shaking my head, trying to discharge the grotesque pictures in my mind. "No. God, no. Nothing like this. I didn't know anything about this."

He stared into space for a moment. "This is pretty tough for Dee to talk about. It did something to her. My brother got a divorce and got custody of the kid, and she and Lionel got married after the divorce, but it wasn't ever quite right. Lionel just never felt right

235

about any of it. I think he felt he should have stayed with Charmaine and let Dee go. Guilt was eatin' him up from the first when he and Dee tried to make a life together after the fire."

"God." I felt sick to my stomach. The whole picture was unraveling.

"Dee's suffered a lot. She's done her penance, I can tell you that. I think she's ready for some happiness, and if you can make her happy, then I wish you all the best. I mean it."

We exchanged mutual looks of bewilderment. "I don't know what to think."

"I don't know what got into her to do something crazy like this." He pushed the bogus telegram across his desk. "Maybe it's just cuz the holidays are comin' on, and the memories and everything made her a little goofy."

We sat without speaking for quite a while.

"Is Charmaine still living in Tacoma?" I asked.

"Yeah. She's in some kind of a home like a convalescent hospital. She can't get around by herself. She's blinded."

"Who is Ethan?" I finally had the guts to ask.

"Lionel's twin."

"Twin?" Oh, sweet Jesus. I could barely swallow.

"He died when he was a baby. Whooping cough. I think he was a year or two old."

"Ethan died as an infant?"

"That's right."

"Delilah never knew him."

"How could she? He passed away when I was just a kid myself."

"Was he an identical twin?"

"Yeah. Why?"

"No reason, I guess." I stood and put out my hand. "Thanks for talking to me, Mr. Goodknight."

He took my hand in a bear-like grip. "Cody. Say, if you can help Dee, make her happy, then whatever Susie and I can do—I mean, she's been put through a lot. If she can be happy, hell, it's her turn." He walked me back through the store and opened the street

236

door for me. "I wish you wouldn't tell Dee you'd been here," he said as I put my hat on.

"I won't."

We shook hands once more. "Good luck, McCarthy. I hope everything works out."

"Me, too." I didn't even bother to stick my thumb out until I had walked halfway around Young's Bay and realized I was headed away from the highway. I took off my hat and let the rain wet my face. While I waited for a kindly motorist to stop and take me in, I wondered what in hell I was going to say to Delilah when I got back to Portland.

# Twenty–Six

I knew before I even opened my door that she was there sitting in the club chair, one hand lazily draped over the arm and my manuscript filling her lap as she smoked and studied the pages intently. A crack of electric light painted a golden stripe on the carpet as I put a hand on the doorknob. I took a fortifying breath and stepped inside my room.

"Hi," she said without looking up. A halo of yellow cigarette smoke hung over her burnished hair. She was wearing a nightgown as pale blue as an Indian summer sky. The material was thin and clung to her body like fresh paint. I could see the outline of her breasts, the circle of mocha brown around her nipples and the curve of her slender thighs.

"Have you nearly finished?" I shed my wet jacket and tugged at my shirt.

"Almost. Is it still raining out?"

"Yes." I sat down on the bed and wiped my lenses clean. I bent over to untie my shoelaces. "I've been hitching."

She flipped through another page and sucked on her cigarette. "Have a hot date, Ethan?"

I pulled off my shirt, kicked my shoes under the bed and ran a hand through my wet hair to tame it. "Why do you call me Ethan?" I hoped she would raise her eyes to look at mine. She didn't. "Do I remind you of someone?"

"Who?"

"The real Ethan. Do I make you think about him?"

She leaned her head back and sucked on a cigaret. "I have no idea. I don't know any other Ethans."

"Then why don't you call me Nathan?"

Because I like Ethan. Is there anything wrong with that?"

"Not particularly. I'd just like it if you'd call me by my real name, that's all."

"Alright. Suit yourself. But I don't like Nathan."

I loosened my belt. "I like *your* name. Why don't you let me use it? Why do you prefer Charmaine so much?"

Her eyes began to smolder. She picked up another page of my manuscript and held it close in front of her face to disguise her annoyance. "I just like it, that's all. Is there something wrong with that?"

"I suppose not. If you have a good reason."

"I do."

"Okay."

"And it's none of your damn business either."

"If you say so."

Her eyes tracked me as I got up and walked to the bureau where I emptied my pockets and tried to catch her reflection in the mirror.

"Where were you tonight?"

"Just out."

"Are you still bussing tables at the hotel?"

"Uh huh. More washing than bussing lately."

"You should get another job. There's openings everywhere with all the good workers gone in the war."

"Uh huh."

The literary 'pregnant pause' hung in the room for nearly a minute.

"The tree looks good." I had seen the lights blazing as I came up the front steps. She had worked all day decorating the house.

Fresh fir boughs and garlands were hung over every lintel and draped above the mantel.

"You'd said you'd help me hang the fir boughs, Ethan."

"Sorry. I had to attend to something else more important." I hung my shirt over the bedpost and stood bare-chested. I felt her eyes boring into my bared flesh while I pretended not to notice her stare.

"I've read through your book while you were gone."

"Uh huh. Nothing else to do?"

"Don't be so damn flippant. I wanted to see if you'd changed anything."

"And what would that be?"

"I don't like the part of your book where Charmaine pretends to be so damn noble that she decides to give him up. I think you should change it."

I shook my head and picked up a pack of Luckies. "I think it's real. She doesn't want to be tied to a cripple for the rest of her life. She's young and beautiful. Isn't that realistic?"

"No," she snapped with her eyes burning. "It isn't realistic at all. I'm surprised you could write something so stupid."

"Stupid?"

"Your very own sister lost her husband this way, and you have the nerve to write this drivel." She flung a page at me. It fluttered to the floor like a wounded butterfly. "This isn't realism. It's shit."

"So you think you'd choose to devote your life to taking care of a cripple?"

"Of course. Anyone would if they were really in love."

"Anyone?" I crossed my arms over my chest. She was radiating hostility. "An invalid who's grossly disfigured?"

"*Yes*, dammit. Don't you think your sister Frances would have accepted Walter and been grateful to have him come back to her at any price? *Any* price?" she begged with moist eyes. "Don't you understand that, Ethan?"

I felt so damned sorry for her, sure she was reliving her torture, blaming herself for driving Lionel away in the end, lighting the fuse that destroyed him. Both of them maybe as it turned out.

"I'm not so certain of that at all." I exhaled smoke at her. "What one in love might say and feel initially when the shock of such a thing is overpowering, is one thing, but to say that a person would commit herself to a lifetime of self-sacrifice because of a rash promise is a bit unrealistic, don't you think? A trifle too maudlin even for a romantic novel?"

"It is not."

"Don't you think in time Frances would have come to hate Walter for making her give up so much?"

"No. Never." She looked away. "You don't understand anything at all."

"Don't you believe that Walter or Ethan," I said tapping the manuscript still filling her lap, "would hate himself for destroying her chance for true happiness?"

"No."

"Wouldn't Ethan or Walter want his sweetheart to be released from such a selfish promise?"

"No. Why should he?"

"Because I thought that was what love was really about. Being bigger than yourself. Feeling so much for someone it can't be contained inside your body, that's the kind of love I'm trying to write about."

"You mean Charmaine is giving him up just to make him happy?"

I held her gaze for as long as I could keep her eyes on mine. "Don't you think that's the ultimate act of love?"

"She's a fool. He doesn't want her to leave him. He needs her. Can't you see that? Can't you write about fidelity and loyalty? What's sacrifice have to do with love? This is a romance story for God's sake not a goddam Russian tragedy."

I raised her hand to my mouth and kissed her fingers. "That's what love is, isn't it? Sacrifice."

She got up and spilled the manuscript onto the floor. "It doesn't have to be that way at all. I think you've ruined the story."

"Okay. You tell me. What should the ending be like?"

In a flash, her eyes brightened; she swung around and put a hand to her hip as she pondered my question. "Well," she started, biting her lip as she turned toward me. "To begin with, Ethan needs to recover more."

"He was very badly wounded."

"I know, but you need to see that he recovers more. He can't be a helpless cripple disfigured, chained to a bedpan for the rest of his life. It isn't fair."

"Who says anything has to be fair?"

Her eyes blazed. "I do. This is a love story not a college sociology course, for heaven's sake. He has to recover. Jesus, everyone in life either gets better somehow or dies. You can't have it both ways."

I gave in and watched her walk back and forth in front of my mirror. The nightgown barely disguised her nudity. Her back was bare to her derriere. I could almost taste the sweet tang of her bath powder as I imagined my tongue running wild along her spine. "Then what?" I coaxed her, slipping into the vacant chair.

"He plans to let her go, release her, as you say. He's going to be noble and pretend he doesn't really love her. But she's on to him, of course, and only pretends to agree to a breakup."

"Uh huh. Interesting. Predictable but interesting, I suppose."

"So he makes up a story about falling in love with someone else. A nurse maybe."

"Uh huh. Some old maid maybe who has a fetish for grotesque invalids."

She ignored me. "Someone who cared for him in the hospital in England."

"Of course."

"And when he tells her, Charmaine pretends to go along. But she knows he's only being noble, and she never believes it for a moment."

"So what happens when he leaves the hospital?"

She kicked a slippered toe at my manuscript. "That's all wrong. You've got it all mixed up. She can't go off and leave him there. That's no good at all. I hate it."

"You'd give it a sappy, Hollywood ending?"

"She only pretends to go, and when she sneaks back around to the front where he's sitting on a lawn chair to take the sunshine..."

My stare was fixed on the delicious swells of her body straining against the blue silk rippling like ocean waves. "Let me guess. She sees him break down and cry."

"He *starts* to cry. Yes. He watched her walk away and thinks she's gone forever."

"But she comes back."

"Yes. And she stands there watching him cry, and then she begins to cry, too." Delilah's face drew into a pained pout, and tears glistened in those wounded, sad eyes. "And when she can no longer stand the sight of him suffering, she rushes out and embraces him." Her arms clenched her shoulders as she shuddered into a climactic finale. "It's the most romantic, saddest ending in the world, Ethan." Her eyes opened and flashed at me. "And it's absolutely realistic."

"I suppose it could be. In a Hollywood tearjerker."

"It *has* to be that way. I hate the way you've written it. It's no good at all. She wouldn't ever leave him. No one will want to read the book if you leave it that way."

"So you think I should rewrite it?"

She flipped the hair back from her face. "I don't care. It's your book. I suppose you'll write it the way you want to no matter what I say."

"No, I won't. I want you to feel it's right, Delilah."

"Well, I don't like your ending. It just isn't right."

"Okay. I can change it."

She crushed her cigarette butt in the hula girl ashtray and nudged my bedspread with a knee. "You got awfully wet, didn't you?"

"I should hang these things in the bathroom to dry out."

She reached over and scooped up my shirt and jacket. "Where did you go today on your day off?"

"I just had a few errands to run."

"I planned on your helping me with the Christmas decorations."

"I'm sorry."

"I fixed some Tom and Jerry batter." She hugged my wet clothes to her bosom and splotched the silk nightgown. "I wanted the house to be just right for Lionel when he gets here. It'll be important for him to see everything is the way he remembered it before he went away."

"I suppose."

"He always wanted the tree to be by a window so he could see it from the street as he went out. He used to get up on the ladder and hang boughs from the eaves with big, red bows tied on. The whole house used to look like a giant Christmas package." She smiled wistfully.

"It looks swell, Delilah. I'm sure he'll be pleased."

"I hope so. I've worked so hard on everything. Tomorrow, I'm going to bake a lemon meringue pie. That's his favorite."

"I know."

She dropped my clothes on the bed, snapped her head around and nailed me with a piercing stare. "How do you know that? What do you know about Lionel?"

"Nothing. I just noticed you baked lemon meringue pies, and you said once it was his favorite."

"I did?"

"Yes. I'm sure you did."

"Oh."

"I helped myself to one, remember?"

"I was thinking I should invite Cody and Susie for Christmas dinner, but since Lionel's been away for so long, maybe we should just keep it for the two of us. What do you think, Ethan?"I took hold of her shoulders. "Delilah, when is he coming home exactly?"

"What?"

"Tell me when."

"Christmas. Christmas day he'll be back in Hawaii. Didn't you see the telegram he sent? He's getting assigned to a new ship. He'll be home just after New Year's. I'm going to bake a ham for him. With all the trimmings, too."

"Did Lionel send that telegram, Delilah?"

"What do you mean?"

"Are you absolutely certain in your heart that Lionel is coming home?"

She shook me away. "Don't be silly. Of course, he is. Do you think I'd go to all this trouble if he weren't?"

"Delilah," I murmured. She wouldn't let me intrude on her fantasy. Not an inch. "Are you sure this is all real and not just what you're hoping?"

"Why would you ask such a stupid question anyway?"

"I talked to someone who told me about the *USS Hammann*." She froze for only an instant, then jerked away and walked toward the door. My voice slowed her movements but did not stop her escape. "He said the ship went down coming back from the Battle of Midway."

"No! That's not true. Lionel's ship was in Australia being repaired. It was struck by a Jap torpedo, but it didn't go down. It was one of the lucky ones. It made it back to port. Now he's sailing home, and the ship will be as good as new. But he's getting a new ship after they get back to Pearl. And another stripe on his sleeve. He's very excited about the next assignment."

"Delilah, for God's sake."

She shoved me back and opened the door. "Don' t talk to me about things you know nothing about, Ethan."

"Delilah, wait a minute."

"You know nothing about life, nothing about love and absolutely zero about me."

"Don't go. Can't you stay and talk to me?"

"Your ending is all wrong. If you leave it that way, the book is ruined."

"I'll change it, if you like."

"If *I* like? Are you writing it for me or for yourself?"

"I wish I knew."

"Well, suit yourself then." She closed the door and was gone.

"Dammit." She was as difficult to hold onto as a greased pole. Just when I thought I had secured a good grip, she would slip from my grasp.

I lay down on my bed and laid the pack of Luckies on my belly. Should I confront her with what I had learned from Cody and make her admit the truth? Or was she too far past the truth to recognize reality anymore? If I closed in on reality, would she slide off into insanity and leave me completely? I had no idea what I ought to do.

I smoked and wondered if I was wasting my time trying to bring her into the real world, destroy her fantasy of Lionel and a romance she was unable to see through to a happy ending. I wanted to know more before I made up my mind. I wanted to meet the real Charmaine for myself and talk to her if she'd see me. It was macabre, but I knew I had to get up to Tacoma and find out for myself where the dream ended, and the nightmare began. I could talk to Francie, and she would understand this insanity as well as anyone could. She might even be able to give me some advice. If anyone could help me, Frances could. She knew about love, real love and how ephemeral and precious it was in the scheme of things. I would pour out my heart to Frances and ask for her advice. And maybe for the first time in a long time, I would listen.

# Twenty–Seven

====================

**The** two of us sat across the kitchen table, munching on Saltine crackers and sipping tomato soup Frances had warmed on the stove. Outside it was drizzling a cold rain, splashing in puddles in the pockmarked street in front of the apartment building. My sister Frances stared out at the dreary afternoon and watched as a fresh shower drenched a straggly rhododendron leaning against the rain spout.

"You know, Nattie," she sighed wistfully, wagging her spoon in the direction of the window, "I didn't even cry at the wedding."

I nibbled the corner off a cracker. I had cried shamelessly as Carla stood in front of the Justice of the Peace and repeated her vows in a voice barely above a whisper. As her nervous groom slipped the plain, gold band on her finger, all I could think of was how Pop would be sniffling into his tablecloth-sized handkerchief and repeating over and over how his little baby girl was leaving him forever. He took all our partings personally.

"I just kept thinking about how happy she was, how radiant she looked." She turned toward me. "Don't you think so, Nattie?"

"Uh huh." I swallowed and reached for my coffee. "She looked real nice, Francie. She was wearing Mom's gray coat, wasn't it?"

Frances nodded. "Something borrowed. Mama would have liked that. It was her favorite."

"She looked real nice."

"Something blue. She was wearing my sapphire brooch Aunt Phoebe gave me for my graduation."

"Uh huh."

"Something old. Something new."

"Uh huh." I washed down the chewy goo from another cracker and dunked a spoon in the soup. There were shreds of tomato skin floating in the foam. Frances had added fresh fruit to the pot just for me.

"I didn't do that, Nattie. I didn't pay that much attention, I suppose."

I had no idea where she was traveling with her reminiscence. I was slurping soup and counting the raindrops sliding down the windowpane.

"Something old. Something new. I was wearing a favorite old suit I bought on sale, lavender blue with white cuffs and a Buster Brown collar."

"You looked great, Sis." I smirked foolishly. We both knew I had no idea what she had worn.

"But there was nothing new. Nothing but the ring, and even that was old. It belonged to Walter's sister. She was a widow at twenty-two. Cancer. I should have realized."

"Uh huh."

Frances was staring out the window, looking beyond the soggy rhododendron bush, beyond the misty street to the stand of fir trees swaying in the storm. Her eyes clouded with a pearlescent veil that instantly made me think of Delilah.

"Sandra Pons. Did you know she died?"

"What?" She caught me with a soup dribble sliding down my chin.

"She had polio and died. She was only nineteen."

"Who died?"

She ignored my query and stared with rock-hard eyes through the splotched glass. "So young. She never had a chance to have even the little Walter and I had."

"Sandra? Do I know her?"

"I had nothing new. Nothing to continue the tradition. Nothing new to carry us forward, Nattie. It was just meant to be. Meant to be from the very beginning."

I started to speak but wisely held my tongue as I saw her expression fade away to one of complete remoteness. I could have been in Africa, and Frances could have been standing in the living room with Walter's arms wrapped around her, waltzing in a dreamy vision only her eyes could see. I put my spoon down and shivered. "Hey, Frannie," I whispered as I touched her forearm lightly. "You okay?"

She didn't answer. Her skin was as cold as the alabaster lamp on my father's roll top desk. Lifeless.

"Francie?" I pecked her cheek.

She blinked then and caught my stare. "Oh, Nattie, it was a nice wedding, wasn't it? Carla was a beautiful bride, don't you think? She's always been the prettiest one."

"She was a knockout, Sis."

She patted my hand affectionately. "Is your soup still hot?"

"It's fine."

Her fingers squeezed mine suddenly. "Nathan, are you alright? Tell me honestly how it's going."

"Fine. I'm great."

"Are you going to make it back to school for the spring term?"

"I think so."

"How's your research coming?"

"Okay." I lowered my eyes, caught in a harmless lie. Frances was never fooled. "I'm having a hard time completing the book, Fran. Maybe it's not what I should be doing right now. It seems like a helluva waste of time, doesn't it?"

"God, no. Why would you think that?"

"With everything else going on."

"Such as?"

"Goddam, Francie." I wiped my mouth and reached for a Lucky. "You and Walter and now Carla." I lit up and sucked in a reinforcing breath of tobacco smoke. "The war— all of it, I suppose."

"Oh, Nattie, grow up. Don't suppose for a minute that any of this has anything to do with you. Whether you get your doctorate or not, finish your book or not has nothing to do with any of the rest of this craziness."

"Look, Sis—"

She shushed me with a glower I had learned to respect. There were days past when it was preceded by a firm slap to my backside. "Don't wallow in a lot of trumped-up self pity and dawdle your life away looking for excuses not to succeed at something."

"Francie, dammit, I just don't know if this is important anymore, that's all I'm saying."

"What's changed? What are you really trying to say?"

God, I wanted to tell her all of it without being forced through a strainer, but the words were stuck in my throat. I smoked in silence and pretended to search for an insightful response. She zeroed in on my ambivalence with sisterly tact I loved her for.

"Nattie, it's that woman you're staying with, isn't it? The one we met at Pop's funeral?"

I didn't even need to muster a feeble nod. The blood began to drain from my face until I resembled the pallor of a fasting vampire. "Jesus, Fran. I feel godawful about this whole damned mess."

"Why?" Her voice lightened, and if I had the courage to meet her gaze, I would have seen the familiar twinkle in her eyes. "Love is wonderful and painful at the same time, Nattie. That's the way it's supposed to be."

"I'm not sure what it is. I'm just confused."

"Confused? About what? She's a beautiful woman, Nat."

"Older than I am." I looked up. "Quite a bit."

"So? What does that matter to anybody? Has Gladys said anything?" she asked suspiciously, rallying to my defense instantly.

"Not yet."

"Forget it. That's not important. Do you really love her a lot?"

I wanted more than anything to say yes, to admit what I could feel eating away at me and turning my heart to mush. But I couldn't get up the guts to answer honestly. "I don't know for sure, Francie."

"What's wrong? Is there someone else?"

"Yes." There was, wasn't there?

Her eyes narrowed. Frances braced herself in the chair and threw her shoulders back. "Nathan, Gladys will have a stroke if she finds out you're involved with a married woman, but, if this is the one you want, if you really love her, then I'm on your side. Remember that, Nattie. I'm always on your side."

"It's not that, Fran. She's not married. She's a widow."

"Oh."

"That's the problem." I rubbed her cheek tenderly. My heroine. My defender. I loved her so much. It was the right thing to be here in her kitchen, sipping her homemade soup and exposing the raw, unpolished parts of my psyche for her wise ministrations. "He's dead. His ship went down in '42, and she's still mad about him."

She expelled a sigh that echoed my pain. "Oh, God, Nattie. I'm so sorry."

"I know."

"I'm just so sorry for you." She leaned across the table and hugged me with both arms. "It's just so sad it has to be this way, isn't it?" She directed her gaze through the window. "What's all this madness going to accomplish? So many maimed, killed, displaced, damaged beyond repair in so many cases. Nations, populations wrenched from their foundations? Why does the world tolerate suffering, destruction, evil? What right do a few mad dictators have to ruin all we've built and cherished? Is there an answer to any of this, Nattie?"

I could only shake my head and shut my eyes to keep the memory of all this world war had caused from flooding my mind. "I don't know, Sis. So far, all Life has taught me is that there aren't any answers. Only questions."

"Walter and I had so much for a little time. Maybe that's enough. So many others have nothing."

"You know, Fran, the way you feel about Walter... Oh, shit. You understand what I'm trying to say, don't you? I don't want to make you hurt, Fran. Honestly, I..."

"I know. I saw an article the other day, and I thought how lucky I was. The letter he sent. It expressed what he was feeling in his heart because he knew he wasn't coming back. Anyway, the article said that the air force crews that went down over the Channel had a good chance of making it if they were wounded. It's the salt water. It helps them to heal and reduces shock. The hospitals are using salt water tubs to treat the burned victims now. It lessens the pain. Treating severely burned victims will be changed for the better after the war. So what happened to Walter and to so many young fliers served a purpose somehow. Don't you think so? Everything does seem to have a purpose in a way." She reached over to pat my hand. "The pain never goes away, Nattie. The wound never heals. She'll love him forever. And not as she might come to love you. You'll get old, lose your luster." She tousled my hair and laughed. "You'll turn into a pot-bellied, thin-haired, cranky old codger someday just like Pop."

"Thanks a lot, Sis."

"But he'll always be the same for her." The eyes grew distant again and misted up. "Always. He'll never age, never stop loving her, wanting her as much as he did the day he went away. It'll always be like that for her, won't it?"

"Something like that."

"Poor Nattie."

"Yeah."

"Tell me about him. What was he like?'

"Her husband?"

She rested her chin in the palm of her hand. "Yes. Tell me about him. What was his name?"

"Lionel. He was an officer in the Navy, and his ship was hit by a Jap torpedo. I guess he was down in his bunk sleeping when it was hit, and by the time he woke up, the ship broke in half, and he went down with it. The guy where I work at the hotel knew all about it."

"How sad."

"He was coming home for a leave at Christmas, and he never made it back. She was crazy about him. She sort of stole him away from his first wife."

"What do you mean 'sort of stole him'?"

"He separated from his wife after an argument, and Delilah kept pulling on him, threatening to kill herself if he didn't come back, leave his wife and kid for her."

"He had a child?"

"A little girl."

"Oh, Nattie, that's wicked, isn't it?"

I ground the butt of my cigarette into my saucer. "She was in love. Desperately, madly, insanely in love. I can understand that. A little."

"I suppose. So he left his wife and little girl for her?"

"Finally."

"And then he goes off and gets himself killed. How awful for her."

"She hasn't been able to handle it, Fran."

"Who could with something like that hanging over you? Can you imagine the incredible guilt she must feel on top of the unimaginable pain of losing him, the person she sacrificed so much to have?"

"She hasn't gotten over it, the shock, I suppose."

"No wonder."

"What I'm trying to say is she's just not able to accept it."

"What do you mean? Is she still too guilty to let herself love you, Nattie? Is that it?"

"No." I sighed and closed my eyes. I couldn't get this out and look my sister in the eye. "She's telling me that he's coming home for Christmas. She bakes pies for him just like he's going to walk up to the front door and ring the bell any day." I checked my sister's expression to see if she was taking this any better than I had.

"What do you mean exactly?"

"Delilah still thinks he's coming home for his Christmas leave just as if the ship hadn't sunk to the bottom of the ocean. She thinks he's coming home, Fran."

"She really believes it?"

"She even sent herself a phony telegram to make it look like he was on his way home from Pearl."

"Oh, lord, how sad. How incredibly sad."

"I can't compete with a ghost, can I?"

"No, of course you can't. But you can't let her bury herself like this, Nattie. You have to help her get over this so she can live again. You have to do it."

"Me? She won't even let me talk to her about it. She doesn't want to hear the truth."

Frances leaned back and crossed her arms in a defensive gesture. "Nathan, do you think she's had a nervous breakdown, gone crazy? Is that what all this is about? The way you've been creeping around, moping. You think she's hopelessly insane, is that it? A basket case who's going to end up in the funny farm, right?"

What more could I say to rebut such simple logic? Of course, that was exactly what I thought. And it had to be true, didn't it? "Well, for crissakes, Sis. She's making up stories about this guy, living in the past and pretending none of this is real. What else would you call it?"

"She's suffering, that's all. I can understand that. There are days when I don't want to get up in the morning and face the fact that I'll never see Walter again. And there are nights when I dream he is still alive and coming home to me. It's just the mind trying to heal the pain, Nat."

"I know that, but Christ, you don't pretend he's coming home on the next train. Set a place at the table every night? What am I supposed to do?"

"If you love her, then you're the only one who can help her, Nattie."

"I don't have any idea if *anybody* can help her, Fran. Maybe she needs a straight jacket."

"You wouldn't be talking to me like this if you didn't know you had to do something to help her. Isn't that true? Let's be completely honest with one another, Nat."

We looked into each other's eyes. "But I swear to God I don't know how, Fran. I can't get through to her. I can't talk to her about this."

"Have you tried?"

"More or less."

"What the hell does that mean? Have you asked her directly to tell you about her husband and how he died?"

"God, no. I can't talk to her like that."

"Well, you'll have to. She's drowning, Nattie, and you have to be the one to throw a line out for her. If you really care for her, you'll find a way." She patted my arm. "You'll find a way, Nattie. We all need help in learning to let go, to say good-bye."

Her soft eyes were moist with tears too proud to roll down her cheeks. I wanted to believe in everything she said, thank her for her compassion and tell her I would do anything to find a key to unlock Delilah's tortured soul, but instead, I just picked up my spoon and buried it in the blood-red soup.

"Fran, she did something really rotten, stealing Lionel away from his wife and kid."

"I agree."

"It gets worse."

Fran folded her napkin and sat back. "Go on. I'm ready for anything now."

"Well, when she threatened to kill herself unless he came back to her, his wife tried to kill herself instead and burned the house down."

Her hands flew up to shield her face from the ugly picture I'd painted for her. "Oh, no, Nat! This is really wicked."

"She burned herself up pretty bad, I guess. Delilah's brother-in-law says she's a cripple now."

"How awful. Oh, God... not *burned*." Her eyes closed.

"Sorry." I had wounded my sister when I could have censored my story to spare her flashbacks of Walter's suffering. "I didn't mean to stir up any bad memories, Sis."

"Well we can't be pussy-footing around the facts all our lives, can we? So... he married her after that?"

"Then he went overseas and didn't come back. She lives this weird sort of fantasy about his coming home any day now like everything is okey dokey. Crazy."

"She can't accept any of it, the guilt, the loathing she must feel for herself."

We sat for a few moments more while I drained my bowl and listened to the sounds of the rainwater tapping against the gutter.

"What are you going to do, Nattie?"

"I want to find his first wife Charmaine. She's here in Tacoma in some convalescent hospital. I don't know why exactly. It's probably a mistake, but I want to talk to her."

Frances slowly nodded her qualified assent. "Be careful, Nattie. Try not to open new wounds in healing the old ones. Do you know how to find her?"

"All I know is that she's somewhere here in Tacoma."

Frances got up and gathered the dirty dishes. "Her name is Charmaine?"

"Charmaine Goodknight. And she's blind."

"I'll talk to Gladys. The Doctor can make some calls for you and find out where she is."

"God, Fran. Is this what I really ought to do?"

She stacked my bowl in the sink and reached for the dishcloth. "Nattie, you love this woman, don't you?"

"I must be crazy, too."

"Then you have to find this Charmaine and talk to her. I'll help you." She thrust a dishtowel at me. "And don't say a word to Gladys."

"Not a word. On my sacred honor."

"You have to have faith, Nattie. Love conquers all."

"How can you say a thing like that?" I shot back angrily.

She pulled her lips back in a wispy smile that warmed my heart. "Nattie, I still have Walter—*here*. In my heart. Nothing can ever take that away from me. For as long as I live, I have that. Just do what you have to do, Nathan. Don't worry about the rest."

She turned the tap on full force and pretended not to notice the tears filling my eyes.

# Twenty–Eight

========================

**Frances** and I sat together in the backseat of the taxi and peered out the window at the clapboard house with wisteria vines hugging the porch. The narrow windows were as gray and forbidding as the cast-iron sky overhead. Paint scales marred the porch rails where red and white ribbons were strung in a festive salute.

I shoved some bills at the driver and opened the door for my sister.

"This can't be it," I mumbled, taking Fran's arm as we crossed the street and stood looking up at the ramshackle porch and dirty window shades. "It can't be this bad for god's sake. I'm pretty sure Lionel had money. They wouldn't let Charmaine rot away in a dump like this."

Frances nudged my side with a gloved hand. "Come on, Nattie. I bet it's nicer inside."

"Are you kidding?" I muttered, following her up the creaky steps. "This place looks like it was decorated by Bela Lugosi."

"Don't be so pessimistic. There's no sense in putting money into the exterior with the war on. There's lots of other things more important than new shutters and fresh paint."

"I'll say. Like indoor plumbing and hot water."

"Remember she's been here for nearly four years. And it's close to the hospital which must be convenient since she probably goes back for surgery to remove excess scar tissue from time to time. Thank god Walter was spared all that."

"Yuck." I kicked aside a soggy newspaper lying like a dead carp against the screen.

"Be kind, Nattie," she reminded me as I rang the bell.

We waited. Traffic passed by in the street. A couple of kids came out in the side yard and started tossing a baseball back and forth. Finally, we heard footsteps, and then the door opened, and a gray-haired woman with glasses as thick as Coke bottles stared out at us.

"Yes? Can I help you?"

"We're here to see Mrs. Goodknight." Frances nodded and clutched her bag as we stood there like a couple of Meier and Frank mannequins on display. "May we come in, please?"

The bug eyes looked us over carefully. "Say, is that cashmere?" she asked, ogling Frances' coat.

"Why, yes."

"Nice. I wisht I could have one like that. Come on in." She swung the screen door aside and let us step inside.

My nostrils automatically contracted as the pungent aroma of stale tobacco smoke, human urine, feces and grease assaulted us. The lace curtains were yellow with age and neglect, but Frances had been partially right. It was better inside than out. At least, they had made an attempt to brighten the place. There was a passable Christmas tree in the parlor, dried pussy willows and twigs standing in a cut-glass vase on a bureau in the foyer where candles lit the dining room. Half a dozen people were seated around the table, some in wheelchairs, some with canes propped against their knobby knees, most with vacant-eyed stares, slack jaws and withering jowls hunched over bowls of what looked like green gruel.

"You wanna see Charmy?"

"Beg your pardon?" Frances asked as several grizzled heads turned to take in my sister's classy figure.

"Missus Goodknight. Charmaine. She's upstairs. She don't get down to supper."

"Oh."

"Come on this way. Mind the rail. The carpet's worn some. Don't want you trippin'."

"Thank you." Frances gave me a reassuring nod as she started up the stairway with the shuffling crone in the lead.

Upstairs we started down a long hallway broken by a series of green doors opening onto the main corridor. The walls were bare. No pictures. Nothing but puke-green plaster and plated, gaslight sconces converted to hold naked electric bulbs. We trod on behind our sluggish guide, turned around a bend, maneuvered by a hissing radiator and stopped in front of an alligatored door.

"Here she is. Talk up a little. Charmy don't hear too good." She winked at Frances. "Course, sometimes she just don't feel like hearin'."

"Thank you." Frances knocked on the door as the old woman clomped back around the bend and left us.

We stood at the door. Kids yelling outdoors, a dog barking, some poor soul wailing and another wheezing and hacking filled the intermittent silence while we waited for Charmaine to answer.

Frances raised her hand to knock again, but I brushed her arm away and grabbed the knob. "Mrs. Goodknight?" I opened the door and went in. She was sitting with her back to us, facing a streaked window with a ragged shade. In the yard below we could hear the sounds of two kids playing catch. "Pardon me, are you Charmaine Goodknight?"

"Who in hell are you?" Her voice startled me. It was a clear and deep contralto with no tinge of disability. Dietrich without a face. I could see only her silhouette, light brown hair frizzed over her ears and broad shoulders covered with a maroon, knit shawl.

"We're friends of Cody's," I lied a little uneasily.

Frances closed the door behind us. "Mrs. Goodknight, my brother's come all the way up from Portland to talk to you."

"You don't say so. What about? You from some charity group wanna give me another goddam pair of slippers?"

"No, Ma'am. I'd like to talk to you, that's all." I fumbled with my hat in both hands.

"What about?"

"About you, I suppose."

Frances shot a look of disapproval my way. "Mrs. Goodknight, the truth is my brother came all this way to talk to you about your accident."

I heard an exhalation and saw the shoulders sag. "Who are you? "You from the insurance company? I already told that bastard not to bother coming around again."

"No, Ma'am. My name's Nathan McCarthy. This is my sister Mrs. Clippendale."

"Never heard of you. Why'd that old bat let you in?"

"We're friends of Cody's, Lionel's brother."

Slowly, a pair of gnarly knuckles groped with the wheels of the chair, and she rotated around to face us. With the light behind her, we couldn't make out her physical features. Only a bent silhouette blocked our view through the unwashed window.

"Did Cody send you?"

"Oh, no," Frances said, stepping forward. "My brother came of his own accord, Mrs. Goodknight. I understand you've been through a terrible ordeal, but Nathan needs your help, if you'll give it."

"For what? I don't have any money left. Jesus, can't you tell by looking around? This is not exactly the Ritz, is it?"

"Mrs. Goodknight, please, just let Nathan talk to you for a few minutes. He needs your help," Frances pleaded my case.

"What kind of help?" she snarled, not seeming a bit inclined to do anything for anybody.

Before I could muster my senses enough to be polite, Frances was edging closer to the dark shadow in the wheelchair. My sister was never afraid of anything or anybody. "Nathan lives in Portland. He rents a room from Delilah Goodknight. I have to tell you, Mrs. Goodknight, that he's very worried about her."

"*Delilah*?" she spat. "Who in hell are you anyway to come barge in here?"

"Please, Mrs. Goodknight, we don't mean to upset you."

"The hell you don't. Get out of here." She jerked her chair toward Frances. "Who asked you to come here anyhow? Did Cody send you?"

"No. Nathan came by himself." Frances backed up only slightly and held her ground.

"Look here," I came to my sister's defense. "There's no cause to be so damned disagreeable. Everybody else is downstairs eating supper, enjoying the Christmas decorations and getting ready to have some eggnog, and here you are all alone up here like a hermit. I came all the way up from Portland just to talk to you. It took me a while to find you in the first place."

"Who asked you?"

"Nobody. But it's important. Whether you like it or not—hell, even if *I* don't like it much, it's important. I need to talk to you. Now will you let us stay or not?"

There was a pause. I could smell the stench of old ashtrays, mold and antiseptic that made my nose sting.

"Gimme a cigarette." She rolled the chair away from the window glare and lifted a stub in front of her. "Light me a smoke."

I reached for my Luckies and dropped the pack on the floor. Frances picked it up. My eyes were frozen on the creature seated in the wheelchair while my sister lit a cigarette and placed it between the gaping orifice in the lower part of the "face" that yawned open to suck the smoke. The lips were burned away, the flesh shiny and raw as a boiled scallop so that the exposed teeth gaped like a skeleton mask. Charmaine was bald and wore on her shiny skull a cheap wig slightly askew and as bushy and silly as Harpo Marx's frizzy locks. There were no ears on her head only a glob of flesh dripping from one side of her jaw like candle tallow. The orbital sockets of her skull were little more than fibrous pits where once human eyes had resided. What I could see of her neck and arms was nearly normal except for the hand. There were no fingers on the right hand. The left arm ended above the wrist, and ropes of scar tissue encircled her bones like gristle bracelets. I felt faint. My lord, had Walter looked this bad? The revelation of suffering, horror and revulsion almost sank me to my knees. What was the sense of living encased in such a misshapen, ugly wreck hidden away from a world which undoubtedly recoiled as much as I had encountering this visage straight from a hellish nightmare?

I thought of Frances then and turned to check her reaction. To my amazement, she was kneeling beside the wheelchair, tenderly tucking the shawl around Charmaine's shoulders and adjusting the Lucky Strike in the scarlet wound below the ugly hole that was her airway.

"Can we bring you something? I saw they're having eggnog downstairs in the dining room," Frances offered kindly.

Charmaine took a deep drag on the cigarette. "I hate that shit. Have you got any drinking whiskey?" The blind eye holes aimed toward me.

Frances stood up. "No. But we can get you some. What would you like, Mrs. Goodknight?"

"Canadian bourbon. Bring me some ice, too."

Frances motioned for me to go. "My brother can run to the store and get it for you right away."

"Why don't you go, Missy, and let me and Nathan here chat for a while?"

"Alright."

"Get a couple pints. I can slip those under the mattress easier."

"I'll be back as soon as I can. Is there a liquor store close by?"

"Ask the old windbag downstairs. It's about four blocks from here. They know what I want."

"Alright then. You stay, Nattie and talk. I'll get the whiskey."

"CC, Honey," she hacked with a stump aimed at the doorway.

"Canadian Club." Francie turned and hurried out the door.

"Well," she snarled. "Sit down. Turn on the light if you want. Doesn't matter to me, of course. Night and day—all the same to me."

"Thanks. It's okay." I sat down on the bed. There was a heart-shaped pillow on the spread. The walls were nude except for an oil likeness of the Virgin Mary staring down with a motherly smile. "How long have you been here, Mrs. Goodknight?"

"Four years in April. Call me Charmy."

"I understand your daughter lives here in Tacoma, too."

"What do you know about Dottie?"

"Cody told me about her, that's all."

"She lives with my folks in Bellevue. I see her one weekend a month. About all I can manage. I get tired out coping with a kid her age." There was a deep rattle in her throat, and I realized she was laughing. "Runs me ragged after a few hours. Hard to stand the energy kids have. Talks a blue streak."

"You must be very proud of her."

"She's quite a dancer. Ballet and tap. She's in the Nutcracker at her school this year."

"Oh."

"What the hell do you want from me anyway?" she rasped.

I looked away to divert my eyes from the faceless creature sucking on the cigarette. I couldn't help it. It was a grotesque gesture I would rather not have to look at, a fleshy orifice puffing hard on the glowing Lucky, smoke seeping out of the single nostril like some misshapen dragon's snout. "God, this is hard for me to say."

"Get on with it for crissakes. So long as you're not here for some goddam charity crusade or prayer group wanting to save my sorry soul."

"Nothing like that. It's worse."

Another gruff chortle filled the room. I lit a Lucky for myself.

"Nothing's worse than sitting here helpless when these preachers and do-gooders get ahold of you and want to preserve your soul for eternal salvation." She laughed again. "So what's your connection to Cody?"

"None really. Except for Delilah. I rent a room in her house."

"You're a boarder with Delilah, huh?"

"Yes."

"And you're here to cure some sick curiosity? Is that it for crissakes?"

"I did hear about your accident from Cody."

"*Accident*?" She shifted her weight in the chair and snorted a curl of bluish smoke toward me. "Is that what she calls it? An accident, huh? A goddam tragic accident?"

I picked up something unexpected in her sarcasm. This was not a helpless survivor, a suicidal victim done in by her own hand. This was something else. "I heard you set the house on fire in an attempt to kill yourself."

Sputum and phlegm gurgled deep down in her chest as she laughed so hard the wheelchair spokes vibrated. "Ha! That's rich. Really rich!"

"It wasn't an accident then?"

Her stump waved wildly in the air. "It was premeditated murder is what it was for crissakes! The bitch meant to kill us all in our beds, me, Dottie *and* Lionel. Are you some kind of a total fool or just plain stupid?"

"What are you saying? Delilah tried to kill you?"

"Any fool can figure that out easy enough. Who else would want to burn the house down in the middle of the night? Look, Mr. McCarthy or whatever your name is."

"Nathan McCarthy."

"Do you think for one lousy minute I would ever want to risk hurting my own daughter? My only child? Hurt Dottie? What sense does that make?"

"Maybe you were depressed. Suicidal, not thinking straight."

"That's nuts. Lionel had come back to me, and I had everything I wanted—my little girl, my husband. He had come back home. Don't you understand? We were all curled up in bed when the damn fire started. I got up and went to get Dottie but didn't make it. Lionel got the baby out. I was trapped when the fire exploded right through the transom and set my hair on fire. Well, take a look at what's left of me for crissakes. You can see it burned me up like a campfire marshmallow."

"Mrs. Goodknight, I don't know what to think." I hung my head and puffed on my Lucky furiously, frustrated by the ring of truth and sanity in her voice.

"Doesn't take a genius to figure out who would want to do a thing like that. If she couldn't have him, she was going to make sure we couldn't either. I know it was her. So did Lionel."

"He knew?"

"He was afraid, I think. Afraid if he didn't go through with it and marry her she'd do something to Dottie. He knew he' be going overseas, and he couldn't stand the thought of leaving his baby girl with that crazy bitch stalking us night and day. Hell, I was already out of the picture. Nobody even expected me to pull through for over a year after the fire. I'd probably be better off dead. Except for one thing. It's what keeps me going, living like this. If you can call it living."

"That can't be true."

"Why not? You got something to tell me I don't know already? I'm staying alive to see that bitch burn in hell. She tried to kill us all, and she did this because Lionel came back to me. I'm the only witness now."

"You mean now that Lionel's dead?"

Her voice nearly broke. She looked down, and the wig slid to a stop on her forehead. "He *knew.* I know he knew the truth, but he protected her. He was afraid she'd do something to Dottie."

"I can't believe Delilah would do anything so evil, Mrs. Goodknight."

"You don't know her, Mr. McCarthy. She gets what she wants, and she wanted Lionel. But she didn't get to keep him did she? She didn't get to keep him after all."

"Mrs. Goodknight, tell me—"

"Charmy. I'm not Mrs. Goodknight anymore, not so long as she has his name. Call me Charmy."

"Charmy. Your brother-in-law said you were depressed over your husband's affair with Delilah and that you tried to kill yourself. You didn't mean to cause harm to anyone else, not your daughter or Lionel—"

She cut me off with a swipe of her stump. "That's bullshit! I was happy, truly happy for the first time in a long time. My husband had come back to us. Don't you get it? Lionel had chosen *us,* me and Dottie over her. He was home. I was happy. I had no reason to want to take my own life. That's crazy."

"Why didn't you tell everyone that?"

"I wasn't in a position to tell anyone anything for quite some time. They all expected me to croak. But I didn't. Because I was out of bed, in the hallway where the fire started, they all supposed I had gotten up and lit it, poured the gasoline on the floor and curtains. But I heard something that woke me up, and I wanted to go and check on Dottie. I smelled smoke, tasted it in my sleep. I got out of bed and tried to get to the baby. But I didn't make it. I was trapped in the hallway outside the bedroom. When the windows blew out, Lionel made it out of the bedroom and got to the roof. He pulled Dottie out through the upstairs window and climbed down a sycamore tree to the front lawn."

"Somebody poured gasoline in the house?"

"Damned right. I'll never forget the smell of it. It woke me up, I think. The fire started so fast one minute there was smoke and the sound of flames, and the next, the heat was racing like a forest fire, exploding windows and racing up the walls. It was just so overpowering. I never had a chance. One minute I was standing in the hallway in my nightgown, and the next my hair just caught fire, whoosh, and I was burning like a Roman candle."

"My God."

"I didn't pass out all the while I was on fire, burning up. I could smell my own flesh sizzling like pork fat in the fryer. I couldn't breathe it hurt so bad. The only reason I didn't get burned to a crisp on the spot is because the floor collapsed under me, and I fell down into the cellar and was covered up with debris. When the firemen pulled me out, they took me for dead."

"You're saying someone came into your house and deliberately set it afire knowing you were all inside asleep?"

"Not someone, McCarthy, for crissakes. Have you been listening to anything I've been saying? Lionel gave her up, turned her down and came home to us. He was at home with *me*. She couldn't stand that, losing him. She didn't want me to have him if she couldn't."

"You don't know for certain it was Delilah. You can't know that."

She shrugged. "I don't know Jesus Christ died on the cross either, do I? But that's what the Good Book says and what everybody tells me happened. Anybody with any brains knows what's common sense, don't they? You tell me, McCarthy. Who else would want to burn us up like that? Who?"

"Maybe it *was* just an accident then."

She sucked air like a blocked carburetor. When she spoke, the glowing tip of her Lucky bobbed up and down like a theater usher's baton. "Jesus Christ. You don't believe me. You can't figure anything out for yourself, can you? Gasoline doesn't get poured on the floor and drapes by accident, does it?"

"But they thought you were trying to kill yourself because you'd threatened to do it."

"What reason would I have to do that? And would I burn up my own house when I knew Dottie was asleep upstairs? What kind of monster do you take me for?"

"Not a monster. Maybe you were just depressed, temporarily out of your mind."

"Why would I be? I may be as crisp as an apple fritter, but I'm not crazy."

"All the stress and pain from Lionel's infidelity, the fear of losing him." The rationality of her argument was sinking in. I couldn't shake it. "Maybe that pushed you over the edge."

"You aren't listening. Lionel was back home with me, wasn't he? Where was Delilah, huh? Did you ask Cody where she was when my house was bursting into flames?"

"No, I didn't."

"Well, you can read the statement she gave to the police."

Of course, I would have to go back to the library and retrieve the newspaper accounts of the fire, see if I could find out what had happened on that night four years ago. Then I could come back with some rebuttal to drench this mad woman's twisted story.

"She told the police she was at Cody's playing pinochle with him and Susie. They swore under oath she was at their place the whole night, slept on the couch because it was too late for her to go back home."

"Cody swore she was with him all night?"

"Playing pinochle. Quiet, little family gathering."

"But why was she friendly with Cody and his wife? Didn't they see Delilah as a threat to your marriage? I'm afraid I don't understand."

She laughed with a crackle as scratchy as an old phonograph. "You don't know my brother-in-law, do you, McCarthy?"

"I've met him. I hitched a ride over to Astoria to talk to him."

Her whole body was shaking as she laughed at me. "Bet he told you how crazy his poor sister-in-law is, huh? Take pity on poor little, miserable Delilah, did he?"

"Sort of, I guess. Something like that."

"Well, you've been snookered, my boy. You just believe everything you're spoon-fed? Good thing you're not a sweet young thing or you'd have a helluva time keeping your legs crossed, wouldn't you, Honey? Hell, you'd fall for every sugary little word some liar like Cody whispered in your shell like ear, wouldn't you, Dearie?"

"Not at all. He understands how difficult it's been for Delilah to deal with losing Lionel, that's all."

"Sure, McCarthy. That's all he cares about, helping her through her grief. Look, why don't you get some straight answers as long as you're butting your nose into somebody else's business?"

"What do you mean exactly?"

She spat the butt of the Lucky onto the floor. "I'm only bothering to keep alive to see the day that bitch lands in jail. If you really want to talk to me, McCarthy, you come back here with some facts instead of gossip."

"So Cody is lying?"

"You figure it out. If you give a shit, you come back here with your facts straight, and I'll talk to you."

"You don't know why I came in the first place."

She snorted and maneuvered the chair back to the window. "Probably something to do with helping Delilah atone for her grief, some shit like that. She traps everybody in her sticky web, McCarthy. What'd you do? Fall for her?"

"In a way maybe."

She laughed. "You're a goddamn silly fool. Her specialty is entrapping witless suckers like you."

"I wouldn't call it entrapment."

"I like to hear the sounds of cars going by and the kids playing ball," she said in a whisper. "I suppose they told you I don't hear so well. Well, I hear what I wanna hear. And one thing I don't wanna hear is bullshit. I can hear you well enough. And you're being taken in just the way Lionel was."

"Mrs. Goodknight, I appreciate your taking the time to talk with me, but I hope you can—"

"You know what I wish the most?"

"Tell me."

"Seeing my daughter dance in her first toe shoes. Everybody says she's lovely, like a floating angel on the stage. I miss that. And being able to be with her, teach her how to frost a cake and baste a hem on her first party dress."

"Mrs. Goodknight, I really am sorry you—"

"She took all that away from me. Took everything away from me, but there's one thing I still have."

The door opened, and Frances came in with a paper sack in her hand. "I got a fifth and some ice from downstairs, Mrs. Goodknight."

Charmaine sighed, and if I could have seen her face, the rigid muscles around her slit of a mouth would have tried contracting in a macabre smile.

"She can hear just fine, and she still can't get it right. I said pint. So she brings me a fifth."

"Oh, I am sorry, Mrs. Goodnight. I asked for Canadian Club, and he just handed over a bottle, and I thought that—"

"Revenge, McCarthy. I intend to live as long as it takes to see her pay for her sins. As long as it takes."

Frances held up the bottle of bourbon and looked at me with a puzzled frown on her face.

When my sister and I waited for a cab outside, she grabbed my hand and squeezed.

"Oh, Nattie,, when I saw her... I mean *really* saw that poor wretch, it made me think..."

I squeezed back. "You don't have to—"

"No, it's alright. What I thought was Walter being like that. Blind, no fingers, terribly disfigured and crippled. I know in my heart now just how much he loved me to spare me all that pain every day of our life together."

"He was crazy about you, Sis. Even after all that, in the hospital, he was only thinking abut you."

She smiled at me. "Yes. It's true. I should quit feeling so sorry for myself and think of what a beautiful, noble, selfless person he was. And I wonder, Nat, could I have stood by him, done enough to help him live a life worth living if he came home to me like that?"

"Sure. You'd be a swell wife."

"Well, maybe not after a few years. We'd miss so much. I'd be a caretaker not a lover anymore. Neither of us would want that."

"Maybe not, but there's a lot of other things in a marriage." I knew that was mostly a lie. "You loved each other so much."

The taxi came around the corner, and Frances stepped onto the curb. "Who can say how much people love? Anyway, seeing Mrs. Goodnight made me think, and I don't fault Walter for that letter after today. I love him even more for it."

She waved, and the taxi stopped. She opened the door, climbed in and never said another word about the pain Walter's letter had caused or the shock of seeing Mrs. Goodnight. Just as she said that day—there is a purpose in everything.

# Twenty–Nine

==========

**The** ride back to Portland, sitting wedged in the back seat of an ancient Dodge sedan with a cranky baby and a wide-eyed four-year old, was one of the longest journeys of my life. I kept my eyes closed and my nostrils pinched tight, but still my space was filled with the stench of sizzling skin, acrid smoke and the pitiful wails of Charmaine as she struggled to escape the licking flames stripping her bones of charred flesh.

How could she accuse Delilah of something so deranged, the plot of a mad woman? It must have been hatched in Charmaine's delusional mind as she lay bound and frightened in a hospital bed facing the awful truth of her mutilation and failed marriage. As the painful days and nights merged, she must have agonized over the continual thoughts dogging her fevered mind imagining Lionel and Delilah together.

Of course, I tried to console my rampaging guilt. The works of an insanely jealous, suffering mind had conjured up this gruesome tale of murder and betrayal. None of it was true. None of it. And as soon as I got home and began to research the plain facts from the newspaper and police records, I would find, with a doleful sigh of sympathy, just how far a poor madwoman's mind could stretch to justify her suffering.

As the old car lurched around a slippery curve and tossed damp toddlers into my lap, I nodded imperceptibly. Of course. It all made perfect sense when I took the time to consider it carefully. Would Lionel's own flesh and blood, his brother Cody, embrace Delilah into the family, welcome her into their inner circle, if they had suspected her of any of this fiendish nonsense? Never. It was an impossible idea. An insurmountable fact which belied Charmaine's tragic account. The marriage must have been doomed long before Delilah took Lionel away from his wife. There was no other way to reconcile Cody's acceptance, even his tender regard and concern for his sister-in-law Delilah. Not to mention the extra groceries and Christmas ham.

I let my head fall back on the seat. Why had I allowed myself to become so upset by Charmaine's tortured tale anyway? Wasn't it obvious how she was consumed by revenge? Wasn't that a normal consequence of marital infidelity and divorce? Wouldn't any woman in Charmaine Goodknight's position hate with as much energy and venomous spite as she did? Wasn't I witness to what I should have expected if I'd given a moment's serious thought beforehand to our meeting?

By the time my highway benefactors let me out on the corner of Morrison and Park, I had myself convinced of the folly of my original disbelief. Certainly Charmaine Goodknight's horrible disfigurement and warped outlook on life had influenced my reaction to her ravings. That's all it was. Once I saw Delilah again and soaked up the loving energy of those fabulous eyes, I would sink into my familiar comfort zone. After all, I needed to keep focused on what I had wanted to accomplish from my meeting with Charmaine, a chance to help Delilah deal with Lionel's death, a way to help her heal the wounds and get on with her life. Which, I hoped enthusiastically, would include me now. Especially, since I felt ordained to be her savior. She was lucky I had gone to such lengths to discern the source of her misery. Now I was able to deal empathetically with her dilemma. Thank God for that.

I pulled the collar of my overcoat up around my ears and headed toward Broadway. The street of prewar days was glitzy now, looking cheap and seedy with its crowded bars, cinemas and cafes jammed with the war's reveling refugees. Servicemen, defense plant workers, hookers and shore patrols passed by at this time of night. I hurried, clutching my bag in one hand and waving a lit Lucky Strike Green with the other as I walked fast enough to cause a stitch in my side by the time I rounded the walk and spied the boarding house. There was a single light on, shining weakly from the sleeping porch on the first floor. Delilah must be there, smoking in the dark, listening to the Philco, dreaming her life away again with her misty stare fastened on Lionel's portrait.

As I climbed the porch steps and set my bag down in front of the locked door, I paused to hunt for my key. Perhaps, she was not alone. Maybe there was company with her tonight, the stench of cigar smoke, the tinkle of glasses, and the smell of bourbon flavoring the draft floating in from the leaky door to the kitchen where I would stand and spy. Not tonight. I was prepared to face her with the truth and heal her. Set her free I reassured myself as the key slipped in the lock, and the door swung open. I had never felt so confident of my chances. Delilah was surely going to be mine, falling into my arms with loving gratitude and moist kisses smothering my hungry lips. It would be a metamorphosis, a true-to-life enactment of the first love scene between my fictional Ethan and Charmaine.

By the time I put the bag down, shed my coat and walked through the darkened kitchen, I was almost bold enough to head out to the sleeping porch and snatch her into my arms, regardless of whether her company was flesh and blood or ghostly.

"Delilah?" I whispered at the doorway. Beyond the tip of my nose, all I could see was the pale, electric light striping a pattern on the rug, a pair of brown suede, platform pumps tossed in front of the wicker chair and a half-empty glass of whiskey with a crimson lip print. A cloud of pungent tobacco smoke hung like a cloud over the room and wafted through the screen. I shivered as a cold breeze blew in from outside and made the shades flutter.

"Delilah?" I whispered again, looking to my right. The Philco hummed. A pack of Camels lay opened on the table. The ashtray still glowed with fresh ashes. "Delilah, are you here?"

I heard a sound behind me and turned around.

"Who in hell are you, Bud?" He was taller than me with a chest like a fullback, a mean, square face with black eyes and uneven teeth. Nothing about him was friendly. I could feel my enthusiasm shrivel. "What're you doin' here?"

"I live here."

A pair of bushy eyebrows squiggled over the coal-black eyes. "You a boarder of Mrs. Goodknight's?"

"Yes." I put both hands in my pockets and took a quick breath. Gallantry gave way to desperation. "Who are *you*?"

He barely acknowledged me. His chin lowered slightly as he reached inside his jacket pocket and flashed a shiny bifold in my face. Before I could blink, the ID was back behind the serge suit and out of sight. "Name's Snelstrom. Northwestern Mutual Life."

"What are you doing here? Trying to sell insurance this late?"

"Not that kind of an insurance man. Special agent. Regional investigator. I'm here to see if Mrs. Goodknight left any incriminating statements behind in a case I've been looking into."

Suddenly, I felt my ears burning. I took my hands from my pockets and looked carefully around the room. "A this time of night? Does Delilah know you're here?"

He dismissed me with a shrug and walked back out to the kitchen. "She knows me, Bud. You better believe she knows me well enough."

"What the hell does that mean?" I was angrier at my own ignorance than his belligerent attitude. "What are you supposedly investigating?"

"There's no supposin' about it, Bud," he snarled. "You ever hear of the Oswego Fire Case a few years back?"

"What's that have to do with Delilah?"

"Our insurance company had the policy on the house, personal property, the automobiles. Worth over seventy thousand, my friend. That's a lotta dough."

"So?"

"It was arson, plain and simple. I've been working on the loose ends, you might say. And this case has plenty of loose ends. None you could give a rat's ass about."

"Look here, you smart bastard, I'm a friend of Delilah's. I want to know what in hell you're doing sneaking around her house at this time of night. And I don't give a goddam who you are or what you're investigating."

He buttoned his wrinkled coat and put a rain-spotted hat on his head. "You're a close friend?" He let the words slide off his fleshy lips with a salacious leer I wished I could have ignored. "A real *close* friend, are you?"

"You might put it like that." My fists balled at my sides. One punch at his prognathous chops, and I could imagine all the knuckles on my right hand smashed like Tinker Toys. "I'm gonna have to ask you to leave, Buddy," I growled in my most menacing tone.

He just shrugged. I wasn't much of a threat. "Don't get yourself in a sweat, Mac. If you're such a close, personal friend," his fat lips curled back in a sneer, "then I'm sure you know she tried to kill herself tonight. Can't stand the guilt, see. It's gettin' to her. Sooner or later she's gonna crack, and when she does, I'm gonna be there."

My eyes bulged. "Tried to what? When?"

"She threw herself down the fuckin' stairs, damned near broke her neck is what I hear."

"How'd you find out?"

"I got my sources, Friend. Ambulance from Providence took her up there not more'n a half hour ago."

"Jesus." I bit my lip.

"Guess she forgot to mention she's a nut case, huh? Cracking up?"

"Get the hell out of here," I shouted at him as I rushed by for the door. At some point, before I ran down the steps, I caught hold of my jacket.

Snelstrom stood out on the porch and raised a hand in my direction. "Tell her I'm still right here, Lover Boy. Right here in her damn kitchen. Sooner or later she's gonna have to own up to what she did, and I'm still gonna be right on her ass, Bud."

The nightmare pursued me as I ran. It was too much to think about all at once. All that stuck in my mind was the look on his face as he described Delilah hurtling down the steep stairway. My spit dried up. My heart was pounding. Fear ran through my guts like castor oil. It seemed to take hours to find a bus, transfer for the ride up Burnside Avenue and then the long walk up the hill to the hospital.

Panting, I waited for the night nurse to look my way. When she took notice of me and came closer, I could see she was only a civilian volunteer, not even a real nurse. The war was changing everything. "Ma'am, can you tell me what room Mrs. Goodknight is in?"

She moved in slow motion toward the patient registry. "Is she a recent admission?"

"Yes. Just tonight." I was still trying to catch my breath.

"Maternity or surgical ward?"

"What?" I panted, trying to read upside down and catch sight of Delilah's name.

A look of terminal boredom fell across her face. "Are you the expectant father, Sir?"

"No, goddammit. She was an emergency. An accident. She fell down the stairs."

"Oh. Let me see. Was she brought in by ambulance?"

"Yes, I think so."

She ran a finger down a page. "Oh, yes. Mrs. Goodknight was sent upstairs to radiography. Would you like to have a seat in the waiting room?"

"Can't I see her?"

"Are you a relative?"

The lie was spontaneous. "Yes."

"Her husband?"

"Fiancé. Please, tell me where she is."

"Doctors orders are blood relatives only." She gave me a quick once-over. "But I guess it'll be alright. Take the first elevator on your left. Go up to the third floor and check with the night nurse. She can direct you to the radiography department."

"Thanks." I dashed off for the elevator and squeezed in as the car jerked upward.

The nurse was squat and starched from her peaked cap to her prickly uniform skirt. She pointed down the hallway when I asked about Delilah. "Go right in, Mr. Goodknight. Your wife is resting now. Nothing's been broken. The doctor wants to keep her overnight to make certain there's no complications, and then I'm sure you can take her home."

"Thank you."

"Room 3B, Mr. Goodknight. Please, don't stay too long." The nurse smiled kindly and poked a thermometer in her starched pocket. "She's been asking for you. I'm sure she'll sleep better after seeing you."

I walked down the hall toward 3B. Asking for me? Nathan McCarthy? Or was she calling for Lionel? What difference did it make? I was real bone and blood come to hold her and keep her safe. Lionel was in a watery grave in the middle of the fucking Pacific Ocean. She really had no choice. It was me or nobody from now on.

"Hello," she whispered when I came in. There was an ugly swelling over her right eyebrow and a gash on her chin.

I crossed to her bed and took hold of the one hand outside the sheet. "You had me so worried. Are you okay?"

A weak smile stretched her bloodless lips. "Of course, I am. I'm fine really. It was such a silly thing to do. I guess I was lucky I didn't break my neck, wasn't I?"

"You certainly were." I kissed her cheek. She had tripped. How simple. How fucking normal to do what hundreds of people must do every week. All the rest of it—Special Agent Sam Snelstrom and his officious bullshit was just a smoke screen for the truth. Delilah was an incredibly beautiful, fragile woman who had been caught up in a tragic, bizarre accident compounded by the grief of losing her husband. And now all her enemies were crawling out of the woodwork to feast on her carcass. Thank God I was here to protect her from these miserable hyenas.

"Darling," she gushed happily, squeezing my hand in hers, "I'm so glad you came. I was afraid I'd miss you."

My heart leapt like a grasshopper at the mention of such an intimate term of endearment. Jesus, Mary and Joseph, I scolded myself. How could I have doubted her for even an instant?

"I just got back. When you weren't home, I didn't know what to think." I decided not to mention Snelstrom and his sleazy snooping.

"I wanted to come down to the station and meet you," she said with her eyes aglow.

"That's alright. I hitched a ride instead."

"Are you very tired, Darling?"

"I'm fine. I'm worried about you. That's all that matters."

She sighed and closed her eyes. "Now that you're home, I'm fine. I'm sorry to cause you all this fuss."

"I was so worried. Did you trip on something? I can tack down the carpet on the stairs."

She looked at me again and widened her mouth in a sweet smile. "I caught my heel in a frayed spot at the top step. Could you look at it for me, Darling?"

"Sure. You bet. Just as soon as I get home."

"It's those darn platforms, the brown suede. The ankle straps are loose. It's so silly."

"Don't even think about it."

Her eyes closed once more. "Oh, Darling, it's going to be so wonderful having you home again. Everything is going to be alright from now on, isn't it?"

"Of course, it is." I nibbled on her fingertips. My gut began to buzz with a swarm of miniature butterflies I tried not to notice. "I'm going to take care of you from now on."

"You've always taken care of me," she sighed. "But now that I've got you back home with me, I'm never going to let you go. Never, Darling. You're mine now." Another long sigh, and the eyes fluttered open for only an instant. "You're mine forever now, Darling. I'm never going to let you leave me again."

"Delilah, I won't leave you. Never, Darling," I whispered back, not certain she could still hear me.

"I knew you'd come home. I always believed you'd come back to me, Dearest. Tomorrow we can open our presents, can't we?"

I put my head down on her breast. "I just love you so much, so incredibly much."

"I know. I'm so sleepy now. I think they gave me a pill." She relaxed her grip on my hand, and her breathing deepened. Sleep took her away from me. I stayed there with my head nestled close under her chin, my hand holding on to hers and listened to the sounds of her breathing, oblivious to my presence, oblivious, in fact, to my existence.

# Thirty

========================

**I** sat slumped in the cushy club chair in my room. A half-spent Lucky drooped from my cracked lips. The smoke burned my eyes as I stared like a dead trout at the lines in the wallpaper. I had been sitting there smoking and arguing with my better reason all night. A shaft of light from the hallway slipped beneath my door and barely lit the carpet at my feet. I didn't even have the energy to get up and turn on the hula lamp.

You see, I kept trying to convince myself, it was easy, very simple really. First, there was no way she could have tripped on the stairs in her chocolate-brown, suede platform pumps, because I had seen them lying downstairs on the sleeping porch when I came home. With the whiskey and the dead Camels in the ashtray, I'd seen for myself all the signs of Delilah's slipping through another evening in her fantasy world. So I knew she had lied. She had not tripped on the stairs. Maybe she fell. Maybe something more sinister. Maybe Sneaky Snelstrom, Special Agent, was right. Maybe my darling was running away from something loosely described as truth.

I ground out my cigarette butt and reached for a match to light off another smoke.

That couldn't be a sustainable hypothesis. First place, Delilah wouldn't lie to me. She had no reason to. She trusted me to help her. Why would she lie about a simple accident?

I struck the match and held it so close to my face that I could feel the heat singe my eyelashes. "Damn!" I yelped, tossing the match into my ashtray. Self-abuse didn't help. I felt so lousy, so beat, so utterly assholian that there was no cure but a full rectal examination, a look way up into my slushy guts to see why it was I had inserted my head so far up my posterior that I could no longer see light in the dark tunnel of love.

Okay, I admitted. Delilah had lied to me. She had not tripped on the stairs. She had taken a flying, lizard leap off the landing and tried to smash her way into oblivion. And at no time had she ever wasted a single iota of time considering my feelings, including me in her universal consciousness at all. Face it. I was fly shit on the window of her life. Maybe even less than that.

The plain truth was that Delilah couldn't face up to the fact that Lionel was never coming home, that she had sacrificed so much to have him, and now he was gone. She had wagered her entire stash, played her trump card, raised the pot and come up a loser. No wonder she was nuts.

At the hospital, while I was gushing like a lovesick puppy, she was slipping away into her dream world without me. She had looked up and conjured a handsome Lionel at her bedside, fresh from Pearl with a sea bag in one hand, perhaps. Not Nathan McCarthy, earnest but boring graduate student resident of her upstairs room. She was playing roles once more—Charmaine and Ethan. I was nobody. Nathan McCarthy didn't even exist in her little melodrama.

An hour went by. I started thinking about the novel. She was making it a replay of her affair with Lionel, a twist of characters, and this time the story would have a happier ending. As if my writing a life for the fictional characters would change her reality. Then I thought about Cody Goodknight, the big-muscled brother-in-law with hands like a butcher and a honey-soft voice who looked at Delilah with such gentle, Cocker Spaniel eyes. I felt a rush of nausea weaken my bowels. I didn't want to think about this part. It was just too goddam sick to consider. But I was thinking ahead of myself, and in another few minutes, I could imagine Delilah being crushed in Cody's sweaty arms, his flushed face pressed against her cheeks. It had to be, didn't it? There was no other way, was there? It wasn't logical. If Snelstrom's implied tale of sordid scandal was bad, what did I have to offer in rebuttal? Did Susie know that Cody and Delilah were lovers? When did they become lovers? Was it before she married Lionel? After? Before the fire? After Lionel went overseas? Was it adultery? Incest? Or just some sleazy shack-up before she took up with Lionel? None of it was any good. Not anything I wanted to seriously consider.

I could see the scene as plain as day in the darkness of my room. Delilah defenseless, miserable in her loneliness for Lionel. Did he forget to write as often as he should? Did she lay in bed at night and cry herself to sleep, afraid he would never come back to her? Was some sonuvabitch like Snelstrom hounding her, accusing her of something she didn't do but maybe had fantasized about in some wild, petulant daydreams when she thought she was losing Lionel to his wife and child? When did Cody take advantage of my angel and get into her drawers? The bastard. The lying sonuvabitch. He must have played on her vulnerability. That was my best explanation.

I suppose the best excuse I came up with that night was thinking how guilt-ravaged Delilah must have been when she found out about the fire and realized that at the same moment Lionel had been fighting to save his life and rescue their child, Delilah had been in bed with his brother. That would certainly drive anyone insane. No wonder she had to take strangers to her bed, drink herself to sleep at night. It was the only way she could blot out the ugly memories and ease the guilt.

By the time the sun poked through the blinds, I figured I had it all sorted out. And none of it made me stop loving her, believing in her. I wanted her that much. She was the embodiment of all my youthful fantasies and aspirations. She was all I wanted. All I was convinced I was entitled to have in this crazy, fucked up world. If I couldn't have Delilah, save her from herself, then I didn't want anything else. Not graduate school, not my doctorate, my novel, Roman History, teaching—nothing. All I wanted was this one woman so wonderfully, tragically, magically insane.

I fell asleep in the chair and woke up with a stiff neck, yellow nicotine stains on my fingers, a thudding headache, scratchy throat and ashes on my trousers. I splashed water in my face, pulled off my shoes and socks and fell into bed. I didn't bother to wake up until three o'clock in the afternoon when my door opened, and Delilah Goodknight walked in. She was wearing blue slacks, a plaid shirt tied in a knot over her navel and a turban. She began to gather up my dirty linen.

"Are you okay?" I mumbled, only half awake. "When did you get home?"

She never even acknowledged my stare as she cleaned the sink, stuffed my soiled towels in her bag and hung fresh linen on the rack. "Aren't you sleeping in awfully late?"

"I didn't sleep too well last night. I was worried about you, Delilah."

She whipped her head around and fastened the swollen eyes on mine. "Call me Charmaine, Ethan. You know I don't like it when you call me Delilah."

"Are you alright?" I asked, amazed at how she seemed untouched by her dramatic brush with death only the day before.

"Of course, I am. Why wouldn't I be?" She looked as unconcerned as a streetcar conductor while she tidied up the room.

"My God. I was afraid you'd broken your neck or something. Did the doctors say you were okay to come home?" I threw my covers off. "Should you be doing that?"

She was slapping the dust from my blinds. "These are filthy. Do you ever open the windows, Ethan?"

"I didn't expect to see you doing housework so soon after your accident."

"Well, I'm surprised to find you still in bed on Christmas day." She straightened up. "Don't you have somewhere to go? Someone to be with?"

"It's Christmas?"

She scooped up the laundry and opened my door. "It's Christmas eve. I'm going to light the tree tonight. I thought you'd go up to Tacoma to be with your sisters."

I scratched my head and tried to clear the cobwebs. "I lost track of time, I guess."

She smiled condescendingly. "I would have thought you'd have at least made plans, Ethan. You know that Lionel is coming home tomorrow, don't you? Did you forget?"

"The telegram said the third, I think."

"Well, it never hurts to be prepared early, does it?"

"I suppose not."

"I'm surprised you forgot about our big homecoming celebration."

The door slapped shut, and I could hear her going down the stairs.

I limped across the room and stepped into my pants. I tugged at the window shades and rolled them up. Sunshine flooded in.

She was as crazy as a hatter. Or she was smarter than I was. I was going to do some snooping on my own. Delilah Goodknight was not going to make me as crazy as she was. In the glare of a bright December afternoon, I decided to get on with the business of finding the source of this woman's madness.

When I got downstairs, Delilah was already busy with her laundry. In the foyer was a large cardboard box addressed to me from Dr. and Mrs. Henry Houghton. My Christmas present. I opened it up. Gladys had included a recent snap of her and Henry with the girls. Very homey. Everybody smiling with identical, stoic faces for the camera. Inside the box was a tin of Gladys' molasses cookies, a pair of Argyle socks way too big for me, a leather bound edition of *Gulliver's Travels* and two new shirts which fit perfectly. A thoughtful gesture on Glady's part. I knew that each of us, me and Carla and Frances, had received Christmas boxes from our older sister. She was still mothering all of us.

When I had shaved, dressed and tried on my new shirts, I went downstairs and looked through the telephone directory for the listing of the Northwestern Mutual Life Insurance Company. I scribbled the number down on a corner of a *Life* magazine page and shoved it in my jacket pocket as I went out the door. The sun was fading away behind the blue spruce tree in the west corner of the yard as I walked downtown.

# Thirty–One

=========

**Sam** Snelstrom's office was on the third floor of the Morrison Building in a corner space overlooking the old Pioneer Courthouse. His desk was piled with manila folders, most branded with circular coffee cup stains. Two glass ashtrays overflowed on the grubby ink blotter. His telephone was smudged with a hundred greasy fingerprints. Both metal wastebaskets were overflowing with sandwich wrappers, cigarette packs, newspapers and eggshells.

When I came through the door, he was sitting with both feet resting on a wire in-basket, a hard-boiled egg in his beefy fingers and the telephone receiver cradled against his fleshy jowls. He looked up for a moment and motioned for me to sit. I had to move a newspaper off the chair first. Then I sat and gazed out the window at the darkening sky.

"Yeah, yeah, yeah," Snelstrom grumbled, peeling eggshell as he listened. "I told you that already. So what's new, Bud? Oh, yeah? Says who? Oh, yeah?" He grinned at me and dusted shell from his sleeve. The bald egg glistened in his hand. "Well, you get that to me in writin', Bud. Got that? In writin'. There ain't no way in hell I'm gonna do a damn thing just on your say so, Bud. You got that?"

He was nodding vociferously as he reached in a drawer and pulled out a saltshaker. He licked the flesh of the egg, sprinkled on a layer of salt and bit off the end exposing the yellow yolk. I looked

287

away as he took another mouthful and chewed and talked at the same time.

"Yeah, yeah. I heard that already, okay? Heard that, Buddy. You get me somethin' in writin', and then we can do bizness, okay?" He listened for a moment more and then slammed down the phone. He had a smear of egg yolk on his chin when he looked up at me. "Hey, Bud. You're the roomer at Goodknight's, right? You check out what I told you?"

"I have some questions I thought you might be able to answer." I folded my hands in my lap and tried to look disengaged. My nonchalance act wasn't very convincing."I'd like to know more about the fire you mentioned last night."

"Yeah? So what about the fire? You heard about it? I don't wanna waste my time talkin' to you, Bud, if you're gonna play some smart-ass games with me. We understand the rules?"

"I think so." I had absolutely no idea what he was alluding to. All I wanted was a chance to pick his brain with my questions not answer his.

"You answer some questions for me first, and if I like the answers, then we'll talk some more. Okay by you, Bud?"

"What's your angle? You think Mrs. Goodknight burned her husband's house down, right? And I presume you have a good motive."

He leaned back and stuffed the remainder of the hard-boiled egg in his mouth. His cheeks ballooned. "Well, well. Ain't this interestin'," he chortled as the glop went down his gullet. "You gettin' a little bit doubty about your lady love, Bud? Think maybe she's playin' you for a royal sucker?"

"I just want to know what you're up to."

"Sure, you do. Sure." He swung his feet to the floor and wiped his mouth with the back of his hand. "Lemme tell you something, Sonny. Mrs. Goodknight is not a lady. She's a lying, scheming bitch. And she's hurt a lotta innocent people. Not the least of her nasty little tricks is to cost my employer a helluva lot of money."

"Why do you think she was responsible for the fire?"

"You got a better theory? Go ahead. Tell me all about it, Bud. I'm all ears. Tell me your smart-ass theory."

"If you think she's guilty, why haven't the police arrested her?"

"The *police*?" His eyes bulged with disbelief. "What do you think, Sonny? You think they just call me up and say, 'Hell, Sam, just tell us who the bastard is that done it, an' we'll go pick 'em up after we finish our java.'" He leaned back in the chair again. "Shit, Bud. You got soap for brains, you know that?"

"You don't have any evidence then. That's what you mean, right? You're blowing pure ass gas, is that it?"

He narrowed his eyes and flared his nostrils. His fingers laced across his ample belly. "You're a wise guy, aren't you, Sonny Boy? What the fuck is it you want?"

"I just want to know why you're convinced Mrs. Goodknight had something to do with burning that house down."

"The hell you do."

"The hell I do."

We stared at one another for a long, uncomfortable moment. His phone rang, and he ignored it. The door opened behind me, and his dour-faced secretary stuck her head in. He waved her away. When the phone was silent, he began to rotate his thumbs inside a loop of rubber band and eye me with a cynical stare.

"Okay," he began cautiously. "Let's talk turkey. I'll spell it out for you, Bud. McCarthy isn't it?"

"That's right."

"Okay, Mr. McCarthy. Let's put our cards on the table. First, what's your angle with Mrs. Goodknight? You and her an item?"

"I'm just a roomer trying to figure out some angles for myself."

He grinned and wagged a finger at me. "Sure. I buy that, Bud. Just a roomer."

"Just a roomer."

"Okay. Well, I been trackin' Mrs. Delilah Goodknight since March of '40. March thirteenth. A house on the lake went up like a firecracker at about two in the mornin'. There was a little girl in the house upstairs asleep. She made it out thanks to her father Lionel

Goodknight who pulled her up to the roof and managed to jump to a tree beside the house. It was a goddam miracle they weren't both burned up."

"It was clearly arson?"

"Let me put it this way." He snapped the rubber band, and it flew across the room and landed on the floor beside the wastebasket. "There was enough gasoline in that house to feed my old Nash from here to Kansas City."

"The newspaper reports said his wife Charmaine tried to kill herself, and *she* set the fire."

"The newspapers don't always get it right."

"Sometimes they do. What makes you think they were wrong?"

"Well, lemme put it this way, McCarthy. Charmaine was crazy jealous alright. Hell, seems normal to me when a gal tries to steal your husband out from under you. But she wasn't so crazy she would have tried to burn up her little girl. She was crazy about that kid. I know. I talked to a lot of people who knew Charmaine Goodknight, and not a single one said she ever did anything that wasn't for that little girl. Ain't no way in hell she would have tried to burn that kid up. Don't make even ordinary sense."

"That doesn't prove it was Delilah, does it?"

"Nope. Doesn't." He picked his front teeth with a thumbnail. "But it gets a fella to thinkin' now, don't it?"

"Maybe."

"And thinkin' is my job, ain't it? Especially when there's seventy-thousand clams involved on the insurance policy. Mr. Goodknight was the beneficiary of the policy. He got the dough."

"Why'd the company pay if they thought it was arson?"

"Hell, doesn't mean he had anything to do with it. Coulda been some nut case on the loose. Lawyers took a look at my file and said we hadda cough up the dough."

"So Lionel Goodknight got the payoff from the insurance policy, and that ended the investigation?"

"Officially. He got every red cent. And you know what he did with the money?"

Suddenly I did. I wished I hadn't been able to figure it out so easily. "He gave it to his daughter."

"Put it in a trust for her. Down to the last penny. Why do you think he did that, McCarthy?"

"You're probably going to tell me it was so he could keep the money out of Delilah's hands."

"You're smarter'n you look, Friend."

"Isn't that just the natural concern a parent would show especially since he was going overseas?"

"Not in 1940, Bud. He was headed for a stateside stint. Shoreside duty sailin' a damn desk. Lionel Goodknight hadda push on a few doors to get himself a warship. He couldn't wait to get away from your landlady."

I felt my toes start to tingle. I hated this smart-talking slob. I loathed his trashy office and his leering smirk. But I needed to know what he knew. "How do you know that?"

He thumped a file on his desk. "I do my fuckin' homework, Bud. That's what they pay me for around here." Not much from the looks of his office, I thought to myself. "He leaned on some political hacks back in DC to get assigned to the *Hammann*."

"Maybe he was just a patriot."

"Bullshit. He had other reasons."

"What sort of reasons?"

"He wanted to look out for his little girl. He wanted to get himself as far away as possible from Delilah Goodknight."

"Sure," I scoffed. "That's why he divorced his wife and married Delilah?"

"Exactly. The fire made a believer outta that poor bastard. As a matter of fact, Charmaine was the one who filed for a divorce."

"Are you sure about that?"

"Check the records. She filed in Multnomah County. I gotta copy of the decree. You wanna see it?"

"It's not that important."

"It ain't, huh?" He flicked egg yolk off his necktie and reached for a cigar. "Look, McCarthy, you wanna help or just get in the fuckin' way?"

"Pardon?" I drew my attention back as he flipped a lighter across his desk and blew a smoke cloud the size of the Hindenburg blimp in my direction.

"I got eyes. I know Mrs. Goodknight is a helluva dish. I'm not blamin' you for bein' stupid, Bud. Hell, I'd give her a roll myself I suppose if I didn't know what I got sittin' in my file."

"What about proof? Is this all you got? Bullshit opinions that aren't worth honorable mention? Where's the proof, Snelstrom, that she's guilty of anything but bad luck?"

"Bad luck?" he spluttered. "You get tangled up with her, McCarthy, and you're the one who'll learn somethin' about bad luck."

I stood up. "Yeah, well, thanks for the bad advice."

"Look, you wanna find out the truth here, maybe we can help each other."

"How do you mean?" I countered warily, coughing on his cigar smoke.

"You scratch my back. I'll scratch yours. Simple as that."

"What do you want?"

"Keep an eye out. That's all. Simple as ABC. Nothin' to it. All you gotta do is keep an eye open."

"Spy on Delilah for crissakes?"

"Just keep your eyes open, McCarthy. That's all. She's crazy like a fox. If she thinks you're a stupid shit, she just might get careless and make a slip with you."

"You're nuts if you think I'm gonna help you pin something on her, Snelstrom."

"Look at it this way. If you think she's innocent, then you can only help me prove it, right? Sooner or later, one of us is gonna get to the truth."

His logic soaked in like dog pee on a new rug. Nothing I could do but watch it trap me in the widening stain. "Maybe."

"Maybe? Hells bells, McCarthy. Use your head. One way or the other, we're gonna prove who did it, ain't we? An' if it ain't Charmaine, then we gotta take a long, long look at your lady friend here. An' if it ain't her, then at least we done our fuckin' best, right?"

"I suppose you could think of it that way."

He stood up and thrust a hand in my direction. I was too far away to reach.

"Have you seen Charmaine lately?" I asked him.

"Hell, no. She won't even let me in the door. She thinks I'm a poor, broken down old pants pisser sleepin' on the job who couldn't find his ass with a ten-foot pole and a flashlight."

"What happened to give her that impression? I'd think she'd be trying to help you prove something against Delilah."

He laughed. "I fucked up. She thinks I'm in bed with the enemy, humpin' your landlady. According to her, I'm about as worthless as the tits on a boar, McCarthy."

"Because you haven't proved that Delilah did it after all this time?"

"You got it. Might say she ain't exactly friendly anymore."

"I saw her myself. She talked to me about the fire. She said if I did my homework and got some facts straight, she'd talk to me."

Snelstrom came from behind his desk and clapped an arm around my neck. "Good work, McCarthy. Tell you what. You follow up. Go on up and see her, let her talk your fuckin' ears off. And anyway I can help, just name it. You need a lift?" He dug in his pocket and pulled out a ten spot. "Here. For train fare. Have a couple beers on me. You scratch my back, I'll scratch yours, McCarthy. We got ourselves a deal?"

"I'm only interested in helping Delilah. I know she had nothing to do with the fire."

"Then you can help me prove it, okay?"

"I will." I headed for the door and avoided his humid hug.

"While you're at it, McCarthy, take a look at these. Might make you a little more interestin' conversation wise up in Tacoma next time you visit Charmy." He pulled out a pile of papers and slapped them down on the edge of the desk. "Be my guest, McCarthy. I got carbons of this stuff. Keep it as long as you like. Just do me a favor and keep everything you see here between us, okay?"

"Sure." I gathered up the papers and left. I was down the elevator and out on the street before I had exhaled all the cigar fumes.

# Thirty–Two

=========

$I$ worked my shift at the hotel and finished a busy evening with my arms reddened like lobster claws from the hot, soapy dishwater. It was amazing there were so many lonely souls on Christmas eve, eating solitary suppers in the corner of the dining room, sipping red wine and staring with misty faces into the fire, missing someone far away. All longing for a reunion and a happy holiday when the war ended. By this time, we knew that our boys were dug in deep in the forests of Belgium, snow piled up to their behinds, frostbitten, hungry, shell-shocked and desperate for relief. It cast a dark cloud over the holiday. The Allied advance which had once seemed so close a month ago now loomed over the Western Front like an ominous storm brewing more death, more months of war to a weary home front.

When I got home, a light rain was swirling overhead, as soft and fine as angel hair. I opened the front door and looked up to find Delilah waiting for me. She was wearing a burgundy, wool drape that clung to her body like pomegranate peel. Her hair was held back from her temples with rhinestone-studded combs catching the faint glimmer and winking like dim stars. Her full lips were the color of beef blood, and the eyes were smoldering.

"Ethan, you've talked to him, haven't you?"

I closed the door behind me. "Talked to who?" My hat came off along with a spray of rainwater.

She put out a hand. A white card slipped from her fingers to mine. I looked at it. *Samuel P. Snelstrom, Special Investigator, Northwestern Mutual Life Insurance Company.* "He was here, wasn't he? I know he was. What did you tell him, Ethan?"

"Nothing."

She turned her back on me and swept into the dining room, continued on to the front parlor and stood facing the window overlooking the rain-slicked street.

I came in and waited with my hands at my hips. "Delilah, I have to talk to you."

"You told him, didn't you, Ethan?" Her voice stabbed at me like nettles.

"What was he doing here? Why does he follow you around and snoop on you, Delilah? What's he looking for?"

She lit a cigarette and blew smoke toward the window. She kept her back rigid, a barrier between us that kept me from approaching any closer. "He's just trying to ruin everything for me and Lionel. It's her who's put him up to it. She hates me. No matter what I do, how hard I try, she keeps trying to ruin everything for us."

"Who?"

"You know who."

"Tell me. Is it Charmaine?" She whirled around and tried to walk past me. I took one step sideways and blocked her exit. "Talk to me, dammit. Stay right here and talk to me."

"Get out of my way, Ethan."

"Nathan," I said, staring back as hard as she was. "My name is Nathan not Ethan."

"Let me go."

"Not until you talk to me."

"Are you working for him?" She pushed Snelstrom's card into my face. "What's he paying you for spying on me?"

"Why would anyone want to spy on you, Delilah? What have you done?"

"Nothing."

"What does Snelstrom think you've done? Why was he here looking for something you might have left?"

"I have no idea. Why don't you ask him?"

"I did."

She drew a hand back and slapped my face before I could raise a defense. Her strength surprised me. She was the only feminine combatant I had encountered in my life so far. Gladys' whacks across my backside hardly counted next to Delilah's full-throttle smacks.

"Get out of my house!" she shrieked, spittle collecting at the corners of her mouth. "Pack your things and get out of my house!"

"Not until you answer me, Delilah. I'm not going anywhere until you answer me."

She pushed against me. I didn't yield. Tears slid down her cheeks, but I refused to give way. "It's Christmas eve, dammit. How can you be so damned mean on Christmas eve? I thought you were a boy who wanted to be kind to people. Why do you want to do this to me?"

Her use of the demeaning word 'boy' stung. "Delilah, tell me what Snelstrom wants from you? Why is he bothering you?"

"It's all because of the money."

"What money?"

"The insurance money he stole from me. Lionel had an insurance policy on Dorothea when she drowned."

She wiped a trickle of tears from the tip of her nose and smeared her face powder. What I wanted most was to hug her and kiss away every dewy drop on her satiny skin, but those eyes were still so threatening, I dared not let up my guard. I sensed that if I showed any weakness, she would slip behind that mental fog and disappear again.

"Snelstrom took the money. He stole it."

"What do you mean he stole it? How could he steal Lionel's insurance money? He works for the insurance company. It was just his job to find out who set the fire."

"He wouldn't give Lionel the money. He kept it for himself. He knows I know about it, and that's why he's after me. I'm the only one who knows he took the money for himself."

"Delilah, that's crazy." I shook my head and turned away. I was starting to feel hopelessly inadequate. "There was no insurance money for Dorothea. She and Lionel were never married."

"No, no," she fumed. "That money was his."

"Snelstrom paid the money for the house after it burned, Delilah."

"Stop calling me that. I'm Charmaine."

"You're Delilah, dammit." I took hold of her shoulders and shook. The glistening eyes looked bewildered as I pushed her back against the window. "Dammit! Listen to me! You're Delilah Goodknight, and Lionel is dead. He's not coming home. Not tomorrow. Not ever."

"That's a lie! How could you be so mean? You sonuvabitch!"

"His first wife Charmaine is still alive. She's in Tacoma."

She struggled to wriggle away, but I held on.

"No! That's a goddam lie."

Our eyes locked. "I saw her, Delilah. I talked to her. The fire didn't kill her. She survived."

"No! Let me go!"

"She told me you set the house on fire. She thinks you tried to kill her and Lionel."

Suddenly, she pulled free with a violent yank and ran out of the room, raced up the stairs and slammed the door shut on room Number 1.

"Shit." I slammed my fist into the curtain, bounced a knuckle off the wooden sill and regretted my rash outburst. It was impossible to talk to a crazy woman. She hated me now. There was no way I would ever get through to her. It was completely hopeless. She was right. I would have to pack up my things and move out tomorrow. What a stupid thing to do, confronting her like that. Force her to face the truth in one big dose. What a fucking idiot. I had ruined any chance I might have had to get close to her. It was all over.

I walked into the dining room. The tree was lit. A fresh pie was on the buffet. Lemon meringue. A fresh sprig of mistletoe dangled from the chandelier. Two glasses were set beside a plate of shortbread cookies. All waiting for Lionel the mystery man whose spirit was to rise from the sea and miraculously appear at Delilah's Christmas table.

I turned out the light and started up the stairs. Another door opened and closed, and I looked up expectantly, hoping to see Delilah coming down to apologize, to ask for my pardon. Instead Miss Virginia Nigh was standing at the landing with a fur-trimmed coat over her arm and a slash of pink lipstick on her puckered mouth. "Good evening, Mr. McCarthy, and merry Christmas."

"Same to you, Miss Nigh. Going out?"

She looked downward with a shy smile and slipped her arms into the coat. Then she put on a silly, striped hat and pulled out a pair of black gloves as she came down the stairs to greet me. "I'm going with Mother to midnight services. Are you coming or going, Mr. McCarthy?"

"Coming back from work, I'm afraid."

"Oh. Well, you can still make the midnight service at St. Mary's if you'd like."

"No, thanks. I think I'll just turn in."

"But it's Christmas, Mr. McCarthy." A bony hand came out from the bulky sleeve and adjusted the veil on her hat. "You should celebrate. Don't you have family to be with?"

"Not here in Portland. Not anymore." In a sudden, unexpected rush of sentimentality, I missed Pop. Right now, if he had been here, we would have been drinking eggnog spiced with rum while he told me how he and Aunt Polly had bobsledded down Council Crest racing the trolley car when they were kids.

"Well, why don't you come along with us, Mr. McCarthy? Mother and I are going to attend the service and then stop in at the Benson for some hot toddies."

"Thank you, but I think I'll turn in."

"Well, merry Christmas then." She snapped her purse shut and went out into the cold, rainy night.

I went upstairs and paused in front of the door to Number 1. I tried the knob. It was locked. Just as well. I went on to my room, undressed and rolled myself up in the covers, too tired to think, too dispirited to care about Christmas.

I woke up when Miss Nigh pounded on my door. "Mr. McCarthy, are you awake? There's a telephone call for you."

I jerked upright and grabbed for my pants. "Thanks, Miss Nigh. I'll be right down."

There was no sign of Delilah when I got downstairs. I picked up the receiver and stifled a yawn. "Hello."

"Nattie? Merry Christmas. Are you alright?" Gladys.

"I'm fine, Sis. Merry Christmas. How are the girls?"

"Marvelous. Henry got Gloria a phonograph, and she thinks she's in love with Frank Sinatra."

"Wonderful. Thanks for the presents, Gladys. That was thoughtful."

"Did your socks fit, Nat? I was afraid they might be too big."

"They're perfect," I fibbed, yawning. I wished I had brought down my pack of Luckies. From the pinkish cast to the light tinting the window shades, I knew it must be much too early to think clearly yet. Gladys never considered the fact that saner Northwesterners were still groggy and sticky-eyed on Christmas morning at the same hour she was bustling with the holiday turkey in Oklahoma.

"Nattie," she hemmed. I knew there was more than a casual holiday greeting initiating her call. Gladys never wasted any energy on superfluous activity. "I want to know if you're going to go back to school after the holiday break. The Doctor and I have been discussing your future, and we're concerned."

"Well, frankly, I haven't made up my mind yet." I scratched. I needed a smoke.

"We've been talking this over, Nattie, and I'm terribly worried about you."

"Me? Why?"

"Frankly, Nathan, Carla mentioned you were serious about some woman, and she was distracting you from your studies."

I smiled. Gladys never gave up, never quit. "Carla said that?"

"Nattie, be serious. Who is she?"

"Who?"

"Is it that woman you live with? What's her name? Desdemona?"

"Delilah."

"Oh, Nattie. What have you gotten yourself into?"

"Nothing much yet," I joked.

"Nattie, for God's sake. Think what're you're doing. What you're throwing away. She's not worth it, Nattie. No woman is."

"You don't know her, Gladys. You make it sound like I'm formerly engaged or something."

"Nattie, are you getting married to this woman?" Her voice had the intensity of an incoming mortar round. "She's so much older, isn't she? I mean, she's quite attractive for her age, I grant her that, but you're so young, Nattie. She's used merchandise to put it nicely."

"Gladys, shut up."

"Don't tell me you're going to marry this woman?"

"Relax. I'm not marrying anybody. Besides, it's absolutely none of your goddam business, Gladys."

"Don't swear at me, Nathan. Now listen to me. The Doctor and I have been talking this over."

"Good for you."

"Be serious, Nattie. And we've decided that the best thing for you is to get back in school immediately and finish your graduate studies and settle down with a respectable, professional position. You know that's what Daddy wanted, Nathan. You know that."

"Uh huh."

"So we've decided that you should quit your job, move back on campus and finish your studies. Henry and I are prepared to send you a monthly stipend for expenses, Nathan."

"Thank the good Doctor for his generosity, but I don't need your charity. I have a job."

"A _job_? You call washing dishes a job?" she spluttered. "Daddy would die if he knew you were slaving in a hotel washing up like a servant, throwing away your education that he worked so hard to give you."

"Gladys, for crissakes, lay off."

"Don't argue with me, Nathan. I know what's best for you. You can't let yourself get mixed up with a woman like that and destroy your future. Daddy worked all his life to ensure you would have opportunities he never had. He wanted one thing more than anything else—to see you earn your doctorate. He was so proud of you, Nattie." She sniffled. I felt only a tiny tickle of guilt. "Promise me you won't marry her, Nathan. Don't do anything foolish."

"Gladys, I'm not getting married."

"You promise?"

"Jesus." I ran a hand through my hair and wiped sand from my eyes. My mouth tasted like rusty nails. I had to pee. Gladys could be a pain in the ass sometimes.

"Then it's settled. You'll move back to the campus, and the Doctor will arrange a monthly allowance check, Nathan. You can forget about all this nonsense of falling in love and finish your education."

"Who said anything about falling in love?"

"Don't tell me this is just about sex. I couldn't bear to hear you admit something like that. That's not like you, Nattie. Not like you at all."

"Okay. It's not romance. Not sex either. It's her cooking."

"What?"

"It's her lemon meringue pies, Gladys. They're absolutely out of this world."

"Nathan, will you be serious? The Doctor and I have this all arranged. Professor Ruth is prepared to help you get settled for the spring term. Don't let us down, Nattie. Don't disappoint the Doctor. He's been so incredibly patient and generous with you since Daddy died."

"Gladys, can't you just let me live my own life? I'm not a kid anymore. Aren't the girls enough for you to mother without trying to smother me?"

"Don't be impertinent. I can't stand to think of you being ungrateful after all the Doctor has done for you. He's willing to support you, Nathan, until you get on your feet professionally. How many brothers-in-law would do the same?"

"God only knows," I mumbled sardonically.

"Well, just pack your things and get back to the campus. I'm wiring you some money."

"I don't need it."

"Don't be silly. How much do you make washing dishes for God's sake?"

"Enough."

"Dammit, Nattie, quit arguing and just do what I tell you. This is what Daddy would want. You know that. You owe us this much, Nat."

Now she had me pinned like a moth to the mat. Stabbed through the heart. All she had to do was to remind me of my abject failure to carry on the family honor, and I was ready to surrender. "Gladys, don't send me any money. Please. I don't want you or the Doctor to send me anything."

"Are you going to return to graduate school?"

"Yes."

"Is that a promise, Nattie?"

I sighed. "Yes."

"And you'll call Professor Ruth and tell him?"

"Yes. Now will you get off my back?"

"Not quite. I want to know about this woman. Will you give her up, Nattie? For the sake of your future and the family?"

"Don't worry about it. It's nothing. We're just friends."

"Carla told me you're madly in love."

"Carla exaggerates. She's a hopeless romantic."

Gladys paused. "Maybe you're right. She does get carried away at times. You're not serious about her then?"

"It's all under control. Don't worry."

"You promise me?"

"For crissakes, Sis, lay off, will you? Kiss the girls for me and wish Henry a happy Christmas and let me go, okay?"

"Remember you promised me, Nattie."

"I promised."

"A little fling is one thing. I can overlook that, Nattie, given the circumstances. I know how hard you took Daddy's death—"

"Gladys..."

"Men do these things when they're young. Henry has explained all this to me very frankly, I assure you."

"I'm glad to hear it."

"As long as you agree to end it, Nattie. And you have promised me, haven't you?"

"Cross my heart, hope to die for crissakes."

"Well, merry Christmas then, Nattie. We love you."

"Love you, too."

"Is Frances doing alright? She hardly ever writes me."

"She's fine."

"She should get out and meet someone."

"Don't worry about it. Francie's fine."

"Well, merry Christmas then."

"Merry Christmas." I hung up.

When I turned around, Delilah was standing there with an apron on and a smear of white flour on her forehead. "Good morning. Would you like some biscuits and eggs?"

I could already smell the fresh coffee bubbling on the stove. "Thanks." I expected her to wish me a merry Christmas, to say something about last night. Nothing. She went to the stove and grabbed the coffeepot.

As I watched her set an extra place at the table, I looked into the dining room and saw the Christmas tree was gone. The boughs were stripped from the plate shelf. Christmas had vanished.

"Where's the tree?" She opened the oven door, hauled out a pan of browned biscuits and set them down on the drain board. "You better go up and wash, Nathan. These biscuits will be cold before you know it."

"Merry Christmas, Charmaine," I said in a voice barely audible.
"Who?"

"Charmaine. It's Christmas, isn't it?"

"Why did you call me that?" she asked with a silly grin on her face. "Go on upstairs and clean up. I'll pour the coffee."

I turned around and went back upstairs. Crazy. Absolutely mad. No way I could ever hope to reach out and pull her back to sanity. I had threatened her fantasy, destroyed her myth of Lionel's homecoming, and now she was somebody else. Delilah. If I had made the picture of Charmaine and Ethan ugly, she would refuse to play the part anymore. I had no idea where I fit into any of this. It didn't matter anymore. She was too crazy to blame for anything, especially my feelings of utter and senseless adoration.

# Thirty–Three

=========

**When** I showed up for work, I wasn't certain this was going to be my last shift in the kitchen of the Multnomah Hotel. As it turned out, circumstances completely beyond my control decided the matter for me. Before I had finished tying on my apron, Mel pushed his way through the swinging doors to the dining room. He had a damp cigarette dangling from his wrinkly mouth and the stench of onions in his breath when he got close.

"Hey, Kid. Bad news. Lousy, rotten luck, but you gotta turn in your time card after the shift tonight. You're gettin' sacked."

"Why?" I asked, not sure if I should welcome the reprieve from a stack of holiday pots and pans crusted with grime tough enough to bust a cold chisel.

"Beats me. You got friends in high places, huh?"

Pimples poked his head out from behind a tablecloth he was folding. "Nathan's gonna be canned? What'd he do?"

"Some muckety futch called up the chief honcho and said you were quittin' and goin' back to college. You got it made, Kid. You ain't gonna hafta work for a livin' like the rest of us poor A-holes." He spat into my dishwater. "You gonna be some professor, huh? Get cozy with some a those little coed cuties?"

"Nathan's real smart," Pimples offered with both arms full of napkins. "He's gonna be a history teacher, right, Nathan? You know all about Julius Caesar and Cleopatra, dontcha?" Pimples was my greatest fan.

"I guess I'll get to these roasting pans then." I reached for a scouring brush.

Mel leaned back with his ass resting against the counter edge. "Tell me, Kid. How's your love life these days?"

I knew he liked siphoning off my romantic fantasies to feed his boredom and frustration with middle-age, and it amused me to humor him. "Great, Mel. She's about to wear me out."

"Yeah? Well, these older gals are hot for it. Did I ever tell you about the redhead in The Dalles who tried to smother me with her pussy?"

Pimples' eyes bulged from their sockets. "Jesus, Mel. How'd she do that?"

I grinned and plunged both hands in the sudsy soup. "I think we heard about that one. I thought you were gonna tell us about the gal who traveled with the carnival."

Mel took a drag on his cigarette and looked up at the ceiling, momentarily distracted by licentious flashbacks. "Owww, Jesus H. Fucking Christ! Now *she* was an animal, pure, raw meat, if you know what I mean. That broad could jump-start a dump truck with one suck."

"Really?" Pimples said in awe.

"She could do it standin' on her hands," Mel bragged as I scrubbed. "Wrap her ankles around my fuckin' ears and do it upside down." He shook his head. "Kee-rist. That was the craziest damn broad. If she didn't screw you to death, she'd turn blue for tryin'."

"So what happened to her?" I asked just to be polite and show some interest in the conversation. "How come you didn't keep her? She sounds like just your type. Perfect wife for you, Mel."

Pimples picked up a stack of folded linens and started for the doors. "I never knew your wife used to be an acrobat, Mel. Can she do the twirling thing with her teeth?"

Mel jerked his cigarette from his lips. "What the hell are you blabbin' about, Stupid? What twirling thing?"

"You know," he said warily, suddenly aware he had offended his boss. "The thing where they hang by their teeth from a wire way up in the air and spin around real fast."

"Are you nuts or just stupid?" Mel spat back nastily.

Pimples shrank against the wall as he slid by toward the doors. "Just askin', Mel. I mean, not everybody can do that, can they?"

"You're too stupid to pour piss out of a boot with directions printed on the heel, you know that?"

"Sure, Mel. I was just askin', that's all," he simpered, making his exit with a swift rear end kick from Mel.

"The one belongs in a fuckin' carnival is you, Meathead. The freak show."

"Hey, Mel, lay off," I said, hoping to deflect his wrath. Pimples was no match for his cruel mouth. "He was just jokin' around."

"Yeah, sure. Kid is plain stupid. If I didn't make allowances for his pinhead brain, I'd bust his mouth in for him. Callin' my old lady a carny whore. Goddammed idiot. Maybe I'll still show him where the bear shit in the buckwheat."

"He was just teasing, Mel."

He let Pimples go. "So you're goin' back to school? Gonna wait out the war in some goddam college, huh?" He still had a mean tone to his voice, sparring with me, hoping he could abuse somebody yet with his sharp-edged wit.

"Can't do any better, I guess. Uncle Sam sure as hell doesn't want me."

"Hell, Henry Kaiser's hirin' niggers and God knows what else. You got a college education, Kid. You—hell, they'd slap you into some office and make you a supervisor. Some a them Oakies and Arkies they got out there don't even wear shoes, wipe their asses with Sears Roebuck's catalog. Hell, I doubt if they know how to read. Goddam white trash. Oughtta send 'em all straight back down South when the war's over."

"They're just trying to earn a living, Mel. No harm in that."

He eyed me suspiciously as I attacked a pan with burned-on meat juice. "Goddam country is goin' to hell in a hand basket, McCarthy. All this trash movin' in here since the war. They see how it's better'n where they come from. Niggers and crackers movin' in on us. Hell, everything north a Albina's turnin' into nigger and hillbilly town."

"I wouldn't worry about it," I tried to dampen his ire.

"Yeah, you wouldn't. What the fuck do you care anyway? You're gonna be livin' the easy life on some cozy campus, teachin' a buncha rich assholes some crap about Cleopatra." He spat into my dishwater again. "Shit. Who gives a fuck anyway?"

"You know, Mel, you're a pretty smart guy. Why don't you try to get a job in a defense plant? You could be a welder or something. I hear they make real good money."

"Shit. Work with all them niggers and white trash? Hell, no. Besides, I got security here. Soon's the Japs and Krauts are beat, these plants are gonna fold up, and all these poor fuckin' s.o.b.'s are gonna be shit up a creek without a paddle. Me? I'll still have a job."

"Your wife works for Jantzen, right?" I knew she was a machine operator at the factory which used to make swimsuits and was now turning out all kinds of military clothing. I also knew she made more money than Mel. No wonder he was so pissed at the world and the pesky usurpers who had displaced the Northwest's finest specimens of manhood, himself included.

"She does alright for a woman. Ain't anything fit for a man, sewin', for crissakes."

"But it must be nice to have the extra dough, huh? Whatcha doin' with it, Mel? Gonna buy yourself a brand new car after the war and travel?"

He grinned and stomped out his cigarette butt. "Shit. Don't need no new car. My old Plymouth's runnin' fine. Me? Hell, I'm gonna get on the train and take a little trip down south to LA., City of Angels, McCarthy. They got the purtiest women down there all you gotta do is crook your little pinkie, if you know what I mean."

"Sounds swell."

"Gonna find me a little stud poker game and parlay my stake up so's I can buy my own place."

I rinsed another gleaming pot under the steaming water. "I had no idea you had aspirations of entrepreneurship."

"What?" he growled, squinting through the steam and smoke. "What the hell's that? One a your two-dollar college words?"

"I didn't know you wanted to run your own business."

"Hell, you think I'm gonna be workin' for these assholes forever? I got plans. You'll have to bring some a your high-spendin' friends to my place, Kid. I'll fix my specialty—baked peppers with Italian sausage."

"Sounds good."

"You know," he said in a friendlier mood finally, "I'm gonna miss you, Kid. You got a brain. Too bad you can't get into the shootin' war, but least ways you can get a head start on some a these A-holes comin' back with medals and ribbons pinned on their shirts like boy scouts."

"Sure."

"You'll make out okay."

"Hope so."

I washed my way through a stack of plates while Mel returned to his butcher block and began slicing a prime rib roast for tomorrow's lunch fare.

I took a break to drain the sink and make my dining room rounds. On an impulse driven more by boredom than necessity, I caught Mel's squinty eye before I unwrapped my wet apron. "Say, Mel. You ever hear of a big house fire in Lake Oswego a few years back. A little girl was rescued by her father when he climbed up to the roof and pulled her out. The child's mother was burned real bad. Everybody said she was trying to kill herself by setting the house on fire because her husband was stepping out on her."

"Lake Oswego?"

"I guess there was gasoline all over the place when the fire department got there."

"I don't pay no attention to those muckety futch's in Lake Oswego." *Whack, whack.*

"I just thought you might have heard something. It was in all the papers." I shrugged as if I were totally uninvolved.

*Thump*. His knife sliced off a band of marbled fat. "A fire, huh? Burnt up a lady real bad, burnt her hair off, did it?"

"I think so."

"I didn't read nothin' about the fire. But I think I remember somethin' afterwards about the lady that got burnt up." He chopped off another blob of fatty meat and began slicing firm, pink strips of roast that fell like cards on his chopping block. "They had a buncha sob stories about the dame. She was some looker. Matter a fact, I saw them pitchures in the paper and told my old lady I think I knew the dame."

"You don't say so?"

"Name's Charmy. Used to have a room in the hotel way back. Before she got married to that rich guy in Lake Oswego, older fella with beaucoup bucks. I knew her cuz I used to take her meals up there. Special room service. We used to do that on the QT, see, for the big shots who didn't want nobody nosin' around in their bizness."

"She was a big shot?"

Mel finished slicing the roast and wrapped the meat in clean butcher paper, opened up the cooler and stacked his work alongside the chops he'd already prepared for the dinner menu. "Well, her old man was. Hell, don't you know who Charmy was?"

"No idea."

"Her daddy was Fitz McCoy, a friend of President Hoover, some bigwig lawyer as crooked as a pig's tail, used to hire out as a mouthpiece for the bootleggers runnin' whiskey through the San Juans."

I feared to move and interrupt Mel's chain of thought. I was taking in every word with both ears. "Interesting. So she got special treatment, huh?"

"Special, my pink, rosy-red ass. She was a spoiled bitch is way I put it. Used to tip me good though. I'd sneak her some booze up there. This was prohibition days. That far back, see. I hadda friend whose cousin hadda boat over at Westport, and they'd bring me some Canadian whiskey now and then. She used to tip me real good for that stuff."

"Why was she staying in the hotel?"

"Charmy McCoy?" As I waited with bated breath, reluctant even to exhale until I had my answer, Mel flipped a pair of T-bones on the board and trimmed the white fat as easily as snipping his nails. He looked over and winked at me. "Why you so interested in Charmy, McCarthy?"

"Just curious. Somebody mentioned it to me is all."

"Bullshit." *Slap, slap.* He slammed two more steaks down on the board. "You got somethin' on your mind."

"Just came across a story about the fire, and it seemed sort of interesting."

"Came across a story somewheres, eh?" He tossed lopped-off fat and gristle onto the floor where it fell through the wooden slats to his slop tray. "Bullshit, McCarthy."

"No, honest. Nothing else in particular. Just seemed like a good story."

"Well, I think you're shittin' me, Boy. You know Charmy?"

"Not personally."

Mel smiled. "Which ain't no. How'd you meet that one-eyed geek? I hear she's up in Tacoma in some sorta freak hospital."

"Why do you call her a one-eyed geek?"

"Cuz her other eye got burnt up. She had one good eye left, burnt up her face pretty bad."

"Well, I understand she's totally blind now."

"No, shit?" He wrapped the steaks and started trimming a huge ham. "Too bad. She was a looker when she was younger."

"So why was she staying at the hotel?"

"What do you think? She didn't want her old man to find out she was screwin' around with some miserable bastard didn't have enough brains to come in outta the rain."

"Before she got married?"

"Hells' bells, even after she married the rich guy and got her hands on his dough. She was screwin' this jerk ever chance she got. Used to have a cab pick her up at Union Station, see." He smirked as he cut around the ham bone. "Her husband was a real sucker, see. He'd drop her off at the station, goin' to see her mama in Tacoma she says. Then she'd duck out the back and catch a cab and come here to the hotel, get a room upstairs. Hell, I even remember the damned room. Always got 707. Lucky number. Registered under the name of Lucy Ranier." Mel stopped and stabbed the knife blade into the wood. "Drank Jack Daniels mostly, but if I got her some CC and Coke, she'd tip me a fiver. In them days, you'd be surprised what a good man could do with five bucks, Kid." A slow, wicked smile spread across Mel's face. "You wanna know the sonuvabitch she was screwin', dontcha, McCarthy? You're about to piss yer britches you wanna know so bad, dontcha?"

"Guess it doesn't matter. How'd I know him anyhow?"

*Whack, whack, whack!* He cut through tendon, bone and muscle with quick jabs of his blade. "Oh, you'd know him. I guaranty you know the bastard."

"Oh, yeah?"

"Guaranteed, McCarthy."

"How's that?"

"That lady you're shackin' up with." He turned his head and spat sideways toward the sink. "Her name's Goodknight, ain't it?"

"Yeah. So?"

"Your lady is a Goodknight. Charmy married a Goodknight. The poor bastard almost got himself burnt up."

I nodded, feeling miserable, like a trout on the end of a fisherman's line. Nothing I could do to dislodge the hook in my mouth. I was being drawn into the net.

"Well, your old lady's gotta be the second missus, don't she? Ain't that many Goodknights around in this hick berg, way I figger it. So you're screwin' the dame who ended up with Charmy's old man. Ain't that somethin', huh? Ain't life strange."

"Suppose so."

"Well, if you're still livin' up there on Broadway with this Goodknight dame, then you know who was getting' in Charmy's panties upstairs in the lucky-number room."

I gulped back a wad of spit. Sure, I knew. It had to be him, didn't it? Why couldn't I have seen it? Why had I assumed the worst, blamed Delilah for the burden of my suspicions? She was crazy but not so clever after all.

"Jesus," I said as the light bulb turned on.

Mel whacked at a joint. *Thump!* "Perzactly," he jibed. "I thought you'd say that, Kid." He winked and flashed a sloppy grin that made the blood rush to my ears.

# Thirty–Four

===========

**Snelstrom's** file was mostly copies of old newspaper clippings about the fire and the heroic rescue of little Dottie from the roof of the burning building plus a few follow up articles about the badly burned mother, Charmaine Goodknight, who was not expected to survive. The longer she survived, through surgeries and skin grafts, the less the newspaper covered. Within a year, she was hardly noteworthy. There was a fuzzy photo of little Dottie being held in her beaming father's arms with firemen in the background. Another interesting photo showed a radiant Charmaine holding a spray of flowers next to a handsome man that matched the portrait on Delilah's Philco—Lionel. Their honeymoon cruise, the article noted. Happier times. The writer referred to Lionel as the son of noted socialite Harriet Harlow Benhurst and Colonel Doyle Adair Goodknight, former investment broker, mayor of the city and founder and president of the First Trust State Bank. Lionel was quite a catch it seemed. He was a scion of the upper-crusted, old money families ensconced on the Heights overlooking Portland's slab town.

The same writer later noted that Lionel's bride Miss Charmaine McCoy, daughter of attorney Fritz McCoy and Sally Owens Loftis, former Queen of Rosaria, had miraculously survived several surgeries and had filed for divorce to free her husband to remarry and live a normal life. The newspaper accounts described an unfortunate event where kerosene lamp oil was spilled on the carpet and started the conflagration. I searched through all Snelstrom's clippings and in only one was the subject of suicide brought up. That item mentioned Mrs. Goodknight was severely depressed since her injury and had been suffering from nervous exhaustion and depression prior to the event which nearly took her life. There was a suggestion of willful negligence, perhaps, but nothing approaching suicide.

Most interesting was a summary of an interview the insurance company investigator had with Charmaine from her hospital bed while she was recovering from her burns. She remembered almost nothing about the fire, only waking up and choking on smoke and then falling through the floor when her hair caught fire. That's exactly what she had told me. She could recall nothing else until she awoke in the hospital, in excruciating pain, numbed with the horror of what had happened to her. There was no mention of Delilah, just a concern for her daughter Dottie. She was suffering so much, but yet she wanted to know first about her little girl. In fact, nearly every other answer she gave was followed by a question about Dorothy. Snelstrom was right about that, too. She was a very concerned, loving mother. How could she ever be accused of trying to harm her own child?

The best part of the material Snelstrom had given me was a few typed pages from a report filed by Lieutenant B.J. Bugsbee of the Portland Police Bureau. Bugsbee had interviewed Lionel after the fire. He had learned about the separation from his wife, and his questions were mostly directed at trying to find a motive for Lionel to destroy his family. Maybe to make it easier for him to take off with his lover, Bugsbee suggested. Lionel was so heartsick, so depressed over the devastating injuries to Charmaine and almost bereft of his reasoning trying to cope with the tragedy that he had no spirited defense to the cop's suggestive questions. Instead, he gave blunt, direct monosyllabic replies, sobbed continually all through the interview and kept repeating over and over how much he loved both his wife and child. Lionel believed it was an accident, a tragic, unspeakable accident with no discernible cause. He never mentioned revenge, motive or bias toward anyone. He praised the firemen who helped save him and his daughter and the medical staff at St.

Vincent's Hospital who cared for his wife. There was nothing disingenuous about Lionel. He was as straight as an arrow. No wonder the police looked elsewhere for their culprit.

Bugsbee also talked to Delilah, the "paramour" as he called her. Apparently when he talked to her, he was mesmerized by those sad, lustrous eyes just as I was. He rambled in his questions, commiserated with her about the loneliness of being "the other woman" who wasn't even able to call Lionel after the fire because of the publicity and harm it might do his family. When it came down to the point of her being thrown over for another woman when her lover returned to his wife, Delilah tearfully proclaimed that she only wanted what was best for Lionel, that he had to think about his little girl now, and if he should ever want to come back to her, she still loved him and wanted to marry him when he became free.

Bugsbee came right out and asked her if she and Lionel had planned to marry. Bugsbee wrote: *"says Mr. G. trying to work things out with wife, had some problems and she wanted to support him in his efforts to save his marriage"*. Sounded pretty altruistic, didn't it? Delilah just wasn't coming across to Bugsbee as the evil other woman scheming to destroy anything or anyone in her path. Where was Snelstrom getting his information which painted Delilah as an arsonist, a raging, jealously insane madwoman with a match in her hand?

There were notes in Bugsbee's file about an interview with Cody Goodknight confirming Delilah's whereabouts the night of the fire. Both Cody and his wife swore that Delilah had spent all day and evening at their house. Firm, solid alibi, Bugsbee concluded.

I tidied up the papers in Snelstrom's file and fit it under my socks in the bureau drawer. Then I ripped open another pack of Luckies, grabbed my jacket and started downstairs. I needed to get answers to some of the new questions I had. If Delilah wasn't the woman Snelstrom thought she was, if she wasn't the witch Charmaine was certain had tried to kill them all, then who was she? The beguiling, loyal lover patiently waiting in the wings for Lionel to work things out with his wife? The shocked victim of a horrible accident conceding that the most important thing was for her lover to devote himself to his little girl and not race into Delilah's arms? Who the hell was Delilah Goodknight? No matter who she was, I knew I loved her. That was the crazy part.

I got to the foot of the stairs, and there she was. Her hair was swept back and held in place with a black snood. She wore a hint of rouge that gave a natural blush to her cheeks. When she saw me, she smiled, and those beautiful, blue eyes were moist and glistening.

"Hello, Nathan. Are you in a hurry to go out?"

"Sort of." I fastened my jacket. I was curious as to who she was going to be today. "Can I do something for you before I go?"

She located a stray strand of hair and tucked it behind her ear. "Oh, I just thought you might like to come in and have a quick bite with me. I made some coffee."

That was an unusual invitation. But she seemed completely without guile and further disarmed me with a shy smile. "I need to get downtown and meet someone," I replied. Then I took another breath and smelled the fruity scent. "Did you bake a pie?"

"A lemon meringue. Would you like some?"

"Sure."

She smiled warmly and touched my sleeve. "Come on in and have a piece. There's no one else around today, and it'll just go to waste, Nathan." She led me to the kitchen. "I enjoy baking. My brother-in-law brought some fruit from the store. I have canned grapefruit, too. Do you like grapefruit?"

"Some," I tempered my reply as I sat down and opened my jacket. Some things were best left out of the can, and that included citrus fruits as far as I was concerned.

"I'm going to make a grapefruit and avocado salad. Cody's got some fresh avocados in from California."

"Oh." It didn't sound too appetizing.

She sliced a fresh piece of pie and set it down in front of me. The egg whites were beaten as thick and high as Mt. Hood snowdrifts. Pale yellow custard oozed over my plate as I picked up my fork.

"You like your coffee black?" She poised the percolator over my cup.

"A little milk, please." I studied her as she pulled open the refrigerator and took out a cream bottle. Today I might as well have been the meter reader stopping by for a quick snack. There seemed to be no recognition of our past collisions with rushed romance. No notice of our fleeting intimacies. I was Nathan McCarthy, a boarder. Period. "Thanks," I said as she dripped cream in my coffee and offered me a spoon.

"I can't eat sweets without coffee, can you?"

"It's great," I admitted, tasting my first mouthful. "Wonderful." It was delicious. Tangy, tart and aromatic as I shoveled in another forkful. The crust dissolved on the tip of my tongue, as light as first fallen snowflakes.

"I'm glad you enjoy it," she sighed, sitting down beside me and watching with wide eyes as I finished off my pie. "It's so nice to see someone with a good appetite."

"Thanks. It was delicious." I wiped my mouth.

"You might as well have another piece if you like."

"No, thanks. I couldn't eat another bite." I drank my coffee and watched her drift off again as if a fog had seeped into the house and enveloped her. She faded away as I finished my coffee. "Well, I have to shove off. Thanks for the pie and coffee."

"Anytime. Stop in if you smell something good. I love to bake, you know, and most of the time there's no one to enjoy it. Miss Nigh is on a continual diet."

"Well, thanks again." I got up. Still no connection. Nothing. A vacant stare out through the sleeping porch was all I got in return for my courtesy.

"You know, Nathan, I haven't asked about your sister lately. How is she?"

"Frances?" I replied, a bit startled by her return to my world.

"How is she?"

"Doing much better, I think. Thank you for asking."

"It's so hard for her, isn't it? She was so young, too. Just like I was."

My heart went thud. Had I heard what I thought I heard? Was she the real Delilah Goodknight now, the grieving widow of the *USS Hammann* officer buried at the bottom of the ocean?

"Yes, it is hard for her. It has to be hard for anyone to lose someone they love. Especially when they had each other for such a short time."

She didn't even flinch when she turned her gaze toward mine. "If only Lionel and I had had more time together, I think it wouldn't have been so hard to let him go. But he felt he had a duty." She smoothed the oilcloth on the table with her fingertips. "I knew he had to go, but I didn't want to face the fact he might never come home to me again."

I sat down carefully so as to keep her eyes engaged with mine. "Delilah, you know he's never coming home, don't you?"

"They tell me he isn't. I know that. But I don't believe it. I don't have to believe it, do I? They might be wrong, and I promised Lionel when he left that I would never give up hoping no matter how long he was away."

My hand pressed over hers. "You loved him very much, didn't you?"

"There was never anyone else for me. Only Lionel. We had to wait so long to be together, and then he was gone again. I'll wait for him as long as it takes, Nathan. Someday, I know he's going to come back. I just have to keep believing."

"Delilah, his ship was sunk. There's no way Lionel could have been saved."

Her eyes hardened instantly. "How do you know? Who told you that?"

"It's just a fact. There were so many casualties. They all drowned, Delilah."

"I know what you're thinking. That I must be crazy to keep hoping, waiting for him."

"I didn't say that."

"But he *could* be alive. No one knows for sure. Maybe he was rescued, and he isn't able to get in touch with me."

I closed my eyes and put my head down.

"Don't you see, Nathan? As long as I keep hoping, there's a chance, isn't there? A *chance*. That's all I'm asking for. Just a chance." She bussed my cheek. "I know you believe in miracles, too, Nathan. Don't you?"

I was too tired to keep fighting. What difference did it make? "Sure," I said, squeezing her hand. "Who knows? Everything's gone crazy since the war. Anything's possible."

She rewarded me with a generous smile. "Oh, yes. That's just what I keep telling myself. It *is* possible, isn't it?"

I took my leave as she cleared away the dishes. Out the door and on my way up Broadway, I kept seeing those sad eyes pleading with me. She needed my faith to sustain her own. I wasn't comfortable telling her lies, sharing in the fantasy she had spun, but I felt so sorry for her. What else could I do? I just felt so goddam rotten for buying into what Charmaine had told me she had done, beginning to believe all the sordid crap Snelstrom had dug up. I should have had the faith and loyalty Delilah showed Lionel. Crazy or not, she was more noble than I.

# Thirty–Five

===========

    **I** caught up with Sam Snelstrom at Murphy's Bar and Short Order Grill. He was sitting by the front window, wolfing his way through a bucket of razor clams sunk in a bowl of butter. He barely missed a slurp as I waded through the traffic and sat down at his table. Droplets of sauce were dribbled on his shirtfront, the tablecloth and spotted his napkin.

    Snelstrom smacked his lips noisily and sucked on a finger. "What's up, McCarthy? You here on a mission or just passing time?"

    I ordered a beer and lit up a smoke. Pulling out his file, I laid it carefully beside the clam pot.

    He belched and leaned back in his chair. "Why is it, McCarthy, I get the impression you just ate the birdie? What's on your mind?"

    "I'm curious. What makes you so smart, Snelstrom, that you know something nobody else does?"

    He grinned. "She's got you fooled too, huh? You just can't see the forest for the trees, can you, Bud?"

    "You tell me. Go ahead. I'm all ears. How do you know you're on the right track?"

    "Who else is there? You learn somethin' new, somethin' I don't know about? You been talkin' to her?"

    "She has nothing to say about it. She still thinks Lionel is coming home."

"That's all an act. She's about as crazy as me. She plays her cards close to her chest, McCarthy. I thought you'd be smart enough to see through all that shit."

"The point is, Snelstrom, she's about as out of touch as you can get and not be in a rubber room."

He laughed and licked another finger. Then he sloshed a foamy slug of beer down his throat and blotted his chin. "So what're you tellin' me? She too crazy to wanna kill somebody?"

"I just don't think she did it. I'm interested in what you have that makes you think differently."

"To be honest with you, McCarthy, I was hoping you'd have figured it out by now for yourself. Let me spell it out for you."

"I know about the brother-in-law Cody."

"You been doin' your homework."

"Enough to know you're fulla shit."

"The point is Charmaine didn't know nothin' about that. All she knows is that her husband came back to her. Delilah was screwin' both brothers, hopin' to get the rich one Lionel to leave mama and the kid. When he threw her over and went home again, she decided to get even. Her own way. Perfect motive. No wrath like a woman spurned and all that crap. Fits like a fuckin' glove, McCarthy."

"She has an alibi. Delilah was at Cody's place the night the fire was set. They both testified to that."

"Sure. But maybe he was just covering for her."

"Why would he do that? Lie to protect the woman who tried to kill his brother?"

Snelstrom pushed his plate away, bit off the end of a cigar, wet the tip with his tongue and pulled a lighter out of his pants pocket. "Because he was takin' care a your dame. He was bein' pressed between a rock and a hard place, see? If he didn't go along with Delilah, she lets the wife and Lionel know all about his sticky dick. You're graspin' at straws, McCarthy. They were screwin' right under the old man's nose. Cody was gettin' in her panties as often as Lionel was. Cody's wife never tumbled to Delilah shackin' up with her hubby. It's Delilah's way of sewin' up an alibi. So Cody covers for

Delilah to save his own ass. You can't trust that bitch as far as you can throw her."

"I don't see it that way."

"You don't see nothin'."

"Tell me more about Delilah. What do you know about her before she married Lionel?"

As soon as I said it, his jaw dropped. He rolled his finger around the stub of the cigar and studied me for an inclination as to my next question. I knew he wasn't sure just where I was headed with this.

"How much do you know about her?" he asked me with one eye closed.

"She's crazy for starters."

"It's an act. A Hollywood agent oughtta sign her up. It's all bullshit."

"But before her husband was killed, I think she was okay. Being accused of something like this and then the circumstances of losing Lionel drove her nuts. That's what I think."

"She's a gold digger. Pure and simple. I've seen a hundred of 'em, McCarthy. My files are full of dames like her. She ain't no different."

"She was in love with Lionel."

"Sure. Maybe. Who wouldn't love a guy leavin' his wife and kiddie and makin' an honest woman of you? She was nothin' but a secretary, typin' up orders for some laundry over on Union Avenue. He was her golden goose. Pure and simple."

"Is it?"

He loosed an unabashed belch. "I know all about you, McCarthy. You work for two bits an hour washin' dirty pots and pans, puttin' up with stale cigars and bad jokes. So what does that tell you, huh?"

"I may not have much credit with you, Snelstrom, but I know a little something about common sense. And what you're telling me stinks. It's so lousy, it stinks."

"Stinks, does it? Well, lemme tell you what I think stinks to high heaven around here. First off, little girls bein' burnt up in their beds, guys screwin' around on their missus with some trashy, gold digger who gets her claws in and won't leggo." He leaned across the table and exhaled a cloud of noxious smoke in my face. "And bitches pokin' both brothers on the sly and then lyin' about the whore who tried to burn the fuckin' house down just to get her rich daddy back. That's the kinda stink I smell around here, McCarthy."

"Why is it the only motive you can see here is Delilah's? How about Cody as a suspect?"

He aimed a finger at my nose. "Hell. Now that's a lousy stink if I ever smelt one. Cody Goodknight? That broken-down produce peddler? He ain't got the guts for it. Kill his own brother? What the hell for? Talk about makin' absolutely no sense, McCarthy."

"If Lionel and his wife and kid died, he'd inherit the family's money."

"He was writ right outta Daddy's will, McCarthy. No dice."

"He'd be the only heir. Since old man Goodknight had passed on, Lionel had the money. So it makes sense that the only people who stood in Cody's way of being on easy street were his brother and his family."

Snelstrom curled his lips back in a gargoyle sneer. "What a buncha crap. Pure crap. You're tryin' to tell me Cody Goodknight is gonna murder his own flesh and blood, burn up his little niece? Bullshit. Him and Lionel were brothers. That's not motive, McCarthy, that's fuckin' fantasy. Nobody is that cold-hearted. Money only drives a man so far."

"He was screwing Lionel's wife for crissakes," I countered angrily.

The cigar wagged from between his lips as he sucked in a breath. "Where'd you hear that for crissakes?"

"I got it on good authority."

"Bullshit. Who told you a story like that? Lemme guess. Your little red-haired honey, huh? She tell you about Cody and Charmaine?"

I challenged his smug self-confidence. "I got a better source."

"Somethin' you better wise up to, McCarthy. I been on this case for a long time. I've been everywhere, talked to everybody who knows a damn thing or might know a damned thing. Delilah Goodknight knows me. She knows I gotta be on to you with your livin' up there in that house with her, playin' footsie. She's gotta figure you and me, we talk."

"About what in particular?"

"Things in general, you might say."

I leaned sideways as his cigar exhaust blew by me. "So she would have told me about Cody and Charmaine? Just to get you steamed? Is that the logic at work here, Snelstrom?"

"Weisenheimer, huh? Don't get smart with me. This ain't a game. I'm talkin' about an attempted murder-one rap. That's felony arson, settin' a fire in the commission of a felony. That's the state pen, McCarthy. Enough time to make her hair turn gray. You get me?"

"So you take this investigation very seriously."

"Damn right. I know the nuts and bolts of this case like I know the back of my hand."

"You knew about Charmaine staying in room 707 at the Multnomah Hotel with Cody Goodknight then."

He swallowed so hard his eyes bugged out. "I make it my business to know the facts in this case," he boasted, puffing out his gut as he exhaled. "But that ain't a fact. That's bullshit from your lady friend."

"You know it's bullshit?"

"Damn right."

"So you already know the name of the guy she was seeing in room 707," I said, hoping to spring the trap. I was positive I knew who was sneaking upstairs to Room 707 and drinking Canadian Club whiskey with Charmaine Goodknight. It just had to be. "And if it wasn't Cody Goodknight, then who was it?"

Snelstrom hid his face behind the cigar for a moment. Stalling, I imagined. "I know everything there is to know about this case, McCarthy."

"You think you know who the guy was?"

"I know who it was," he bluffed. "But it ain't important to the case."

I made a steeple with my fingers and stared at the smoky ceiling. "Seems to me that you might want to know about everybody with a motive, Snelstrom, and if Charmaine Goodknight was seeing somebody on the side, that should figure into your formula."

"There's no proof Charmaine Goodknight was seein' nobody. You got the wrong lady."

"I'm a little surprised you didn't figure it out, Snelstrom."

"How's that?"

I could see it in his eyes now. I had called his bluff, and he was one card short. "Well, you're the professional, right? You make it your business to learn these things."

"Who gives a shit who she was seein' before she settled down? Lotsa them society dames run around when they're just outta the startin' gate."

"I suppose so. But she was seeing this guy after she married Lionel."

"Says who?"

With a cocky grin I pulled a slip of paper from my pocket. Triumphantly, I unfolded the wrinkled page and laid it flat across his plate.

"What the hell is this?"

"A page from the Multnomah Hotel Register. February tenth, 1940."

He leaned over and examined it. "So what, McCarthy? It's a fuckin' page with a fuckin' date. What's your point?"

"This." I thumped my forefinger over the signature swirled in black ink. "Lucy Ranier. You can check out the handwriting. It's Charmaine Goodknight's signature."

"Why the fuck do I care who it is?"

"Because she married Lionel Goodknight in September of 1935."

"So? What the hell does this prove?"

"It's Lucy Ranier. A phony name to conceal the fact that Charmaine was staying at the hotel with someone shortly before the fire."

"So what does that prove?"

"Lucy Ranier met her lover at the hotel, Snelstrom." I refolded the page and put it back in my pocket. "She was there in 1937, a year and a half after Charmaine married Lionel Goodknight. She was also there in February of 1940. She went there to see her old lover."

He rolled the cigar around in his fat fingers. "What're you gettin' at, McCarthy?"

"This guy she was seeing, her lover, had a motive, didn't he? The jilted man, thrown over for Lionel. Maybe he decided to get even."

"Yeah? Who is this mystery stud, and why would I give a fuck?"

I stood up and threw down a fifty-cent piece for my beer. "I thought you said you knew all the facts in this case like the back of your hand, Sam."

"Damned right."

"So what're you asking me for, huh? You know all the fucking answers. You tell me."

"She's gonna make a mistake one a these days, and I'm gonna be there to nail her ass, McCarthy. Count on it."

"You're wasting your time. Chasing down dead-ends. That's what you're doing, Sam. I can't believe your employers pay you for this nonsense."

"Hey, wait." He threw down some bills on the table and reached for his coat. "Tell me one thing before you go, McCarthy."

"Yeah?"

"Why should I give a shit who Charmy was screwin' around with? So who was this guy? What's the angle?"

I didn't need to depend on Sam Snelstrom anymore. "See you around, Sam."

I left Murphy's and headed for the train station. I intended to put Sam's ten spot to good use. I wanted to see Francie and check on her. She'd also be happy to hear I was returning to school to complete my education. More importantly, I could tell her what I had learned about Charmy and Delilah and see if her reaction was the same as mine. I couldn't wait to talk to her.

# Thirty–Six

========

**The** second time I paid a call on Charmaine Goodknight, I didn't have to take a cab. Carla's husband Philip had his kids for the weekend, and he and my sister were taking them up to a cabin on Mt. Rainier. Philip dropped me off at the convalescent center, and Carla wished me well.

"Are you sure you wouldn't like us to wait for you, Nattie?" she asked me.

"No. Go on. Thanks for the lift."

"Take care of yourself, Nathan," Philip saluted me as he put the car in gear and drove off.

I waved to Carla and walked up to the front door. The lady who answered recognized me from my last visit.

"You've come back to see Charmy?"

"Yes, that's right. I'm Nathan McCarthy."

She pulled the door back and stepped aside. The house smelled like garlic simmered in antiseptic.

"Go on up. Charmy don't get many visitors. She'll be pleased to see you."

"Thanks."

"You remember the way?"

"Sure. Thanks."

I put a hand over the bulge in my coat and went upstairs. I followed the long, winding corridor and knocked on Charmy's door.

No answer. I wasn't really expecting a cordial welcome. "Mrs. Goodknight? Hello? It's Nathan McCarthy. I'd like to talk to you."

I could hear the wheelchair squeaking as she propelled it over the noisy floorboards. She was in there, the sightless pockets in her hideous face as bleak and barren as the surface of the moon. I knocked again harder.

"Mrs. Goodknight? I brought something for you." I put my cheek against the wood and listened for some sound of recognition. "Charmy? Please, let me come in for a few moments. I brought you a little refreshment."

A gruff voice boomed through the door. "What'd you bring me, McCarthy?"

"A fifth of Canadian Club, a bottle of Coke and some ice. You'll have to provide the glass."

Another squeak and a scuffing sound as her feet padded across the floor and moved the chair forward. "Open the door. It's not locked for Pete's sake. Quit standin' out in the hall makin' such a damned racket."

I came in. She was sitting in her chair in front of the bed. Her head was tilted back. Her wig was on the bureau. Her pate was crimson and purple like a rotting carp's belly, rippled and gnarled with scar tissue. I looked away, knowing she sensed my repulsion although she had no eyes to see my rejection. I pulled out my paper sack, put the whiskey and cola on the dresser and looked for a water glass.

She read my mind. "On the sink in the bathroom. Don't get carried away with the cola."

"No, Ma'am." I took a glass from the shelf and emptied in my ice cubes borrowed from Carla's GE, poured in a trickle of Coke and sloshed in a half glass of Canadian Club. When I came back into the room, I realized that she had no fingers to take the glass from me. I stood there like a lamp pole, uncertain of what to do next.

"Just give it to me. Make sure it's not filled too full. I hate wasting good whiskey."

I held the glass out until her stump rose and touched me. Then she clamped her knobby stumps in a clumsy embrace around the glass, lifted the whiskey to the slash of a mouth and flicked out her tongue to test my mix before dribbling it in.

"*Ahhhh*, damn. That's good whiskey. Thanks, McCarthy. Hits the spot."

I sat down on the edge of the single bed and tried to see out the window. Not much of a view looking at the shingles of the house next door with its blinds drawn. Charmy was living life imprisoned in a grimmer cell than a death row inmate.

"So you came all the way up from Portland just to see me?"

"I wanted to talk."

She sucked up more liquor. "You do your homework like I told you?"

"Yes, Ma'am. And I have some questions."

"I thought you might." She sighed and let her head fall back and rest against the high back of the chair.

"Tell me about Lucy Ranier."

I could see the muscles in her neck tense, cords bulging in the shiny flesh. Her knees pressed together, and the wet tongue flicked out like a rattler's tracking the scent of a mouse. I had touched a nerve. I was pleased.

"You knew Lucy Ranier, didn't you?" I pressed on.

"That goes back aways."

"Before you married Lionel Goodknight."

She drained the glass. "Fill this up, McCarthy. My brain needs a little lubrication."

I poured her another double. "Tell me about Lucy," I said once she paused to take in a noisy breath.

"What the hell do you want to know about her for?" she grumbled.

"You said to do my homework, and I have. I found out about Lucy Ranier. So I'm here to get some answers. That was the bargain, wasn't it?"

"Nothing to tell. Can't you come up with something better to talk about?"

"I want to know about Lucy. She's the price of that Canadian Club."

"Good for you, McCarthy," she rasped. "You're a hard bargainer, a real tight ass."

"Why did she stay at the Multnomah Hotel? Was it to keep a secret from her father?"

"Maybe."

"Why was it necessary for her to do that?"

She laughed in a voice as thick as chowder. "You never knew her daddy."

"He was a lawyer, wasn't he?"

"Old school, ran his house and his family like a military camp. He wasn't the kind of man who could accept imperfection, even in his only daughter."

"So Lucy needed to hide her private life from her father?"

"If she wanted any private life at all, she had to keep it to herself. That's just the way it was." She flicked out her tongue and lapped at the rim of the glass. "That was a long time ago. It has nothing whatsoever to do with the fire or the fact that Delilah tried to burn me up and kill my baby girl."

"Did anyone else ever know about Lucy and how she spent weekends at the Multnomah Hotel?"

"It's an old story. Who'd give a damn now? You're off on the wrong track, McCarthy."

I reached out and took hold of her glass. My fingers collided with her stumpy arm. "Charmy, I kept my part of the bargain. I'm here to see you keep to yours. Maybe you were just feeding me a line, playing on my sympathy, any sob story for some company and free booze, is that it?"

She jerked the glass away and kicked at the floor so the chair rolled backward. "Just leave me alone then. Who asked you to butt in?"

"Nobody. But you said you wanted me to help you prove Delilah set your house on fire. And I did my homework. Now are you going to help me or not?"

"You don't need to know about Lucy Ranier. That's not part of the story. Who told you about that? Was it that sonuvabitch Snelstrom?"

"I have my own sources. I know that Lucy Ranier stayed at the hotel in room 707. I know she ordered Canadian Club and Coke all the time she was supposed to be on the train to Tacoma to visit her mother."

"You don't say."

"Maybe she was there to hide her affair from her father. Or maybe it was for some other reason."

"Like what for instance?"

I hoped I was reading this right and fitting the pieces together. It had taken me a while to get this far. What I dreaded was Charmy's throaty laugh to let me know I had missed the mark. "Lucy was at the hotel with someone no one ever suspected she'd be with."

"Could have been anybody. In those days, Lucy was a free spirit unfettered by marriage or children. What she did and who she did it with were nobody's business but hers."

"Maybe."

"Damned right."

"And maybe not."

"What's that supposed to mean?" she asked with a slight lisp. "If you have something to say, spit it out."

"I think Lucy was seeing someone her father disapproved of."

"Could be. He was the kind of man who would have asked Jesus Christ for references if he wanted to ask his daughter out."

"I think it was more than that. I think it was someone who could have caused Lucy a great deal of trouble if anyone found out about the affair."

"Is that so?"

"Not just because it was a man her father would never have approved of as his son-in-law," I said slowly, watching her feet twitching in the pink socks. "I think there was something more than that."

"What makes *you* so damn smart, Mr. McCarthy?"

"It took me a long time to put the pieces together. I thought all along that you had to be the wronged woman, and Delilah was the cause of your marriage breaking up."

"She was. Jesus, do you need a signed affidavit? Isn't it clear enough?"

"Not anymore. It's not clear at all."

She shrugged her shoulders and brought the glass up to drink again. "You're not as bright as I gave you credit for, McCarthy. That's too bad. I thought you might be able to help."

"I think Lucy was seeing the same lover even after she married. Her husband never knew who it was."

"What's that have to do with anything? Even if it was true, and it's not, who cares? What does that have to do with anything? The fact is that Delilah broke up our marriage. She tried to take Lionel away from Dottie and me, and when she discovered she couldn't do it, she was eaten up with hate and revenge. She did this to me. If you can't see that, then you're as blind as I am."

"I know who the man was in room 707, Charmy."

The glass tipped and dribbled whiskey down her legs and splotched her pink, cotton stockings. "What a bunch of horsecrap. Look, McCarthy, if she was there, it was because her daddy never allowed her to have any personal kind of life worth living. And then her husband was the same. She never had a chance for freedom to make her own choices. She had to resort to deception and secrecy if she ever wanted a chance to have a little happiness. That's all there was to it."

"Was she in love with her husband? Or did she love the other man, the one she really wanted to spend her life with?"

"Maybe in the beginning, that's how it was. But then after she was married, she had to keep on seeing her lover. He was the one worth living for."

"Did she ever care for Lionel?"

"She did once, I suppose. But it was different. She sneaked off to the hotel and the room on the seventh floor to be with her lover, using the name of Lucy Ranier so her husband wouldn't find out. That's how simple it was."

"Charmy, you don't have to tell me who he was. I know."

"Then why drag all this out in the light of day? What's the use? Lionel's long gone, and I'm everything but buried."

"Lionel never suspected you were unfaithful. He must have loved you very much."

"Like he loved his sports cars, his yacht. The one he really loved was Dottie. He'd do anything for her."

"All the time you and Cody were lovers, nobody knew. Even Delilah never figured it out. You were in love with one brother and married to the other one, the one with a promising future. Cody was already married, working in a produce warehouse."

"He had to marry Susie. She was pregnant."

"I should have been more curious about why Lionel had all the opportunities and family money when his brother Cody was lugging melons back and forth across the Cascades. I should have asked myself why."

"And why *is* that then? Why is it that Cody Goodknight slaves like a Negro in that stupid store for peanuts when his parents had so much? What's the answer to that one?"

"His father cut him out of the will, cut off his allowance, made him drop out of school and get a job."

"Nonsense."

"Professor Ruth told me that. Cody was his student."

Charmaine let out a sigh and sagged like a pricked balloon. "They cut him out of the will when he got Susie in a family way. That's all it was. His parents just couldn't stand the scandal. It wasn't even his fault. Susie lied just to get him to marry her. That's all it was—a trap. But he went ahead and did the honorable thing, married her. He was like that— honorable. Cody wasn't cowed by all that family money. He never was. I admired him for that. But that's all it ever was. He was my brother-in-law. That's it."

"Cody was the one you really loved."

"You figure it out. Why would I cash in a Lionel with money in the bank for a green grocer with a dowdy wife and holes in his socks?"

"Love does crazy things to people."

"You're not the only nosy bastard, McCarthy. Somebody found out about the Multnomah Hotel and Lucy Ranier."

"How?"

"Not a clue. Never knew. I think it was Lionel's father, Colonel Goodknight himself who put some private dick on my tail. He threatened Cody, I know that much. Not just the will, but from the whole family and letting Susie know about Lucy. That's why Cody got cut off from everything."

"And they made him marry Susie, I suppose. Or did he marry her out of spite when you told him you were going to stay with Lionel? Had he asked you to divorce Lionel?"

"I suppose he expected I would. But I knew it would never happen."

"Because of the money?"

"To hell with the money!" she spat. "The dirty bastard would have taken my little girl, kept me from Dottie. He had powerful connections, and I was an adulteress. I could never let that happen."

"Did Lionel go along with that?"

"He didn't want to, but he was afraid of his father. We all were. He chose Dottie over me. Over Delilah too."

"Cody wanted you to leave Lionel and marry him, didn't he? You must have broken his heart."

"He already had a wife."

"People do get divorced. If they want to badly enough."

"He thought it was all about the money, but it wasn't. It never was. It was about Dottie."

"But you had to keep seeing him."

"It was the only way Lucy could keep on living."

"The hotel registry. Lucy Ranier kept on going to the Multnomah Hotel long after she was married to Lionel. As a matter of fact, she was with him shortly before the fire. Was that when you told him you were taking Lionel back, Charmy?"

"Before that. There was a fellow at the hotel who took care of things. I gave him some money, and he reserved a room and kept our identity secret. Lionel never knew. Susie didn't either. Nobody ever knew."

"Delilah didn't steal your husband away. You left him really."

"He was cheating on me behind my back with that floozy all the time I was so worried about his finding out about Cody and me."

"How did you find out about his affair with Delilah?"

She snorted in the whiskey glass and finished it off. "He didn't keep it a secret. Son of a bitch bragged about it. Had her use our beach house. Delilah took advantage of him. That's all it was at first. Gold digger making a play for an older man. For once, Lionel played the fool. But I was stupid and still naïve. I told my father-in-law, and Lionel tried to break my neck when he found out I'd snitched. We had quite a row, and he left that night and moved in with Delilah at our apartment in Seattle."

"Did he walk out on you for good do you think?"

She was nodding in the semi darkness. "I'm sure he wanted to, but his father had other ideas. He didn't want a scandalous divorce with all the nasty infidelity and so on. So I had a pretty good hand to play after all. I got to stay with Dottie and didn't have to pretend I loved Lionel. I had the whole house to myself, and all. But I had to give up Cody. My father in law knew about us after all, and he made it plain as day what would happen to me if I saw Cody again. So we broke it off. For good."

Now I was confused again. I needed a villain to complete my script. If not Delilah, then who? This helpless wretch sitting in the dark like a French-fried Quasimodo? How could Charmaine Goodknight turn out to be a compassionate, caring human being when I had already assigned her to the role of a miserable, hate-mongering witch locked up in this drab room day and night to dwell on her sins? She had turned out to be twice a victim. First of love and then attempted murder.

"Did you still love Cody? Please, help me to sort this out, Charmy. I want so much to find the truth."

"Why? What does truth matter to anybody now?"

"I don't know exactly. I just know that I need you to tell me. Delilah is crazy, you know. Completely insane. She accepts guilt for all of this. All of it. Don't you have any compassion for her at all?"

A brittle silence smashed against my ears. How could I have the audacity to confront her with her rival's anguish when she was so completely ruined herself?

"It's because of her that I'm here like this. I can never forgive, never forget. Not for a single minute. Never."

"Did she start the fire? I just can't accept that."

"Don't you understand? Cody and I were in love. All Delilah knew was that Lionel and I had a beautiful little girl, and he came back to me for reasons that had nothing to do with her. But Delilah's the one who destroyed it all. I'm sorry if that's not the answer you want, Mr. McCarthy, but you wanted the truth, and that's it."

She raised her head as if she could see. Despite the disfigurement, there was a tinge of pride in her posture. "I may have been rash when I was young and beautiful. My father-in-law made sure I suffered for that. But nothing will ever change the fact that I didn't marry for love, but I did love a good man very much. More than anyone else."

"Why did you divorce him after the fire? Was it because you wanted him to be with Delilah?"

"That's not it at all. I was afraid she would do something to hurt Dottie, be a cruel stepmother. I had to do it. I didn't want her to have bad feelings about me. Besides, Lionel couldn't be with me after this. Nobody could."

"Did he ever find out about you and Cody?"

"I don't want to talk about that."

"Please. Just tell me the truth. I need to know."

"No, you don't! You're not listening to what I'm telling you. I loved Cody not Lionel. Delilah hated me because she thought Lionel wanted *me* not her."

Suddenly there was a loud thump. Charmy beat on the arms of the chair with her elbows and scooted around so her back was to me. The glass rolled to the floor. "Go on and get back to Portland now. I never asked you to come, and now you've heard the whole sad story.

There's not a damn thing more to tell. I'm worn out. Leave the whiskey and go on home."

"I had to find out if I had it figured out."

"She's still crazy as a pet coon. It's karma in a way, don't you think?"

"I don't even know what that is. I do know she's living a fantasy. But I still don't think she set the fire."

"You're as much of a fool as Lionel was."

"Then who *did* set the house on fire?"

"You tell me. You're so goddam smart. You figure it out."

"I keep coming back to your little girl. You both loved Dottie so much. I think that's why he could never have done it, risked his daughter's life like that."

"Lionel is innocent. No matter who he really was or what he did, he loved that little girl. Of course, he didn't start the fire."

"So who's left?"

"You think I didn't love Dottie? You think I could have tried to burn her up in that house? If you think that, then you're crazier than Delilah is."

I wasn't sure I had an answer for her. "I'm trying to help Delilah. Trying to find the truth. Maybe that will cure her somehow."

"*That* bitch. Her cure is in the grave."

"I don't think she can be cured until she discovers the truth. She thinks it's all her fault. Everything's her fault. And it isn't."

She strained forward so hard the wheels skidded across the floor. "The hell it isn't! Look at me!" She whirled the chair around to face me. "For God's sake, *look* at me!" she screeched. "Look what she did to me!"

I stood up. "I'm so very, very sorry for what happened to you, Charmy. But what did she do? She fell in love with your husband after you had cheated on him. You're the one who drove him away in the first place. That's your fault not hers."

"That's a filthy lie!"

"And then when he came back to be with his little girl and try to save his marriage, she gave him up. Is that so evil?"

"Who told you this drivel? She's insane. She tried to murder us all!"

"I don't believe that."

"Then get the hell out of my room," she ordered. "Just get the hell out and don't bother coming back."

"If that's what you want."

"She's got you under a spell, McCarthy. You're nothing but a goddam fool."

I walked to the door and opened it. "You may be right. But I just don't believe you, Charmaine. I'm sorry."

"I'm gonna get that bitch. You'll see, McCarthy. If it takes me a hundred years, I'll outlast her. I'll see her in hell before I forgive her for this!" She lunged forward and bent her head like an angry rooster. "In *hell*, McCarthy! Tell her *that!*"

I closed the door and left her ranting and screeching. Downstairs, everyone stared at me as I pulled my coat closed and went outside. I didn't expect to come back.

# Thirty–Seven

===========

**Francie** greeted me at the door and ushered me into her tiny kitchen where the coffeepot was still bubbling.

"You look awful, Nattie. How was she?"

I sank in the nearest chair and put my head back. Frances poured me a cup of coffee and sat down beside me. "She's an evil, mean-spirited lying witch," I mumbled.

"Oh, Nattie. How can you say that about Charmy after what she's been through?"

"It doesn't matter," I sighed, reaching for the hot brew to warm my leaden innards. "She's still a witch."

"What did she tell you? Did you find out about the man in the hotel room?"

"She admitted everything I already had figured out. I could tell I hit a nerve."

Frances sat back and crossed her arms over her chest. She nibbled on her lower lip pensively. "So it was a waste of time, wasn't it?"

"I suppose not. She drank the whiskey."

Frances grinned. "I thought she would. Did you bring back Carla's ice tray?"

"Sorry. I forgot it."

"Carla will not be pleased with you, Nattie."

"Sorry. I just took off and didn't even think about it."

"Well, what now? Are you going to talk to the insurance investigator again?"

I lit a cigarette and drank my coffee. "No. He's got a one-track mind. I'm beginning to think it's because he was attracted to Delilah himself, and she gave him the brush off."

"Hmmm, could be. You know, Nattie," she mused, "she is stunning."

I blushed. "I *have* noticed."

"So where do you go from here?"

"I don't know." I gave her a weak smile. "To bed, I think. I'll get a ride back to Portland in the morning. Do you mind if I camp out on your davenport tonight, Sis?"

"Of course, not." She refilled my cup, always looking out for my needs, the eternal big sister, mothering me. "What are you going to do when you get back?"

"I'm going back to school."

"Oh, Nattie. I'm so happy for you. If it's what you really want to do."

"What do you mean?" I was naturally suspicious of her condescending response. I knew Frances better than that.

"You're sure Gladys didn't browbeat you into this decision?"

"Who? Me?"

She tousled my hair playfully. "Well, it's probably the best thing for you, Nattie. Maybe what you need is an objective outlook on everything. It might help to have some space between you and the situation in Portland right now."

"What the hell does that mean?"

"Sometimes you need to stand back a little, that's all I'm saying."

"Yeah, I suppose so." I gave up trying to be coy. Frances was right. No matter what happened, I just couldn't stay in the rooming house with Delilah. My painful impulses to act out my romantic fantasies were turning me into an emotional zombie without direction, spinning in my own tracks. Gladys was right about that. I didn't have to quit loving Delilah or trying to help her, I just needed to answer the voice inside my head that kept reminding me of the days and weeks slipping by with no sign of progress on either the domestic or academic front. Something had to change. Maybe Delilah could love me better as a professor than a dishwasher at the Multnomah Hotel.

A gentle kiss warmed my cheek. "I'll get you a pillow. A hot bath sound good?"

"Sounds swell."

She stood up. "I'll get you Walter's robe."

My hand came out to catch her wrist. "No, Sis. Don't bother."

Our eyes met for an instant. There was a reflection as deep as an Artesian well in my sister's eyes that reminded me of Delilah's far away stare at the Philco and Lionel's portrait.

"Don't worry. I like it when you use his things. It shouldn't all go to waste. Don't be so sensitive. It's fine. Really. Don't be such a worry wart."

"Are you over it, Fran? Is it finally okay?"

"It'll never be okay. But every day I'm better able to handle it." She winked at me. My indomitable heroine. "Don't worry about me. I'll get the robe and slippers."

My heart sank. I could feel hot tears stinging like rubbing alcohol behind my eyelids. "Jesus, Fran. I feel so goddam rotten." I massaged my temples trying to ease the ache.

"What is it, Nattie?" Her hug was spontaneous and curative. "Tell me."

"I can't."

"Of course, you can. Don't be silly. You tell me everything. Remember the first time you had a wet dream when you were twelve?"

I felt my ears turning crimson. "Ten."

"You were always so precocious, Nat."

"Jesus, Fran, this doesn't make any sense at all."

"Tell me what's going on."

"I feel lousy. Rotten. I'm so crazy about her, Fran. And I don't know what I'm supposed to think. Christ."

She named my torment immediately. "You think she's responsible for setting fire to Charmy's house? Do you really think that, Nattie?"

"Not anymore. She couldn't. She's crazy, losing Lionel, thinking she caused it all. She's as nutty as a fruitcake, Frannie, but she's not a murderer. At least not in my mind. But that doesn't mean she's innocent either. I don't know which side of the fence I'm on. It's one side how I feel emotionally, and the other is where the factual side lives. I can't ignore that. I want to. But I can't."

"I'm so glad to hear you say that. What I think is that if you love someone and believe in them, then that's all that counts. You don't have to prove anything to anybody, Nattie. So long as you believe, that's enough."

"No, it isn't."

"I think it is."

I looked up at her. Pale freckles were sprinkled across her cheeks like flecks of nutmeg. "They all think she's guilty. Even she believes it, I think. If I can't prove to her she's wrong, then I might as well give up."

"Oh, Nattie. Don't say that. You'll figure it out. You always do."

"Sure," I grunted sarcastically. "Nathan the boy genius."

"Remember the time you got locked in Mother's dressing room?"

"Carla lost the key."

She giggled. I loved to hear the sound of her laughter again. Sometimes I despaired of ever hearing it since Walter had died. "Well, you figured out how to take the door off the hinges using some hair clips, a rat tail comb of Mother's and a pair of tap shoes. You impressed the hell out of all of us."

I pecked her cheek. "My cheerleader."

"You'll figure this all out, Nat. I know you will. Have a little faith."

"Sure."

"Look at it this way. The insurance investigator has been working on this case for four years, and he hasn't been able to prove she did it, right?"

"True. Not yet."

"Well, it seems to me that if she were guilty of anything, he'd have come up with something by now, wouldn't he?"

"Maybe."

"He hasn't. So why should you expect to find out what he hasn't been able to learn in four years?"

"There must be something."

She rubbed the back of my neck. "Don't be so hard on yourself. Just go with your feelings. Trust yourself, Nat. Trust *her* a little bit, too, why don't you?" She tweaked my ear.

"She's really crazy, you know," I confessed dolefully. "Sometimes she's one person, and sometimes, she's somebody else altogether."

"Well, we're all a little crazy. I wouldn't hold that against her." She stood up. "I'll get the bedding and Walter's things for you."

I finished my coffee, sank into a warm bathtub and soaked while I smoked Luckies and read the newspaper. I soaped up my hair, dunked beneath the bubbly water and came up feeling ready for sleep. When I crawled onto my sofa bed, the apartment was dark. Frances was in the bedroom, alone with her toes finding only cold, empty sheet beneath her covers. Life was so goddam unfair. The scales so out of balance. What sense did any of it make? I went to sleep long before I came up with an answer.

The next morning, I enjoyed a hearty breakfast Frances prepared for me, hugged her good-bye at the front step and started out for the highway to thumb a ride back to Portland. I got lucky. A traveling huckster in a salesman's special, an oxidized-blue Plymouth coupe with a crack in the windshield and bald tires picked me up and took me all the way to the St. John's Bridge. I thanked him as I climbed out. In ten minutes, I hitched a second ride with a beer truck which dropped me off in front of the Smith Block downtown and a short walk home.

I turned up the street and stopped. I pulled my hat down and rubbed my hands together to ward off the chill. It was there. Parked at the front curb was Cody Goodknight's old truck with the tarp covering a load in back. Things did have a way of fitting together, opposites attracting, comets and planetary bodies meeting in the universal void. I was going to have to meet my destiny head on. Ready or not.

I went up the steps and hesitated just a moment at the door to eavesdrop. I heard nothing and went inside. As I entered the foyer, I could hear the pipes singing in the walls. Water was rushing into the claw-footed tub upstairs. I walked down the hall and looked into the kitchen. Cody's broad butt was poking out of the Frigidaire. He didn't even hear me come in.

"Hi," I said, shedding my coat and hat at the kitchen door. "Gotta problem there?"

He was bent over the condenser. A pair of pliers and a screwdriver were stuck in his belt. "Uh, hi. McCarthy, isn't it?"

"That's right. How's it goin'?"

"Oh, damn icebox shorted out on her. Little electrician's tape oughtta fix it up."

"Need any help?"

"No, thanks. I got it. I just stopped by to help her out with a few chores around here before I head back."

I circled around the work area, watching as he spliced two wires together. "You carrying produce in the back of your truck out there?"

"Huh?" He looked up briefly. "Naw. Just some paper stuff, toilet tissue and crap. Hadda go up to Camas to get it from the wholesaler up there." He dropped a roll of black tape on a rack and straightened his back. "I like to help Dee out when I can. She said you were up in Washington visiting your sister."

"Yeah. I just got back."

"She's a war widow like Dee, huh?"

"Yeah."

"Shame. Damned shame. This war stinks. So many good guys like Lionel never comin' back home."

"Yeah. Damned shame."

"Hand me that knife there, will ya?" He pointed at the penknife on the kitchen table. I retrieved it for him, and he snipped the tape. "That oughtta do it. Go ahead and plug it in."

I snaked the cord behind the pie cupboard and pressed it into the outlet. The old condenser began to rumble and hum.

Cody gathered up his tools. "Just caught up on a few odd jobs for her. Things always need fixing in a place like this."

"Uh huh."

"I keep tellin' her she oughtta move into an apartment. Better for her, too. She works too hard around here."

"She likes this house. I don't think she wants to leave it."

He hitched up his pants and accepted a Lucky Strike I offered. "Well, she works too damned hard around here. Taking care of boarders is too damned much for her. She should sell this heap and move into a nice little apartment with new plumbing and a decent furnace."

"I suppose so."

"I try to tell her to forget about all this, but she's stubborn as a mule. It's hard to get through to her sometimes."

We adjourned to the sleeping porch where Cody climbed up a rickety stepladder and unscrewed the porch light. I watched him as he put in the replacement bulb, yanked on the chain and stuffed the throwaway in his back pocket.

"Do you know someone by the name of Ranier?" I asked him suddenly.

He took a step down the ladder. "Who?"

"Ranier."

"No. Don't." He came down and folded the ladder. He was headed back down to the basement, and I followed him.

"Lucy Ranier," I called out after him as we thumped down the stairs. Below, the furnace was belching and roaring like a drunken bull. "Did you know her?"

He put the ladder back behind the stairs, set the tools down on the bench and slicked back his oiled hair. My Lucky dangled from his mouth. "I said I didn't know her." His voice tightened.

"I thought you might remember the name."

He turned around, and I saw the combination of fear and hatred blazing in his eyes. I could visualize electric sparks flying from his nostrils, flames shooting from his mouth. A dragon about to slay a hapless knight with one fatal blow. "I said I didn't know her, McCarthy."

"Okay. Just curious."

He clamped both hands on the bench and leaned his weight forward. "Who wants to know? Where'd you hear that name anyhow?"

I spoke before I had time to consider my options trapped in the basement with this hulk of muscle and bone. "Charmy told me about her. I saw the name on old registers from the Multnomah Hotel."

He raised his head slowly. Very slowly. When he looked at me, I had the sense to be genuinely concerned for the first time. He looked as if he was going to lunge at me and tear out my throat with his bare hands. I could count the individual pores on his swarthy skin, identify each strand of greasy hair hanging limply over a bushy brow. Bluto in person.

"Tell me, McCarthy, now why in hell would anyone want to do that?"

"Pardon?" I strained to hear his voice. His lips were barely moving.

"Why would anybody but a fucking idiot want to go around looking at old hotel registers, huh? You trying to dig up some dirt on somebody? What the hell's the matter with you?"

"You knew Lucy, didn't you, Cody?" I held my ground as he took one step toward me even though I wanted to turn around and race up the stairs to safety. As I watched his ropy muscles flex under the flannel shirt, I could see myself being hurled against the wall, my guts ripped from my body with one punch as my teeth flew out of my head and clattered onto the concrete floor. Nobody would ever find the remains after Cody hauled me across the Coast Range mixed in with the rolls of toilet paper and bury me in a gravel pit somewhere. Oh, my God. My sisters would never forgive me.

"Who says you gotta right to talk to Charmy?" he snarled.

"I know about Lucy Ranier and the Multnomah Hotel. I know who was in Room 707."

He advanced with one more step to put him in arm's reach of my face. I closed my eyes as he lowered his chin and drew back his right fist like a sledgehammer aimed at the middle of my forehead. My entire body would probably end up in a plaster cast with both legs in traction for six months.

"Cody?" The bell sounded from the top of the stairs. In a voice as clear as an angel's song, Delilah had come to my rescue. "Is that you? Who are you talking to, Cody?"

"Nobody, Dee. Go on back upstairs. I'll be right up." Cody pressed a hand against my chest and pushed me into the wall.

"Delilah!" I shouted out. "It's me. Nathan."

She came down the stairs and looked at us with a puzzled frown on her face. "Nathan? I didn't know you were home."

"I just got home, Delilah. I was... uh, helping Cody fix the icebox."

"Oh." She checked with her brother-in-law who stepped back and tucked his shirt in. "Cody, are you done?"

"Uh, yeah. It was just a short. It's okay. I changed the light on the back porch, too."

"Well, why don't you come up then? Can you stay for supper?"

Cody shot me a look of disgust which translated as *"Don't worry, Sucker, I'll get you later,"* and squeezed by me for the stairs. "I'll be right up, Dee. We gotta finish something down here before I go, okay? We'll be right up."

Delilah studied my face, probably whiter than pure cane sugar, and then looked back at Cody. "I heard you talking about someone," she said warily, watching for either of us to give her a clue.

"We were just passing time," Cody interjected. "You go on. We'll be right up."

She took another step down. I took a step up in her direction, just far enough away to be out of Cody's grasp.

"What's going on?" she asked with a prescient frown at both of us. "Is something wrong?"

"Naw. Nothin', Dee. Go on up and give us a few minutes, okay? Me and McCarthy got somethin' to discuss, that's all. It doesn't concern you."

I looked up into those wonderful, radiant eyes and pleaded my case. "Delilah, it's *all* about you. Believe me. Cody isn't telling you the truth."

"You sonuvabitch," he slurred, making a grab for my collar.

Delilah held onto my arm. "What do you mean? Cody, tell me what he's talking about."

"Nothin', Dee. Don't get upset."

"Ask him about Lucy Ranier. Just ask him, Delilah." I watched her eyes grow dim, fading away where I couldn't intrude. "Delilah! Please, just listen to me. Cody has something very important he needs to tell you. Ask him about Lucy Ranier."

She averted her gaze to study Cody's sweaty jowls and snake-eyes. "Cody, what's he saying? What does he mean?"

"Nothin', Dee. It's a lotta bullshit. Don't listen."

"Who is Lucy Ranier?"

"How the hell should I know?"

"I heard him say something about the Multnomah Hotel. What is he talking about?"

So she had been listening from the top of the stairs. She had overheard it all. Then she knew Cody was lying. She had to. I could see the revelation in her eyes.

"Delilah, Cody knows who Lucy Ranier is. She was a lady he loved. Someone he met secretly at the hotel for years. Nobody ever knew until Lionel found out about it."

"What are you saying? Cody has been cheating on Susie?"

"Lucy wasn't a real person," I told her. "That was a name Cody's lover used when they met secretly at the hotel."

Cody tossed a wrench on the cement where it slammed into the furnace box. "Don't listen to this, Dee! There's no point. This doesn't concern you. It was a long time ago."

"What's Lucy Ranier's real name?" she asked him.

"It's just a lady, that's all," he hemmed, pulling at his neck. "It doesn't have a thing in the world to do with you."

She descended another step so she was at my level. "Nathan, tell me. What is this all about? Does it have anything to do with Lionel?"

"Yes."

Cody lunged at me. "You miserable bastard!"

"Cody!" she shrieked, tearing at my shirttails as he hauled me back down the stairs and thumped me on the back with a fist as hard as a major league fastball.

I ducked my head and avoided a punch that would have landed me in the emergency room of St. Vincent Hospital. Before Cody could rewind, Delilah was between us, yelling at him and shielding me from another blow.

*"Leave him alone! Stop, stop!"* Delilah tugged on her brother-in-law's arm. "Tell me what he means, Cody! Don't lie to me! Don't you dare lie to me, dammit!"

"I have nothin' to tell you, Dee. I swear. Nothing. So help me God," he heaved, holding up a saintly salute.

She whipped her head around and drilled me with a diamond-hard stare that wrenched the words from my throat.

"Delilah, Cody was meeting Lucy Ranier in the hotel. He loved her, but he was married to someone else, and then so was she."

"Who's Lucy Ranier? Are you trying to tell me something about Lionel, Nathan?" she wept. "For God's sake, then tell me. Is that why he hasn't come home? Has there been someone else all along, Nathan?"

Oh, shit. I folded my shaky arms around her and cradled her like a baby. She cried pitifully while I tried to comfort her. Cody had deflated his chest and stood looking like a shell-shocked soldier, without speaking, without meeting my eyes.

"No, no," I whispered. "Nothing like that. Lucy Ranier was really Charmaine Goodknight. And she and Cody were lovers."

I could feel Delilah shudder in my arms. But she didn't speak. Cody turned away and slammed his fist against the furnace door.

"Cody? Is that true? Is it?" she asked in a little girl's voice. "Can it be true?"

He broke down and began to shuffle his feet and wring his hands. "Yes, dammit. It's true." He turned around. He had soot streaked across his cheeks. "That was a long time ago, Dee. Long time ago. Before you knew Lionel, believe me. This doesn't concern you. I don't know why this sonuvabitch would want to bring up this shit. Maybe just to get back at me for some reason, to hurt Susie. Hell, how should I know?"

"Why would he want to hurt you?"

"How the hell should I know?"

She looked up at me. "Nathan, tell me the truth. Does this have something to do with Lionel?"

I couldn't answer her immediately. I had to be sure. I wanted to be dead certain I finally had it right.

"Nathan? It does, doesn't it?"

"Yes. It does. You need to know the truth, Delilah. It's your only chance to get well, the only way to help yourself."

"What do you mean?"

"Delilah, you're sick. I only wanted to help you, can't you see that?" I buried my face in her hair and held on.

"Don't listen to this bastard, Dee." Cody jerked her away from me, like taking candy from a baby. "Go on upstairs now like I told you. You don't need to listen to this guy."

"Let me go, Cody." She freed herself and stood between us. "I want to know about Lionel."

"This has nothing to do with him," Cody whined belligerently.

"I have a right to know. Tell me, Nathan."

I did. "Charmaine fell in love with Cody when she was engaged to Lionel. They began an affair but had to keep it secret from Lionel and his parents. Then when Cody got Susie pregnant, he had to drop out of school. When his father found out, he cut him off in disgust without a cent. And so Cody had to get married, then with a wife and child to support, he took a job in the produce warehouse, and he was trapped. But he still loved Charmaine. And she loved him. But Lionel was going to inherit everything not Cody. Lionel finished college and went to work in the brokerage house while Cody was washing cabbages at the produce warehouse with a wife and baby to support. So Charmaine married Lionel. And Cody and Charmaine continued as lovers, meeting secretly at the Multnomah Hotel for years until the fire."

"Dee, for crissakes," he interrupted. "Don't listen to this jerk."

She was shaking her head, prepared for more. "Tell me about Lionel. I know about Cody's problem with his father. He was angry and disappointed because Cody got Susie in a family way. They never approved of Susie because she was a nobody. Her father was a drunk, and her mother was arrested for prostitution once. Cody's father considered her nothing but trash and cut him off when he married her. Mr. Goodknight was like that. So it doesn't matter about Lucy then, does it?" Her eyes questioned mine.

"That's not the only reason Cody's father cut him off completely. It had to do with his affair with Charmaine."

"You goddam bastard!" Cody growled like a junkyard dog. "What the hell do you wanna go and tell her that for?"

"Is that true?" she asked her brother-in-law. "It is, isn't it?"

I had to tell her the rest. "Delilah, you think Lionel left Charmaine because of you."

Her eyes closed now. "He loved me. I know he did. But he had to go back to his little girl. Don't you understand that, Nathan?" She turned. "Cody? You understand that, don't you? He had to."

"It doesn't matter now, Dee. Forget about it. It's all in the past. Over and done with. Ancient history."

"Lionel left Charmy because he found out his wife was sleeping with his brother all the time they were married," I told her gently, hoping it was sinking in. "You had nothing to do with their marriage failing. Cody and Charmaine broke up Lionel's marriage, not you, Delilah."

I saw a new clarity shining out at me. "Lionel knew that? He knew that Charmaine was seeing Cody, Nathan?"

"No!" Cody spat at us. "That's a bunch of crap, Dee. Don't listen to this sonuvabitchin' liar. Lionel never knew anything. Nothin'. *Not a goddam thing.*"

Delilah stood between us, looking first to me then to him. Her face never betrayed her judgment. Nothing. No anger, no tears. Nothing. "Cody, tell me the truth. Were you having an affair with Charmaine all those years?"

He hung his head, bit his lip and dug his heel into the cinders on the concrete. It was answer enough for her.

"Lionel would know, wouldn't he? He must have known." Then she looked back at me. "That's why he left her?"

"Yes," I told her. "It had nothing to do with you. Nothing at all. You just happened to be there when he needed a place to land."

"Thank you, Nathan," she murmured, stroking my face with the coolest, tenderest touch I could remember receiving from a mortal. "How very kind of you to let me know that."

As Cody and I stood there like chimneys, she glided gracefully up the stairs, pushed open the door and left us in the dark with only the creaking of the floorboards overhead to mark her departure.

# Thirty–Eight

===========

**"Is** he gone?" I sat up suddenly, feeling the blood rush to my head.

"Yes. He's gone."

She closed the door and sat on the edge of the bed that shrieked in protest at the extra burden.

I switched on the hula girl lamp and brushed the hair back from my eyes. "Are you alright, Delilah?"

Tenderly, with slow-motion grace, she reached out and touched me. "I'm fine. Don't worry about Cody. He's always protected me, looked after me since Lionel's been away."

"I know, but..."

Her hand pressed lightly over my lips. "It doesn't matter about that. It was a long time ago. They were so young, Nathan. They were in love, weren't they?"

"Yes, but they let you think it was all your fault for everything."

"So much in love for such a long time."

"Charmaine was cheating on Lionel all along," I protested.

"It doesn't matter anymore. Don't blame Cody. He's been punished enough, hasn't he?"

Maybe she was wiser than I. Or maybe just crazier. I couldn't figure it out. I was only relieved that Cody Goodknight had climbed in his old truck and made himself disappear back over the mountains for the coast. I could sleep in peace without wondering if I would wake up in a hospital room with every known bone in my body broken. Delilah had calmed his temper and fed him some supper while ushering me upstairs to pace in my room until he left. I had lain down on the lumpy bed, tried editing my manuscript and fallen fast asleep.

Delilah put a hand on a typewritten page that had fluttered onto my pillow. "Why don't you finish the book, Nathan? I wish you would."

"I don't have an ending."

"You're not going to let them be happy, are you? Ethan and Charmaine."

"I'm not sure they deserve to be that happy."

"Does anyone deserve to be happy?" Her clear eyes blinked back a bottomless sadness behind the thick lashes. "Who says anybody deserves anything anyway?"

"I hope it's not so bleak as that."

"Then why can't you give them a happy ending? Why do love stories always have to be so sad?"

"I don't know. Why are you so sad?"

"It's just that it's so empty here. Especially at night. I get so lonely sometimes, Nathan."

I drank in her musky taste with my mouth pressed close against her cheek. Both arms went around her and meshed our bodies in a slow, careful embrace. She was wearing the blue, satin nightgown that slipped like melting butter through my hands. "I swear I want you more than anything in this world. All I want in this life is to protect you, look after you, keep you safe forever, Delilah."

"You mustn't blame Cody. He was just trying to protect me."

"I never want you to be so sad again."

"Cody looks after me, Nathan. It's so lonely with Lionel away. You understand, don't you?"

My lips swelled with a longing about to be freed as I kissed her warm neck and lapped at her silky cheek. I could have devoured her whole and infused my body with her incredibly luscious scent and still been half-empty. My need was so great that this incredible, fortunate moment was about to eclipse my expectations. It had been too long anticipating the taste of the fruit, too long pining over my poor fantasies held up to the ridiculous light of morning's reality. This couldn't be real, couldn't be happening to me at last. Delilah was not succumbing, surrendering in a sweet, passionate swan dive into my squeaky bed. This was more. Much more. This was not conquest. It was completion. It was a gracious gift to treasure, the granting of a beautiful dream, a wanting so pure and painful I can still recall the spark in my fingertips when I touched each virginal spot on her body for the first time.

Somewhere, far away from my pulsing libido, I understood that she must be trying to tell me that Cody's alibi was for the best, a demonstration of his devotion and loyalty. But it didn't register immediately.

"Did he lie for you, Delilah?" I whispered smothered beneath her plush lips trembling against mine. "The night of the fire were you with Cody all night like he said?"

"He was only trying to do what he thought was best for me, Nathan. You understand that, don't you? He didn't mean to hurt me. Cody would never do that."

Her eyes looked straight through me. She disengaged as suddenly as she had reached out a moment before to connect with my flesh and bone. Now she was halfway lost somewhere in space, physically there beside me on the bed, incredibly irresistible and vulnerable, but spiritually on a solo flight across the Pacific Ocean on a mission to mate with a kindred lost soul. I was being abandoned, left behind once more.

"Delilah?"

Those brilliantine eyes looked up at me, shone like welding sparks and left me breathless. It didn't matter anymore, did it? Who was lying, who was telling the truth. If Cody was lying to save himself or save Delilah. If Delilah was with Cody or alone all night vulnerable to creeps like Snelstrom wanting to hang her from the nearest tree, wasn't important. None of it mattered. I was in love. Completely, insanely in love. And love conquered all, didn't it?

Wasn't that what Frances and Professor Ruth were trying to tell me? What mattered was my faith. I believed. God, I believed. With all my heart. With every inch of my quivering self I believed and prayed for the strength to keep on believing.

I tried to suck the life from her body as we kissed with open mouths then held my breath and dipped below the waves as she clung to me. We sank to the covers. I had both arms and legs wound tightly around her. My hand reached up and switched off the hula lamp.

"Delilah," I gasped in the darkness as I felt her hips undulate beneath mine. There didn't seem to be a matter of seconds ticking by, minutes and hours passing away as I fondled her and caressed every curve, every hollow and slender dip of her belly and breasts rising like fresh bread dough under my exploring fingers. "I love you... I love you. That's all that matters."

She never answered me. Never spoke a word as we made love on the gossiping bed springs. Suddenly, seemingly with no forethought, no clumsy machinations of belts, suspenders, snaps and silk, I was released from my fantasy and glided into her. My whole body froze for an instant, paralyzed in her sultry embrace. Then I rushed her into the abyss and hung on like a drowning man in a cyclone as we thrashed on the mattress. The bed screamed. The hula lamp swayed on the nightstand and shook the grass skirt. All the while I exulted in my delirium, I heard nothing except the whisper of her breath on my chest and the sharp slap of our sweaty flesh as we were swept toward the tidal shore.

When the ultimate moment arrived, I threw my head back, closed my eyes and moaned like a milk cow, but she never made a sound. I kicked with both feet as I shuddered with the aftershocks and gasped for breath while Delilah turned her face away and clutched the sheet. I remember that and the disappointment on opening my eyes again and seeing her staring blankly at the wall. Not at me. At something only she could see. As if I hadn't really been there at all, inside her, part of her even for that brief moment in time.

I had Delilah. For this one moment in 1944, she was mine. It was delirium, raw ecstasy and the purest form of unrestrained lust. The fact it was unrequited was not crucial to my pride. Youth forgives many things, among them the blind optimism that leads young men into such hopeless affairs in the first place. Planting my seed in Delilah was proof enough of my belief in her and my place in her life. And there was absolutely nothing else that mattered. Only this woman glistening like oiled marble, painted with a scarlet flush as she clasped my shoulders. All I wanted or ever hoped to possess was a part of me at last. Only Delilah Goodknight inhabited my world. She was enough for now. Partial payment for a future lifetime yearning to return to this moment with such blind devotion, pure faith and total absolution.

But those moments are not repeated. They never come again to replay with better instincts, a smoother technique, the right word or nuance. It's useless to imagine them as anything other than what they appear to be with the passage of time and wisdom: miracles. And as wonderful as they are, time never improves on their performance. It is enough to experience them in the innocent spontaneity that rewards young lovers so generously. Time only makes the longing for their truth even more painful. But that's the way of miracles.

# Thirty–Nine

===========

**I** woke up. My head felt like a drugstore cotton ball. I had no spit in my mouth. Both ears were ringing off the hook. My body ached as if the Russian Army had marched over my backbone. My balls felt as shriveled as last year's jack o'lantern. I licked my cracked lips, reached out to touch Delilah and recharge my batteries and grabbed only a clammy pillow. She was gone. My bed was cold.

I sat up, groggy and momentarily disoriented. This was not a dream. This was real. My bed was still damp with our juices. I was worn out from loving her all night long. But my feast had only whetted my appetite for more. Waking up to find myself sleeping alone was confusing. Where would she be if not curled up in my arms where I had left her before I succumbed to a stupor paralyzing my limbs still locked in a wrestler's hug?

I switched on the hula lamp. My room was empty. No Delilah. A rosy tinge of dawn was shading the window. Morning already. God, I was tired.

I blinked back the crusty sleep in my eyes and listened. Tinny, radio music was coming from the sleeping porch below my room. The Philco radio played a serenade. Voices floated up through the screens to my window. Someone was downstairs playing the radio, laughing.

Crawling out of bed, I groped for my trousers. I jumped into my pants, grabbed my Luckies, lit one as I went out the door and tossed the dead match in my pocket. I walked to the stairs and stood for a second, sucking in the tobacco smoke. I could hear a woman's voice from downstairs and knew it must be Delilah's.

I made my way quietly down to the foyer. The clink of glasses as an orchestra began a Glenn Miller swing tune wafted from the rear of the house. I walked through the dark kitchen. The glow from the old Philco radio barely illuminated the room. A glimmer of sunlight was breaking through the naked tree in the backyard, painting the wicker furniture with false whitewash. I took a cautious step forward and stood halfway in the doorway. Then I heard her voice caressing her lover with tender murmurs and purring endearments she had withheld from me.

Polar icicles stabbed my heart as I stood transfixed, trying to catch my breath. How could she leave my bed and be with someone else? Were my worst nightmares coming true? Was there no God in heaven to save my ego? What was I supposed to do, storm in and kill the sonuvabitch holding her? Declare my undying love in some corny, Paramount scene and play the sap? Never had I been made to feel so worthless, so shamed, so completely humiliated. Balls-ass naked in the classroom with the whole assembly laughing at my puny appendage—the ultimate nightmare come true. So powerless to control my own emotions, I was devastated, destroyed, consumed with a fiery jealousy which had to be avenged.

Deaf and half-blinded with rage, I burst in and whirled around to face the sonuvabitch snuggled up to Delilah on the sofa. I was prepared to kill anyone within my reach. My lips curled, my fists drew back, nostrils flared, and the veins in my neck bulged like Chinese noodles as I yanked at a handful of shirt and prepared to rip some rival's heart out with my bare fingers.

*"What the hell are you doing, you sonuvabitch?"* I yelled, effortlessly jerking the silly bastard up from the couch with one hand. *"Take your filthy paws off her!"*

My heart skipped a beat. I froze, every tendon and muscle in my body hanging in the void by a slender thread of reality. There he was at last. My rival. Staring at me with sullen, glassy, shoe-button black eyes and sculpted, chiseled features like Dick Tracy.

"Everything's going to be alright now. Don't pay any attention to him, Darling," Delilah crooned into his ear. She stroked his shellacked hair lovingly with her crimson-tipped fingers and kissed a painted curl. "You know you're the one I care about, and it's been so lonely without you." She was trying to straighten his jacket. "You understand, don't you, Darling? You won't be angry with me, will you?"

My heart was pounding so hard, my eyes hurt. I let go and bit down on my lower lip until I tasted blood. "Don't do this, dammit. Stop it!"

"I love you so, so very much," she cooed lovingly, nuzzling his neck.

He never moved, never uttered a reply, never held her, cupped her childlike face in his hands and kissed away her tears. He just slumped on the cushions, filled the space beside her, stolid, rigid, cold and unfeeling dressed in his rumpled dress whites with his gold-braided hat on his lap and a full glass of whiskey at his elbow.

"Tell me you love me. I love you so," she pleaded softly. When he didn't answer, tears streamed down her cheeks and made my heart bleed.

I began to shake until my teeth chattered. I had no idea what to do. I was totally unprepared to deal with this. Only hormones were operating. Anger, rage, humiliation, fear, all these things overwhelmed me at once. Here was the object of my adulation, my first real love, acting as if I didn't exist. This was my anonymous rival beside her. Sitting there like a lump of laundry with a phony smile painted on his face. The stealthy lover who crept up the stairs to room Number 1 and spent the long nights lying like a piece of firewood next to my darling. The interloper who masqueraded as a Naval officer, sat on the sleeping porch in the wee hours of the morning with an untouched whiskey at his side, cigarettes smoldering at his fingertips and a stare as lifeless and vacant as Delilah's was now when she finally looked up at me standing there.

I started to blubber like a baby. "Delilah... Oh, Jesus. Delilah, don't. Don't do this. Please, don't do this."

"It's been so lonely, but he's come back to me. I told you he would. Can't you leave us alone now?"

"Delilah, don't. Please, for God's sake." I tried to pull her away.

"No! Don't touch him!" She clutched at his sleeve and hung on until she yielded to my fierce yank. Then she fell back with his plaster hand caught like a prize in hers. She put both arms up to shield her face and began to shiver and moan. The molded limb clunked to the floor and rolled under the sofa.

Delilah howled like a wounded animal captured in a trap and made the hair stand up on the back of my neck. I had never heard a human being make noises like this. It was like the cries of madness echoing from the dungeons of an asylum.

"Delilah, for God's sake stop it! Stop!"

She kicked, scratched and sank her teeth into my hand. I was struggling to restrain a wild animal who only an hour before was an angel in my arms. I had no idea what to do to calm her down. Her eyes were dilated, and after a while spittle glistened on her cheeks. I didn't recognize this mad woman anymore. I didn't know her. And I couldn't seem to reach through the madness no matter what I tried to do. Delilah didn't see me or hear me as we fought like feral cats.

"Delilah, it's me! Nathan! Stop it! *Stop it!*"

She wrenched free for a second and slapped my face so hard my nose spurted blood. I grabbed hold again and pinned both arms to her sides as she shrieked and keened like a banshee. We lurched across the room and fell against the Philco, knocked it over and toppled the floor lamp.

As we grappled and staggered like drunken boxers trying to survive until the bell, we bumped against the wicker sofa, and her lover slumped to one side, bowed his plaster head and slid to the floor. There he lay on the rag rug like a broken toy, a dismembered department store mannequin with glossy, black hair, glass eyes and ruby lip prints on his lifeless mouth.

Suddenly, Delilah quit fighting, quit yelling and went limp in my arms. She sagged to her knees and fell over the mannequin, drew her knees up in a fetal curl and shut her eyes. I was trying to catch my breath, wipe the dripping blood from my lip and suck on the painful bite at the web of my right hand while I watched her whimpering on the floor like a whipped dog. God, this couldn't be happening. Not to my beautiful, mysterious Delilah, my dream lover.

"Delilah?" I called softly.

There was a noise at the door, and when I looked up, Miss Nigh was standing there with her hair in rag curlers, cold cream on each cheek. She clutched the throat of her robe and stared at Delilah with eyes as big as jumbo ripe olives. "Good lord in heaven, Mr. McCarthy. Is she alright? Should I call somebody for you?"

"Call the hospital. You better call an ambulance, I guess."

"What's wrong? Has she been hurt?" She turned halfway around and bit her lip as she looked down on poor Delilah cuddled against the broken mannequin.

"I don't know, Miss Nigh," I snapped, wanting help desperately, but angry as hell for this nosy crone to see Delilah like this. "Just please call for the ambulance, will you?"

I stood there for a moment. I could hear Miss Nigh dialing the number from the hallway. I was hoping maybe this was a bad dream, another crazy episode that would pass in a few minutes and return Delilah to me, demented and in disarray but a part of my world again. As I waited and watched her, she gave no sign of even wanting to rejoin me. She seemed peaceful finally. Her eyes stared off into space and looked right through me as if I wasn't there.

I knelt and touched her gently on the shoulder. She was as rigid as stone. "Delilah?"

She never even blinked. Only the mannequin returned my incredulous stare as I waited for the ambulance to come and take her away from me.

# Salem, Oregon 1974

# Forty

===============

**Delilah** never spoke to me again. Never uttered my name or looked me directly in the eye. The nurses said she would curse when they took her down the hall for her weekly shower and got soap in her eyes, but otherwise she became mute. The medical diagnosis was catatonia, and when I was absorbed with the tragedy of her case, I poured through every book I could find at the library that described the clinical prognosis of her illness. The volumes offered little hope. Whatever it was that caused her to close her mind to reality, to refuse to accept incoming stimuli and live her life like a stalk of celery, was beyond my understanding or that of the doctors as it turned out. All I was ever able to determine for myself was that whatever private demons had been torturing her, she seemed to be at peace with them in her limbo. For all I knew, she was carrying on a happy, active existence somewhere else where I could never gain admission. All I could see was the shell she left behind. That's what I liked to think had happened to Delilah as the years went by. It helped me cope with the pain when I watched her withering away.

Whenever I came to visit her, she would sit listlessly with her knees locked together, both hands folded in her lap and stare right through me. What she saw with those wonderful, radiant, sad eyes only she knew. I always imagined she saw Lionel standing tall and proud like a Viking in his Navy dress uniform, waving from the bridge of the *USS Hammann.*

"How are you feeling today, Delilah?" I began another visit as I pulled up a chair. "I brought you something." I set down a white bakery box. It was her favorite—fresh, lemon tarts with meringue. "Would you like one?" I tempted her.

Her eyes blinked once. No other sign of recognition came from the placid face. Only the hands would move and betray the faintest hint of sharing my dimension. Otherwise, she was a perfect, polite listener as I rambled on about my students, the doctoral dissertation committee I chaired for the history department of Willamette University, the birth of my third son Harold, the assassination of John Kennedy, my sister Francie's bookseller's award for her fifth and most successful romance novel, Gladys' Doctor boasting about all the celebrity patients at his private clinic, Carla and her husband now grandparents of an expanding brood living a good life in the burbs. Delilah just sat there like a sphinx while I gabbed on, flashing photos of the latest addition to the family tree, looking far beyond the present to somewhere with perennial blue, sunny skies and happier people than those poor, lost wretches at the Oregon State Hospital who surrounded her now.

I always made it a point to stop by at Christmas time. Somehow I suspected it was always the worst time of the year for her. And whether she sensed my presence or not, I felt better sitting there holding her hand, tempting those once strawberry lips with the scent of fresh lemons and hoping she could remember what she was still waiting for this holiday season.

"It's almost Christmas, Delilah," I said, opening the bakery box. "No snow again this year, I'm afraid. Laura is making pies, and the boys and their wives are all home again trimming the tree tonight. We'll have a full house."

Her mouth barely opened as I offered a tasty tart. First her tongue flicked out to taste the custard. Then slowly, her lips parted, and she accepted a tiny bite of my treat.

"You know, Delilah, they make these just for you," I said, watching her chew noiselessly, cheerlessly.

"Nat, maybe you shouldn't try to make her eat," Laura scolded. "It's such a waste anyway, isn't it?"

My hand shook as I held up another morsel and waited for her mouth to open. Tears flooding my eyes blurred my vision. "It's alright, Laura. It doesn't matter. If she enjoys it, so what?"

My wife snapped her purse closed. "Nathan, haven't you ever wondered about her?"

"What do you mean? Wondered what?"

She puffed her cheeks and lowered her chin, her favorite expression of frustration with my responses. "Well, think. Don't you still wonder who really set that fire?"

"I never think about it anymore."

"I suppose we'll never find out then, will we?"

"I suppose not."

Laura rolled on fresh lipstick and snapped her compact closed. "Well, still, Nat. One wonders after all. Either she did it, and that's what drove her crazy or Cody did it all. Either way, it's so tragic, isn't it?"

"Uh huh."

"Does she know Cody's dead?"

"I have no idea," I lied. I knew she must have understood me the chilly day I sat on the bed and told her that her brother-in-law had driven his Ford off the cliffs at Oceanside. Nobody knew if it was a suicide or an accident. Susie said he had been declining steadily since his sister-in-law's mental breakdown, and then after Charmy died, he started drinking. The day I brought Delilah the sad news, she refused to open her mouth for a single bite of lemon meringue tart. She knew.

"She's the last one now. When she dies, nobody will care anymore anyway," Laura sighed.

"I suppose not."

Cody dead. Charmy had died some years before. Pneumonia took her off one evening with nobody at her bedside. Her daughter Dottie was now a nurse at St. Vincent's in the burn unit. Sam Snelstrom I completely lost track of until Frances spotted his obituary in the *Seattle Times* and called me. Old Sam spent his last years playing bingo and drooling on himself in a seedy rest home just off the Kelso I-5 exit. Never did close the case, I guess.

"Well, we should go. You promised Marcus you'd be home in time to help him wrap his presents. He's really all thumbs. I know what it is. A new mixer with all the attachments that I'll probably never use."

"He's an engineer, Laura. He can't help himself."

"But you have to admit, he comes in handy when something breaks down," she teased. "It's a quarter after, Nat, and you know what the traffic is like."

"In a minute, Hon." I wiped the corner of Delilah's mouth.

Laura siphoned a noisy breath, impatient with my tardiness. "I hate to leave the boys too long on Christmas eve. Rosemary and Professor Garland are coming over if you forgot."

"I didn't."

My wife's gloved fingers tapped on the bedside table and fiddled with the Christmas tinsel hung over the iron bedstead. "I don't know why you keep coming here, Nat. This whole place gives me the creeps."

"Me, too," I admitted. How could I ever make my wife understand why I had to come? It wasn't a pleasant experience. Never. But it was necessary. I'd tried to explain this a thousand times and failed. I suppose I should have been more grateful for Laura's forbearance.

"Do you suppose any of these people ever snap out of it?"

"Who?" I asked over my shoulder.

"These people like her. Do they ever just wake up one day and say 'Where am I?' Something like that?"

"I have no idea."

"How long's she been here now?"

I hated to tally the time lost. The years and days since I had watched the ambulance attendants wrap a sheet around her and carry her out of the house as if she were a Persian rug. I told Laura all about the screaming and kicking, the mannequin with his arm pulled off. I did not tell her about the wonderful, beautiful gift she had given me moments before. I never could. But of course, I always suspected she sensed the real reason for my faithful visits. It had to be more than pity. Laura was smarter than that. And yet she still let me come, often made the trip with me and pretended to be interested. Maybe it was curiosity on her part wondering what I could have seen in this strange, mad woman to have given away such a large part of myself to her with no hope of return.

"It must be almost twenty years, isn't it? Maybe more? Twenty-four?"

I knew to the day. But out of respect for Laura, I shrugged my shoulders. "About that."

"What would you say to her if she did just wake up one day, Nat?"

"God, I haven't any idea."

"Haven't you?"

Her stare made me turn away. "Not really."

There was a heavy pause while her gaze lingered on my hand spooning the lemon custard. She barely touched my shoulder with her fingertips as she passed by. "Well, I'll just wait in the car then. Don't be too long."

"I won't, Hon."

Laura's heels tapped down the polished hallway and left the two of us alone.

I sat there drinking in the soulful reflection from those eyes, duller and even more distant now but still summoning me to mysterious memories which refused to fade away. I scooped the last of the custard into the spoon and placed the tart shell on the bedside stand. Then I smoothed her hair, a tarnished silver now, and planted a kiss on her tissue-paper cheek.

"Merry Christmas, Delilah."

She opened her mouth, took one last lemony spoonful and closed her eyes.

The last time I saw Delilah, her wheelchair was by the window so she could look out on a planter full of daffodils. It was a sunny, spring day with just a whiff of April breeze fluttering the flowers. For a moment as I moved my chair to sit close to her, I imagined a sparkle in her hooded eyes. Maybe she had seen the colors of Mother Nature waking up, absorbed the sunshine as I did. But nothing ever happened of course to bring her closer to the real world I was in. Sometimes I liked to think she was with Lionel, happy, young and in love.

That last visit before she died, I held her hand and told her about the novel. About Charmaine and Ethan. The love story she told me I had gotten all wrong. After I was at the University and Laura was pregnant with our first child Conor, I finished the story. And Delilah was right about my draft of the original ending. It wasn't right. The lovers did walk into an uncertain sunset. Readers were left to wonder if their devotion survived the long night.

When the last page was written, I had paced in my office and let my mind drift away at the supper table trying to find the title of my opus. I could never seem to grasp it. The manuscript occupies a space in the lower drawer of my desk at Willamette University History Department, known only to me and Delilah. 'A Portland Melodrama' is scribbled on the title page in pencil. Maybe that's enough.

CPSIA information can be obtained
at www.ICGtesting.com
Printed in the USA
BVHW030852040821
613615BV00008B/191/J

9 781647 195526